KINGDOM

BOOK ONE

Shawna Ryan

KINGDOM
Book One

By Shawna Ryan

Cover Art:
Select-O-Graphix

Publisher's Note:

This is a work of fiction. All names, characters,
places, and events are the work of the author's
imagination.

Any resemblance to real persons, places, or events
is coincidental.

Solstice Publishing - www.solsticepublishing.com

Dedication

I Dedicate this book to my grandmothers,
great-grandmothers,
And great-great-grandmothers,
Courageous pioneers all,
Whatever their religion.

Chapter One

Present Day
3:00 a.m.
April 13

Beneath a moon that was but a slit in the sky, a hundred miles west of Tucson and deep inside a desert wilderness, Arthur Johnson knelt in powder dry dirt at the edge of his grave. The night air was cold and filled with the yap of nearby coyotes. Saguaro cactus boldly loomed above him. Yet, as if not to witness what was to come, the desert lilies and tumbleweed blossoms had closed their petals.

He was about fourteen miles west of State Route 85 at the north foot of the Growler Mountains, twenty miles northwest of Ajo, and about seven miles south of Tenmile Wash. But, what did it matter? No one would ever find him.

There were only animal trails nearby. As he casually examined them, he hoped the animals who made them would not bother him.

He shuddered, silently praying, Please God, let this place of my eternal rest be good to me.

In a tidy pile next to Arthur were the change of clothes his wife had freshly washed and ironed for the occasion. On top of them, were his empty wallet and a picture of his wife and grandchildren. He had left all of his cash and his credit cards with her.

Several yards in front of him, bats the locals called Leptos swarmed, harvesting nectar from the bright yellow blossoms of a twelve-foot-tall mescal agave. Knowing the agave was about to die too, Arthur stared.

Half-a-dozen yards behind him was the white Impala which had transported him there. Standing on either side of him, were the two men who had brought him.

The men wore ankle-length ponchos, stark white against the night sky, revealingly open over their naked and barefoot bodies. Covering their heads, were white, pillbox style caps with something white dangling from one side.

The man on Arthur's right, a redhead, clenched his muscled jaw. He was a head taller than his companion and stocky. His face was freckled and His buttocks and chest were furred with thick patches of graying orange hair.

The bloodless complexion of the shorter man on Arthur's left glowed almost as brightly in the night as his bleached white poncho. His head was bald, and his body virtually hairless. His muscles were large and overdeveloped, and he bore the large crater of a war wound in his thigh.

"Are you ready?" the tall redhead asked Arthur.

His emotions welling up inside him, Arthur tried to speak, but he could only nod.

The two men stepped away from him, silently walked to a blanket they had spread several feet behind him, and disrobed. Neatly folding their ponchos, they set them side by side on the blanket, laid their caps on top of them, and put on the vinyl gloves awaiting them there.

The bald man returned to Arthur first, standing very close to his left shoulder. The other man went to the Impala, took something from under the driver's seat, and holding it behind his back, positioned himself on Arthur's right.

Arthur was terrified. His legs and buttocks trembled. His hands shook in prayer, and he wet himself.

The two men stepped closer and from behind the tall man on Arthur's right came a knife, razor sharp and as long as his forearm. A hand grasped Arthur's hair, lifted it, and yanked his head back.

He felt a slitting, – a slight separation, – an excruciating sting. His trachea popped, then split, and he tasted blood. Abandoning old, familiar channels, the warm fluid gurgled as it rose in his throat, deserting him as it gushed into his grave and mixed with the dirt.

Crickets sang to him. Purgatory beckoned. His body melted, and the powdery earth beneath his knees gently received him.

His mind in mortal haze, he bore witness to his death.

Chapter Two

Present Day
Salt Lake City, Utah
April 14

The chamber where the brethren were speaking to their God was dark. There were twelve of them kneeling, pressed in a circle so tightly together that each had become as the same flesh of the men beside him, — all becoming one. They were servants of Elohim, the Lord. They were instruments of a priesthood with power over life and death, but in the dark they were shadows, — waiting for the accused who was just outside the chamber door.

An open hand was raised, and they were silent. Clothed in darkness, they each turned toward that door. Having been disrobed and dressed in white, as he would have been for any other ritual, the accused entered the chamber from the lighted hall, setting in motion the ritual of the trial. Head bowed, hands at his side, he was trembling.

There was no need to restrain him, for he was a believer. As he stood in the center of the circle, his heart and head pounding, sweat dripped from his every pore. He was so close to his accusers, he not only felt their breaths but tasted the rancor in them. The man who escorted him inside stood to his immediate left and was also dressed in white.

"Are you the man we call 'Min'?" the escort asked the accused.

The accused turned and faced him. "Yes, I am Min."

From behind the accused, a voice, gravelly and old interrupted. "Do you understand why you are here?"

The accused turned toward the voice. "Yes, I have been summoned to appear before the Tribunal, and I have come."

"Did you come here willingly?"

I wasn't dragged here, if that's what you mean, the accused thought to himself, while he said what he was supposed to say, "Yes, I am here willingly."

"Have you been told the charges against you?" the gravelly old voice continued.

"No."

"You have been charged with disobedience for failing to follow a direct order. You have also been charged with breaking the oath of secrecy. How do you plead?"

"I have never divulged a secret I have sworn to keep. Nor have I ever disobeyed an order that followed my heart or that I believed came from God. I am innocent of the charges against me."

"Very well, then. Let the witness come forth," the old man ordered, his voice ripe with anger.

Suddenly and without cause or warning, a hand seized Min's arm. He heard two clicks and felt the cold lips of a double action revolver press against his ear.

"Say nothing, or I will kill you," his escort, the man they called "Michael," whispered.

The door to the hallway, which was now darkened too, opened. With the gun to Min's ear Michael pulled him to the edge of the circle, and the witness entered.

Something small and hard was stuck in the sole of the witness's street shoes. It scraped against the old stone floor as he slowly walked through the darkness into the center of the circle.

"You understand that the penalty for false testimony is death?" the gravelly old voice asked the witness.

The witness's shadow was tall, and his voice emanated from above them. "I understand." The cheap, peppery and leathery cologne he wore had completely absorbed him and was now consuming the room, its heavy toxin familiar to them.

The old man grumbled, "Then, give your testimony."

"Min, the accused, attended the March 2 Project meeting," the witness began. "At that meeting, and before everyone present, I issued him an order for the good of all and for our future. I ordered him to immediately surrender his vessel. Before all in attendance, he promised to obey. That was weeks ago. Though Min has never specifically refused to surrender it, after several requests, he has still failed to do so. It's obvious he treasures that vessel more than he treasures us and would risk his life to keep it from us. Clearly, Min has ignored my order and ignored the command of our Priesthood. Even worse and unforgivably, to protect his vessel he intends to make the details of the Project public. We have proof that Min has, without legitimate cause, traveled to the East Coast on at least three occasions in the last two months, – first on February 22, – then on March 12, and again on April 6. During the April trip, he met with a man known to us only as Henry Blanchard, a man who has connections to some kind of watch group. Min has not only failed to obey the order I gave him, but he has engaged in overt acts in which it appears he divulged one or more of our most precious secrets. By doing so, he has greatly endangered the Project and our security."

The old man's gravelly voice was strained as he asked, "Have you recorded any of these events or put any of this in writing?"

"No."

"Good. Is there any other evidence that might be used against us? Any that Min might have given to this Henry Blanchard?"

"We don't know what, if anything, Min gave Blanchard. Nor do we know whether Blanchard has put anything Min told him in writing."

"Sloppy. Very sloppy," the old man criticized the witness. "We must know if there is anything out there that can hurt us." Threateningly, he added, "Immediately after this matter of Min is resolved, you and I will talk. In the meantime, you are excused."

Passing through the circle of silence, the witness retreated toward the door and into the darkened hallway. When the door closed behind him, the gravely voice spoke again. Appearing to give the accused one last chance, he asked him, "Min, did you hear and understand the testimony against you?"

"Yes."

"Have you delivered the vessel in question as ordered?"

The mouth of the revolver dug deeper into Min's ear.

No longer able to deny his sin of disobedience, he took a very deep breath and exhaled, "No, I haven't."

"Why not?"

"There just didn't seem to be a right time," Min responded, though that was not the truth. He worshipped his vessel. There would never be a time in which his heart and soul would be ready to relinquish it.

"Then you do intend to deliver the vessel?"

Min had not considered the possibility there may still be a way out. Was the old man throwing him a lifeline? Was he giving him one more chance? – Or was it a test to see if Min would admit his flagrant disobedience. Knowing all other options were closed to him, and that if he was punished, the vessel would fall to them anyway, Min chose to lie. His heart was in his throat. His voice was a whisper, as he told them, "Yes, I do. I will deliver it in the next few days."

Even to Min, his testimony seemed unconvincing, and his expectations fell.

"The witness testified that you met three times with a man named Henry Blanchard. Have you been meeting with Blanchard?"

"Yes, he's a good friend of mine."

"Where did you first meet him?"

"He was my roommate in college."

"Is he a believer?"

"No, he's a Gentile."

There was a collective sigh from the circle of men around him. Min had made a mistake, and he knew it. Identifying Hank as a Gentile was sufficient in-and-of itself to convict him.

The old man too sighed, and as if resigned to Min's fate, ended his questioning. "Has anyone else anything to add?"

But for a single cough, perhaps born of out of awkwardness and regret, there was silence.

"Do you understand the significance of the charges against you and what will happen if you are found guilty?" the old man asked.

Min involuntarily shuddered. His voice quavered as he stammered, "Y..y..yes."

"Then take him away, Michael. We are done with him."

The man holding the revolver to Min's ear crooked his other arm around Min's neck, yoking him. Ordering him to "Move," he forced him to the left. Directing him between two men in the shadows, he pushed him toward a thick, pine door.

"Let the door be opened," the gravelly old voice ordered.

A hand bearing a ring of keys more than a century old, dangling from the fingers, reached in front of them through the darkness. Holding a three-inch-long brass key between the index and thumb, the hand slid the key through the hole between old tumblers, and effortlessly and quietly unlocked the door. The hand then turned the nob, and the aged pine door creaked open.

Holding the gun barely an inch from Min's ear, the assailant squeezed the arm around Min's neck and nearly strangled him. Pressing him through the doorway, he forced Min into a tiny, dark room made of stone.

Min swallowed hard, inhaled, and a thick odor of undiluted bleach burned his lungs. He coughed, and Michael tightened the grip around his neck.

Min panicked. There was another odor lingering in the room, of a more egregious stench other than the bleach. Searching for a way out, his eyes already accustomed to the dark, Min quickly defined the room's windowless walls and knew there was only one way out. He tried to turn toward the closing door, but Michael held him. Min tried to squirm his way free, but Michael so brutally tightened the grip around his neck it nearly crushed his windpipe, cutting off his air. He struggled, but the exertion without air was too much, and he faltered.

Michael shoved him to the floor. "Kneel!"

Even with Min's abrupt descent to the stone floor, the revolver never wavered or moved from his ear. Infuriated he tried to turn his head, but Michael was ready. Savagely jamming the barrel down Min's ear and through its narrow canal, Michael drove Min's head into the floor, rammed the barrel against his eardrum, and burst it.

"A-a--agh!" Min cried.

Michael covered the gun with his hand and drew back the hammer, clicking a pronouncement of death.

In agony and fear, Min closed his eyes and shuddered. "Oh, God...!"

A cruel reality was exposing itself. "Is this the verdict?" he implored.

Unfeelingly and without removing the gun from Min's ear, Michael watched him suffer without responding. Long seconds past, then slowly and casually he wrung the gun from Min's ear, telling him, "No, I'll let you know when there's a verdict."

Michael was only steps from the doorway. Slowly and deliberately backing though it, he closed the door behind him. As the ancient key turned in the lock, half his hearing gone, Min barely discerned the old tumblers turning. Frantic and in excruciating pain, the incessant pounding of his heart interfering with his breathing, Min tried to catch his breath but choked. His trial was not yet over.

Slumping to the stone floor which was frigid against his buttocks, he tried to calm himself. His testimony was feeble — his plea of innocence a lie.

He stared into the impenetrable darkness. This was where he would die.

He twisted the gold ring on his left hand and pictured the woman he loved. Regrets mingled with memories, and he swore to her that if he were to have their marriage to live over, he would do whatever he could to make her happy. She was his life, their children his blessing, and he would elevate them above everything else. Vividly remembering their courtship and marriage, his breathing became easier and more consistent, and his heart beat started to return to normal.

In desperation, he began to search in the dark for a way out. The frigid, stone floor was as smooth as glass and sloped slightly. He crawled forward. About a foot away, he felt a steel ring about six inches wide crisscrossed by bars, — a drain. He tried to force his fingers through the holes hoping to yank the grate out, but the bars were too close together and there was no room. He dug at the edges with his fingernails until they broke and started bleeding, his efforts futile. Unable to dislodge the grate, he crawled over the drain and in a zigzag pattern crossed and recrossed the room, feeling every inch of the floor and walls for any defect or deficiency that might offer him a way out.

Hours passed. Defeated, Min sat motionless for what seemed forever and thought of his wife, trying to adjust to what he knew to be inevitable.

They had taken his watch and phone when they abducted him, and there was no sense of time in this place. Yet, Min knew instinctively morning was approaching, and he was ready for whatever fate awaited him. His mind and body exhausted from the mental and physical trauma dealt him, he fell into a deep and troubled sleep. His wife was on fire. His children were being forcibly taken away. He heard the tumblers roll, and he jumped. Fully awake, his heart pounding, he stared wild-eyed when the pine door opened and Michael appeared, ominously silhouetted in the doorway.

The lights were on in the windowless room which that night had held the circle of brethren in darkness, but the room was now empty. Michael stared at Min for a moment, his expression as cold and hard as his revolver had been the night before. He seemed to hesitate and when he was ready, almost reluctantly, announced, "The verdict is in."

Anticipating the worst, Min took a deep breath and held it.

"Go home."

Chapter Three

The middle of the North Atlantic
April 6, 1854

The winds blew light in the predawn skies, barely enough to half-fill the twin sails of a steamer, seven days out of Liverpool and bound for Philadelphia. Two hundred Mormon converts were on board. As the skies turned orange, a harbinger of trouble, and as calm waters masked a savagery below the waves, the converts slept peacefully.

Beneath blankets awkwardly tented for privacy among crowded rows of bunks where anyone could hear them, Erich's long, slender fingers lifted the hem of Anna's thick wool nightgown and tenderly drew it up the length of her shapely leg. "Is there something you want?" she whispered, teasingly.

His playful, deep blue eyes enticing her, he grinned. "Ah-huh."

The close quarters, the prying eyes of the righteous among them, and the rigid expectations of elders determined to keep order had, until that moment, stripped Anna of desire. Out of complete embarrassment, she had not let him make love to her since just before they left Liverpool.

"What if somebody hears?" she whispered. "What if they tell Brother Jacob?"

His breathing rapid and shallow, Erich lifted her nightgown over her full, bare breasts, passionately enfolded her in his arms and pressed her against him. "What if they do? I'm your husband, aren't I?"

He was much more than her husband. He had been everything to her for eight years, her only love from the moment she first saw him. The physical confirmation of his love was her sustenance, and without it there was a void inside her. She ached for him.

His hands sure, his touch familiar and gentle, his long and sinewy body in fleshly harmony with her own, he moved subtly about her body, his attentions sensuous and unselfish. Unable to deny him any longer, she invited his legs to slip between her own. Eager to feel him inside her, with grasping fingers, she demanded he penetrate her.

Thrilling and exciting her, raising within her passions that gripped her very soul, his rhythm became her rhythm. Caressing her, pleasing her, he moved up and down with the beat of her heart.

Erich's love was a cushion upon which her life rested, and her contentment with him was an indescribable joy. Absorbed in his impassioned lovemaking, Anna forgot everyone and everything about her and did not see or feel through the protection of the darkness, disapproving eyes watching her.

Calm only an hour earlier, the wind that awakened at dawn was angry. On deck with some of the other converts, equally mesmerized by the erupting sea, Anna and Erich stood hand in hand. Unlike the others, their heads were uncovered, their hair flying out of control at the mercy of the wind. They were the picture of strength, fearful yet courageous as they stood gazing wide-eyed at the viperous waves crashing against the gunwale, – she mimicking the romantic figurehead on the prow, he the stalwart bow. Erich wrapped his arm around her waist and grabbed a mast line as the ship rose and shuddered to the wrath of a wave breaching the gunwale, sending everyone else quickly below.

The sea was unpredictable and deadly, but in their youthful exuberance, they were courageous. Like the strands of a good rope, each was interdependent upon the other for strength.

Never having said it, Anna knew if either of them failed it would be her. That had become her private fear, and one she shared with no one. Wanting to appear as brave as Erich, she stayed with him at the gunwale until the sea began to calm. Leaning against him, holding onto the rail with a white-knuckled grip, she kept her wide, aqua-colored eyes locked on the horizon.

Her curly, copper hair was tied in a single braid, rippling down the back of her neck to her shoulders. Her feet were spread for balance. Struggling to keep the contents of her stomach down, she quietly watched with him as the wind blew itself away and the sun crept through rainless clouds into morning.

The dying wind and the opposing force of the ship plowing through the waves buffeted Erich's blond hair as he quietly beheld the ocean's power. Grinning, his love of the adventure a sparkle in his eyes, he leaned into her, tightened his grip and protectively whispered, "Hang on. I've got you."

As the sea appeared to be calming and the waves begin to recede, the sun fully breached on the horizon with the promise of a good day. Anna felt completely safe with Erich at her side, with his arm wrapped tightly around her waist. She had successfully tested the breadth of her courage, and the danger seemed to have past. Daring to trust the sea, she began to relax and enjoy its power until a giant wave battered the bow. The ship shuddered. Its hull moaned and cracked as if it was being pulled apart, and terrified, Anna cried.

Standing by her side, his arm nearly crushing her, Erick held her tight against the wave reaching out to sweep them overboard, through the sounds of the ship breaking apart, and through her terror, strong against the murderous forces that would destroy them. Then as suddenly as the fury came the wind and waves died down, and the sea settled. The threat was over. His hand shaking, he wiped her tears and grinned. The adventure over, the danger behind them, she laughed with him.

The converts who had taken refuge below returned to the deck. A small hand touched Anna's arm and gently squeezed. Kristina Tuttle was normally bright and cheerful. Her complexion was usually ruddy and her eyes clear, but in her early pregnancy she suffered what seemed endless bouts of seasickness, and she was very pale. Her eyes were dull and were framed by dark, gray circles. She looked utterly miserable. Her voice was weak and hushed, her smile faint and unsure as she greeted, "Good morning."

Kristina was sixteen and would not be seventeen for months. She was the youngest sister of one of Anna's childhood friends, and was one of only twenty other Swiss **converts** on board.

Very short cropped, copper hair feathering the edge of Anna's cheeks was barely displaced by the wind as she turned to greet her. Anna was immediately concerned when she saw that Kristina looked even worse than what she did the night before.

"How are you this morning, Kristina?" she gently and caringly asked.

Before Kristina could speak for herself, a bearded man at least twenty years her senior dressed in a black, wool suit spoke for her. "She's feeling just fine, thank you.

"Aren't you, Sister Kristina?" he asked without looking at her.

"Morning, Brother Jacob," Erich said.

Anna acknowledged Jacob with a nod, but did not take her eyes away from his young wife. She reached for Kristina's hand. It was pale and limp. "When was the last time you were able to eat anything?"

As if silently asking her husband's permission to speak, Kristina looked up at him. When he gave an approving nod, she responded, "Why, just last night, I was able to keep my supper down. This morning, I may even manage breakfast."

"She's getting stronger by the day," Jacob proudly announced to everyone within hearing distance. "She's already stronger than she thinks she is."

"Yes," Kristina confirmed. "I'm so much better."

Elder Jacob Tuttle was thin. His tailored black suit, which was once properly fitted, now hung loose all the way to his polished shoes. He was not tall, but he had a large head, overemphasized by a long, square jaw. The round, broad brimmed hat he had pulled down over his forehead kept his eyes in the shadow. A short, black beard obscured the deep cleft in his chin. As he was standing there, he clenched his teeth, a habit which made his neck and jaw taut and unyielding.

"Are you sure you're better?" Anna asked Kristina.

"Brother Jacob is so wise in these matters," Kristina told her. "He knows better than me, and I'm just sure he's right. I might not feel better this minute, but I know I will in a few minutes more."

Her pale hand reached for the gunwale and she steadied herself. "Just hearing Jacob say I'm getting stronger makes me feel stronger," she reassured everyone.

As Anna's critical and unwavering gaze met Jacob's dominating stare, Kristina looked uneasily away, following the water line to the brilliant hues on the horizon at sunrise. The rough sea was behind them, and despite its rage against them only moments before, she seemed completely unafraid of its immensity. "Isn't it beautiful?" she raved, a little too enthusiastically.

Unsuccessful in intimidating away the defiance in Anna's eyes, Jacob looked away and instead took control of every convert on board by gesturing to a man standing at the stern holding a bugle. In response and without a word, at the instant of Jacob's signal, the man put the bugle to his lips and blew, rigorously summoning the converts to discipline and order.

It was time for the morning meeting. Crowding amidships, facing the stern, the two hundred eager converts waited as Elder Jacob Tuttle pompously moved through the gathering. Making his way up the stairs to the quarter deck aft, he turned and faced them. The words rumbling from deep inside his throat, he addressed them, "Saints, – converts chosen by God to build His Kingdom, – listen."

Jacob paused. When the only sound was that of the ship gliding through calm waters, he continued, "Do you hear? Do you hear God's breath upon the waves? – Look!" he pointed to the horizon. "Can you see Him?"

Anna looked at the sea with the rest of the two hundred mesmerized men and women, but try as she might, she neither heard nor saw Him.

"Where is He?" a woman behind her asked, almost in desperation. "I can't see Him."

"He's there!" Jacob said, continually pointing. "He's always there, with us and beside us. We are His people. He buoys our ship in the cup of His hand for our safety. Close your eyes and picture Him. Then open them and look again."

As if sealing an image within them, the woman behind Anna tightly closed her eyes. While everyone watched her, moments past, and her expression changed.

Brilliant with excitement, her eyes snapped open. She ran to the gunwale, gripped the side of the ship, and peered overboard. "I see Him!" she shouted, pointing. "He's there!"

Anna and dozens of others crowded next to her, all of them searching.

"Look!" the woman shouted, pointing at the hull. "I see His fingertips."

Pressed against the gunwale, crushed among others eager to see, Anna searched the hull directly beneath them. Yet, she could not see God's fingertips.

"There they are!" another woman beside Anna exclaimed, pointing in the same direction.

Struggling to keep her place, praying she would see them, Anna stared expectantly, but saw nothing. Disappointed, she allowed herself to be pushed aside and away from the gunwale.

Erich was waiting for her. "Well?" he asked, gently.

Sadly and slowly, she shook her head.

"Maybe another day," he comforted, slipping his arm around her.

As the other disappointed followers rejoined them, the two women blessed with His vision stayed at the gunwale praying.

"Why didn't all of us see Him?" one of the men asked, as the congregation regrouped.

"You did not see Him because you did not truly believe you would see Him," Jacob told them all-knowingly. "Your faith is not yet strong enough."

"When will our faith be strong enough?" the man challenged. "Haven't we already proved ourselves by leaving our homes and coming this far?"

Jacob stared at him, his glance condemning the man for his impertinence.

"You know nothing of proof. What you have done is only the beginning. You won't see Him until you believe in Him and in His Prophet without question."

Intimidated by the exchange, Anna stepped a little closer to Erich, relieved she had not asked.

"Let me show you true faith. Let me introduce you to Him. Come to me," Jacob beckoned the two women still hanging over the gunwale. "Who did you see?"

"Why, God," one of the women responded, somewhat puzzled by the question.

"Do you know His name?"

Seemingly confused, she momentarily went blank, then ventured, "Elohim?"

"No!" Jacob's directness, his rebuke, stunned her to silence.

"Jehovah?" she then quickly offered.

He lowered his head and peered at her. "No, not Jehovah."

Bowing her head, she meekly stepped back into the gathering.

"God is not 'Jehovah!' Nor is He Elohim, the Father in Heaven. He is Adam. Adam is our Father and our God."

All former Protestants who had become the converts gasped. Most had heard of Jehovah as God. Some had heard of Elohim, another name for God in the Old Testament. None of them had heard that Adam, a man, was God.

"Adam of the Garden of Eden?" Erich shouted. "That's blasphemy!"

Cold fire leapt from Jacob's eyes as he lifted his hand, pointed at Erich, and accused him through clenched teeth. "You are the blasphemer! I am the voice of the Almighty. You shall not question me or any of the other elders. We are your priests. You – all of you, are here to learn from us, – and you will!"

"You told us God had promised us His Kingdom and that He would always care for us if we came to Utah,'" Erich argued. "You didn't tell us the god you spoke for was not a god at all but a man, – a false god."

"False god?" someone else shouted.

Fear and betrayal, confusion and panic tore at the converts who had given up everything, left everything they had to follow this god. Whispers of,

"What have we done? Where are we going?" echoing through the crowd.

Another man stood, demanding, "What do you mean? Our god's a man?"

The elders who surrounded the converts stepped closer while two of the youngest and strongest moved in to flank Jacob.

"Steady," Jacob ordered, his voice deep and commanding. "There is no 'false god' here." His eyes still shadowed by his hat, he waited, saying nothing further until the converts quieted. He then turned to Erich. "Until you learn and believe what we will teach you, you know nothing of what we say. We told you from the beginning that to inherit God's Kingdom, you must listen to us and obey. You have done what you needed to do to this point, but there is much to do before you earn the keys to His Kingdom. Much to learn before you earn his notice. This we will teach you beginning today." Jacob silently surveyed the converts. "Adam," he said, when they were settled, "was a celestial being when he came into the Garden of Eden, bringing with him Eve, who was one of his wives."

There was a rumbling through the converts, and somewhere within the body, a woman gasped, "'One' of his wives?"

"Quiet!" Jacob ordered, as the elders closed ranks around the edge of the gathering, moving ever closer.

The elders were warriors as well as priests of the faith. They were survivors in a deadly, ongoing struggle against people who did not believe, people they called "Gentiles". They did not suffer skeptics, and they hated those who mocked and persecuted them.

Yet, as if nothing had been questioned, Jacob continued. He went on to tell them that when the Garden of Eden was destroyed, Adam made this world and became its God, and that Adam was the only God the Mormon's had anything to do with. Adam became mortal when he ate the forbidden fruit. Years later he appeared to the Virgin Mary as Michael the Archangel and begot Jesus Christ. As Adam's son, Christ is our brother."

"What?!?" Erich shouted, enraged. "I've never heard such drivel! You're all cranks."

The elders surrounding the converts immediately converged on him. Pushing Anna aside, one of them grabbed Erich's arm, yet Erich did not stop. "What have you gotten us into?"

Jacob's jaw visually buckled as he seethed, "Thou shalt not question the Lord or his priests. For if you do, you will be damned. All of us will be damned!Silence him before God abandons us," Jacob told the elders surrounding Erich. "Take him below and reason with him. He is endangering our souls."

Jacob's brother was murdered by Gentiles at Haun's Mill, Missouri in 1838. His father was lynched by Gentiles when Gentiles drove the Mormons out of Missouri two months later. He hated Gentiles. He hated Gentiles who only pretended to convert even more. Paranoia and intolerance were Jacob's legacies. His heritage was murder. Like the elders with him, Jacob was born in the faith and raised defending its beliefs with blood. Finally earning the rank of priest, he did not tolerate know-nothing converts questioning either him or the Church teachings.

While the other converts watched dumfounded, elders tied a bandana over Erich's mouth. Restraining him, six of them picked him up and carried him below.

"Erich!" Anna cried, helplessly watching as she was restrained by two others.

Stunned, the other converts said and did nothing. When the immediate shock was over, the women around Anna tried to comfort her. "He'll be all right," they told her, all the while nervously staring at the open hatch through which Erich had been taken.

As if the scene they just witnessed was normal, Jacob calmly told them, "This was but a small test of your faith."

Most of the converts turned back to him. "Because Brother Erich could not accept the truth about our God, he failed the test this time, but he will have other challenges. Many others. Just as all of you will have challenges. You must forget all that you have previously learned about God, for you have been taught by heretics. No matter how well meaning those heretics were, they knew nothing of God, our Adam. Only we, Adam's priests, have the keys to His Kingdom. Only those among you who come to believe without question will come to know and see Him. From now on, you must learn the truth and adapt. You will be asked to endure and pass many tests to prove you are worthy. Only through obedience and unquestioning belief will you then be allowed to enter His Kingdom."

The converts were lured to the faith by the elders' promises of a life and eternity better than what they left. Seemingly fascinated by what Jacob was telling them about what they must do to earn it and apparently eager to show him they believed, the converts quietly listened. The women beside Anna turned back to him, and only Anna looked away,

still anxiously watching the hatch to the darkness
below.

"Your pilgrimage to God's Kingdom will
not be easy," Jacob continued. "Until God is certain
you are worthy, He will try you at every corner. He
will search your spirit and, if need be, will take your
soul in His hands and crumble it, so He can remold
it. You will suffer fire and deprivation, hunger and
sickness. You will survive only if you are strong
and live by His orders, — the orders we, his priests,
pass on to you. Only if you prove you believe in
Him unquestioningly and do as you are told, will
you share the glory of His Kingdom."

Jacob's tenor markedly shifting from that
of a disciplinarian to that of a nurturer, his voice
softened. He became like a father reading a fairy
tale to his children, describing to them the Heaven
on Earth to which he was taking them. "The Utah
Territory is His chosen land," he began. Describing
deep canyons of orange and red clay with piers
stretching to the sky; timber and granite with which
they would would build their cities; mountains full
of game and life sustaining waters; and an inland
sea, beside which they were building His temple, he
painted a paradise.

He told them not to worry about leaving
their loved ones behind in Europe. Their loved ones
would also be saved. If the converts measured up to
the hardships before them, God's ordinances would
be revealed to them and they would be given the
keys to His Kingdom. Those keys would not only
open God's Kingdom to them but to all those they
left behind. "No matter what comes to you, whether
at sea or on your journey overland, persevere and be
determined. His Kingdom awaits you."

Chapter Four
Present Day
Provo, Utah
Tuesday, April 20

As Sharon Marshall drove into the hills east of Provo, the sun glared off the hood of her leased, red convertible, blinding her even in sunglasses. Large, stone and clapboard, look-a-like houses, equally spaced and with immaculate yards, banked each side of the freshly laid black top. Their occupants bound by unbreakable covenants, this pristine neighborhood in the hills of the Kingdom of God was seemingly perfect.

Near the end of a block just like the other blocks in the neighborhood, she turned into a drive, left her car, and knocked at the oversized front door of that stone and clapboard house. "Kim," she called. The door was locked. "Kim." She rang the doorbell. "It's Sharon. I'm here."

The door opened and a woman appeared. She was tall and slender, blond and beautiful, and her blue eyes were smiling.

"I came," Sharon announced, as she embraced her. "Got your note." Sharon was three years younger, not nearly as tall or as slender as her older sister, and brunette. Was she to love Kim any less, she would have been envious. "Where are the kids?"

"Wayne took them to Portland to visit Mom for a couple of weeks."

Kim and Wayne had four children. Martha was five. Keith was four, and Philip was two. Emily was the baby. They would have had five children if Kim's first had not been born prematurely and died.

"To our Mom's?" Sharon was astounded.

"Yeah."

"I thought Wayne didn't like the kids around her because she wouldn't become Mormon."

Kim shrugged. "I thought so, too."

"He even took the baby?"

"I tried to talk him out of it, – thought she might be too much for Mom, especially with the boys. But, she wanted her, and – well. Come on in."

The floors inside were red clay tile, matching the upscale southwestern theme of the house's interior. The reds and browns, oranges and yellows were subtle and warm like the clays in the desert canyons a hundred miles south of them. Their treasure was a small carpet, hand woven by the Anasazi hundreds of years ago. It was framed and hung on the wall to the left. In the living room, where the upholstered furniture was soft, yellow leather, tall windows flooded the room with sunlight. Dominating the room, was a floor to ceiling, tempered clay fireplace. On small tables and in cabinets, where Kim did not allow a single particle of dust to fall, were assortments of genuine and replicated desert artifacts. Off to side was a small room Wayne used as a study.

"The kids don't spend much time in here, do they?" Sharon observed. Single and childless, her law practice and her penchant for travel dominating her life, even she could appreciate the risk.

Kim laughed. "No, not unless we're in here with them."

"That's an interesting piece," Sharon observed, gravitating to an urn enclosed in a small, glass cabinet outside Wayne's study. "Looks more Egyptian than Native American."

The urn was a foot tall and about eight inches wide. It was fired clay with blue and black geometric designs and there was a wide band of hieroglyphics around the circumference. Seemingly depicting a parade, people and birds were bunched behind two men. The first man seemed to be a Pharaoh, the second a servant carrying a large, red crown.

"Do you know what the hieroglyphics mean?"

"Just what Wayne told me."

Noticing the lock on the cabinet door, Sharon asked, "Can I take a closer look?"

"No, he won't let anybody touch it. Not even me. I can't even get in there to dust it."

"Don't worry, Kim," Sharon soothed, "I doubt if any dust could get in there." Sharon studied the urn from outside the glass. "It's pretty old, isn't it?"

"He said it was really old. It's the most valuable thing we have in the house."

"How much does he think it's worth?"

"He told me, 'Tens of thousands.' He said we could almost retire on it."

"What did he say the pictographs mean?"

"Apparently, they depict people migrating to Egypt from Asia. Wayne says they're the people who brought civilization to Egypt.

"Do you see that red crown?"

"Yes."

"The red crown means they are carrying with them the Cult of the Honey Bee. See the antennae rising?"

Sharon hardly believed something so miniscule could be there, but as she got as close to the crown as she could, she saw what looked like tiny antennae.

"That crown is the symbol of the bee and is called 'Deseret'," Kim continued.

"What's the 'Cult of the Honey Bee?'"

"That's where it gets really interesting," Kim told her. "The bee was supposed to have granted the secret of reincarnation solely to the Pharaoh. That meant the Pharaoh had the power over death! The cult began when Adam and Eve came out of the Garden of Eden because the bees came with them. The bees provided them honey, – delicious food in their new world. I suppose, they might not have even survived without it."

"Isn't the bee a Mormon symbol, too?"

"A-huh, Joseph Smith made the bee a symbol not long after he founded the Church. Utah made the beehive its emblem when it became a state. The bee symbol is everywhere."

"And, did Joseph Smith wear a red crown and know the secret of reincarnation?" Sharon asked, sarcastically.

"Of course not?" Kim said, impatiently. "But, when our people took his body to his mansion after he was murdered, I guess they did put a bee house on his grave."

"Who's this guy?" Without looking at him too closely, Sharon pointed to the figure carrying the red crown.

"That's 'Min, The Beekeeper.'"

More interested in finding out why she was there than in learning more about the urn, Sharon turned to her sister and, deeply concerned, asked, "So, what's going on, Kim? What's happened?"

Kim had called late last night, didn't want to talk about what was bothering her over the phone, and told Sharon she needed to see her immediately. Frightened by the urgency in Kim's voice, Sharon had cancelled her appointments for the day and gotten on the first flight out of San Francisco that morning.

Kim's entire demeanor instantly changed. Her eyes teared. Her mouth quivered, and she almost cried. She looked worried and frightened. Putting her finger to her lips, she silently asked Sharon to say nothing more. Wrapping her cold, sweaty hand around Sharon's arm, she suddenly pulled Sharon out of the light streaming through the windows and into shadow. As if she was talking to someone in another room, she said noticeably louder than in her normal tone, "Just wanted to see you. If I hadn't made it sound important, you'd have begged off. "Wait here, and I'll go get something for us to eat."

Great, Sharon thought when Kim left her. She drags me all the way over here in the middle of the week then abandons me in a dark corner of the living room for a cookie. When Kim came back, Sharon started to protest but Kim put her hand over Sharon's mouth, again drew her finger to her lips, and silenced her. Pulling Sharon around the corner, she dragged her down the hall and into the bathroom. Shutting the door behind them, shushing Sharon every time she tried to speak, Kim blocked the opening beneath the door with a thick, brown, bath towel.

"What are you doing?" Sharon blurted. She was frightened. What could be making Kim act like this?

"I need to talk to you," Kim whispered.

"I know that, but why are you whispering? Why are we in the bathroom?"

"Wayne and I always come in here when he wants to talk in private."

"You can't talk in your living room?" Sharon asked, incredulously.

"No, they're listening."

"Who's listening?"

"I don't know."

"Then why do you say, 'They're listening?'"

"Wayne told me we're under observation."

"Is he in some kind of trouble?"

"He won't tell me."

"Do you think the police are after him?"

"I don't know, but he's acting very peculiarly. He sees things that don't seem to be there and thinks somebody's following him. When I ask him what's wrong, he says I don't need to know. He just brings me into the bathroom, closes and muffles the door like I did, and sobs.

"I'm really worried, Sharon. What if he's going crazy?"

"He hasn't said anything about what's bothering him?"

Kim shook her head. "Nothing."

"Maybe he's told you something without you realizing it. Has he done anything new or different with the kids?"

"Just taken them to Mom's."

"You've got to admit, that, in itself, is unusual."

Kim nodded.

"How did his taking them come up?"

"Wayne had been working and sleeping at the lab for several days. When he came home, he told me he needed to visit a clinic in Connecticut right away and that he'd dropped the kids off to visit Grandma."

"Why would he want to go out of his way to take them to Oregon? Sharon asked. "Even if he liked Mom, he wouldn't usually do that. What clinic was he visiting in Connecticut? Could he be sick?"

"No, he's fine. He's been working with an obstetrician or somebody like that back at the Zion Clinic in Hartford. They've been working on some kind of vitamin or something he says will prevent premature births."

"Given your baby died because it was premature, that makes sense. Has there been anything specific? Any one incident you can recall that didn't ring right?"

Kim's eyes teared and looked down. "Just one," she whispered. "It was a couple of days ago. A few hours after he got back from Connecticut." She sighed, looked tearfully at Sharon, and told her, "He hit me."

"He hit you!" Sharon shouted, incensed. "Did he hurt you?"

"Sh-h-h. Not really."

"What do you mean 'not really'?"

"He slapped me."

"Why? Has he ever hit you before?"

"No, he's never even threatened me."

"So what happened?"

"I don't know. The next day, I found a strange medallion when I was cleaning up one of his drawers. When I showed it to him and asked him what it was, he exploded. I've never seen him so angry. He told me to stay out of his business. To keep my hands off his things and not to tell a soul what I saw."

"What did the medallion look like?"

"A solid gold coin. About the size of one of those old silver dollars."

"Were there any inscriptions or designs?"

"Oh, yeah. There was a big, flying bird on one side and the Egyptian red crown on the other. But the figures were nothing special. They were no different than anything we already had in our living room."

"Was there anything else on the medallion?"

"Not that I saw."

"Then why did he get so upset?" Sharon asked.

"I wish I knew.

"Anybody home?" a deep voice called from the living room.

Kim immediately panicked. "He's home! Do something. He'll know we've been up to something if he sees both of us in here."

Wayne's footsteps were heavy as he approached.

Reacting, Sharon jerked something off Kim's hand. She then yanked the towel from the threshold, kneeled next to the toilet, and stuck her head in the bowl.

"In here," Kim quavered.

Chapter Five

The middle of the North Atlantic
April 6, 1854

In the hold where the trunks and ship stores were stowed, where no one on deck could hear, the elders who wrestled Erich down the ladder were giving their own sermon. Tying Erich to a column and gagging him, they forced him to listen.

"You pledged to follow the teachings of Joseph Smith, whatever they be, yet at the first chance, you deny him. You pledged to help build the Kingdom of God, yet when you hear the truth about Him, you object. You endanger all our souls by questioning Him. You damn your own with your denial. All we ask is that you listen. Will you try, Brother Erich?" Though one of them untied the gag that filled Erich's mouth, no one released him from the column.

Angry, but willing and afraid, Erich nodded. He realized he had no choice. He also knew they might be right. "Maybe the idea of Adam, as God, is just too new to me. I promise I'll try."

They stepped away from him, murmured among themselves, and then returned. "Good. Come with us and join the others."

The converts' religious instruction for that morning ended three hours later, and as part of the daily ritual, the converts divided by ward. On schedule, within the time allotted and in their groups, they disrobed and scrubbed themselves with lye soap, – men on deck, – women below. This being a designated day of fumigation, they then powdered their bodies with lime. Thereafter, for hours through the afternoon in the sun, they met in small groups with the elders to learn more about their new religion.

"Our universe has many gods, and Elohim rules over them all," Jacob began. He was speaking to a group of about twenty converts who included Erich and Anna. He went on to tell them that each of those gods rules over his own planet and that Adam was Earth's Supreme God. These planet gods give birth to spirit children who then attach themselves to human bodies in the form of babies.

When Jacob came to Weiningen, Switzerland, Erich and Anna's hometown, he talked of one god, and, it wasn't Adam. Now, he talked of many Gods. Comparing as equals Joseph Smith and Brigham Young to Jesus Christ and Muhammad, Jacob called them all lesser gods. Their duty was to give birth to the spirit children who would inhabit the humans on earth.

Erich shuddered but said nothing. His face was flushed, and his brow was wrinkled. His lips were taught and slightly curled, and he began taking slow, even breaths.

"The Christian Bible you studied as children is not completely accurate because there were mistakes in its translation," Jacob continued. "The Book of Mormon corrects most of those translation errors. The other errors were corrected by God himself in His revelations to Joseph Smith. One of the errors in the Christian Bible is the way it identifies Jehovah. Jehovah is actually Jesus Christ, the Son of Elohim. Both Elohim and Jehovah are men like us, but right now, they are in their celestial state. Satan is Christ's brother. He is also in his celestial state. Satan fell from Heaven because he was jealous of Christ and became his enemy."

Blood rushed to Erich's face, and his fists clenched. His fingernails began digging into his palms.

"As Mormons, we are all saints. As saints, we reign with Christ in this temporal Kingdom of Earth," Jacob continued. "Our church is the Church of Latter Day Saints. Our primary duty is to conceive and bear the children to whom gods' spirit children attach. Our glory in Heaven will be equal to the number of children we conceive and bear. Women cannot be saved except through their husbands. That is why they must be sealed to their husbands forever."

Jacob's gaze fell on Anna, who appeared to be listening intently. He glanced at Eric, then turned away. "A man's salvation depends on his unquestioning belief in our faith and his strict obedience to the Priesthood. Without total devotion, he is damned. The founder of our religion, Joseph Smith was the only 'Prophet of the Living God.' All other religions, including those in which you all were baptized, belong to Satan."

By now, Erich's breath was coming in bursts. "Excuse me a moment," he said to the converts next to him. He made his way through and around the groups on deck, walked to the rail at the stern, and pretended to urinate over the gunwale. No one else heard as he swore under his breath, "Enough of this! I'm taking Anna home."

Though he glanced repeatedly and disapprovingly at Erich, Jacob continued his instruction without pause, telling the converts, "A man's route to salvation also requires that he be baptized in Salt Lake City where Adam's apostles dwell. Any man who fails in these matters will be damned." His expression softened as he gazed at his wife, Kristina, saying proudly, "My son will be baptized there, and he will learn obedience to the Priesthood from me."

Returning to his lesson, Jacob told his converts, "We call the people of Satan's churches, all churches other than our true church, 'Gentiles.'"

"Are we Jews, then?" a German woman, her eyes wide and amazed, asked.

"No, we are not Jews," Jacob answered, impatiently. "Jews are heretics and unbelievers. They are Gentiles, just like the rest of the world – Catholics, – Protestants – Muslims. They're all the same. You must fear and hate them. Gentiles do not understand us and are our enemies."

Seemingly ashamed of her ignorance, the woman who asked the question lowered her eyes, bowed her head, and protectively crossed her arms.

"As Joseph Smith's successor, Brigham Young is now the 'Prophet of the Living God. He is the president of the Church and is our supreme authority. Every elder, including myself, is a priest. And as priests, we speak for both God and the Prophet."

Jacob glared at Erich who was still at the gunwale, his back to them. "To find salvation you must obey us." He then paused. Night was falling, and the bugle that had called them to meeting that morning announced supper.

The converts and elders ate in shifts in the clean and organized galley below deck. In the commotion of them being served and of them chattering about the day, no one noticed hands deeper below deck dip a tin cup into a vat of lye and fill it.

Chapter Six

The Middle of the Atlantic
April 6, 1854

As the sun descended into the troubled sea that evening leaving behind the turmoil that threatened, most of the converts not yet eating came on deck to watch its departure. Preferring not to challenge the almost rail high waves hitting midships, Anna and Erich joined the converts at the stern.

Gazing at the dark violet sky left by the sunset and watching gray clouds form, Anna bid goodbye to the day. No matter what happened that night, it marked the end of one more day she would have to face the violence of the sea. She could handle almost anything on land, for the earth gave her strength. The sea did not. Its infinite depths were treacherous, unpredictable, and terrifying, and she would be glad to leave it forever.

In his always intrusive way, Jacob Tuttle joined them. "I'd like to talk to Sister Anna for a moment," he told Erich, his voice rich with timbre. "Would you go down to storage and ask Elder Caswell if I can meet with him a little later?" Jacob's tone made it clear this was not a request. "It'll only take a few minutes."

Already frightened by the sea, Anna did not want to be alone with Jacob. She took Erich's hand and squeezed.

"I don't think I should..." Erich began to argue against leaving.

"Nonsense," Jacob said. "Sister Anna has to learn to face her fears, not pamper them. I'm here if she needs help."

"Very well," Erich said. In a sweet, caring voice he assured her, "I'll be back as quickly as I can."

With a nod from Jacob, the converts beside them stepped away. Standing alone on deck with him and without Erich by her side, Anna was certain the sea was growing more threatening. Nervously stealing glances at Jacob, who was examining his thumb and picking at its cuticle, she gripped the rail and winced as wave after wave crashed against the hull beneath her. Knowing the deep, gray waters, on whim, could swallow her, pangs of disaster roiled in her stomach, and her anxiety swelled with the waves. If only Erich had not left her.

"What did you want to talk to me about?" she pressed, hoping the sound of Jacob's voice would distract her and that what he said would be of some comfort. Always in the company of other converts, she had not had a chance to learn from Erich what happened below decks that day, and as he lingered below this evening, his departure began to worry her.

Keeping his head down, raising his eyes to peer at her from beneath thick, dark brows, Jacob issued not comfort but criticism. "I was awakened a little early this morning by a disturbance in your bunk. I could not help but hear." He paused, then said with emphasis, "Everyone could not help but hear."

Anna flushed with embarrassment.

"It is to the glory of God that man and woman join," he continued, raising his head and glaring at her, "but you should not flaunt your pleasure in such a joining before others." He screwed his lips in disgust. "You were cooing and writhing like animals."

Utterly humiliated, not daring to defend herself, she mumbled, "Yes, sir."

"What is remarkable is that someone as healthy looking as you, having been married so many years and having had such opportunities, has no children. Most women of your age and build would have five or six by now. There isn't anything wrong with you, is there? There isn't anything you should tell me?" Peering at her all-knowingly, his pallid, brown eyes widened then winced. Until Anna bore a child, her life was universally considered purposeless. Her worth, not only as a woman but as a human being, was in question.

The converts in the stern moved closer to listen. By morning, everyone on board would know.

Back home in Weiningen, Switzerland, her infertility was an embarrassment to their families: – their fathers always asking Erich, "When?;" – their mothers and sisters asking her time and time again, "Why?" there was no baby. She and Erich ran out of excuses. In coming West, they hoped to leave the accusations behind.

Anna did not know what was wrong, why she had not conceived, but even if she did know, she would not tell Jacob. "No, nothing."

"Good. A man's worth before God, his glory, is in large part measured by the number of children he spawns. He must have a wife who will bear them for him. I suspect, though, in your case, there is more to the problem than that." He leaned uncomfortably close. "Maybe all you need is a man already close to God."

With an oily smirk he nodded, turned and bid her, "Good evening." Leaving Anna at the stern, completely disgraced and demoralized, he walked toward the bow and joined the pregnant Kristina.

Desperate for Erich, she was in tears as spray from a wave crashing against the bow showered her. Why doesn't he hurry? she thought, turning away from the converts still staring at her. Where is he? Staring at the stairwell, she shivered. Something was wrong.

In the darkness of the hold, – from behind rough hewn and ancient oak posts as broad as a strong man's chest, – and from a tiny space beneath the stairs, four men rushed Erich. Savagely throwing him to the floor and sitting on him, they held him as one of them forced a cup of liquid down his throat.

"My God!" he screamed, as the fluid burned his flesh. His mouth, his throat, and all the living conduits leading to his poisoned stomach were melting.

In an instant, he could scream no more. Incapacitated, unable to fight any longer, like metal fired and liquified, he collapsed.

"Let's go," one of his attackers said.

They released him, and Erich heard them walking, unhurried and confident, from the hold. He heard their footsteps on the stairs, and then nothing. He was three flights below deck and what seemed a hundred miles from the stairs. Anna, he thought, for he had no organs left with which he could speak. Anna, help me. Struggling to his elbows, he rolled onto the stomach that was dissolving inside him and crawled with all his will to the stairs. Fighting off the ravage inside him, desperately searching for the hatch to the deck, he pulled himself up one step at a time.

Death crawled behind him, chewing at his feet, as he made the first flight and reached for the second. His tongue and esophagus half gone, his throat filled with fluid, he began to bark. His body was trying to force him to stop, to writhe in agony, but his love for Anna was driving him on.

The wood of the stairs was cold, its taste and smell briny. He felt himself climbing with his chin, catching it on the stair above him and pulling. He was but feet from the open hatch, in hearing distance of everyone on deck, yet he could not summon them. Imagining Anna beside him, he pulled himself inches closer, then all function stopped. Staring toward the sky, making gurgling noises, gagging sounds that only he could hear, he prayed for her to come to him.

Synchronized with the waves, Anna's spirits rose and ebbed as she fought the desire to search for him, to face the consequences of interrupting something she knew was only for men. Finally quashed as the wind kicked up and the waves swelled higher, her spirit faltered. The sea was at hand, and theirs was the only ship in sight. Fighting waves trying to swamp it, the ship bucked, and she could wait no longer. I've got to find him. With the roll of the ship, she staggered toward the hatch. "Erich!" she screamed, when she saw him sprawled on the stairs, his feeble hand reaching up for her. "What happened? Mrs. Tork, help!"

Mrs. Tork and a dozen men and women nearby came to her assistance. While Erich made burbling noises, seemingly trying to tell them what had happened, the men carried him back down the stairs to the second deck and to his bunk.

He convulsed, and Anna cried, "What's wrong with him?"

Feeling for a pulse, Mrs. Tork touched his neck with her stubby fingers. As he convulsed again, she wrapped her copious arms around him, holding him tight until he quieted.

He whimpered and inhaled a trickle of air, but he could not exhale it. He could not take in or release any air at all. His legs stiffened. His fists clenched. His arms and hands went limp, and he slipped into unconsciousness.

Her world crashing around her, Anna screamed, "No! Please, no!" Unable to control herself, she madly sobbed. Her life was shattering. Her love was dying before her eyes.

The agony on his face evaporated. In what seemed only seconds, he was still.

Pushing Mrs. Tork aside, Anna grasped Erich's shoulders. "Erich!" she shouted, shaking him, trying to wake him. "Erich!" He couldn't be dead. Yet, she could feel no life in him. Her light and her darkness, the substance of her soul, was gone. She looked desperately to Mrs. Tork for an answer.

"Something must have ruptured," she told her. There was no need to look into Erich's mouth and see the destruction there, the charred remains of burned flesh. The blood flowing from between his lips was evidence enough. "I'm sorry. Sometimes these things just happen."

Women swarmed about Anna, wanting to help, praying for her, and seeing to her comfort, but she was barely aware of them. Buffeting voices fell silent, and only lips moved. Comforting arms dried like winter leaves and crumbled. Her mind occluded by an intensifying fog, she was isolated from everyone and everything about her. The commotion around her dreamlike, the bunk on which they sat her a cloud on which she wept with despair, she was neither whole nor half. She was nothing. Her mind was in twilight. Her grief was an impenetrable cell, and she did not feel time pass. Yet, an hour later, a hand reached for her and pulled her away. The women around her were but shadows, the stairs to the hold but ridges down which to be guided. The ship and all about her were blurs until she saw Erich.

His body appeared out of nowhere stretched across three large casks. He had been bathed then wrapped in canvass. His face was exposed for her. A single lantern, its light a beacon for his soul, hung from the bulkhead behind him.

Seeing only him, unaware the room was full of women there to comfort her and prepare Erich for burial, Anna knelt at his head. His cheeks were pallid, his eyes closed. He seemed to be as she had so often seen him in sleep.

Putting her arms around him, she embraced him. Pressing her cheek to his, she suddenly pulled back. His flesh was like stone. He was nothing as she remembered him, and his touch left her cold. Cut through the heart, she realized at last, he was gone. The reality too much for her, she sobbed inconsolably.

Chapter Seven

The Middle of the Atlantic
April 7, 1854

For Anna, the dawn was scattered with light and shadows, confusion and silence. Barely aware of those busying themselves around her, she was dressed by them in black and then scurried upstairs to attend Erich's funeral on the main deck. Unwilling to feel, she hardly noticed the rocking of the ship. Unwilling to hear, the congregation's singing was muffled. She looked away as Erich's body was carried on deck, the canvass shroud closed about his face. As he was laid on crates lashed to a mast, she stared at her feet.

The sea had awakened in a mood, and if was raining. As the ship rolled the crates shifted, and each time they shifted, Erich's body moved back and forth. Shrouded in a daze, Anna saw and heard nothing as the singing built to a crescendo then fell into a slow, melodious dirge.

Two men moved to hold Erich's body down, and Jacob began. "Erich Baek was a good, hardworking man. We will miss him for what he might have been and for how he could have helped us build God's Kingdom. Born in Weiningen, Switzerland, the son of a carpenter and raised in that trade, he could have contributed much to our community. But there was something missing in Erich, – something crucial to his having a place in our midst. Brother Erich swore to us that he believed in God. Yet, he did not. That is why he is dead. Because he refused to believe, Adam struck him down.

"But, do not fear for him, for he will find a Heaven. There are three heavens to which we may go. There is first the 'Telestial Heaven' where heathens and those who are in Hell pending Judgment Day go. Second, the 'Terrestrial Heaven' for Gentiles and Mormons who aren't obedient to the priesthood or loyal to the Church. If God so wishes this will be where Erich spends eternity.

"Brother Erich will not reach the 'Celestial Heaven' which is the greatest of heavens. Only obedient Mormons are rewarded with that. The Celestial Heaven has three more levels, and they are the highest levels to which a Mormon man can aspire, his success depending on the strength of his belief in the true God and his obedience to the Priesthood. If a man is unquestioningly loyal to the Church and obedient to the Priesthood in all things while he is in this world, he will be deified at death. He will rise to the highest level of Celestial Heaven and become a God like Adam. He will have his own godhood and his own planet on which he will build his kingdom. He will populate his godhood with his wives and the children he has spawned. He will rule as Adam rules Earth, and his descendants will worship him. For this and the glory of our God, you are journeying to Utah, the seat of His Kingdom. You and your children will never want for food or shelter, and in time, all the riches of the world will be yours.

"Brother Erich did not pass his first test of faith. Because he failed, he will never rise to Godhood. We are sorry for Brother Erich. We are most especially sorry for his wife, Sister Anna, whom he left with no children and no means to salvation. As I have taught you, a woman cannot be saved except through her husband."

Jacob looked at Anna and made her a solemn promise. "Don't worry, Sister Anna. We will remedy that."

Yet, Anna was not thinking of her own fate. Publicly confronted with Erich's blasphemous transgression, she hung her head. Accepting that the fault was his, she accepted God's punishment and was heartbroken.

"This is a lesson in what will happen to you and yours when you are not utterly faithful and do not obey," Jacob threatened. "Adam has no patience with doubters and will not help them either in His Kingdom or in the hereafter." He glared at the congregation. "See that He never doubts you." He paused for maximum effect, then came to a close, motioning a group of men to pick up Erich's body. "We have much to think about this day. Brother Erich's life on earth is over, but yours is not. It is time to prove yourselves. Best you get started."

Anna watched as the men awkwardly carried Erich's remains to the gunwale. Her gaze froze when they fed him to the sea.

She was given the day to mourn, her only duty prayer. After that, she was expected to fully participate in the convert's activities. Sitting and brooding, allowing melancholy to control her, were not healthy. Refusing to go back to the bunk where she and Erich last made love and where he died, Anna spent nights sitting quietly in the galley, thinking about him, suffering her pain and despair alone.

Within a day or two, the women were pressuring her to go through Erich's things. The community could use them. So one day, after morning meeting and during the scrubbings, she and Kristina went to the hold for the trunks.

"Do you need any help?" Kristina asked her.

"Thank you, anyway, but I'd rather be alone."

Kristina nodded and handed her the lantern. "Just call if you need me," she said, as she climbed the stairs.

The hold was dark, and overpoweringly musty. Passengers' trunks were stacked in stall like holds. Sisters eager to help had already retrieved Anna and Erich's trunks and set them aside for her, so she had no difficulty finding them. Ignoring her own trunk, she hung the lantern next to Erich's.

Inside the trunk, on top, shirts she and his mother had made by hand for him were neatly folded, just as she had packed them. Carpenter tools his father gave him, his best wool pants, and his new boots were also there. Everything brought back memories. In the right hand corner of the trunk, wrapped in a leather strap was Erich's old straight razor, its ceramic handle worn in the shape of his hand. Taking comfort from its touch, she held it to her breast. Unable to sort through the rest of his things, she left them as they were, and closed the lid. Erich's only other possession was his rocker, packed deep in the hold. Except for the razor and the rocker, the community could have it all.

Exhausted, the roll of the ship inviting her to sleep, Anna crawled into a nearby corner and closed her eyes, clutching Erich's razor in her hand. She would be missed on deck, and in a while, someone would come looking for her. Until then, she could rest.

"Anna," a voice, soft and gentle, called.

"Wake up. Jacob wants to see you." Kristina was leaning over her, a second lantern in her hand. "He's been looking for you.

"Are you all right?"

"Yes," Anna said. While she slept, she had clung to Erich's razor, and her fingers were numb. Shaking her hand, she added, "Just a little stiff."

"He wants to see you right away," Kristina hurried. "He's waiting in the galley." She offered Anna her hand and helped her stand.

"Must have been colder down here than I thought," Anna said, as she strained to straighten joints nearly frozen.

"You didn't even have a blanket," Kristina observed.

"I'll be all right. What does Jacob want?"

"He didn't tell me. Just said for you to come. I'd go with you, but I have laundry to do."

"Get your things sorted?" Jacob asked, when Anna came into the galley. He was sitting at a heavy, oak table and did not stand.

"Yes."

"Good. I know the brothers and sisters will appreciate anything you donate.

"Sit." He motioned her to the bench across from him, and she sat down there, submissively folding her hands in her lap. Except for the two women chopping salted pork and reconstituting desiccated beans on the other side of the room, he and Anna were alone.

"I want to talk to you about your pilgrimage," he began. "I don't want you worrying."

Hesitant to interrupt him, to tell him she had decided to go home and knowing he would not like the idea, she determined to wait until he was finished.

"I've gone through Erich's lock box," he continued, "made sure all his papers are safe, and will see that his money goes to a good cause. You needn't worry about a thing."

Puzzled, Anna tried to understand what he was saying. Yet, nothing he said made sense. Erich had no papers. Their money box was in their bunk, wrapped in canvass and sewn in the mattress.

Jacob smiled, reassuringly. "When we get to Philadelphia, I'll donate his money to the Perpetual Emigrating Fund."

"The what?"

"The Perpetual Emigrating fund. It is a reserve we keep to help our poorer converts emigrate to Utah, – people who would not otherwise be able to come."

"But, why Erich's money?" she asked, a little frightened. "Now that he's gone, isn't his money mine? I'll need it."

Jacob laughed. "Don't be absurd. Women can't inherit money. We're in America now. In America and its territories, and in God's true church, women are property, the same as horses or houses. They can be bought or sold, given away, or promised – but they can't own property. That would be ridiculous. How can property own property?

"When Erich joined the Church of Jesus Christ of Latter Day Saints and became a saint himself, he implicitly bequeathed to the Church you and all he owned in the event he died."

"But, I want to go home to my family, and I need the money!"

In complete control, not only of the money, but of Anna, Jacob reached across the table and patted her hands. Half comforting her, half threatening her, his glance left no room to argue as he told her, "The Church is your family. Utah is your home. We promised Erich that we would love and protect you, and that is what we will do.

"The life you left in Switzerland is over. You belong to us now."

Chapter Eight

Provo, Utah
11:30 p.m.
April 20

In a large, modern kitchen, with an island at which people could sit and watch the cook, Kim was washing dishes in steamy, hot water and a thick bath of soap, preparing them for the dishwasher. The phone rang, and she picked it up.

"Hi," Sharon said. She was already in her motel room ready for bed. "Did I wake you?"

"No, I was just finishing up."

"I wanted to tell you how much I enjoyed the day with you. I'm sorry I haven't been paying closer attention."

"That's all right. I know you're busy. Thanks for helping me with Wayne." Kim giggled, "I think he really believed you were fishing my wedding ring out of the toilet. Didn't even question me."

"I'd have been all right," Sharon quipped, "if the bleach you used to clean it hadn't about asphyxiated me. Where is he, anyway?"

"In bed. He turned in right after you left."

"Any new problems?"

"No. Just a couple of remarks about how you weren't married and why he thinks you belong in the kitchen and not in the courtroom."

"You'd think by now he'd stop singing that tune," Sharon said in disgust.

"I know, but that's all he knows," Kim excused.

"Rather narrow, don't you think? Maybe I should do more to broaden him."

"No, please, don't do that. Your pressing just causes problems." Deftly changing the subject, Kim added, "Did you know you forgot your iphone?"

"That's another reason I'm calling. Where'd I leave it?"

"On the mantle in the living room, when you were getting in touch with your assistant before supper."

"I've got a meeting with Transamerica's CFO tomorrow night, so I'll have to leave here early. Do you mind if I drop by first thing in the morning?"

"No. Is six early enough?"

"Just right. Thanks. It'll give us another chance to talk."

"Okay. I'll see you at six."

"Good night."

As Kim hung up her hard wired phone, she smiled. At last, she had someone in whom she could confide. Comforted, she sighed. Finishing the dishes, she turned the lights out and started up the stairs. She was halfway up when the front door bell rang. Not expecting company so late at night, she went to the door and cautiously peered out one of the long, bronze tinted relights. A black van was parked at the curb. Two men in business suits were standing on her front steps. "Who is it?" she asked.

"Me, Kim. Frank," the man nearest the door answered. He moved closer, so his face was illuminated by the porch light.

"Frank?" she asked, as she opened the door and let them in. "Is something the matter?"

Frank was one of Wayne's best friends and golfing buddies, his best man at their Temple wedding. Kim did not know the man with him. What could they want at this hour?

"Where's Wayne?"

"He's in bed. Why, what's wrong."

"We have to see him."

"Go on into the living room, and I'll get him," Kim told them. Spurred by the seeming urgency of her errand, Kim hurried upstairs, opened the bedroom door, and turned on the overhead light. "Wayne," she called, shaking him. "Frank's here. He needs to see you."

Wayne's grogginess immediately left him, as did all the color in his face.

"Should I make tea?" she asked, nervously.

"No."

Slowly, as if he was moving through waist deep sand, Wayne put on his pants, a shirt, and his favorite sandals. "I'm sorry," he said, standing next to her but not touching her. "I tried. I put them off as long as I could, but I failed."

"Failed in what?" He was scaring her. "What are you talking about? What do they want?"

He took Kim in his arms, uncharacteristically stroked the back of her head, and said, "You know I love you. I'm sorry I've taken this all out on you. I should have made this easier for you, not harder. I should have spent more time with you."

"Wayne!" she protested. "What's going on?"

"Probably nothing," he told her, with a shallow smile. "Just stay in here and keep the door closed. I'll take care of them."

"No! I'm going with you."

Piercing her with a steel hard stare, all compassion gone out of it, Wayne reminded her, "I said, 'Stay!'"

Backing off, she succumbed, "All right."

"Just do as you're told, and you'll be fine."

Downstairs, outside Wayne's study, fingers touched the glass on the cabinet that housed the urn with the hieroglyphs.

"Why are you here, Frank?" Wayne asked, standing just inside the room.

Frank was next to the Egyptian urn, the locked cabinet now open. The curly, sandy hair of his youth was almost gone. The characteristic grin that always made him appear so harmless forgotten. He did not look like a friend but like a messenger with bad news. "You need to come with us."

Wayne nodded as Frank approached and took him by the arm.

"Is this it?" Wayne asked.

There was no answer.

As the three men stepped outside and walked across the lawn to the unmarked, black van, Frank made a call on his cellphone. "We've got him," he said.

"Is the vessel there?" the voice on the other end asked.

"Yes." Even before Frank disconnected, a second black van, lights out, silently pulled up behind them.

Not a word was said while the black van in which Wayne was held traveled for hours: – first down freeways; – then over rough, gravel roads, always climbing, the roads getting progressively worse; – up primitive, dirt roads with great swells worn by logging trucks. Finally, at 4:00 a.m., on a mountain peak deep in the wilderness, the van rolled to a stop. Nudging Wayne with the back of his hand, Frank ordered him to, "Get out."

Wayne complied. The side door slid open, and as Wayne stepped down, the man who had come to the house with Frank stood there and watched. A third man, the driver, walked around the front of the van to join them.

"Put your hands behind your back," Frank ordered. He then bound Wayne's wrists together with a long zip tie.

While Wayne stood there, Frank busied himself unpacking the articles he would need. Not wishing to see them, Wayne looked away, quietly and resignedly waiting in the darkness for what was to come.

They were in a mountain bowl dotted with Douglas Firs not far beneath the snow line. Their only light was by the stars and a kerosene lantern, turned down low, on a stump beside him. After a few, very long moments, the other two men approached him, cut off the zip ties, and took off his clothes. They then pushed him to the nearest tree, turned him facing outward, and tied him at the chest and at each of his thighs to the trunk.

The rough scales of the bark dug into Wayne's back. The ropes around his wrists cut off his circulation and made his hands swell, but he did not notice. Spread eagle and naked, a cushion of needles beneath his bare feet, he was terrifyingly aware that he was at the precipice. He was at the end of all he would ever know, the tree to which he was tied the closest thing he had to God.

From the edge of the lantern light a voice came, "I am Michael," Frank began, standing in shadow.

Wayne already knew Frank was the ritual "Michael," the man who held the revolver to Wayne's head at trial. He was Wayne's friend, his best friend. – Yet, he was the man who was going to.... Wayne could not even think about it.

As Michael proceeded with the ritual, he was cold and formal. Cloaked by spiritual duty, it was as if his conscience and their friendship were forgotten. "The Tribunal has made its decision," he said. "It has found that you, the man known to us as 'Min, the Beekeeper,' failed to surrender the vessel as ordered. It has also found that you, most likely, revealed to a Mister Henry Blanchard and possibly others secrets you have sworn before God and the Priesthood to keep. The Tribunal has therefore ruled that you have violated the covenants of secrecy and obedience to which you swore. Though Christ died for all men's sins, His blood can never wipe away what you have done. The only way you can earn salvation, the only way you can have a place in His Kingdom, is if you atone for those sins. In order for you to atone, your blood must be shed."

As if suddenly struck by the gravity of what he must do, the man Wayne knew as Frank paused. His voice trembled as he continued, "I am here to help you." Instantly returning to his role as "Michael," Frank ceremoniously donned a long, white apron and gloves, ritually sharpened a ten-inch knife, and stepped forward.

Wayne's legs were shaking. His mouth was as dry as dust.

Michael grasped one of Wayne's testicles, pulled it hard, and sliced it off.

Wayne's scream was blood curdling. It traveled for miles, but there was no one to hear it. He begged Michael to stop. He pleaded with him not to do it. Yet, Michael grabbed the other testicle, raised the knife, and cut it off too.

Quivering, his body in a tailspin of horror and shock, Wayne felt the knife then arc across his belly, slicing it open. He felt and saw his guts unwind and slither to his feet. He panicked. If only he could walk, stumble away. If only he could go back to yesterdays and see Kim again, he would gladly give up Heaven. Yet, as his tethers were cut and as he felt his hands freed, all he could do was slump to the ground like soft mud. No longer feeling or able to speak, his heart beating against his chest as if trying to get out, he gasped. As his executioners gently and professionally stretched him out and gathered his pieces, he could do nothing.

Helplessly lying there, Wayne saw Michael coming at him again with his knife. He felt his wind escaping as the knife slid across his throat. No longer caring as they dug a grave beside him, he forgot everything he knew, even Kim, and drifted away.

"Wayne?" Kim whispered, hearing someone at the bedroom door. "Wayne?" she asked aloud, as the knob turned.

Chapter Nine

Iowa City, Iowa
June 1854

Days toiled into nights, and weeks were enveloped by them. Time seemed of little importance as Anna continued her journey to the shores of America and then into its heart. Near Iowa City, at a staging point for Mormon wagon trains, she and the converts with whom she traveled joined hundreds of other Mormon converts headed west, across the wilderness to Utah.

Out of the long, marshy grass near the river and from the woods, clouds of mosquitoes rose at dawn and at dusk to harass them. The converts were mostly British, Scandinavian and German. There were more women than men, and many of the women had children. Many of the adults were over fifty and had brought with them a wealth of Old World trades, necessary skills for quickly civilizing a wilderness. Prepared to travel nearly 1,400 miles west, across rough mountains and vast prairies to what they believed was Zion, their Kingdom of God on Earth, they were excited to get started. Two wagon trains had already departed that spring. A third was being organized.

Without having the means to feel anything but grief, the ache deep inside her constant and heavy, Anna was getting used to doing what she was told to do by Jacob and the other elders. She never questioned them, and she never hesitated. Grateful to Jacob for taking her under his wing and for not having to make her own decisions, she was completely dependent on him. Who better to trust than a priest of her church? Switzerland seemed very far away. Lulled by a sense of Mormon community and caring, enthralled that their Prophet had the power to speak to God, she felt part of a great movement west and gave up on the idea of going home.

Jacob had required Anna to sign a promissory note in the amount of twenty dollars to buy a cart and provisions for her passage west. To repay that debt, she was to bake bread on the trail for the other families.

"Can't I use just some of the money my husband left?" Anna had asked Jacob, when he demanded she sign the note. They were sitting with Kristina at his campsite before a tent provided to them, next to the fire Anna had built. "I'm sure Erich told me he had enough to buy oxen and a wagon for us. He even said there'd be enough left over when we got to Utah to build a house and buy cattle."

Jacob's eyes narrowed as he glared at her. His voice was ragged with impatience, as he reminded her, "I already told you. I gave that money to the poor. It's in Europe by now, furthering God's work. You don't need money, Sister Anna. All you need do is work hard and do what you're told, and the Church will provide for you."

Heavy in the pit of Anna's stomach was a new and troubling realization that she had nothing, not even choices, unless Jacob and the Church gave them to her. While light, imperceptible shackles closed about her ankles, her indenture secured, suspicion crept through her. Her gut tightened, and she stared into the cooking fire. Maybe Jacob took Erich's money for himself.

She thought back. When the ship landed in Philadelphia, Jacob left for two days. He could have done anything with Erich's twenty dollar gold pieces.

Then Anna reconsidered. Doubting Jacob only increased her distress. Jacob was a missionary of God, a priest. If she couldn't trust him, how could she trust the Church? She reasoned. How could she trust anyone or anything? If she questioned her faith, she had nothing, – not even an afterlife. She trembled with fear as she envisioned what would happen to her, and that brought her to her senses. If I mistrust them, I'll only make myself miserable over something I can't do anything about. The money's gone, and I'm out here in the wilderness alone. I can't alienate these people. I can't leave them. They're all I have. If I'm ever to be at peace, I must put all doubt out of my mind. I must trust them.

Tiny bits of light filled the late night sky, while beneath them, the runoff swollen river churned downstream. Seeking a diversion, Anna left the huge encampment and walked toward the bank. Busy and noisy, the campground was usually a welcome distraction from her grief, but tonight her heartache was especially acute, and she needed some privacy. The stars were friends to her. The river was consuming. As the moon reflected off the fast moving water, she watched and allowed herself to cry.

"Is there anything I can do?" a voice, distinctively English, interrupted her. "I came out to check the river and saw you here." Though ample in girth, the woman who approached her was petite, barely five feet tall. Bright in the moonlight, her eyes were wide and peaceful. Her soft, round face was a well of strength and understanding. "I don't mean to bother you, but you look like you need someone to talk to."

The women with whom Anna traveled across the Atlantic had tried to help her, but their talking incessantly of death, God's will, and of the trials and sacrifices expected of all of them had been no comfort. Most often, she felt better when she was by herself. She could tell this woman was different. Even beside the swollen, threatening river, her mere presence and the sound of her voice instantly calmed Anna.

"I've got some water for tea. Would you like me to make you some?"

"I'd like that very much. Thank you."

The pot was warming over the woman's fire, the water beginning to steam, when someone sneezed in the tent behind them. "That's Lizzy, my granddaughter," the woman explained.

"Where are you from?" Anna asked, although there was little doubt the woman was English.

"From Grimsby on the Humber. My son was a fisher there, the last of a score of generations of men in our family who made their living on the sea. We came to America last year and have been living in New York. There's just the three of us, you know. Lizzy's poor mother dying when Lizzy was born and there not being any more children. Poor child. The only parent she's got is her father. All the mother she's had these past ten years has been me.

"I'm Hattie Wickens. My son is John Wickens. And, your Anna Baek, aren't you?"

"You know me?"

"When your group arrived, your story spread all over camp. I'm sorry if I've offended you, but I wanted to help. When I saw you wandering out of camp, looking so lonely, I followed you to make sure you were all right. I lost my husband when I was about your age, just as suddenly, so I know a little of how you feel."

Anna politely watched as Hattie rolled tea leaves between her fingertips, sprinkled them in the bottom of two plain, tin cups, and poured the now boiling water over them. "What were you doing in New York?"

"Earning enough money to pay our way to Utah," Hattie told her.

After a moment, Anna asked, "Do you have a daughter?"

"No, Lizzy's as close as I've come to that dream. – I barely knew her mother."

"Any other sons?"

"No, just John."

The fire was soothing. The moon and stars were a still, peaceful cover. As the hours past, a bond grew between them. With gentle encouragement, Anna told Hattie about Erich and the sea. "I have nightmares," she confided, her voice quavering in distress. "I see him in a violent sea. He's thrashing for breath, fighting to stay on the surface and live. Fish are surrounding him in a frenzy and tearing him to pieces. He's calling for me, begging me to help him. But, I can't move. I can only watch as what's left of him sinks into the darkness."

Hattie put her arm around her, comforting her. "Now, now," she said very sweetly. "I guess I didn't realize how frightened you are. You see, I lived at the edge of the sea all my life. My family lived or died by what it provided. I never even thought how terrifying a burial in its depths could be to someone who knew only the land. Where did you say you were from?"

"Weiningen in Switzerland." It was about as far and fortified from the sea as a European could get.

"Many a man I've known has been buried at sea," Hattie assured her. "Burials there as natural as those in the ground, no more or less tragic to the ones they've left behind. What happened wasn't your fault. That's just the way thing's are done," she said, not belittling Anna's feelings. "There's no way to, ahh – keep – a body at sea. There is no choice."

"The bible talks about 'ashes to ashes' and 'dust to dust,' but where is there anything about the sea?" Anna argued. "What if Erich's burial wasn't holy? What if God doesn't find him? What will happen to his soul?"

"There, there. I'm sure God will find him. "There must be something about that in the bible. I'll ask John."

The next evening after supper and prayer, Anna looked up from her cooking fire and, for the first time, enjoyed seeing the scores of other converts in the campground, – listening to their music, – watching them gather to visit and get acquainted. She had nothing to bring Hattie but a small bunch of wild flowers she had picked that afternoon. With the flowers in hand, she went to see her.

"Why, thank you, dear," Hattie said. "Come join us."

At the edge of the small fire, on bright orange coals, rested an iron pot in which water for tea was boiling. A few feet further from the fire's edge, a man was on his knees working on a huge length of canvas. He had shoulder-length, dark brown hair, and his sleeves were rolled to his elbows. A little girl about ten sat next to him.

Hattie introduced her, "John, Lizzy, this is Anna Baek."

Long, curly bangs tumbled over his brow as John unwrapped himself and stood. "Pleased." A dark beard covered his cheeks and throat. A mustache masked his lips. He was big and muscular, yet there was gentleness in his eyes. He extended his scarred and calloused hand to her.

Hattie beamed as she touched his shoulder. "Anna, this is my son, John, and his daughter, Lizzy."

Lizzy's dark hair was like her father's, curly and unruly. Cascading over her shoulders, it reached halfway down her back. Her cheeks were gently rounded, but her chin came to a finely chiseled point. Framed in long, black lashes, beneath delicately arched eyebrows, her regal, walnut eyes, sparkled. "Hello, Mrs. Baek. Glad to meet you. Can I get you a cup 'a tea?"

"I'd like that very much, Lizzy. Why don't you call me Anna?"

Lizzy's full, pink lips spread to a grin. "You can take my stool if you want. That way you'll be next to Papa."

John was polite but was clearly impatient to get back to his work. He waited for Anna to sit down then resumed working on the canvass that would ultimately cover their wagon.

"What are you doing?" Anna asked him when she sat down.

"Sewing a channel for the tie rope." He lifted a corner of the heavy canvass between his fingers and showed her. "Like piecin' shark's hide together."

"Papa always liked fish nets better," Lizzy explained, while she prepared Anna's tea. "Only patched sails when he had to."

In deep concentration, his big fingers tying off a stitch, John did not look up but managed to add, "Yup."

"Why don't you put that down for a while, John?" Hattie gave him an encouraging, nudging glance. "Maybe Anna would like to hear about the sea." Hattie had told him what happened to Erich and how Anna felt and had asked him to try to make her feel better.

As if he suddenly remembered what he was supposed to do, he set the canvas aside, licked his fingers, and brushed the hair from his eyes, casually starting, "Hear you lost your husband at sea. That he was buried there."

Anna caught her breath, lowered her eyes and nodded.

Seeming to realize the extent of her suffering, John softened his voice. "I'm sorry, Mzz Baek, I didn't mean to be so ...." Looking very uncomfortable, unable to finish his thought, he sighed. "You shouldn't be afraid for him, you know. The sea's an honorable graveyard."

"But, the bible...," Anna began.

"I don't know much about the bible, but I can guarantee you God is on the sea," John said very firmly. "I've faced Him a hundred times. Every man who's ever sailed has faced Him, – and none of 'em would deny it. Any man who's buried a mate there will swear God attended the funeral. Why, God's been receiving good men there for hundreds of years, and I swear, – when the world ends, He'll come for them."

When Anna did not respond, John hesitated. When Hattie nodded, encouraging him on, he told Anna, "The sea is all and everything to a man who sails. It's kinda' like his search for God. It's brutal, with fluky currents that drag him this way and that. It draws him first close to God, then shoves him away. It tempts him to places he should not go, then punishes him when he is enticed by them. It sometimes lures him into thinking he is in control, but then destroys him. Every man who sails it lives at the edge of both Heaven and Hell, – fighting it, then knuckling under its urgings."

A fierce struggle between love and fear was raging in John's deep, steely eyes. "If a man wisely chooses the waves on which he searches for God, the sea will calm, be a friend to him and provide sustenance. If he chooses unwisely, the sea will turn on him in rage. Men who rest at the bottom of the sea are at the end of their search, and God embraces them."

Hearing the affection and enchantment in John's voice, Anna began to feel better about Erich's fate, yet she was concerned for John. "If you love the sea and your search for God was there, why did you leave it and come here?"

"Because there are other ways to find God, – and because there's something I love more." He looked at Lizzy and smiled. "I didn't want my daughter orphaned."

"Tell her, John," Hattie encouraged.

"I'd been out two months," John told Anna. "Fishing was good and our hold was full. We were comin' home. As we passed east of Flamborough Head, the wind blew to a gale and riled the surface. It sent waves as tall as temples over our bow. We took on water and toppled." He paused, keeping his gaze on Lizzy. "We were suddenly under." He looked briefly at Anna then stared blankly into the fire. "We were in the water a couple a' days before another fishing boat picked us up, – only three out of the ten of us surviving."

He smiled reassuringly at Lizzy. "We took Elder Damon, our missionary, as a sign from God to go to Utah. So we left the sea and set a new course."

Chapter Ten

Iowa City, Iowa
June 1854

Targeting the poor, who were bereft of opportunity in Europe, the hopeful, and the adventurous, the Mormons offered glories greater than all the other churches. They offered wealth and sainthood on Earth, sister and brotherhood, and a community that would forever take care of them and their families. People flocked to them. Converts gave up their lives to come to America and go west, despite the dangers. For men, the ultimate reward was Godhood. Where else in Christendom, could a man become a god?

Once Anna got over the initial shock of their god being Adam, thereafter being indoctrinated to it by instruction every day, she also believed in the religion. Why couldn't God be Adam and Michael the Archangel? Why couldn't God be a man, and other men become gods?

Beside the camp, the river was deep and treacherous as it flowed south and away from the long, wilderness road the immigrant converts would take to Utah. They had been organized in groups of ten, fifty and a hundred. Five groups of fifty had been chosen to make up the next wagon train west, and a meeting had been called. It was sunset, and as the river rushed past the trailhead, a ribbon of light shimmered through it. Nearby, the two hundred and fifty chosen to go enthusiastically crowded together waiting for instructions from the elders.

Jacob stood in front of them on a wooden crate, his head above the crowd. Anna and Kristina were only a few feet away, yet Anna's back was turned to him. She was searching for Hattie. When she saw her with John and Lizzy, standing at the edge of the crowd near the river bank, she waved until she caught Hattie's eye.

"This is Brother Ned Haight," Jacob began as the crowd quieted. He motioned to a rugged, grizzled man standing on the ground next to him. "Brother Haight is to be in command of your wagon train. You and he will get along fine if you remember two rules: Whatever he says goes. And, whatever he wants gets done. Brother Haight was one of the men God chose to lead the first group of Mormons to Utah. In the last seven years, he has brought thousands more to its sanctuary and light. He is Brigham Young's envoy, and is a conduit to Heaven. Through him, God will guide you. Above all, you must respect and obey him."

Brother Haight's suit was black like Jacob's, but unlike Jacob's, it was old and rumpled, sorely faded, and covered with dust. His flat brimmed, high crowned hat was cocked back on his balding head. There was a deep, ragged scar on his stubby cheek. He was sullen, almost contemptuous of the people watching him, – the people who would depend on him for their lives.

"Brother Haight has made at least a dozen trips across this continent to the Great Salt Lake. Nobody knows the route better," Jacob continued. "I can't begin to stress how important he will be to you. If you listen to him and do everything he says, you'll have a safe and passable journey. If you do not, you will die. Brother Haight?"

His feet spread apart, his knees locked, and his hands resting on his hips, Ned Haight faced the crowd squarely. Exposed beneath his coat were two old sidearms, the barrels half as long as his leg. Hanging from his belt was a fifteen-inch Bowie knife with an elk horn handle tucked in a buckskin sheath. "Brother Jacob's speakin' ya the truth," he began, ignoring Jacob when Jacob stepped down and offered him the crate. "You people listen to me, you'll get through this. You don't, I'll leave yer fannies behind. No tellin' what'll happen to ya then.

"That prairie yer crossin's dangerous. Them mountains is killers. Many of our people have gone before ya leavin' rafts and sign posts to show the way. That'll make the goin' easier. So long as ya do what I tell ya, you should be safe.

"We'll be leavin' in a couple a' weeks. The elders here'll give ya a list of everything ya'll need. Once we start, the wagons'll travel in close order, every man walkin' beside his wagon with a loaded gun in reach. At night, the wagons'll be corralled with wheels cuddlin' and tongues hangin' out. Every mornin' 'afore dawn, ya'll be woke by a bugle. By the next time ya hear the bugle at 7:00, yer ta be back on the trail and ready ta move out. The women folk'll cook dinner 'fore we leave, 'cause we ain't stoppin' more than an hour at noon. We'll go as far as we can each day, and at 8:30 every night, a bugle'll let every man know it's time ta go to his wagon 'n pray. Yer all ta be in bed with campfires out by 9:00. Daylight's long this time a' year, so with God's help, in a few months, you'll be lookin' at the Great Salt Lake. Anybody got questions?"

Hands were raised, and as Brother Haight explained the details, Anna thought back. The rules were strict. They had been since she left Weiningen, but she was getting used to them. Everything was structured, so there was little room for doubt as to what to do and when. A dangerous, life altering journey was ahead of them. Having everything decided by men who knew what they were doing was reassuring. If she trusted Ned Haight, Jacob, and the other elders to take good care of them, she should not have to worry. She looked around for Hattie who was coming toward her through the crowd. Spirits were high, and the converts selected to go were noisy as they started planning.

"We'd like the three of you to come to dinner," Hattie invited, as Jacob joined them.

Kristina did not respond. She was a dutiful wife, clearly afraid of her father-like husband who seemed to avoid casual chats.

"We'd be pleased," he said, to her obvious surprise.

The night air was thick with moisture, the humidity a curtain in which thousands of flies and mosquitoes bathed. The moon was a slender sickle, its companion stars faded by the fire light. In seventy degree temperatures, Anna, Hattie, John, Lizzy, Jacob and Kristina sat away from the fire as the water boiled for tea.

"Tell us again about the revelations that first led our Prophet to God and the golden plates," Anna asked Jacob.

Jacob reverently began, by telling them, "Joseph Smith was only fifteen when the gods Elohim, Adam, and Jesus Christ came to him. The three gods talked to him in length, bidding him to restore true Christianity to the world." Stretching out the great saga of their prophet, Jacob described in detail how, stunned by the responsibility the

Gods bestowed on him, Joseph had a seizure. Jacob did not tell them that Joseph Smith had many visions in those days, just like his parents and grandparents, – divine revelations which were always accompanied by seizures, – visions that made those who did not believe call him a "charlatan.

"A few years later," Jacob continued, "the Angel Moroni appeared and told Joseph about the 'Bible of the Western Continent'. It was buried on Cumorah Hill in New York, and it would clarify the meanings of the New Testament."

"Who was Moroni, again?" Anna asked. Mormon teachings were still new to her.

"You should already know that," he scolded. "Moroni is the glorified son of Mormon. The two of them were the last survivors of the Nephites, whose people came to the Americas from Jerusalem in 600 B.C. The Lamanites, who came with them, strayed from the faith. Because they strayed, the Lamanites' skins turned dark, and they became the red skin savages of the west."

John started. "You mean the Indians?"

"Of course, but that's enough of them. What's important is that our Prophet Joseph Smith found the Bible of the Western Continent just as Moroni told him he would."

"What did the new bible look like?" Hattie asked.

"It was made of thin, gold plates bound together by three gold rings and etched with small characters the Prophet recognized as reformed hieroglyphics. It was eight inches high, seven inches wide, and six inches thick.

"If the bible was written in hieroglyphics," Anna noted, "how could Joseph Smith read it?"

"The bible was buried inside a stone box. With it was a gold breast plate and a pair of very special glasses called 'Urim and Thurmmin.' These glasses were twice as broad as a man's head and were shaped like a bow. Their lenses were made of crystal. By looking through them, Joseph was able to translate the hieroglyphics into the Book of Mormon."

"Have you ever seen the gold plates?" John asked. "Are they kept in Utah?"

"No, when the Prophet completed translating the historical plates, Moroni reclaimed them. The breast plate and spectacles disappeared, too."

"Didn't anyone but the Prophet ever see them?" John asked.

"Only the Prophet was allowed to see them. Only he had the power to translate the inscriptions through the mystic eyeglasses. The Curse of God was on anyone else
who looked upon them.

Chapter Eleven

Provo, Utah
6:00 a.m.
April 21

Night was fading, and day was just beyond the Wasatch Mountains as Sharon turned into Kim and Wayne's driveway. On the nearby foothills a trace of moisture was awakening the blossoming sagebrush, and the air was lush with their fragrance. It was the only time of day the ever present wind did not blow, and the stillness was Heaven like. "Kim," Sharon whispered, as she gently knocked at the front door, the house closed and quiet. "I'm here."

Guess she didn't hear me, Sharon decided. Giving up on being quiet, using the brass knocker, she banged against the richly stained door four times. "Are you there?" There was no sound, no sign anyone heard. "Wayne!" she called, loud enough for even the neighbors to hear. That's odd, she thought, when still no one answered or came to the door.

The door was locked and bolted. I'd better go around back. Around the corner of the house and through the gate of a six-foot-tall, redwood fence, she followed a granite stone path to a massive, three tiered deck. The sliding doors that led into the kitchen were also locked. A fear was growing inside her. "Kim! Wayne! It's Sharon. Where are you?"

Lights came on in the house next door. A man came to an upstairs window, angrily stared at her, and then retreated. From the house on the other side, a woman about Kim's age, barefoot and in a knee-length, dark blue satin robe tied tightly about her, came outside to look.

"They're not answering. Do you know if something's happened?" Sharon asked her.

Her lips never moving, the woman slowly shook her head and went back inside.

Looking above the slider and to the second floor, Sharon saw that Kim's bedroom window was open. Picking up a few small rocks from the garden next to the deck, she tossed them at the open window. Something moved inside the room, and she sighed, "At last."

After only seconds, there was a thud. "There they are. Kim!" she called, but no one appeared. Something was wrong. She had to get inside. Where does Kim keep that extra key?

Trying to remember, she looked about the yard spotting a birdhouse attached to a young willow ten feet off the deck, the only tree in the yard. There, that's it. The extra key was hooked on a nail driven into the back of the birdhouse Wayne had made for the children. It stuck in the sliding door's lock, and Sharon fumbled with it. "Kim?" she shouted, when she finally stepped onto the kitchen's red clay, tile floor. It looked like nothing had been disturbed or used, or that they'd had breakfast. The tea pot was on the stove, empty and cold. She must not be up yet. "Kim! Wayne!" Sharon shouted.

Still no response. There is something wrong. I know it. Sharon ran up the stairs and to their bedroom. "Kim!" she called, as she knocked on the closed door. "Are you there?" The silence was frightening as she turned the knob and slowly opened the door.

Chapter Twelve

Iowa City, Iowa
June 1854

The sun was broiler hot. Anna's eyes stung with perspiration as she swung a long, twenty pound ax over her shoulder, splitting a four-inch log into kindling. A sawed off old stump was her prop, the swollen river her company. Her flesh was sticky and inviting to a deer fly, bigger than her thumbnail, that landed on her arm and bit her. "Ow-w," she said, swatting at it.

Reaching for mud to ease the sting, she was startled when a hand suddenly touched her shoulder. It was Jacob's. He must have enjoyed sneaking up behind her, because he startled her often. In no mood, she turned on him. Yet he surprised her with a smile.

"I brought you something," he proudly told her. "A woman's ax." Small and razor sharp, the instrument he handed her was three feet long and weighed only eight pounds. It was the perfect size for her. "I've seen you struggling with that big one of mine and thought you might like something lighter," he said, uncharacteristically generous.

Disarmed, she smiled back at him. "Thank you, Brother Jacob."

"I had one of the farriers make it 'specially for you." He took her hand, turned her away, and before she knew what was happening, enfolded her, drawing her close to him. "I'll show you how much easier it is." Thin fabric was all that separated them.

Through her skirt and the flimsy protection of her petticoat, his members pressed against her.

She was shocked. Yet, believing his touch was inadvertent, unable to believe anything else of a disciple of God, she tried to move subtly forward and away from him, without embarrassing him or provoking him to anger. Shifting her hips, tucking her buttocks to gain a modicum of distance between them, she quietly struggled to pull away, but she gained no ground. No man but Erich, had ever been that close to her. What is he doing?

As Jacob tightly wrapped her hand around the handle of the ax and pressed against her even harder, she suddenly realized he was doing it intentionally and forcefully twisted herself away. Her face flushed, her palms sweating, she faced him. "Thank you for your help, Brother Jacob, but I'm sure I'll do just fine without any instruction."

Seemingly amused by her resistance, with a distasteful, overbearing smirk he conveyed to her how foolish she was. Don't you know I own you, came his silent message. Lustfully examining her with shallow, malicious eyes, he told her, "Walk with me. I want to show you something."

A warning bell louder than a fire wagon's rang inside her. Only if you drag me, she thought. Ready to defend herself, she braced against him, and reminded him, "Kristina wouldn't like that."

"Nonsense," he told her, "Krisitina will have no opinion at all." He ripped the ax from Anna's hand, tossed it aside, and grabbed her, his long, steel fingers like vices around her upper arms. "When I tell you to move, you move. When I tell you to come with me, you come with me. Now move!" He released her left arm, turned her upstream, and dragged her away from camp toward a dense clump of trees.

Stumbling over brush and rock, unable to stop him, Anna tried falling, but it didn't work. She tried turning, using her left arm to push him away or strike him, but he would not let her turn.

Staring, his eyes like an animal's ready to strike, he neither looked at her nor changed his course, always and unrelentingly forcing her toward those trees.

"Stop, please stop," she begged. "You can't do this? You just can't!"

"Hi there," John said. He was suddenly behind them, walking toward them, acting as if nothing unusual was happening. "Mum sent me for you," he told Anna. "She needs your help with something. I'll finish up for you here." Whether deliberate or fortuitous, John's timing was perfect.

"If you want wood, go cut down a tree," Jacob snarled. "Leave the kindling to her. This is woman's work, not man's."

"Only in your family," John said, smiling. "In mine, we share the chore."

"If you insist," Jacob growled, "but when you're done, I expect to find the kindling at my fire, not yours."

"Don't worry," John told him, his voice almost threatening, "you'll not only get a fair share, you'll have luck you don't get something else." He turned to Anna. "I think Mum needs you right away."

Grateful and relieved, Anna smiled. Yet, there was no getting completely away from Jacob. As she hurried away, slowing only to pick up her new ax, she heard him bellow after her, "You're to be back in time to help Kristina get supper. Hear me? Don't make me come after you."

Attempting to rape her, then treating her like an incorrigible child, he was in every way demeaning her. He could do anything to her. He was dangerous. She must be very careful not to let him find her alone again.

Ox stew in an iron pot awaited Jacob when he came back to the campsite for supper, its cornbread crust steaming over an open fire. He had been gone all day but, as usual, did not tell them where he had been or what he had been doing. Anna had seen him only when he brought her the ax.

Seeming especially irritable, perhaps because of John's earlier interference, Jacob picked up the iron lid with a stout stick and peered into the pot. "Put in enough sugar this time?" he questioned Kristina. He liked his cornbread sweet but not too sweet, and Kristina seemed always to get it wrong.

"I put three tablespoons in, just like you told me," she timidly defended.

"Good." He replaced the lid, and while Kristina and Anna stood at the fire watching, he inspected and evaluated the camp. "This kindlin's too big. That wood's too green. They'll take all night to start burnin'. Worse yet, their smokin'll draw every hostile within a hundred miles."

Anna reminded herself Jacob told them he wanted everything done right so they wouldn't have trouble on the trail. But, the wood was dry. There'd be no smoke, and there was nothing wrong with the kindling, either. He was just mad because he didn't get his way with her upriver. She stared at Kristina. Poor thing, being married to a man like that. Thank heavens Anna was with her. "I'll try to do better next time," Anna interjected, trying to change

Jacob's angry focus to her. She did not like making him mad. She was not only indebted to him, but she was still dependent on him for her livelihood. Yet, she could not tolerate him bullying Kristina.

Ignoring Anna, Jacob continued his inspection. Finding the lid to the cornmeal ajar, he again struck out at Kristina. Threateningly shaking his finger at her, he shouted, "I told you to be careful. Do this on the trail and we'll lose our food." He removed the lid and carefully sifted the meal through his fingers. "You were lucky this time," he said, replacing the lid and putting the tin away. "Ever see what silverfish can do?" His temper fully inflamed, the scope of his inspection became broader and his standards increased. The flour was out of place. The water barrel was only half full. "I don't care if we are right next to a river. That barrel is to be topped off every chance you get." By the time he was finished, Kristina was in tears as she silently served him.

Expecting him to yell at Kristina because the stew did not have enough beef or had too much salt, or because the cornbread had too much sugar after all, Anna did what she could to help her. Yet, their best was not good enough, and when they sat down to supper, neither of them ate.

Jacob stared at their plates and rebuked them, "You took it. You eat it. There'll be no food wasted here."

His treating them like children unsettled and infuriated Anna, but she was in no position to argue. Lucky to be supported by Jacob and the Church and to be learning now about the trail so mistakes could be avoided, she forced herself to remember he was only trying to keep them alive. Completely dependent, self-esteem becoming a luxury in a place where there were no luxuries, she filled her spoon with stew and responded, "Yes, Jacob."

The next morning, when Jacob came back to their campsite, Anna and Kristina had just finished filling the water barrel. "Your cart's ready," he told Anna.

"My cart?" She was very excited. Finally, she could get some peace away from Jacob. Her own wagon and supplies would make that possible. "When can I see it?"

"Right now. Let's go." He seemed excited too.

She gave Kristina a hug then followed Jacob across camp to the wagon yard which was on the outskirts. Dusty, crowded with men and materials and with wagons in varying stages of completion, the wagon yard was a maze through which Jacob led her. When they reached the forge, a man was fitting wheels on a full-sized wagon. A few feet away, standing by itself, was a small, two-wheel cart that was no more than a wooden box covered with ticking. "There it is," Jacob announced.

Its rawhide wrapped wheels were taller than its sides. A crossbar extended from the front. Its bed barely four feet by five, minute compared to the giant wagons all around, the miniature wagon was dwarfed by them. Having expected something more, Anna sighed. "Is this all I get?"

Her disappointment obvious, Jacob offered encouragement. "That cart might not be very big, but it's made of fine, dry wood by skilled craftsmen. Don't worry, it's plenty strong enough to get you to Utah."

She ignored him.

Doing something she had never seen him do, explaining himself to a woman, he told her, "I wanted to give you something bigger, but I couldn't. Hundreds of converts are coming after you, and there has to be money for them." Circling, making a show of examining the wheels, seeming to be stalling, he finally said, "You've got to be realistic, Sister Anna. You wouldn't be able to push a bigger or heavier wagon. Your food and belongings are going to be heavy enough."

"Push? Don't I get an ox or a mule?"

"No, they're too expensive. We use them only for the heavy wagons."

"But, there's fourteen hundred miles between here and Utah," she complained. "I can't push this thing that far. "And I won't!"

The man at the forge had stopped working and was staring at them. A man planing his wagon's yoke, was watching them, too. Jacob saw them and was clearly embarrassed. Anna was making a spectacle, challenging Jacob in public. Before she realized what she was doing, Jacob rounded the cart, drew back his hand, and struck her, his open hand a sledgehammer against her left cheek and eye. "You'll take what you get and be grateful for it! You'll do just fine," he then quietly told her. "Others have succeeded, women a lot less hardy than you have made it." He raised his voice and fell into preaching. "Remember, only through hardship and sacrifice will you find God and a place in His Kingdom. Only through enduring the hardships put in front of you will you prove your worth. Whining will get you nowhere! Now, take your cart back to camp while I arrange for your provisions."

Thoroughly discouraged, her face stinging, her courage waning, she felt her strength weakening, too, as Jacob walked away. How am I ever going to do it? This is a garden cart, and there are deserts and mountains out there. She circled the cart, then looked about for help. The men around were no longer paying any attention to her. Realizing she would die if she failed, her heart buckled in despair. Tears filled her eyes. She felt terribly alone. She yearned for Erich, but he was not, and never would be, there for her. No one was there but Jacob and the Church. She was at their mercy, and she should not have provoked him.

She brushed off the pain of her cheek and squared her shoulders. If other women had pushed a cart across this continent, she could do it too. Even as a child, a Lutheran, she was taught that God would not put a trial before her if He had not given her the strength to overcome it. As she pictured what the women who went before her must have gone through, she borrowed strength from them and became more understanding of Jacob. He is only doing what he has to do. He wouldn't ask more of me than he would ask of himself if our circumstance was reversed. I know he only hit me because the other men were watching. Finally receptive to the idea, she ran her fingers over the cart's dried hickory frame and wheels. Crawling beneath it, she inspected the axle and was satisfied. The cart was not much to look at but at least it was hers.

Empty, the axles just greased, the small, well made vehicle easily bumped behind her as she pushed it through camp, the crossbar across her hips. At once excited and disappointed, courageous and frightened, she moved quickly. She knew that all of her belongings would not fit, but she was not yet ready to think about what she must leave behind.

Late that afternoon, while men worked in the wagon yard and women started the cooking fires for supper, Anna split with one strike of her new ax a four-inch log. Dead and dry, if divided into small enough pieces, this wood would make kindling acceptable even to Jacob.

Having argued with Jacob in public was an embarrassment not only to Jacob, but to Anna. His slapping her was justified. Not wanting anyone else to know what happened, she had told Kristina she fell and hit her head on a rock. Not wanting to be accused of "whining" again, she suffered her headache in silence.

Jacob's thermometer, nailed to a nearby tree, showed a temperature of over ninety. As the humidity closed around her, stifling her, she dreamed of the green valley in Switzerland she once called home, vividly imagining a cool, mountain breeze through the still, smothering air of Iowa. Closing her eyes, taking a moment to prolong her dream, she hummed a tune her mother taught her.

Although Anna's daydream was comforting and serene it was not lasting and was abruptly interrupted when Kristina asked, "Who's this?"

She raised her head. Kristina was looking at a small, black dog not more than a few feet from them, sitting with its head cocked and ears alert. There was a patch of white on its chest and a tiny, white goatee on its chin.

"Why, hello," Anna greeted, gently holding out her hand.

Hesitant, yet curious, the dog neither moved away nor came closer.

"Try a biscuit," Kristina suggested.
"There's one left from dinner." She went to the tent,
handed the dry biscuit to Anna, and stepped back.

"Come on fella,'" Anna called. Her voice
was apparently threatening, and the dog backed
away.

"Look," Kristina observed. "It's starving. I
can see its ribs."

"Must be a stray." Anna took a closer look.
"A little girl dog." Hoping the needy dog would not
run away, she slowly stepped forward and left the
biscuit on the ground several feet in front of it.
"We'll see if that interests her."

Never taking its dark brown eyes from her,
the dog waited patiently for Anna to walk back to
the fire. Yet even as Anna retreated, it did not go
any closer to the biscuit.

"Let's ignore her," Anna suggested.
"Maybe she'll eat if she doesn't think we're
watching."

Working at a small table, Kristina began
cutting potatoes for a stew. Anna returned to
splitting wood. The next time they looked, the dog
was gone and so was the biscuit.

Early in the morning, a few days before
their wagon train's departure, Jacob picked up his
wagon at the construction yard and drove it into
camp. It was a mammoth vehicle pulled by four,
well fed oxen. The bed was at least five feet wide
and a dozen feet long, and it could carry nearly two
thousand pounds. Already strapped down inside the
wagon were some of the new furnishings Jacob had
bought for his home in Utah: a velvet sofa from
London; a sideboard, hand carved from walnut,
from a small village in the Alps; and an Elizabethan
clock he got at discount from the mother of a

sixteen year old girl he had converted on his last trip and who had married in Utah.

His purchases had been packed by professionals in Plymouth before their departure from England. On their arrival in Iowa City, the oak boxes in which they were packed were resealed. The boxes had been kept so secure from damage even Kristina had not seen their contents.

"I've already instructed Kristina how to pack the supplies," Jacob informed Anna, after he had positioned the wagon at his campsite. "I know you've got your own wagon to worry about, but I'd like you to help her first. I've got heavy sacks and barrels coming, and I don't want her lifting them alone. I wouldn't have you do it, but she's kind of limited in what she can do. I don't want anything happening to that baby. I'm taking the oxen to the farrier to have their hooves examined."

Kristina was six months pregnant and clearly showing. Sick most mornings, she looked almost as pale and unthrifty as she had looked onboard ship. Despite Kristina's condition, when the big sacks and barrels of flour, sugar, beans and salt pork arrived, she and Anna got them strapped to or into the wagon by themselves. By midday, they were finished.

That afternoon, while Kristina repaired a tear in her conjugal mattress, Anna sorted her own belongings. No longer able to postpone it, she had to decide what she would take and what she would leave behind. Fully loaded, her little cart could carry only four hundred pounds, and then, only if she was able to push that much. Jacob had told her that after she packed her food stores and water, after she packed the utensils, pots and pans he had ordered for cooking and baking bread to pay her way, there would be only sixty pounds of room left for her personal things. Preparing for the inevitable, she had traded her big steamer trunk for a wood box less than half the size. Deciding what she would leave behind was not easy. Already having given up so many precious things, what remained was especially dear to her and seemed indispensable. Again pulling her life apart, she clung to everything she touched. Everything she saw reminded her of Erich or someone else she loved. Parting with them would break her heart.

The two porcelain cups and saucers her mother gave her from the family's set, a framed picture of her father, and Erich's razor and rocking chair were essential. She would skimp on clothes if she had to, but not on her few remaining treasures. Two travel dresses, a going-to-meeting dress, a wool coat, a hat, and one good pair of walking shoes would do. She would also take two wool blankets and a pillow. She had but one pair of pantaloons fit to make the trip, and those she would wear.

Over the next few days, Anna watched for the little black dog with the white on its chest and chin. It came back after two days, only to be scared off by a neighbor swearing at his wife.

The beans Anna and Kristina set out for it every day dried up and blistered in the hot, afternoon sun, but Anna did not give up. Picking them up and hiding them before Jacob returned for supper, afraid that as frugal as he was he would not like them giving even scraps to a dog, she waited each night until he went to bed. Adding what little was left of supper, she put all the scraps beneath the cart, and on the fourth morning, the scraps were gone.

Chapter Thirteen

Present Day
Provo, Utah
6:00 a.m.
April 21

Kim and Wayne's bedroom was as orderly and still as the rest of the house, but Kim and Wayne were not there. No one was there when Sharon came in. The movement Sharon had seen in the window was the sheer curtains waving in the developing breeze. The thud she heard was a small, wood carving of a horse Kim had made as a child falling off the bed stand. It was on the floor, lying next to one of the rocks Sharon had thrown. The bed was made. A rust brown and blue, patchwork quilt in Navaho patterns was neatly folded at the foot. Pillows with matching shams were fluffed and in their place at the headboard.

"My God, where are they?" Trying to find a clue, Sharon searched the house, but is seemed nothing had been added or taken away. Nothing was missing but the Egyptian Urn from the now unlocked and open cabinet in the living room. Maybe they were robbed. But, why isn't anything else taken? Maybe there was an emergency, and they're at the hospital, she thought. No, Kim or Wayne would have called.

Sharon reached for her neat, compartmental purse and smart phone. As she began to dial, the front door opened.

"What are you doing here?" a deep and unfriendly voice challenged. A burly man with arms as big around as Sharon's waist was standing in the entryway glaring at her. He wore matching khaki shirt and pants, and his sleeves were rolled up. "We were told everybody was gone." A younger man with even tauter muscles, dressed in an identical uniform joined him.

"Who told you that?" Sharon challenged.

"Isn't this Wayne Hoffel's house?"

"Yes."

"Well, he told me, that's who."

"Who are you?" she asked. "What do you want?"

"Best tell me first who you are," he demanded.

"I'm Sharon Marshall, his wife's sister."

"Maybe so, but you're not supposed to be here."

"Why not?"

"'Cause we're here to move 'em, and our orders say there won't be anybody in our way."

"Move them where?" Sharon asked, her fear mounting.

"He told me they were goin' to Central America."

"Central America? That's ridiculous. When did he tell you that?"

His lips skewed, his eyes rolling, the burly man mocked her. "When he called. When do you think he told me?"

Sharon paid no attention. "When did he call?"

"Don't remember. Been quite a while ago though. Scheduled the move a couple weeks ago.

Said something about doing some research down there."

Sharon looked beyond the big man and through the open front door. A large moving van was parked in the driveway immediately behind her car, tail to tail, its ramp down and only a few feet from her bumper. The signage on the side panel identified the van as belonging to, "Deseret Moving and Storage." She could not make sense of it. What is this? Kim and Wayne would have said something. They would have told me last night they were moving out of the country this morning. Something has happened to them. I know it. "You're not to touch anything until I get the police," She told the movers.

"You got something in writing signed by Wayne Hoffel?" the burly man demanded. "Well, I do." He flashed a clipboard at her with an order slip bearing Wayne's name, address, telephone number, and moving date. At the bottom was a signature that appeared to be his.

If only I had seen Wayne's signature more often, Sharon thought as she studied it. I just can't be sure.

The young man brought a dolly up the steps that he had left on the front walk, and the two of them pushed passed her and into the living room. When they returned with the leather sofa and chairs, Sharon blocked their way and refused to budge. Shoving her aside, the movers took the furniture outside and returned. She stood her ground as boxes full of art and knickknacks were packed and whisked around her and away on a handcart.

"My sister and brother-in-law are missing," she told the dispatcher when she called 911.

"What are their names?"

"Kim and Wayne Hoffel."

"And, your name?"

"Sharon Marshall."

"When was the last time you saw them or talked to them?"

"I talked to my sister on the phone last night just before midnight. I had dinner with both of them."

"Ma'am," the dispatcher sarcastically began, "that was only a little over six hours ago. Don't you think calling them 'missing' is a little premature?"

"No, I spent the entire evening with them, and they never said a thing about moving today. When I called last night, Kim told me she'd see me this morning at six. But, no one's home, and a moving van is here."

"Let me see if we've had any advanced notification. Hang on please."

Moments past. "Ma'am, I'm transferring you to a non emergency line. Please hold."

While Sharon waited on hold, the soft, slow background music coming from the phone was increasingly irritating. Without even being slowed, while she was standing there, the movers lifted the dining table and chairs over and around her and moved them out of the house and into the van.

When the background music finally cut off, a voice said, "This is Sergeant Franklin speaking. I understand you're a relative of Mr. Wayne Hoffel at 4568 Valley View Drive. Is that right?"

"Yes, I'm his sister-in-law."

"Our records show that Mr. Hoffel came into this station on April 15 and informed us that he and his wife were moving out of the country and that they could be called to leave at any moment. He told us Deseret Moving and Storage would be moving the contents of the house to storage and not to be concerned."

"But, they would have told me!" Sharon protested.

"I can't speak to that. I don't know why they didn't tell you. There is nothing in the record to suggest to me that Mr. Hoffel and his wife are missing. Only that they planned to move and expected to leave suddenly.

"I suggest you calm down. I'm sure they'll be in touch with you when they get settled." Click.

"What the hell?" Sharon said, increasingly frustrated and troubled.

I wonder if their cars are still here? she thought. Her mind was struggling to reconcile the panic in her heart with the protestations of normalcy everyone around her was making. She went into the kitchen and out the door to the garage. The garage was empty. The new, light brown Avalon; the family van, big enough to seat twelve; and the jeep Wayne used for off road driving were gone.

There was only Kim and Wayne, Sharon reasoned. How could they drive away three cars? Then, I didn't see the cars last night. I didn't even see Wayne's. Maybe the cars had already been shipped or sold. Then again, if Kim and Wayne didn't know they were leaving until after I talked to Kim, why would they have already arranged for the cars to be shipped? They would have kept at least one. She hesitated. Maybe they did keep just one, and that's the car they drove away in. This is no help at all.

Frustrated and confused, Sharon went back into the house to see the movers bring down the bed from Kim and Wayne's room. Where am I to look? They're gone with no trace, and all the evidence is being removed right from under my nose. Maybe there's something in Wayne's desk, a note, a destination, anything. She hurried toward the study, but when she got there, his desk and credenza were gone. His file cabinet was on the way out.

"I want to look at Wayne's desk," she told the burly mover as they came back for Wayne's books.

"Not without written authorization. As long as I'm responsible, nobody touches this stuff but us."

Sharon bristled, then forced herself to calm. Belatedly as it was, she began taking notice of every article boxed, every dish wrapped and packed, and anything not fixed that was moved out of the house and into the Van. Since her car was trapped by the van, the movers would think her staying until they finished was quite natural. She followed them from room to room, inspected the bathrooms in case Kim had left something for her there, put to memory everything they took, and waited. By one o'clock in the afternoon, the house was bare, the only clues to Wayne and Kim's disappearance packed away and out of reach.

"You can leave now," the burly mover told her. "We're done."

A light breeze stirred the fine veneer of dust covering the hood of her red car as Sharon got into the driver's seat. Thinking a red convertible made her too obvious, she delayed in putting up its thick, black top until the van was around the corner and out of sight. There was only one way down the hill. She counted to twenty, put the car in gear, and slowly followed the van out of the neighborhood, down a narrow, winding road, and onto a two lane, two way road, heading south. She let a black, Cadillac sedan and a gray, Toyota sports car pass her. When they passed the van, she pulled back, always watching.

Traveling into the countryside, where there was little traffic, they continued south between irrigated, green pastures. To her left, were the foothills of the Wasatch Range and the edge of Uinta National Forest. She followed as the van drove into dry, natural areas where brown was dominant and every other color was muted, then into rough areas where sagebrush and tall brown grasses bordered scrub oak and trees ladened with dust. Bud's Diner, a wood shack out of the 1930s and in serious need of paint and repair, was off the road to the left. The van pulled into the unpaved, dirt and gravel parking lot and the movers went inside.

Unless they turned back the way they came, there was only one direction to go from there, so Sharon continued south. Less than half a mile further, she turned onto a dirt road and turned around. Parking in the shade of several scrub oaks, facing the highway, she waited.

An hour later, the movers drove out of the parking lot and toward her. When they passed, she pulled out behind them. After another five miles on the isolated road, through high desert country with granite mountains in the distance, the van turned left into a driveway and into what was clearly a storage facility crowded with little garage like compartments.

Inside the facility and on the right, were a dozen long rows of one story, concrete masonry buildings. The buildings were situated west to east and each had at least fifteen units. There were just as many one story buildings and units to the left, behind the main office. At the back of the facility, perpendicular to those buildings, were another six rows with at least thirty units each. A ten-foot chain link fence crowned with four strands of concertina wire surrounded the facility. As the van drove inside, two armed guards in private security uniforms locked the gate behind it.

Just before she reached the drive, Sharon pulled off the main road, got out of the car and watched. As the van drove between the rows of buildings, she could barely see the tip of the radio antennae. Heading along the lane that divided the two east/west sections, the van turned right, drove about seventy feet further, and stopped.

Half an hour later, it emerged from the facility and turned north toward Sharon. Having found what she was looking for, she did not care if she let the movers know she had followed them and stayed where she was, boldly meeting the burly man's glare as they drove past her. When she drove into the storage facility, one of the security guards was at the locked, steel gate. His hand was on his hip resting on a holstered revolver. His partner was behind him at the office door.

At her most coquettish, Sharon got out of the car, her hips in full play, and walked toward them. "I'm moving into Provo," she began, "and I'm looking for a place to store my things until my house is ready. I was wondering if I could have a tour." She smiled. Like a teen trying to get a date for the senior prom, she drew her hand across her face and through her satiny, dark hair.

Stone faced and somber, his hand never retreating from his gun, the guard's bullet gray eyes stared at her. "This facility isn't open to the public."

As charming and innocent as she could be, she pushed a little further. "This is such a nice complex – and big! Don't you make any exceptions?"

Clearly charmed by her flirting, the guard lowered his hand, grinned and talked freely. "No, I'm afraid there are no exceptions. This facility is only for tithing storage."

"What's that?"

"Tithing is kind of a church tax. Members can pay either by cash or by non cash donations. We store the non cash stuff here: clothing, jewelry, antiques, furniture, everything you can imagine. Estates mostly. When they're auctioned off, the proceeds go to the Church. There's no room here for anything else.

"You staying around here?" he asked, his eyes showing particular appreciation for Sharon's ample breasts, tucked out of view beneath her sapphire blue, silk blouse.

"Not yet," she said, trying to stay friendly.

"Too bad." Tearing their gaze away from her breasts, his eyes hungrily followed the curves of her waist and legs.

Repulsed by him, Sharon forced a smile. "Are any of these things for sale now? I might like to buy something."

"Only a bishop or somebody like that can buy directly from the tithing office. Everything else has to be auctioned."

"Doesn't anybody just store things here and pick them up later?"

"No, once here, all property belongs to the Church. I've worked at this gate eight years, and in that time, nothin's ever been reclaimed."

What the guard was telling her could only mean one thing. Kim and Wayne were not coming back. Gravely disturbed by the realization, her voice level fell to a whisper, and she sighed, "Oh. Can I just take a look around then?"

Her question was apparently one too many. The guard's leering smile disappeared, and his hand returned to his revolver. "Who are you, anyway?" he demanded.

Realizing she had said too much, she retreated to her car, smiling and saying, "Never mind. Guess I'll have to look for storage closer to town. Know any place?"

He was glaring at her and did not answer. The other guard was reaching for the phone. It was time to get out of there.

As she started the car and backed toward the highway, the guard behind the gate took a pad from his pocket and wrote down the number on her license plate. She knew she had made a mistake. Quickly pulling away and onto the main road, Sharon drove north toward Provo. Somebody is lying, she thought. But, who? Why are Kim and Wayne's belongings to be auctioned as Church tithing? Their things aren't an estate.

Or, are they? She choked as she was reminded Kim and Wayne were probably not coming back. Arguing with herself, trying to explain away the grim possibilities, Sharon was less than two miles up the road when a white Chevrolet Camaro passed her going the opposite direction. It had a multicolored band of emergency lights on top and a cartoonish, honey colored beehive on the door.

She watched in the rearview mirror as the patrol car turned around and followed her, the words "State Trooper" printed between its headlights. Maybe he can help me, she thought. She pulled onto the graveled shoulder, got out of her car and waved him down. She waited while the officer adjusted his high crowned, wide brimmed, gray blue hat in the rear view mirror, reached for a baton-like club, and got out of the patrol car. His square, well groomed face was without expression as he walked toward her.

She smiled. "Thank you for stopping, Officer. I wonder if you could help me."

A gust of wind buffeted the brim of his hat. From either side of the road, from out of the sage and scrub, the dust swirled all around them as he put black, impenetrable sunglasses over his ghost blue eyes. "Hands on the hood. Feet spread," he ordered, his voice stern and impatient.

"Have I done something?" she asked, taken by complete surprise.

His face was locked in anger, "Just shut up and do it."

Disturbed by the suddenness of his anger and not just a little scared, she turned toward her car.

Not quick enough, he grabbed her shoulders and forcibly turned her.

"Now, just a minute," she began, the lawyer coming out in her.

He was not listening. "I said spread!" His size fourteen boot kicked the side of her ankle, knocking her foot out from under her. She stumbled. As she reached for the hood, his giant hand gripped her head and pushed, violently shoving her cheek against the sizzling hot metal. She was sprawled over the car, his full weight suddenly on top of her. "Your driver's license," he demanded.

"In my purse on the passenger seat," she said, her voice muffled by his hand pushing against her face.

"Don't move," he ordered. He left her, found her purse, and dumped its contents on the road. Picking up her wallet, he examined every card and picture she kept in the folds. Afraid to move or lift her head, barely able to see him, she checked his badge and uniform.

He's a cop all right. If I could only read his badge number.

He brought her driver's license to her, grabbed a handful of her hair and yanked her head back. "San Francisco, huh. What's your business here?"

"I came to see my sister."

"Way out here? Who do you think you're fooling?

"Suppose you do everybody a favor and go back to that iniquity you call a city. We don't want you here. You understand me?" He tightened the grip on her hair and pulled harder, forcing her head further back and over her shoulders. He shoved his knee hard against her back and forced her chest to rise. Nearly breaking her back, he then flung her to the ground. "Don't come back," he growled, as he returned to his car.

Tires squealing, gravel churning, he sped onto the highway, the beehive on his door missing her head only by inches.

Chapter Fourteen

Iowa City, Iowa
June 1854

About midmorning, two days before the
wagon train was to depart, ten women from Anna's
group of one hundred met in a weed patch near the
wagon yard. Their wagons would be among the first
in the train. Their duty to the train would be to build
the earthen ovens in which the community's bread
would be baked at campsites along the trail. Under
an elder's direction, the women practiced by
building six of the earthen ovens, each time a little
faster. They were told that after they arrived at each
community campsite, they must build the ovens
before doing anything else. Anna was to fuel and
fire them and, when the ovens were hot enough,
bake whatever bread was needed for the entire one
hundred. It was all to be done in the few hours they
would have until supper.

Before the train moved out each morning,
she and four other women, chosen because they
were traveling alone or with other women, so no
family would be neglected, would make the dough
for that day, knead it, and shape it. The dough
would rise during the day as they traveled and be
ready to bake when the earthen ovens got hot.

To Anna, baking bread for a hundred
people every day in the time allotted her seemed
impossible. She was completely overwhelmed. She
stewed and worried about it all night, but by
morning was resigned to it. What did it matter? It
was part of the price she had to pay to reach the
Kingdom of God. It was payment on her debt to the
Church, and she must do it.

That night, Kristina asked Anna to go for water, motioning to a wood-swollen bucket near one of the huge wagon wheels. The big water barrel was full, but Kristina did not want to have to fill it again before their departure.

The sun was setting beneath bright pink clouds as Anna dipped Kristina's bucket into the river. In the marshy grass nearby a frog skittered away. The winds were still, and the community was quieting. Instantly aware she was not alone, Anna turned around.

"Why, hello." The little, black dog was sitting quietly by a tree, its brown eyes steadily gazing at her. Unconcerned about the mud, Anna crouched, the hem of her ankle-length dress immersing in it. "I wasn't sure I'd see you again." She picked up a stick, stripped of bark, and held it out to her. "Want to play?" She tossed the stick to the side, but the dog did not go after it. "No, huh?"

Aware Kristina was waiting for the water she carried, Anna stood and started toward camp. "Coming for supper?" She called, wanting the dog to follow. She looked back as she walked away, but the dog did not come. Hoping it would come back to their camp, she saved a biscuit and a bit of gravy from supper and put them beside her cart that night. She tried to watch for the dog but fell asleep. In the morning, she was both pleased and sorry. The biscuit and gravy were gone but so was the dog.

At midday, as she finished loading the cart, the dog reappeared, carrying the stick she had thrown the night before. "Well, aren't you a good girl." Anna knelt. "I won't hurt you," she promised. "Come." There was salt pork in the supplies Jacob had obtained for her. "Want a piece of meat?" She reached into one of the small barrels and held a strip of meat out in front of her, but the dog came no closer. "Don't worry. You'll get some anyway." She tossed the meat, watched while the dog ate it and then went back to work.

The wagon train would depart tomorrow. Hundreds of miles of wilderness awaited her, over which she must pull everything she owned. Like the rumblings of thunder in a vicious lightning storm, a paralyzing fear rumbled inside her, warning her she would not make it to Utah. Dispirited, she longed to have Erich there to help and protect her. Clinging to her memories of him and believing she was doing what he would have wanted her to do were her only solace, – until she looked up.

To Anna's surprise, the little dog had stayed and was sitting nearby, quietly watching her, offering its companionship. Its presence immediately calmed her. Her fear instantly dissolved, the overwhelming journey before her suddenly became possible. She put her hand out to it, but the dog neither came to her nor moved away. It stayed with Anna until late afternoon, but by supper, it was gone.

The next day, those who were to leave with the wagon train woke hours before dawn. Men shouted at their animals, scuffling with them to get them hitched. Women tried to control rambunctious and disorderly children while banging and clattering belongings not yet packed. Excitement peaked, and the camp got very noisy.

By the time the first wagons rolled into their pre-assigned traveling positions, the vivid, purple hues of dawn were already breaking. Dust was everywhere. Watching wistfully, the hundreds who were to be left behind stood in groups on the sidelines, wishing they were going too.

In Iowa City, Gentiles who provided the Mormons supplies were just rising, their pockets full, their futures secure as long as the Mormons kept coming. As long as they kept moving west, the Gentiles welcomed them.

Anna braced the crossbar against her hips and pushed the cart into the third place in line. A prairie barge packed to capacity was in front of her. It was Jacob and Kristina's wagon. She looked behind her for Hattie. She was reassured when she saw Hattie waving from beside the wagon three back from her own.

A meeting was held in which every member of the train, and even those not members of the train, prayed for God's help in the journey. The travelers went back to their wagons and a bugle sounded.

With Kristina standing beside him, Jacob snapped his whip over the oxen and his wagon pulled slowly away. The crossbar squarely over her hips, her hands around the side bars, Anna pushed, and her wagon followed. As the sun became fully visible, one by one, the wagons moved out and down the trail west.

Believing she was part of something great, something special in history, Anna trembled. Excited and terrified, her heart weakened. Her eyes clouded with tears. She was at the edge of a deep crevasse, and she would find there either Heaven or Hell.

Chapter Fifteen

June 1854

The trail was well worn, and at first, the traveling was easy. Anna's confidence grew, but the cart's weight and the strength it took to push it was wearing. By noon, her hip bones hurt where the crossbar rested against them, and she was tired and thirsty. By mid afternoon, she was miserable. Worn to threads, her arms became useless, hanging behind the crossbar like limp, wet rags. Her legs struggled with the load. Her feet were throbbing, and every step was bone crushing agony.

The entire weight of the cart had been trained on her hips, crashing against them every time she hit a rut. Her hips and all the flesh around them were severely bruised. She tried holding the cart away from them but did not have the strength to keep the cart at bay. All she could do was try to protect them, inserting her hands between her pelvis and the bar as cushions. Dust swirled about her face, and through the cloud, she saw a countryside no different from the one she had just left. Frustrated and miserable, she stared at her feet, her mind trying to detach itself so she would not feel them. Concentrating on taking one step at a time, she made herself numb to them.

In late afternoon, thirty miles west of Iowa City, the lead wagon turned off the trail and into the pre-established campsite. Anna moved her cart into position, walked to the river for water, returned, and sat down. After drinking her fill, she poured what was left of the cold water into her washbasin, took off her shoes, and soaked her feet.

She was grateful to Jacob for requiring every family in the wagon train to bake bread enough for three days before they left, so she need do nothing that first night. Sitting in the dirt, her back against the wheel, she dozed.

"You all right?" Hattie was kneeling beside her with a plate of stew and a slice of bread. The camp was quiet, and it was growing dark. "I brought you something."

Anna smiled. "Thanks."

"You poor thing," Hattie soothed, examining the bruises and blisters on Anna's feet. "I'll tell you what. I'll send Lizzy to you in the morning to help you. It's going to take all of us awhile to get used to this." Having walked all day in ill-fitting leather shoes, Hattie had her share of blisters too.

"Eat hearty now. You'll need all the strength that stew can give you." She took a blanket from Anna's cart and covered her. "Sleep tight."

After eating only half the stew Hattie brought her, unable to eat more, Anna put the plate on the ground, closed her eyes, and went to sleep. She woke in the middle of the night to find the campfires out and the stars bright above her. Cuddled next to her, head resting on the empty plate, was the little, black dog. Thrilled the dog finally trusted her, she reached for her and cooed as she gently petted its neck.

Lizzy awakened Anna before dawn and invited her to breakfast. By seven, Lizzy was in the train behind Jacob's wagon, helping Anna push the cart.

The little dog had left before Anna woke, but Anna was certain she was somewhere in the long grass watching her, following her. She could not see her but knew she would be back.

With Lizzy's help, Anna could hold the crossbar a little higher, where her arms could bend and brace it and her forearms bear the load rather than her hips. As the train moved out, she could barely get her sore legs and bruised feet moving, but as they did, they began to feel better. By the end of the day, another thirty miles west, she had enough strength left to bake half a dozen biscuits and take them to Hattie with her thanks.

The river next to the campsite that had hosted hundreds of Mormons before them was serene. Grass was in seed, and a light breeze blew.

"I've changed the system a little," Jacob told Anna. He was standing in her camp, his back to the setting sun, his face obscured by its intensity. She shaded her eyes to see him.

"Before we left," he began, "I bought the Church a dozen Dutch ovens. I was going to save them new until we got to Utah, but I've decided they will better serve God if they help get us there. So, I'm going to let you use them. Since they sit on the coals from open fires," Jacob told her, "the women who were going to build the earthen ovens won't be needed and can go back to their own work. They and all the other women can make their own dough before we leave in the morning and bring you their already leavened loaves when we make camp at evening. All you have to do is maintain the fires and bake them." He moved out of the sun and approached her. "That should make things much easier for you."

All at once, Anna's work seemed achievable, and she was grateful to him.

He glanced at her smoldering fire and at the pot still simmering. "Looks like there's still coffee," he observed. "Think I'll have some." Without invitation, he sat in Erich's rocker and watched her pour.

Fearfully remembering his advances in Iowa City, Anna was afraid to be alone with him. Glancing toward his wagon, she saw Kristina at his campfire and breathed a little easier. All around her there were wagons, and people at their campfires. He would not dare put his arms around her here.

Taking only a sip of coffee, then putting the cup on the ground, Jacob rocked back and forth, casually smoking his pipe as if he belonged there.

What does he want? What else could we have to talk about? Anna thought.

"How's Kristina?" she asked, reminding him of her. She looked toward the river from which Kristina was lugging two buckets of water to their wagon.

"Not well, I think." Jacob stopped rocking and relit his pipe, throwing the twig he used into the fire. "She's not as strong as I would like her to be. She's small, and I worry the baby's not sitting right."

His pipe went out. He tapped it against his boot then carefully packed it with fresh tobacco. "Many of our women have given birth on the trail, but she's not as strong as any one of them. Not nearly as strong, and I'm afraid she'll have trouble."

"Is there anything I can do?"

He found another twig, held it to the fire, lit the pipe, and puffed. "I want you to spend more time with her. Help her do chores in the morning.

Keep an eye on her." He leaned forward as far as he could. "Don't stray from us too often." His constricting eyes locked her in their gaze, then relaxed. "She may need you."

Anna pictured Kristina lugging those heavy buckets while Jacob sat there. Wanting to get rid of him, Anna proposed, "Maybe I should go over there now?"

Jacob refused her. "No, no, Kristina's fine. Let her finish her own work tonight. Labor like that will help her get stronger. She'll go to bed after she washes up. She can rest then. Just check on her in the morning."

He sat at Anna's fire for the longest time, smoking his pipe and only occasionally sipping the coffee she had given him which, by then, was cold. As he told her about the beautiful paradise awaiting her, his eyes reflected the firelight.

Listening intently, she searched them. She had lost everything, including Erich, and she prayed with all her heart that someday, she would reach that paradise.

Chapter Sixteen

426 West 92nd St.
New York, New York
5:04 p.m.
April 21

Dirty, smoke stained windows through which sunlight only trickled and old wood floors worn deep with depressions made the corridor dark as Alex Caldwell walked past offices occupied and busy to Suite 810, where the signage on the door read:

ASEG
Henry Blanchard
Branch Manager

ASEG was the acronym for the American Society for Ethics in Genetics. The main office and funding for the ASEG, a very unpopular organization in the science community, was in Washington D.C. Hank was given a tiny budget but was responsible for all investigations conducted by ASEG in the tri-state area.

"Hank?" Alex called, as he opened the door and walked inside. The receptionist was not at her desk.

Alex and Hank had lived in adjoining rooms in their college dorms and had been good friends for nearly fifteen years. Alex was tall and slender, his black hair just long enough to show off his curls. Long, deep dimples flowed down his cheeks to his jowls, framing his narrow lips. Wearing blue dockers, a tee shirt, and a worn Knicks Explorer Jacket, Alex was there for a guys' night out. Knicks first round playoff tickets, floor side, were in his jacket pocket. "Hey, I'm here. You ready?" he called in his baritone voice.

Hank's office was only slightly larger than a rich man's walk-in closet, with only Hank and Julie, his receptionist, occupants. Guess Julie took the day off, Alex thought. He strode the six feet to Hank's private door and knocked. Maybe he's on the phone, he thought, when Hank did not respond. Checking the phone on Julie's desk, Alex saw that the lines were clear. Must be on a cell. Not wishing to interrupt Hank if he was conducting business, he listened at the door for Hank's voice. Yet, he heard nothing. He knocked again. "Hey, Hank, if we don't get to The Garden soon, all the beer'll be gone."

There was an odd smell around the threshold, a heavy, pungent odor that made Alex's skin crawl. The glass doorknob to Hank's office, which had always before been grimy and disgusting, was clean and clear. "Hank?" Alex called, before he gripped the knob and turned it.

"What in the world?" he gasped, as he went inside. The office looked like a great wind had come through it, scattering its contents. Papers and files in disarray covered the desk and floor. Books were on end and opened. A cup of coffee was spilled next to Hank's computer. A half eaten sandwich rested on top of the keyboard, and Hank was not there. Alex took a step, pushing papers aside with his foot. "Where are you?" he whispered. Whatever happened here, Hank left in a hurry.

Alex suddenly felt a light pressure against his ribs. He started. He was not alone.

"All right, raise 'em," a voice behind him ordered.

"What do you want?" Alex asked, complying.

"My ticket. What do you think?"

Immediately dropping his hands, Alex turned around. The voice was Hank's.

"Ready for the game?" Hank asked, playfully waving the long, foam finger he had stuck in Alex's ribs.

"Very funny."

Hank was an avid Knicks' fan. Like many spectators, he was overweight. His torso was ball-like, and his physique was not at all like the athletes' he adored. Alex was his best friend.

"I thought this place finally ate you," Alex told him. "It gets messier every time I see you. How do you work in here?"

"It only looks sloppy. Every note and every piece of paper in this office has its place. It's a filing system that's stood me good for years."

"Don't know about the 'good' part, but I certainly can speak for its longevity," Alex teased. He pictured the room Hank shared with Wayne at Harvard. Hank's half was a garbage pit. Wayne's was a model of good housekeeping. Each of the four years Hank and Wayne congenially roomed together was a small miracle.

Alex and Hank's bargain $3,330 seats in Section 18, court side, were very near the opposing team's bench and within twenty-five feet of the key. As the seats around them filled, they watched as number ten, Skip McVee, thirteenth leading scorer in the league, took his first practice shot.

McVee's easy lay up bounced up and off the basket.

"Gees!" Hank gasped, "He missed. No wonder the Nets beat us two games in a row." He swallowed the last bite of his second kielbasa and started on the second of the three beers he had lined up at his feet. He hesitated, thought for a moment, then in all seriousness told Alex, "Wayne came to see me. He needs our help."

Hank would never have mentioned it if Wayne did not seriously need them. "Why, what's wrong?" Alex asked.

"He's gotten himself into something he says he shouldn't have – and he can't get out of it."

"What?"

"Don't know. He came into town about a week ago. Said he didn't have much time and that he thought someone was following him. He didn't want to lead them to my office, so he met me at Bogie's down on West 85th Street. I've never seen him so nervous. He was spooky. He kept looking around like he expected somebody was going to shoot him. Handed me an envelope under the table and said if anything happened to him to come looking for him then laughed like he'd just told a joke. Couldn't get another thing out of him."

"He didn't tell you anything else?" Alex was a senior reporter for the New York Post. He could smell a story. A troubled friend combined with a mystery, peeked his interest on several levels.

"Yeah, that was the strangest part of all," Hank continued. "He told me that when I came looking for him, I was to search for the bees. That the proof was in the envelope."

"Proof of what? What did he mean, 'bees?'"

"Don't know."

"What was in the envelope?"

"Can't talk here. Wayne made me promise not to tell anyone but you and to tell you in private."

"Where is it?"

"In my office. Tucked inside that half eaten hoagie on my keyboard. Didn't figure anybody'd look for anything important in pastrami."

"Why didn't you show me when I was there?"

"Too many people in the building. Not enough privacy."

"But, there was just you and me in your office."

"Still, – Wayne told me to be very careful."

"Think he's off a bit? Did you see anybody following him?"

"No. When I asked him, he told me the men following him traded off, so he was never certain who they were."

"He wouldn't tell you anything more?"

"He said he'd explain everything to us next week when he came back. He'd bring us the rest of the evidence then.

"I think he intended to hopscotch across the country to lose the guys following him, so he'd have time with us. He wants the whole matter exposed and ended."

"So, when do I get to see what's in the envelope?"

"I'll take you back to my office after the game."

After a heartbreaking one point loss, Hank and Alex joined the crowd flowing through the nearest exit. Caught in the cross currents of an otherwise orderly flow, Alex and Hank got separated. Spilling out into the corridor, Alex worked his way across and out of the crowd. He waited next to the wall for Hank to emerge. Moments past. The stream became a trickle but still no Hank.

Alex had waited too long.

Chapter Seventeen

Oregon Trail
June 1854

When Anna woke a couple of hours before dawn, the little dog was lying beside her. Anna stroked her. "How's my little Angel? How's my girl?" As if Anna was the most wonderful being in the world, Angel cuddled into her.

Breakfast was hardtack, a biscuit made of only flour and water, and Anna willingly shared. "Come on, Angel. Let's go help Kristina." She stood to go to Jacob and Kristina's wagon. "Come on, Angel." Yet Angel did not come. Preferring to remain in a secluded spot beneath the cart, she simply wagged her tail.

"Don't want to meet the neighbors, huh? I guess I can't blame you. Stay here, though, please. I'll be back in a little while." Wanting Angel to stay on her own and not because she was tethered, yet afraid Angel would leave and not be there on her return, Anna left reluctantly. When Anna reached Jacob's camp, he was waiting for his breakfast. Kristina was in the bushes throwing up.

"She all right?" Anna asked him, silently observing it seemed late in Kristina's pregnancy for morning sickness.

"Yeah," he sighed, matter-of-factly. "Does this every morning. Doubt she'll stop 'til he's born. Don't worry about it, she'll be fine in an hour or two."

Anna ignored him. "Can I do anything for you, Kristina?" she asked from several feet away.

A weak, unsteady voice responded, "No. Thank you. I'll be all right in a minute." The conversation apparently too much for her, Kristina coughed and threw up. Embarrassed, she walked further into the bushes.

Anna fixed bacon, potatoes, biscuits with gravy, and black coffee for Jacob's breakfast, then mixed and kneaded two loaves of bread, setting Jacob and Kristina's loaf in their wagon to rise. By the time Anna had cleaned their campsite and packed for them, Kristina had returned. Though she wanted nothing to do with anything to eat, she claimed she was well enough to travel.

As Anna helped her up and onto the wagon seat, Jacob laid down the law. "It's all right for you to ride occasionally for now," he disciplined Kristina, putting his hand on the nearest oxen's haunch, "but this is good trail. When the team has to work to make way, you'll walk like the rest of us. Do you understand?"

Kristina nodded. She was pale. The circles under her eyes were dark and puffy, and she was in no condition to walk.

"She won't hurt anything by riding," Anna defended.

Infuriated, Jacob turned on her. His eyes were cold. His voice was stern. "That decision is mine, not yours. Not Kristina's. These oxen have to carry two thousand pounds over a thousand more miles, and they're not going to carry her! Other pregnant women are walking, and she's perfectly capable of it, too. I can't make exceptions for her just because she's my wife." He looked up at Kristina and reminded her, "I am an elder, a priest. My wife has to be an example of strength, not of weakness. Anna will give you any help you need.

He paused. "You can ride for a day or two when the baby comes due."

Kristina tried to force herself to stand, but her arms would not bear her weight. "I just need to rest a few minutes, then I'll be able to walk," she promised, her voice faltering. "Don't worry, I won't fail you."

Jacob nodded his approval then turned to Anna, and dismissed her. "Better get on your way, or you'll be late."

It was nearly seven o'clock. The wagons were getting on the trail in their assigned positions, and just as Hattie had promised, Lizzy was at Anna's cart making friends with Angel. "Where'd she come from?" Lizzy asked, not having seen Angel before.

"She and I made our acquaintance in Iowa City. Looks like she's decided to come to Utah with me."

Upon arriving at their prearranged evening camp, Anna gathered wood and built three large fires. As women in her group of a hundred brought her leavened loaves, she baked them in the Dutch ovens Jacob loaned her. Needing regular and repeated fueling, the fires generated heat like a giant furnace. The summer air all around them simmered and was stale. The work was hot and tiring.

The perfect companion, Angel sat quietly nearby, accompanying Anna on every trip she made into the brush for fuel. By the time the entire train arrived, the camp set up and the stock taken care of, it was time for supper, and all the bread for which Anna was responsible was baked. As her share of supper, Anna took the loaf she had made for herself to Hattie. "I want you to meet Angel," she told

Hattie, as the dog cautiously followed her into Hattie's camp.

"Lizzy told me about her." Trying to make friends with Angel, Hattie knelt, holding out her hand. "How do you do?"

Angel did not go near her. "Guess she likes Lizzy better."

"Welcome, Angel," John said, bringing Anna a stool.

Protectively showing her teeth, Angel growled as he set the stool next to Hattie's.

"Think I'll let you get to know me better before I offer you my hand," he joked. "Might have a use for it later."

John was especially cheery and talkative that night, and during supper, with an amusingly exaggerated accent, he entertained them with humorous stories. One was about a sailor who was always "sportin" women while his wife stayed home."Told everybody his wife was dumb, and he thought he was foolin' her.

"When he was leavin' home one night to go to his favorite tavern, a big, scruffy dog started followin' him. Close like. Pretty soon, there was another. 'Fore long, there was a whole pack'a dogs followin' him, – sniffin'at his heels, – and howlin', always growlin' at each other for position.

"He got scared and started runnin', the dogs runnin' after him, collectin' others as they went, all the while gettin' frenzied and bitin' at him. When he got to the tavern, the dogs was scratchin' and yowlin' and carryin' on so at the door everybody inside stopped drinkin' to look. The louder the yowlin' and scratchin' got, the louder their laughin' at him. Jake was so humiliated he snuck out the back door with those dogs right on his tail.

"Only place he could go was home. And, there he stayed. Trapped, – those dogs howlin' and scratchin' at his front door 'til the day his ship sailed. Every dog in town had set his sights on him, and he had to run all the way to the dock to board it.

"Lived that way for years, Jake did. – Goin' to sea for months, then returnin' to face the dogs. He never sported with a girl again."

"His wife didn't have anything to do with that, did she?" Anna suspected.

The twinkle in John's eye got brighter as he told her, "Course, nobody knew for sure. But, there was rumors that his wife'd go about the neighborhood at night when he was home searchin' for bitches in season and rubbin' his trousers 'tween their legs. Never noticed the smell himself, cause He never took a bath."

"Oh, John," Hattie said, giggling with the rest of them.

"You're so naughty," Anna told him. She was finished eating and, having left plenty for Angel, set her plate on the ground. "Tell us another one," she encouraged, as Angel ate.

It would have been a wonderful evening, if a voice, sharp and disapproving, bellowing from outside the circle, had not instantly turned the mood glum. "What are you doing with that food?" The spoiler was Jacob. "Whose dog is that?"

"She's mine," Anna told him, standing between them.

"Yours? I made no provision for a dog. You don't have enough food for a dog. You'll have to get rid of it." His reaction seemed wholly out of proportion to the problem.

"If Anna doesn't have enough food, we do," Hattie defended, standing beside her. "We can help. She's just a little dog. She won't eat much."

"You don't know if you've got enough food for this journey! None of us know." Jacob was in no mood for compromise. "Get rid of that dog, – or prepare to have to eat it when your starvin'.

"Here now," John said, protectively stepping in front of Anna and Hattie. "There's no reason to scare her. I'm sure we'll have enough food to take care of the dog. We brought extra."

Jacob scowled. He was not used to being refused and did not like it. "Very well, but don't come running to me when you get hungry, – when you see that dog wasting away and suffering because you don't have enough food to feed it anymore. Whatever happens to it will be your fault, not mine. What are you doing here, anyway?" he demanded of Anna, again taking control. "You should be with Kristina. She needs you."

Jacob treated Anna like his slave, but she owed him too much to argue. She was in enough trouble over Angel without pressing him further. "I'll be right there."

Having at least retrieved Anna, Jacob left seemingly satisfied.

"Guess I'd better go," she said. "Come on, Angel."

Angel followed Anna but would not go with her into Jacob's camp. Sitting outside the camp, just feet away, she quietly watched as Anna joined Kristina by the fire. Kristina was alone, sitting on a small stool, mending one of Jacob's cotton shirts.

"Have you seen Jacob?" Anna asked, hoping he had not followed her.

"No – he went off somewhere," Kristina responded, seeming not to care.

"Need any help?"

"I'd just like some company."

Anna was angry Jacob lied to her about Kristina needing her, upset he had ruined her evening, but she kept those feelings to herself. Kristina was a beautiful young woman forever entrapped by him. Idly studying her, Anna could not help but ask, "Are you happy with him?"

To Anna's surprise, Kristina responded frankly. "To tell you the truth, I don't know. I think it's because I don't know him very well." Her brows wrinkled as she considered her feelings further. "He's not exactly what I thought he'd be when I married him. I wasn't interested in any of the young men who came calling. They seemed so purposeless and immature. Jacob seemed to know everything. He was closer to God than anyone I'd ever known." She sheepishly smiled. "I suppose I got all mixed up with what he said about God and Zion, – what he told me about the big house he owns in Utah and all the jewelry he was going to give me when we got there. I don't think I ever saw him the way he truly is. I only saw what I wanted him to be." There was a quiet thoughtfulness in Kristina's eyes, a wistfulness in her expression. It was as if she wished she was somewhere else. "But then, that was my fault."

She paused, then perked up a little. "No use worrying about it now. I'll get used to him."

Knowing Jacob, Anna was not surprised Kristina felt that way. She was only surprised Kristina had told her, and she ventured to learn more. "Are you sorry you're having his baby?"

As if all doubt suddenly melted away, the light came back into Kristina's eyes. She smiled. "No, not at all. Because Jacob is his father, my baby will be among God's most fortunate. He will be baptized in the Temple by an apostle and will live in the Kingdom of God as one of His children. He will grow up to be a leader in the Church and, like his father, will someday be a god. Whatever happens to my baby in this life, I know someday he'll have a place in the highest rank of Heaven." She put her hand on Anna's knee, leaned forward, and whispered, "This baby is what I was created for, why I gave my body and soul to God and to Jacob. He is the reason I'm here."

Jacob walked into the firelight and headed for the wagon, ignoring Anna. "Time you go to bed," he told Kristina.

"I'll see you in the morning," she told Anna. She dumped water on the fire, collected her sewing, and climbed into the wagon with Jacob.

Anna sensed that Jacob was still angry over Angel, and she was worried. What if he makes trouble? What if he cuts off my supplies? I'll die out here.

A few yards away, Angel was waiting for her. Though their lives had been entwined only briefly, this dog was the only family Anna had. No matter what Jacob said or did, she would not let her go. As they bedded on the ground beneath Anna's cart, wrapping themselves in her blanket, Anna pulled Angel close and clung to her.

At Sunday worship, as the entire community gathered by the river for prayer and sermon, Jacob made his thoughts known. His loud, deep voice demanded obedience. "The voice of God comes to us through our leadership, and none of you

shall disobey Him. God has spoken through
Brigham Young and has laid down His law. Each
day, a man has a duty to ask, 'What is God's will?'
Each day, a woman's duty is to ask, 'What is my
husband's will?' There must be no questioning of a
husband's authority or of our leaders. Our
community, our Kingdom, will not be threatened
from the kitchen." He glared at Anna and Hattie
who were standing together on the river bank with
Angel at their feet, and the whip of his authority
stung.

"What should I do?" Anna asked Hattie,
when services were over. "I can't leave Angel out
here in the wilderness. I can't leave her at all. Do I
have to?"

Hattie was strong, her voice sure as she put
her ample arm around Anna. "No, darling. You
keep your dog. Jacob's just jealous. It's obvious to
all of us he doesn't want you depending on anyone
or anything but him. Just let him get used to her.
You'll see. He'll forget all about her in a few days."

Hattie's jaw was set and determined. There
was enough boldness in her hazel green eyes to stop
an entire army of Jacobs. "Don't you worry, Anna,
you don't have to leave your dog. Jacob can't hurt
you. If he won't help you, we will. You and Angel
can travel with us and share our food, the two of
you can be part of the family. Now, you and Angel
come have supper with us."

Chapter Eighteen

Madison Square Garden
New York
11:30 p.m.
April 21

The corridor outside the arena was dark except for spotlights aimed at a still, lifeless body sitting on the floor, its back propped against the restroom wall. The Crime Scene Unit was at work, and a middle-aged NYPD Sergeant of Detectives was demanding of Alex, "Tell me again where you were." The sergeant's tan, for every season suit, was worn and rumpled. His pants were at least three inches longer than his short, plump legs. As if issuing a traffic ticket, his brown, nondescript eyes, used to such drama, were uninspired.

"I went out of the arena with the crowd and was in the corridor waiting for him," Alex responded.

With thumb and forefinger, the sergeant stroked the bushy, grizzled mustache inhabiting his upper lip. He then wrote something on a notepad.

Fifteen minutes earlier:
The two sauerkraut smothered, knackwurst dogs Hank ate after the kielbasa roiled in his stomach, and he belched as he casually followed Alex out of the arena and down the corridor. In flow with the other spectators, he did not at first notice he was being cut off from the throng by two men. One had sandy hair, the other light brown. Dressed in dark suits with white shirts and narrow, black

ties, they were crowding in front of him. At first slowing him down, they then cut him off, maneuvering him out of sight and earshot of Alex.

Irritated, Hank tried to pass them, but they did not let him pass. After several attempts, his patience spent, he pushed between them and triumphantly got one step ahead. Thinking he was free of them, he stepped out, but then they were beside him. "Hey," he muttered, thinking the problem was just part of being in a crowd.

He was stunned when they gripped his arms, and the one with the light brown hair pressed a knife to his ribs. "What is this?" He was scared. "My wallet's in my pocket. Take it."

"Shut up," the sandy haired man whispered. "You're coming with us."

Guiding Hank out of the flow, squeezing him between them, the two men hurried him through the crowd and forced him into the nearest bathroom, where there were three men at the urinals. Suddenly, the man with the light brown hair tripped Hank. Hank fell forward, only to be be rescued by the man who tripped him, who joked "We'll help ya this time, Al, but ya gotta lay off that stuff. If it don't kill ya, Donna will." As he helped Hank regain his balance, he pressed the knife against one of Hank's ribs, and pricked it.

Hank groaned. He opened his mouth to cry for help, and the blade turned deeper into his side. The man with sandy hair subtly pushed him, and he almost collapsed. Holding him up, pretending he was too drunk to stand on his own, his captors laughed.

Sweat beaded on his brow. He tried to pull away, but the knife bore even deeper. He could only watch as the men at the urinals wiped their hands on their pants and left. I've got to be smart about this, or they'll kill me, he thought, taking the pain in his ribs as warning. "There's no need for this," he told them, trying to sound reasonable. "What do you want? I already said you could have my wallet."

"Not looking for your wallet," the man with the light brown hair said, matter-of-factly.

Hank looked at their faces trying to find any distinguishing features, but there were none. There was nothing exceptional about them. He braced his legs against them, but they overpowered him and pushed him to the last stall. "Then what? What do you want?" He grabbed the stall door and held tight to it, but the knife turned deeper and their steel grips forced him inside. He realized they wanted to kill him. Panicking, he kicked at them. No longer caring about the knife digging into his rips, he twisted, trying to break away. By some miracle, his body recalled from his college days some judo. His knee sought and found the firm, fragile balls of the man to his left, and he jammed it into them.

"Aghh," the sandy haired man cried. Helpless, he doubled up then fell to his knees.

Swiftly turning, gripping the wrist of the hand that still held the knife, Hank desperately clenched its handle and wrestled the brown haired man for its possession. Pushing and shoving, kicking and twisting, each man trying to dominate the other, the two fought their way through the bathroom and out into the corridor.

"Help!" Hank yelled, but there was no one left in the corridor to hear, nothing there but scattered garbage.

Their arms and hands cut, the knife in their grasp committed to murder, one of them surged with strength, turned the blade and shoved, finding the heart of the other.

"Hey, you know this man?" the sergeant repeated, demanding Alex's attention. He pointed to the corpse.

"No."

"Ever seen him before?"

"No."

There was nothing exceptional about the dead man on the floor, flashes from cameras bursting in his face. He had light brown hair and was about forty. He was well groomed and clean shaven, though with a starched shirt and narrow tie, Alex thought he was overdressed for a basketball game.

"Know of any reason he or anyone else would try to kill your friend?"

"As far as I know, nobody would want to hurt him," Alex said. "These guys must have tried to rob him."

"See the Rolex on the dead guy's wrist?" the sergeant asked him, unimpressed with Alex's conclusion. "Why would this guy try to rob him? What possible reason could he have for trying to stab him? It just doesn't ring right."

In custody, restrained, his hands cuffed behind him, Hank was standing just a few feet from the body, the glare of the spotlights in his eyes. He was being interrogated by the sergeant's partner.

The only witness to what happened in the corridor, a uniformed security guard, was yards away. He was surrounded by fellow guards, his statement already taken. Consumed by curiosity, their adrenaline high, his fellow guards kept urging him to tell them more, and he obliged, embellishing the story each time he told it.

Coming back through the corridor, Alex came along just after the man died. He found Hank standing over the body with a knife in his bloody hand.

The witness security guard said he had seen everything: Hank pushing the victim out of the bathroom; his hand shoving a knife into the man's heart and killing him for no apparent reason. Yet, the guard had not seen it at all. Calling for and receiving assistance at a minute after the stabbing, that guard and another guard surrounded and restrained Hank while the police and EMS were summoned. They held Alex too, as a possible accomplice, off to the side where he could not talk with Hank.

His face stark white, his hands trembling, Hank was in shock, and there was blood on his shirt. Stunned and exhausted, he had watched the sandy haired man he kicked stumble out of the bathroom, reach for his accomplice's corpse, and take from around its neck a gold medallion. He could only stare as the sandy haired man staggered away and out the nearest exit before the guard arrived.

When the security guard came toward him, Hank was standing over the body, blood sticky and growing cold on his hand. He quietly gave up the knife and, as he blankly gazed down the hall, saw Alex. "What have I done?" He murmured.

Chapter Nineteen

Oregon Trail
August 1854

It was the end of summer, and there had been no rain on the prairie in months. Oxen, horses, and converts on the move, and the ever-present wind stirred the deep, powdery dirt beneath them into curtains smothering and enveloping the wagon train. Trudging through the dense air, their eyes stinging, their faces masked with dirt, the converts could breathe only through cotton handkerchiefs tied over their noses and mouths. They could see only through eyes squinting and lashes caked with it and from beneath broad brimmed hats. Most walked with their heads down, only occasionally looking up to find their way.

Like a donkey powering a millstone, monotonously following the donkey in front of it, Anna followed Jacob's wagon. Her faded cotton dress, her limp, copper hair, and all but the deepest hollows of her face were coated with dirt. Her shoes, designed to be worn on either foot and fitting neither, without cushion and worn out, were nearly full of powder, and with each step more dirt collected inside them. With water scarce and to be used only for drinking, she had not bathed in weeks. Yet, she allowed herself a handful to wipe her face with her hands and to wash them before supper.

Keeping her head down like the others, she guided her cart between the tracks the wagons in front of her made, seldom looking up. Day after day the scenery, when she could see, was the same, – endless horizons of dry grass, – land so flat there was no character to it, – and the sun, vague in the dust choked sky. Always at her side, Angel never strayed while they were traveling, waiting until they camped in the evening to go off hunting. Not knowing what dangers there were beyond the camp boundaries, Anna fretted about her at first, but after a week or two, did not worry as much.

As usual one day, Angel was walking beside her, the only other passenger in the wagon train Anna could see. Anna's head was down. Her mind was on anything she could think of but the dust and the heat. Only when Angel stopped, her ears alert, her nose sniffing, did Anna suspect something was wrong.

About half a mile behind her, a horse was screaming. Cows were hysterically bellowing. Hooves thundered, and the stock stampeded. The dust cloud behind her widened, and above the cloud, she saw smoke. It was a wild, raging fire.

Someone in their train or in one of the Gentile trains following some distance behind was careless, either not burying their campfire deep enough or burying it too close to a dry, dead root. Already miles wide and moving quickly, the fire was chasing Anna's wagon train with nothing between them but the inexhaustible fuel of the tinder dry prairie grass.

"Come on!" she shouted to Angel. In a torrent of panic, she started running, pushing the cart as fast as she could in a race for her life.

Wagons pulled by terrified oxen who had long since left their drivers on foot barreled by her. Crazed cattle, men chasing wagons, women carrying babies and pulling children by their hands swept past her, – all frantically running from the flames. Caught in the stampede, terrified she and Angel would be trampled, she ran faster. Unable to see through the dust, she was following blindly, when all at once, the wagons in front of her stopped. Men and women who had passed her reversed their course and ran by her again, this time toward the fire. "Bring your shovels!" someone shouted. She grabbed hers and followed.

The fire was less than a quarter mile away, quickly moving toward them. They must make their stand here. Quickly organizing in row after row, four abreast, everyone started digging. By the time the fire reached them, a five-foot-wide trench a foot deep was dug. Behind the trench, they readied themselves to face the fire head on.

Her shovel full of dirt, Angel beside her, Anna waited, sweat pouring from her brow. The flames coming at them were two feet high, the line of defense a hundred yards across. Shovel to flame, she fought as the fire surged to devour her.

Failing to see the sparks that got her, failing to see them creep along her dress and flare, she was ignited. "Oh-h," she screamed when she realized it, slapping at the flames, fighting them alone.

Someone grabbed her, knocked her to the ground, and rolled her. It was John. "You all right?" he asked, still on top of her.

"I don't know."

He helped her stand, brushed the dust and ash from her skirt, and smiled. Studying the charred remains of her dress, he sighed, "Looks like you're all right." Then he grinned. "But your petticoat's a mess." He glanced back at the fire line. The swath they had cleared was wide enough, and the fire was going around them. They were safe.

Hattie was there in an instant, Lizzy at her heels. "Oh, Anna, are you hurt?"

"No, – thanks to John."

"We were over there," Hattie gestured, pointing to two abandoned shovels about fifty feet away. "When I heard Angel bark, I looked up, but if John hadn't moved, hadn't been as quick as he was...." Her voice trailed off, and she sighed, "I'm so glad you're all right."

"Looks like we're all lucky," he said, looking back up the trail.

Hundreds of feet away, tipped over on their sides, two wagons were ablaze. The people who had gone to help had been forced back by the flames and were just watching.

"We've got a couple of blankets we can spare and a sack of beans," John said. "Those families probably lost everything."

"Not everything," Anna said sadly. She looked toward a crowd gathering nearby, around a small, lifeless boy. His mother was holding him and praying. His father was standing over them, his eyes dark, his lips gray. He covered his face with his hands, dropped to his knees, and sobbed.

"What happened?" John asked a man coming from that direction.

His face smeared with dust and ash, his eyes red and sore, the man stopped. Sadly looking back at the scene, he told them, "The boy got run over by their wagon."

Chapter Twenty

Oregon Trail
August 1854

At the crest of the Rocky Mountains, on the Continental Divide, in what would become Wyoming Territory, rip-rap skirts of solid rock rose thousands of feet into the sky creating the Wind River Range. The Oregon Trail crossed the range over South Pass. Over seventy-five-hundred feet high, the trail was one of broken stones and buried roots and was brutally jarring. As the Mormon wagon train descended into a lush, mountain valley on the western side, where grass was cropped by stock in passing wagon trains, the trail became a carpet of dried mud. In comparison to the broken stones and buried roots, it was a cushion.

A mile ahead, the trail branched. Pioneers bound for Oregon and California took Sublette's cutoff north. The Mormon train continued west. As the Mormon train approached the cutoff, at the side of the trail as if waiting for them, a man and a woman stood. They smiled and waved. Their morning campfire was still smoldering. A hobbled team of four, well bred, bay mules was grazing nearby.

"Are we glad to see you," the young man told Ned Haight. The wagon master was approaching them on horseback. Jacob was hurrying over to them on foot.

"What ya doin' out here?" Ned asked. He often saw black men on the trail traveling with Gentiles but seldom saw them alone. He glanced at the young man's companion, a white woman who looked younger than him. She was obviously pregnant. The man was dressed like a farmer. He wore a straw hat; a beige, homespun shirt; brown cotton pants; and faded red suspenders. The woman was wearing a straw bonnet and a plain, blue dress, loose over her bulging stomach. Their clothes were trail worn and dusty.

"Got trouble?" Ned asked.

"Yeah," the young man responded, his brow deeply furrowed. "Our train got some ahead of us a few days ago. We were trying to catch up with it when our axle broke."

"Where's your wagon?" Jacob asked.

"Bout five miles up that direction." The man gestured north toward the mountains. "Took a turn too fast and straddled a rock. Can't get it loose. We walked down here 'cause we knew somebody'd come along." The black man grinned, "Jesus be praised. He sent you to us now."

"We'll get a couple of men to help you," Ned promised. "Need food or water, or anything?"

"No thanks, we've got all we need."

"Get Elders Yost and Baines, and Brother Hawkin's buckboard," Jacob told Ned. "I'll get my irons and ax and join them. We can take care of this couple and meet the train up trail tonight."

Less than half an hour later, Jacob drove Brother Hawkin's buckboard onto the cutoff. It was loaded with axes, hammers, a variety of hand saws, Brother Hawkin's forge, and two iron rods for lifting. It was pulled by two big, sorrel mules. "My names 'Tuttle'," Jacob told the young man as he and the young woman approached him. "These are Elders Yost and Baines," Jacob said of the two men to the right of them on horseback. Yost was a straw thin man with a long, red beard. Baines was rather dumpy. "We'll have you off and up the trail in no time."

The young man sighed, "Thank you, Mr. Tuttle. My name's Palmer Washington." He put his arm around the woman's waist and stepped closer to the buckboard. "This is my wife, Elizabeth. Mind if she rides with you?"

"Not at all," Jacob said. He offered her his hand and helped her onto the seat beside him. "Pleased to meet you both," he said. "Ready to go?"

Palmer had already buried their fire in dirt and packed their things on the back of the second mule in his string. Taking hold of the halter of the first, he swung his long leg over its back and climbed on. "Ready."

The sky was as vivid as the mountain blue birds. The sun was halfway to its crest. It was midmorning. The Mormon train continued its slow and steady journey west. The rescue party traveled north.

The trail to Palmer and Elizabeths' covered wagon was a steep, rocky, switchback trail, cut into the ten-thousand-foot mountain by hand. The wagon was about six-thousand feet up, and it took hours of climbing for the rescue party to reach it. Snagged on a craggy boulder a few feet from the edge of a steep, forested drop, the wagon was tipped awkwardly on its side toward the mountain.

"You're lucky you didn't roll off," Jacob observed to Elizabeth, peering over the edge. Hundreds of feet below them were the shattered skeletons of wagons not so lucky. While Jacob secured the buckboard, Palmer, Yost and Baines watered, then tied the horses and mules to trees a safe distance down the road.

"What can we do?" Palmer asked, when the men had examined the rock, the road, and the wagon.

"What you got in that wagon?" Elder Baines asked, his fleshy forehead creased, his full, unruly eye brows lifted. "Looks full."

"Got everything we own," Palmer told him. "Food, clothes, bedding, a couple of trunks, and a dresser."

"We'll have to get all that out," Baines told him, already unloading.

Yost and Palmer joined him. They worked until Palmer and Elizabeths' every possession was unloaded, carried, and stacked on the trail behind the buckboard.

"Here, take this," Jacob said, handing Palmer one of the two, six-foot-long, iron bars they would use as levers. Jacob pointed to the edge of the drop-off next to the front wheel. "We'll have to stand over there to get the wagon off the boulder because we need a sharp angle. When you get over there, put the bar well beneath the wheel so we'll have plenty of lift on that wagon. It'll take both irons and all four of us to do it. Elder Yost will be with you. Baines and I'ull take the rear."

Palmer dutifully carried the heavy rod around the crippled wagon to the treacherous edge next to the front wheel. He securely tied the wheel to the bed frame, brought over a boulder about two feet in diameter, quickly figured the angle that would make the boulder a good fulcrum, and dropped it on the ground just inches from the brink. He placed one end of the iron rod beneath the wheel and rested the center of the rod on the boulder. The rod was at a thirty degree angle as he waited for Yost to join him.

Yost took one look at his work and told him, "The rock's too far from the wheel. The angle's not steep enough.

Without argument, Palmer handed Yost the rod then knelt, put his hands on either side of the two-foot boulder, and started working it closer to the wheel. "There," Palmer announced, as the back of his skull was caved in by the butt of an ax.

Elder Yost was standing over him. The bloodied ax was in his hand.

Crumpled onto his side, Palmer dazedly looked up at him, a questioning look in his eyes. He gasped. Helpless to move, he watched Yost calmly and quickly turn the ax in his hand, edge down, and grip it with both hands. He cried as Yost swung high and drove the blade into his throat.

Elizabeth was near the buckboard fifty feet down the trail and did not hear the crack of Palmer's skull, blood bursting from his jugular, or the rattle of his death. She was reorganizing their things, getting ready to repack them. She suspected nothing as Yost dragged Palmer's body to the front of the covered wagon and out of sight, its near-severed head bouncing independently from its neck, leaving a wide trail of blood. She did not see Jacob quietly approaching her from behind, holding a well worn Walker Colt behind his back, raising the revolver to within inches of the back of her skull, and firing. She saw and felt nothing. She was dead before she hit the ground.

Sexual intercourse between a black man and a white woman, between any black and white, was an unforgivable sin in Mormon eyes. Their Prophet, Joseph Smith, had told them that those who committed the atrocity must die. He had said that, like the American Indian, black people had been cursed by God with dark skins. Indians were cursed for their apostasy and evil deeds. Blacks were cursed because they were direct descendants of Cain, earth's first murderer. Jacob and the other elders who murdered Palmer and Elizabeth were of God's chosen people, doing what their Prophet had taught them to do. As they cooly moved the bodies into the covered wagon, there was no guilt or remorse. Intentionally separating the two in death, they laid Palmer's body on the seat and Elizabeth's near the tailgate so the couple could sin no more.

The decision to kill Palmer and Elizabeth had been made by the elders before they left the wagon train. They did not kill them at the cutoff because the converts in the wagon train were not yet conditioned to the way things had to be done and would not understand their motives. The Gentile trains coming behind them were also a problem. There could be no evidence left near the trail of the executions. Experience had taught the elders that, guilty or not, the Mormon train would be blamed. There was also, as always, the issue of waste. There would be stores in Palmer and Elizabeth's wagon their own people could use. Perhaps there would be money.

The elders were implements of God, keepers of the converts they were bringing west. They loaded into the buckboard all the young couple's belongings they found useable and for which there was room: food, clothing, tools, a gun, and eight hundred dollars. They would conceal it from the converts and divide it later. They threw the rest of Palmer and Elizabeth's possessions into the covered wagon.

Though personally repulsed by the mixed couple, the elders were performing only their duty to God in murdering Palmer and Elizabeth. There were no regrets or words of compassion spoken as they pushed the wagon and its contents over the edge of the mountain. There was no remorse of any kind as they watched it tumble hundreds of feet down the steep and treacherous slope to the bottom where it joined the scattered skeletons of other wagons and passengers the mountain had claimed in death. God's will had been done.

Chapter Twenty-one

Oregon Trail
August 1854

It took nearly a month of navigating the steep, mountainous trail before the Mormon wagon train reached Fort Bridger, a pole stockade in the foothills of the Uinta Range, elevation a little less than 7,000 feet. Scattered about the supply post were several Indian lodges belonging to Shoshone, stragglers from the band of Eastern Shoshone who camped at the fort during the winter.

Anna's wagon train was still over a hundred miles from Salt Lake City and had yet to cross the twelve to thirteen-thousand-foot ridges remaining over the Rocky Mountains. Jacob had gotten over his objection to Angel some time ago, and each time the wagon train stopped for supplies, he saw to it that Anna had enough food for Angel. Yet there was a condition to Jacob's generosity. He required Anna to sign a second promissory note for an additional two dollars, requiring her to work the debt off by doing more of Kristina's chores.

The agreement increased Anna's workload by an hour each day, but as far as she was concerned, Angel was well worth the extra effort. Despite the additional debt, she was very grateful to Jacob for giving his permission to keep her. Even though Hattie had offered to help, Anna wanted no trouble with him. Hattie had John to take care of her and could afford to be a little troublesome. Anna could not.

Fifty miles up the trail from Fort Bridger reveille broke the stillness of the crisp, predawn morning, as Angel shifted slightly beneath Anna's thick, wool blankets. The blankets were warm, and neither she nor Anna hurried to leave them. The rocky banks of the stream that rippled beside them were laced with ice. It was the end of September. After weeks and months of bone aching travel, along with everyone else in the train, she was exhausted.

Not wanting to get up, but knowing she had to, Anna rolled over, told Angel to, "Look out," and threw the blankets off them. "Sorry, girl, but that was the only way." She shivered, jumped to her feet, rubbed her hands together, and blew on them. There would be time and fuel for only a small cooking fire. She and Angel would have to warm themselves with that.

Later, as Anna and Kristina cooked Jacob's breakfast, Anna noticed how pale Kristina was. Trudging behind the wagon every day on steep, rocky trails, Kristina's body had become like an old woman's, thin, except for the baby, and frail. She was so slow some days, Jacob let her ride, a decision, he told them, he did not make lightly. At the higher elevations, where the trail was steep and often unsure, the weight his team already carried was treacherous. Kristina added more than a hundred pounds.

Vaguely aware of the danger, Anna was even more concerned about the baby and kept Kristina in sight. She was ghost white this morning. "Why don't you let me take care of the milking?" Anna offered.

"No, I'm perfectly able to do my own work," Kristina protested. "I feel fine. Besides, I'd like to get away from the wagon for a while."

Maybe it's Jacob she needs time away from, Anna thought. "Okay, but let me know if you change your mind."

In the mountain meadow where the wagon train had camped, frost coated the ground and clung to knee high grasses. The willows following the course of the stream were bare, and the fall day looked very much like winter. The herd of cattle driven behind the train was grazing about fifty yards outside the wagon circle. It was Anna and Kristina's turn to help milk the cows, and as they ventured into the meadow, each of them carried two buckets.

It was cold, and the air was thin at that altitude. Kristina was obviously in pain and short of breath, yet she forced herself to go on. Not paying attention, she approached a cow nursing a calf. Ignoring the swish of the cow's tail and her pinned ears, Kristina walked behind them with her bucket. Paying no attention to the cow's warning snort, she nudged her. The cow spun.

"Look out!" Anna yelled.

It bucked and kicked Kristina hard, knocking her to the ground.

Anna ran to her. "Shoo!" she shouted, as the cow and calf ran off. "Are you all right?" she asked, as she knelt at Kristina's side.

Kristina's eyes glazed over and teared.

"Where'd she get you?"

Seemingly only half realizing what had happened, Kristina slowly shook her head. "I don't know, but I feel a little crampy." She rubbed her brow, drew her hand across her mouth, and looked down. She grabbed her stomach and screamed, "My baby! She kicked my baby!"Hysterically weeping, Kristina frantically rubbed her belly. Then as if soothing the baby inside, she rocked back and forth. "What do I do?"

"Let's get you back." Anna reached to help her up, but Kristina rejected her assistance. Before she could stop her, Kristina was up, stumbling through the grass, and running back to the wagon.

"Not so fast." Anna caught her by the arm. "You might make things worse."

Fear commanding her, Kristina stopped, afraid to move at all. "Help me. I don't know what to do!" She was not much more than a child herself.

"Does your stomach hurt?"

"No, not now."

"Then, you're probably all right. Try to stay calm and walk slowly." Anna put her arm around Kristina's waist. Setting a gentle, deliberate pace, she guided her back to the wagon.

They were within feet of it when Kristina stopped. A warm, sticky fluid was running down her legs. "I think something broke."

"Just a little further," Anna assured her, noting Kristina was leaving a narrow trail of blood.

"John!" He was grazing his oxen nearby. "Get Mrs. Tork. It's the baby."

He hurried his team into the circle of wagons, dropped their leads, and ran for Mrs. Tork.

At the wagon, Kristina and Jacob's mattress was already rolled, tied and packed for that day's journey. First propping Kristina up against the wheel, Anna hurriedly threw enough of their things out of the wagon to make a space. She then spread the mattress on the wagon bed. Mrs. Tork arrived just as she was helping Kristina inside.

"Get me a towel. Now!" Mrs. Tork ordered, as they lay Kristina down. Blood was pooling on the mattress.

Anna handed her the towel hanging on a nearby nail.

"Get me more," Mrs. Tork ordered.

Two additional towels were folded and packed in a chest near the seat. Anna brought them to her and another from the cart. "What else?" she asked, as Mrs. Tork stuffed the towels between Kristina's legs.

"Get me plenty of water. Boil some. I've got to get her clean before I can see what's wrong."

Suddenly caught by a violent contraction, Kristina sat up, opened her mouth, and screamed. She continued screaming as Anna added fuel to the fire.

Mrs. Tork stuck her head out the back of the canopy. "Better get Brother Jacob."

Anna looked for him everywhere, among the men grazing oxen and all the way around the circle of wagons, but could not find him. No one had seen him. He returned on his own an hour later, after most of the wagons in the train were hitched and ready to go. He and Ned Haight had been scouting the trail ahead.

"She can't be moved," Mrs. Tork told him. "You've got to hold the train."

"I can't hold the train," he said, off handedly. "What's wrong?"

"Sister Kristina's got serious trouble."

He peered into the wagon. Both Kristina and the mattress were soaked with blood. Writhing in pain, sweat pouring from her brow, she cried, "Help me, Jacob. Help me."

Clearly concerned, he looked at Mrs. Tork. "She isn't right, is she?"

Mrs. Tork solemnly shook her head and frowned.

"I'll ask Brother Haight, but I don't think he'll delay. We've got to get to Salt Lake before winter, or we'll die in the mountains." Desperation was in his eyes as he whispered, "Is my son going to die?"

Mrs. Tork was not encouraging. "Let's see what happens in the next few hours."

Anna dutifully boiled as much water as she could, storing it, as best she could, in the pots and pans other women brought her. As Jacob suspected, Brother Haight would not delay the train because of one sick woman, and at precisely 7:00 a.m., at the bugle's command, the wagons moved forward.

As Jacob's wagon pulled out, Mrs. Tork stayed inside it with Kristina. Anna followed, keeping her cart within a few feet of them.

Like recurring blasts of harsh wind, shrill and terrifying, Kristina's screams went on all morning. When the train stopped at noon, ever vigilant of Kristina's condition, Anna gathered fuel and boiled more water. There had been no time to prepare dinner, so Hattie brought the food she made for her own family. She stayed to help until the bugle sounded and the train moved on.

As if he could not bear to be near, Jacob stayed some distance from the wagon yet never diverted his eyes from it. Once the train was moving, he walked next to the oxen, and though it was obvious from his expression his attention never wavered from what was happening inside the wagon, he never looked back.

Hours before dusk, when the animals could go no further without overstraining them, the train stopped for the night. It had traveled fifteen miles over steep, rugged trails that day. Kristina was exhausted. Yet through her exhaustion and pain, she kept screaming, almost without pause, until dark.

"What can I do?" Anna asked Mrs. Tork, checking on Kristina one more time.

"Won't be long now."

Hattie and several other women were gathered at the campfire. They had come to help if it was needed and to bring food to those waiting. They kept the fire going and the water boiling while Anna baked the one hundred's bread, and together, they held vigil. Jacob had apparently gone off somewhere to pray.

"It's time Hattie," Anna called.

Anna and Hattie climbed onto the front of the wagon and over the seat, then crawled over Jacob's crates to get to Kristina. They were at her shoulders when the baby's head crested.

"Hold her! Hold her!" Mrs. Tork ordered.

"Not too fast," she told Kristina, in relative calm. "Let me get ready. – Now push! – Good. – I can see the baby's eyes. – Steady. – It's Almost over. She glanced up at the three women, "Only God can stop the birth now."

The contraction that would finally drive the baby out surged through Kristina's shoulders, pushing Anna and Hattie aside. Then suddenly, all was over. A blood stained infant about a foot and a half long lay in Mrs. Tork's hands. She held it up by its ankles, and swatted.

Breathless, they waited for a sound. She hit it again, and again they waited.

Then, the baby cried.

Barely able to lift her head, Kristina smiled, and Mrs. Tork placed the infant on her stomach.

There was a hush outside as everyone
paused to hear what happened, the silence broken
only by the tumbling stream. One of the women
peeked inside and, when she saw the baby, burst out
laughing. "It's a boy!" A cheer went up. Those
silent only an instant before chattered with joy. As
if he had been present all along, Jacob came out of
the shadows. With him, came two dozen men with
several jugs of whiskey and a couple of fiddles. The
celebration had begun.

The center of attention, the hero of the
night, Jacob announced his son would be named
"Joseph," after their founder, and "Samuel" after
one of Jacob's uncles. "Joseph Samuel Tuttle"
would be his name.

With the baby tucked peacefully in her
arms, Kristina slept most of the next day. Keeping
the cart pressed against the back of the wagon as
they traveled, Anna tried to keep an eye on her, but
was able to see only the top of her head. With other
women bringing Jacob and Kristina food, Anna was
free to do other things. She looked in on them at
dinner and again when they camped for the night,
waking Kristina only to make sure she had eaten.
The baby was quiet, fussing only occasionally.

Because the road was steep and narrow,
Anna dropped back to a safer distance the next day
and did not see Kristina until after supper. "How's
everything?" she asked her. "I can take care of the
baby if you want to get out for a minute and wash
up."

Kristina had not been out of the wagon
since the birth, and though Mrs. Tork had cleaned
her as best she could, the wagon was musty. Most
women would have wanted a break but not Kristina.
Her arm tightened, and she drew the sleeping baby

closer. "No thanks. I'll go down to the stream after everybody's gone to bed. I can take him with me."

"Anything I can get for you?"

"No. We're fine. We just want to rest."

Anna took the hint and left. New mothers were often possessive of their babies.

The next morning, she fixed Jacob and Kristina breakfast and prepared their dinner for the noon stop. The climb was steep and rocky, the going slow that day, and all she could do was manage her cart. When she finished baking bread that evening, she accepted Hattie's invitation to supper. She and Angel did not visit Kristina until after dark. "How is he?" she cheerfully asked when she saw her. The baby's head was covered with a corner of the embroidered quilt Kristina had made for him, and he was sleeping. "He's sure a good little fella. Don't think I heard him cry all day."

Kristina lovingly gazed at him. "He's the most precious thing I ever saw. Do you think, if I asked, Brigham Young would personally bless him?"

Anna had no idea, but since Jacob was an elder, she thought it was certainly possible. "I don't know why he wouldn't."

There was a strange urgency in Kristina's voice as she asked Anna, "As long as he's baptized by one of the apostles, he'll see God, won't he? He won't be damned, will he?"

"That's what Jacob told us," Anna assured her, attributing Kristina's anxiety to the trauma of the birth.

Kristina was tired and pale, yet there was tempest in her eyes.

"If you want to take the baby outside, I'll clean the bed for you," Anna offered, reaching in his direction. The odor in the wagon was getting stronger, almost insufferable.

As if Anna was trying to wrest him from her, Kristina grasped him. Completely out of character, her answer was sharp and abrupt. "No!"

"What's wrong, Kristina?" Now, Anna was worried.

"Nothing. I'm just tired. Go away and let me sleep."

Anna backed away. This was not like Kristina.

Jacob was at the fire, and she joined him, bluntly asking, "Is something wrong?"

His face was drawn. His eyes were fraught with worry, and he had not touched his supper. "I don't know. She won't let me anywhere near her."

"Have you seen the baby?" Anna asked. "Smells very odd in there."

He sighed and shook his head. "I think there's something the matter, but she won't tell me, and she won't let me look."

"I'll get Mrs. Tork."

When Anna returned with Mrs. Tork, Kristina would not let them into the wagon.

"Come on, Kristina," Jacob urged. "Mrs. Tork just wants to check him. Make sure he's healthy."

Anger flashed in Kristina's eyes, and her face turned red. "No!" she screamed. "You're not touching him!" Clutching him to her breast she scooted away from them. "He's dead, understand?" She sobbed. "He's dead! Now leave us alone." Still and unresponsive, like a cloth wrapped stone, the baby showed no sign of life. By his color and rigor, he had died some time ago.

"Just leave her be," Mrs. Tork advised. She escorted Jacob and Anna to the fire and to a place she thought was out of hearing distance of Kristina. "We'd better leave her alone for a while. Let her get used to the idea he's gone."

Jacob's eyes filled with tears. His voice was choked with emotion. "But, he'll need to be buried."

"I know," Brother Jacob. "But, not now. Maybe tomorrow."

That night, when the community came to pay their respects, the women brought food, comfort, and prayer. Kristina wanted none of it. Huddled defensively in the wagon, refusing to see anyone but Anna, she growled at anyone else who approached. When all retreated to the fire, she quieted but did not rest.

Despite Anna's assurances the women had not come to take the baby, Kristina did not believe her. Frightened and suspicious, her eyes vigilant and restive like a trapped and wounded animal's, she frantically searched for intruders.

"At least let Jacob see you," Anna pressed. "He's worried about you."

Kristina glared at her. "I don't want him. I don't want anybody. I just want to be left alone with my baby."

"But, he's your husband, the baby's father. He wants to comfort you."

"I heard him talking to Mrs. Tork about my baby. He wants to bury him! Send him to Hell without baptism!" she cried, rocking back and forth as if the infant was crying.

"No one's going to take your baby," Anna soothed, "not if you don't want them to." She smiled. "Jacob knows you need more time. We all do."

Kristina was not comforted. "Keep them away from me." Terrified, she looked toward the campfire as if she knew those around it were quietly plotting to take her baby away.

"Why don't you get some rest?" Anna suggested. "I'll keep watch for you."

As if Anna was a stranger not to be trusted, Kristina glared at her then at the women around the campfire. After that, Kristina stopped responding to her at all.

Unable to abandon Kristina to join the community, Anna found herself keeping her promise. Posting herself at the wheel, she took watch with her.

The next day, Kristina refused to say anything to anyone and, until supper time, refused to listen. Jacob was losing patience. The odor near the wagon was unbearable. "We've got to bury him," he told her, as he and Anna stood outside. His voice was strained. "You've got to give him to me, Kristina. It's time."

Her eyes sparked. Her cheeks flamed red as she told him, "No, our son is going to be baptized by an apostle, and before he's buried, he's going to be blessed by Brigham Young. Not even you will damn him!"

Jacob was incredulous. "You mean you want to take him all the way to Salt Lake City?"

Anna put her hand on his back subtly reminding him to be patient. Flustered, Jacob stepped away.

"Forgive him, Kristina," Anna said, trying to calm her. "This has been very hard on him. He loves you both and only wants to do what he thinks is right."

Kristina was not convinced. "Then why is he so determined to damn our son?"

"I'll talk to him, maybe I can make him understand."

Anna followed Jacob to the campfire. "Can't you wait a little while longer?" she asked him. "You told us a baby has to be baptized by one of the apostles to be saved. Kristina can't deprive her baby of its soul."

Jacob's frustration was uncontrolled. "But, he deserves a decent burial. I can't just let him rot in there." He looked sadly at the wagon.

"He's only been dead a few days, Jacob. A few more might not hurt."

Still staring at the wagon, he cupped his hands over his lips. The lesson Jacob had taught them was absolute.

"We've given up all we have to be baptized in God's Kingdom," Anna reminded him. "Did our sacrifice not matter?" A man not baptized by an apostle in Salt Lake City would be damned, no matter who or how old he was. If Jacob buried his own son without being baptized, it would diminish the ritual's importance, convey a message to the converts that baptism by an apostle was not that important after all and that their sacrifices in journeying to Utah were meaningless.

He turned toward her, murmuring, "All right, I'll wait."

In the days that followed, as the odor of death and decay from Jacob's wagon became worse and the community less tolerant, Anna repeatedly argued with the complainers to give Kristina time, – to let her decide what was best for her son. Yet,

Anna's arguing only delayed what had to come. After two weeks of climbing, Salt Lake City another two weeks away, the odor drifting over the train was like a poisonous vapor, and scavengers were hounding their trail. Fed up with Jacob's pampering, the wagon master, Ned Haight, issued an ultimatum. If Jacob did not bury the baby immediately, he and Kristina would be left by the wayside to travel alone.

"I know you think she's right," Jacob told Anna that evening, when she came to cook their supper. "But, I don't have a choice any longer, and I want you to help me."

"I can't, Jacob."

"Don't worry, Anna, I'm not going to do anything that will hurt my son any more than he's already been hurt. I've been thinking. I'll see that he's not damned. I'll see Little Joseph gets his place in Heaven even if we bury him here. He WILL be baptized by an apostle."

Anna did not believe him. "How is that possible?" She gestured around her. "We're in the middle of the wilderness. We'll probably never even find him again."

"Not here. In Salt Lake City. In God's Kingdom."

"But, how?"

"Another baby can take his place in the baptismal, and he can be baptized there."

"He won't be there?" Anna said, pointing out what she thought was obvious.

"His soul will be," Jacob argued. "Little Joseph's soul will be blessed through the substitute baby, and he'll be saved. My son will be accepted into God's Celestial Heaven just as if he was there himself."

Jacob's eyes were a deep, thoughtful brown. His plea was earnest. "Once Kristina sees his baptism, she'll believe it too."

"What if she doesn't?"

"She'll believe. I promise. And, she'll forgive us."

Jacob was more compassionate than Anna had ever seen him. She found herself wanting to believe him, wanting to know that Kristina's suffering could be so easily quelled, but she would not take the risk. More fearful of what would happen to Kristina than of Jacob, even when she knew how dangerous he could be, Anna took a stand. "I'm sorry. Unless she changes her mind, you'll have to get someone else to help you."

Jacob did not like being refused, particularly by a woman. His face turned a furious crimson. His stare bore through her, as with clenched teeth he reminded her, "God imposes on you a duty to do whatever I tell you to do."

Conscience or duty was Anna's choice. If she yielded and did what Jacob demanded, she would have no trouble with him but would be condemning Kristina to a lifetime of torment. She had defied Jacob once before over Angel, and he had forgiven her. Maybe, he would forgive her this time too. "I just can't."

Not wanting any part of what he was going to do, knowing she could no longer prevent the burial or protect Kristina, she turned her back on both of them and walked back to her cart. Sitting on Erich's rocker, holding Angel on her lap, not wanting to see or hear what was happening, she waited.

Less than half an hour later, Jacob came back to the wagon with Mrs. Tork and waited outside near the wheel while she went inside with a cup of tea. When Kristina refused to let go of her baby and take the tea, Mrs. Tork cooly put the cup down and pretended to look for something. "Let me get you another blanket."

Suspicious and agitated, Kristina scooted to the other side of the wagon as Mrs. Tork opened the trunk. "What do you want?" Kristina challenged, glaring at her.

Mrs. Tork smiled. "Just to make you more comfortable."

Inside the trunk, next to the blanket, was a coiled rope. "Here," she said loudly, giving Jacob his cue.

While Mrs. Tork reached for the rope, he leaped into the wagon. Pushing the baby aside, he grabbed Kristina's wrists. "Tie them," he yelled. As Mrs. Tork tied Kristina's hands together, Jacob grabbed the baby and hurried away.

"Don't!" Kristina screamed after him. "Please, don't!"

Chapter Twenty-two

Provo, Utah
9:00 p.m.
April 21

That evening, as Sharon turned the key to Kim and Wayne's house, the tumblers were silent. The lock easily slipped open. She was using the key she had taken from the birdhouse in the back yard that morning.

Her blouse was torn. Her knees and arms were badly scraped. She had picked herself off the side of the road where the cop had thrown her, stopped at a gas station for antiseptic and bandages, and checked herself into the nearest motel. Physically and mentally shaken, she had rested, waiting until dark. She had telephoned her assistant and, without saying why, rescheduled her appointments for the week. The procedural hearing before the United States District Court for the Northern District of California on a motion to quash evidence could be handled by one of her associates. Her social engagements, her date with Jeremy, was to be canceled or postponed.

She approached the house with the headlights off, entering the empty house in darkness. There were no coverings on the windows, so she kept her back to them, doing the best she could to block the beam from her pen-sized flashlight.

The house was eerie in the dark, nothing like it had been in the sunlight. Not knowing for what she was searching, Sharon moved slowly through the living room and into the kitchen. She looked through cupboards and drawers for anything that might be taped on the inside, outside, or anywhere around them. She found nothing. After searching the downstairs' closet and bathroom, thinking Kim might have left something upstairs, she examined the children's bedrooms and bath, hopeful, but not expecting to find the beginning of a trail. Resting all her hopes on Kim and Wayne's bedroom, Sharon searched in, under and around everything she saw: behind the mirror affixed to the wall and the pipes under the bathroom sink, in the gaps and grooves of the baseboards and the window sills. Yet, the bedroom was as empty as the rest of the rooms.

An hour after entering the house, she was sitting at the top of the stairs, out of ideas and discouraged. Knowing something terrible was wrong but having no place to go, the improbable happened when the wall phone in the kitchen rang. Irrationally hoping the caller was Kim or Wayne, or someone who knew where they were, she leapt down the stairs, two steps at a time, and rushed into the kitchen. "Hello!" she shouted into the receiver.

"Kim?" a baritone voice asked.

"No," Sharon sighed. "I'm her sister," she said, flatly, adding with a trace of hope, "You don't know where Wayne is do you?"

There was a deep, worried, "No," on the other end. "I was just calling to see if he was all right."

"Why do you ask? Who are you?"

"A friend of his, Alex Caldwell," the man said, somberly.

"I remember you from Kim and Wayne's wedding reception," Sharon told him, a bit brighter. None of the Gentile guests had been allowed in the

Temple to attend the wedding itself, not even Kim's mother. "You're that reporter from New York, aren't you?"

"Yeah, so where's Wayne?"

"I don't know. I was supposed to meet Kim early this morning, and when I got here, she and Wayne were gone, – supposedly to have suddenly moved to Central America. A van came, emptied their house, and took their things away for auction." She paused. "Alex, I think they've been kidnapped."

Clearly alarmed, Alex demanded, "Where are the kids?"

"At my mother's. Wayne took them there last week. Why did you call? Did you know something was wrong?"

"Someone's been killed," he blurted.

"Who?"

"He didn't have any I.D. I only know he tried to kill Hank."

"Hank Blanchard?" she recalled him from the reception. Hank had caused quite a stir among Wayne's Mormon relatives when he spiked the punch. "Is he all right?"

"Yes, but he's in custody, pending an investigation. Police think he was the aggressor."

"Does what happened to Hank have something to do with Wayne?"

"I wasn't sure until I called."

"What connection could there be?"

"I don't know, but I think the answer's in Utah. Hank told me he'd met with Wayne and that something was up. Wayne was scared and was being followed. Delta should have a flight to Salt Lake first thing in the morning. Meet me at the airport. I'll be on it."

On the four-hundredth block of West 92nd Street in New York City, Alex had no trouble getting past the security guard with Hank's key and written authorization. Expecting Hank's office to be as messy as it was when they left it, Alex was surprised to find the files and documents scattered about that afternoon were now in neat, organized piles. My God, they've already been here! he thought. He anxiously searched for anyone who might still be there. Satisfied he was alone, he looked for Hank's half eaten sandwich.

The hoagie was gone. The desk was clean and dusted. Obviously someone had tried to hide their search by putting everything in order. The janitor had not yet dumped the wastebasket, and Alex searched it. There were cans; a bottle of seltzer; potato chips; days old spaghetti; chicken bones; paper; and finally, one lone, half eaten hoagie. The pastrami was spoiled, and its contents were sealed together by melted cheese and mayonnaise.

Chapter Twenty-three

Outside Salt Lake City
Fall 1854

Early in the morning, two and a half weeks after Kristina's baby was buried, the wagon train entered Emigration Canyon, the threshold to the Great Salt Lake Valley. When they reached the overlook, Anna rushed with others to see. They had given up nearly everything they had. They had left their homes half a world away and traveled thousands of miles on promises of hope and salvation. Below them, was the Kingdom they had been promised.

They gasped. With everyone else, Anna stared. God's Kingdom was but a sagebrush-choked desert with a massive dead sea in the distance. A thin film of fog covered it. Bleak and gray, it seemed not a Kingdom of God but a place abandoned by Him. John, Hattie, Lizzy and dozens of other arriving converts joined them on the overlook. Uniformly and in silent concert, the reaction was the same. The gravity of their disappointment was palpable. Expecting a garden paradise like that of Eden, – anticipating a city paved in porcelain, they gazed in disbelief, and no one spoke. The joy that should have marked their arrival hung dismal in the heavy air, their distress a dark, malignant shadow. A collective sigh, unheard but felt, rippled through the train.

After long moments, someone quietly made a cautious observation. "It's like the land described in the Old Testament, isn't it?"

"Abraham's land," another added, hopefully and insightfully. "God has brought us to the New Jerusalem."

"Aaah." Suddenly everyone saw, and someone shouted, "God is here. This IS His Kingdom."

"Look!" someone else shouted, as the bright, orange sun peered through the lifting fog. "He's opening His door to us."

A cheer went up, loved ones hugged loved ones, and in a joyous rush, they returned to their wagons. Eager to descend, ignoring Ned Haight's warnings to slow down, they raced down the mountain, into the valley, and to the city's edge where they were greeted with cries if hosanna and offerings of melons. Scores of men, women and children, forewarned that they were coming, escorted the converts and their wagons through town while hundreds more applauded.

Divided in ten acre blocks, the city was drawn in precise measurement. Every street was wide enough for a team of four oxen and a wagon to turn around in without backing. Each lot was designated by number, and there was a plot of land for every man willing to earn it. In a long parade, the crowd led the wagon train to the center of the city to a giant, open space, where huge blocks of granite arranged in orderly rectangles, nine feet thick in places, were erected. Standing alone on a stage in front of the granite rectangles was a paunchy, regal man, their Prophet, Brigham Young.

Brigham was portly. His hair was wavy and brushed back from his face. His beard was well groomed and curly. He was dressed in a tailored, black suit with standing white collar and black, bow tie, appearing to be not only a man of God but one of property. He was the epitome of what most of the men there wanted to be. As God's Living Prophet, as President of the Church and of the Quorum of the Twelve Apostles, Brigham Young was the most powerful man in the West. To all who surrounded him, he was the voice of God.

He only faintly smiled as they approached, yet his expression was one of great satisfaction as he saw their numbers. He had the air of a man completely in charge, and he critically and intensely studied them.

The new converts approached him with awe, Anna with Hattie, John and Lizzy. Elevated head and shoulders above them, the Living Prophet silently and haughtily waited while everyone from the train gathered before him. He was as a king to his subjects, and when he spoke, he spoke like a king. "Welcome to the Kingdom of God."

He paused, as if giving the newcomers time to absorb the significance of the moment, and then he spoke again, "Seven years ago – on July 24, 1847, God led us, His Latter Day Saints, to this valley. And, in this Great Salt Lake Valley we reside, here to build His temple and the New Jerusalem.

"When we arrived, Gentiles and other heathens had already laid claim to this land and all the territories around it. Yet God did not want Gentiles on these lands and gave those lands to us: – all the land, – water sheds, – mountains, – deserts – and settlements of the Great Basin. Territory as far north as the Columbia River in Oregon, – as far east as the Continental Divide of the great Rocky Mountains, – southwest through the Gulf of California, – and east into the Colorado River shed. Almost 200,000 square miles, and it is all ours.

"We have named this land, our land, the 'State of Deseret', and I have been elected Governor. Here on this land we will be free. Free from Gentiles like those in Missouri and Illinois who forced us from our homes, – murdered our brothers and sisters, – destroyed our City of Nauvoo, – and drove us west. Free from the United States and the dictates of the scum that govern it." He proudly gestured to the huge, granite blocks behind him. "This will be our Temple!"

A big, brass band began playing a hallelujah tune, and citizens, new and old, gathered around the stage and briefly introduced themselves to one another. After a few minutes, Brother Brigham raised his hands and called them back to order. "Let everyone who has come here today bow their heads to God and pray.

"Welcome to the City of Zion," he said, when their prayer was through. "You, our new and most glorious converts, have endured many trials in your long and difficult journey, but those trials are merely a down payment for your admittance here. The rewards and opportunities that await you are a thousand fold. You, – we all, – are God's chosen people. The riches we will inherit from Him are boundless, but you must earn them.

"As successor to our Prophet, Joseph Smith, I have been anointed with God's power and have been given the keys of the Priesthood. Through me and, by extension the Priesthood, God will command you. No man shall come unto God save through obedience to those commandments. The great knowledge the priests and I will impart to you will be for your glory and happiness. Do not close your hearts to it. If you reject our testimony of God's word and will, – if you do not heed to the principles we impart to you, – He has ordained that you will be damned.

"Open your hearts to our testimony, follow His word, and you will inherit thrones, kingdoms, principalities, dominions, and unlimited powers. You will become gods yourselves and have no end. You will be eternal, your life everlasting, and you will be above all things.

"God has commanded us to do much, and the price of His rewards is high. "Through revelation, God revealed to Joseph that a man cannot be saved unto Him without a woman by his side. A woman cannot be saved except through her husband. He also revealed that there are thousands of spirit children begotten by the gods of the universe, – children who are drifting, hovering at the doors of bad houses, unable to enter tabernacles of the body. God's will is that we, his chosen people, open tabernacles to these spirit children. Because we are Adam's chosen, the best place for these spirit children to take up their tabernacles is among we saints, through our wives. This is their primary duty.

"Several years ago, God revealed to Joseph that if a woman is not sealed to her husband for eternity by our Priesthood, the man can never be a god. He and his wife will be in servitude forever as angels. Know also, that any marriage performed by a Gentile is invalid!"

Among the new converts, married men stared blankly at him. Wives gasped. Their shock was electrified by single men chuckling. Virtually all the new converts had been married by Gentiles!

"Then, what do we do?" a woman clutching her four children, shouted.

"Your marriage will be sealed by the Priesthood, and you will be remarried under the authority of the Church," Brigham Young replied. "You should know God has also commanded that a man be sealed to many wives."

There were murmurings of disbelief through the crowd. Brigham raised his hand to silence them. "This," he said loudly, "is for the benefit of spirit children awaiting tabernacles of the body and for the glory of Adam, our God."

Single men amused by the notion of voided marriages and the prospect of numerous wives broke into laughter. Married women and their husbands stood stunned. Staring at the unruly in the crowd, his eyes locked in a stern and mortal gaze, Brigham Young, God's Prophet, demanded, "Silence!"

The disruptive sheepishly obeyed and quieted. Despite a few lingering sniggers, he continued. Addressing only the men, he told them, "God commands that a man earn his godhood and build his own kingdom. God also commands that he take enough wives and produce enough children to populate it. A man's glory is proportionate to the number of wives and children he has. The more women sealed to him, the more he can save to his kingdom. The more wives he has, the more children he will bear.

"Even Jesus Christ must have married a number of women. There were just too many women following him, pampering him, for it not to be so. Had he not married them, there would have been scandal.

"In 1835, while our Prophet, Joseph, was translating the Book of Abraham from papyrus found with Egyptian mummies, our God came to him. God told Joseph that to serve Him we, his chosen people, must engage in celestial plural marriages. Brother Joseph was stunned at first. Wrongly influenced by his Gentile upbringing, he hesitated and delayed in following God's instruction. Then one day an angel of God appeared to him with drawn sword and told him that if he did not establish plural marriages, his priesthood would be taken from him and he would be destroyed." Studying the faces of the newcomers, Brigham looked down and at a young woman standing next to Anna. She was crying.

"What is your name, child?" he asked.

Men allowed to have multiple wives? Anna could not believe it. Along with everyone else in the crowd, she turned and stared at the young woman.

The young woman's usually amber eyes were red. Her face was puffy. Holding tight to the toddler in her arms, she was sobbing as she said out loud that which was on all the women's minds. "If my husband marries more than one wife, we will all be whores. Our babies will be bast...."

"No!" Brigham shouted, before she could utter the word. "Neither you nor the other women your husbands take as wives will be whores. Nor will your babies be bastards. The boy babies you bear are destined to be gods, – the girls their wives and the mothers of their children.

"If a man marries a woman, and that woman gives her consent for him to take another wife, then he is justified. He cannot commit the sin of adultery for his wife or wives agreed to his taking another. The children they bear are legitimate." Brigham was losing patience. His eyes frigid, he glared at the young woman for her ignorance. His voice was dark and foreboding as he continued, warning her, "However, if a man's wife withholds permission, God will destroy her." He paused again, glaring in turn at Anna and Kristina and all the other women near him. His message was clear: No woman dare refuse her husband.

A very old looking woman, gnarled from years of hard work and harsh weather, her face hidden from the newcomers by an all encompassing bonnet tied over her ears, glared at him from the front row. She was Emma Hale Smith, Joseph Smith's first wife, the woman he first told of God's revelation demanding plural marriages. She was his only wife at the time, long before he took so many others. Her eyes were squinted, and the corners of her dry lips were fixed in a long, deep frown. Her anger at Joseph had fomented for years, and she had made no secret of her disdain for the dogma Brigham was spouting. Plural marriages were a sin against God.

Emma had suffered Joseph Smith's philandering for years before he brought her the document describing God's revelation encouraging Joseph to bring his whores home with him. The document had specifically addressed her by name and threatened to destroy her if she did not consent. It promised to bless her, multiply her, and make her heart rejoice if she forgave him.

Furious with him for what she perceived to be a vile trick, she had crumpled the dictation, thrown it in the fire, and burned it. Though she could not stop Joseph from marrying scores of other women or initiating plural marriages in the Church, at least she forced him to bed his other wives in secret. She kept herself at a distance from them, but after Joseph was murdered, she was defenseless.

She was pressured into marrying Brigham Young and was one of his twenty-three wives. Now she, too, was a whore, and like so many other women in the community had to hide her feelings and pretend acceptance.

"Oooohhhh." Anna shivered aloud at the thought of multiple women bedding with one man. To Anna, a man was entitled to only one wife, and their marriage was to be entered under the eyes of God until death. Having more was wrong.

Then it struck her. If marriages performed by Gentiles are false, what was her marriage to Erich? Anxiety pressed against her heart, and she felt faint. Tears came to her eyes, and she swallowed hard. Was she his whore? She was confused. How could so many things she thought were good and right be condemned by God?

Puzzled by the strange revelations Jacob, and now Brigham Young, were telling them, she no longer understood God's ways. Her confidence was shaken. She no longer knew what God expected of her. With nowhere else to turn, she, like the other converts listening, had only Brigham Young to explain God to them.

Confusion obvious in their faces, he took advantage of their weakness and continued, "Your rewards in eternity will not only be dependent on the number of wives you take and the number of children you bring into the world, but will also depend on the strength of your faith and your obedience to His word. While you are a saint on this planet, your responsibility is to build Our Lord Adam's Kingdom. Your personal glory will be in proportion to the degree of your success. In the years to come, you and your children will spread His Kingdom north into Oregon, Idaho, and

Wyoming, west to the Pacific, east to the other edge of the Rocky Mountains, and south to Mexico. As His chosen people, you will ultimately hold and inhabit, rule and govern the entire world."

Chapter Twenty-four

Salt Lake City
Fall 1854

It was late afternoon by the time all the speeches were given, the prayers said, and the ceremonies adjourned. As an announcement was made that there would be a dance on Saturday night to celebrate the converts' arrival, Jacob disappeared into the crowd.

"Where do you think he went?" Kristina asked Anna. They were standing next to Jacob's wagon. The other wagons had moved out, headed to the edge of town to a campsite that had been set aside for them.

"Maybe he went to see that his house was ready for you," Anna offered, as she kept her company. She could tell something more was bothering Kristina. "Is anything wrong?"

Kristina's brow wrinkled. Her eyes filled with tears. "You don't suppose he has another wife, do you? "What if he's gone to get her?"

"Surely he would have told you by now if he had another wife," Anna reasoned.

"Maybe but, what if he didn't tell me? What if he made me his whore before I even left my parent's house in Switzerland?" Tears flowed down her cheeks. The Prophet didn't say a man taking more than one wife was all right in Switzerland. Only here. Didn't Jacob have to have his other wife's permission to marry me? If he didn't have it, wouldn't our marriage be adultery? He didn't even know I existed when he left here."

A stern and condemning Jacob, coming up behind her, answered, "God commanded we take our wives from anywhere we find them." He was standing at the wagon wheel. A tall, older woman, a woman several years her junior, and a gaggle of children were behind him. He gestured toward them. "This is my family."

There were eight children, three boys and five girls. The oldest was a girl about fifteen, the youngest was little more than a toddler. The older of the two women was as tall as any woman Anna had ever seen. She had broad, manlike shoulders and brilliant red hair. She looked to be at least five years older than Jacob. The younger woman was not much older than Kristina, maybe even a little younger. Her face was rich with freckles, and she had dimples. Gesturing toward the older woman, Jacob introduced her first, "This is Sister Sarah." Turning to the younger woman, he said, "This is Sister Rachel."

Smiling pleasantly, the two women nodded but said nothing.

"Sarah and Rachel are my celestial wives. These are my children."

The breath sucked out of her, Kristina gasped. Her fears were being realized in multiples. "But, what about me?"

"You shall bear no shame nor shall anyone look down on you. Our marriage will be blessed by God and confirmed by the apostles, and you will be sealed to me as my celestial wife for eternity. You will be as much my wife in the eyes of God as Sarah and Rachel, and they no lesser." He paused, took her hand, and told her, "You will forever be dear to me, Sister Kristina, and I will always take care of you."

Kristina paled. Her eyes glazed, and she was speechless.

Horrified, Anna stared at the children, blurting, "Do you all live together in the same house?"

His eyes biting, Jacob angrily responded, "Of course we live together. I love my family. It's my duty to care for them. Not only did God decree that we marry many times to populate the Church, He demanded that those of us who can support ourselves take care of those who cannot." He drew Kristina toward him. His expression softened, and in a controlled voice, he told Anna, "There are many more women in the valley than men. The women need to be cared for, and I must do my part."

"But, why didn't you tell me before I married you?" Kristina asked.

"I couldn't tell anybody."

"Why not?" Anna demanded. It was not right to keep his other wives a secret from Kristina.

"If I had let my situation and our doctrine of plural marriages be known to anyone, even Kristina, I would have compromised my mission to bring converts to Utah. Kristina would have told her parents, and they would have told others. Word would have spread. I couldn't take that chance. People not used to the idea would have hated me, – would have hated all of us elders. They might even have killed us. People close to converting might have objected so much they would not have converted and would have lost their opportunity to come to God. It was better to wait. Let those who believe in our faith come here first where they can see plural marriages work. We do it that way, so the unfaithful will not hurt those of us who go to distant shores to spread His word."

Jacob's voice was like cream thick with sugar as he told Kristina, "If you are faithful to the Church, you will come to love your sister wives and be happy."

They look normal, Anna thought of Jacob's wives and children. Yet this was so strange, so contrary to everything Anna had been taught by her parents. Bigamy was a sin under her old God. Now it was Kristina's duty? Anna studied her.

Slowly, as if restrained by heavy chains, Kristina's gaze fell first on Sarah, then on Rachel, – then, one by one, on Jacob's children. The God to whom Kristina now prayed had spoken through Brigham Young. Her husband, Jacob, commanded it. If she resisted her plural marriage, she would be damned. When she finally spoke, her voice was weak and trembling, and all she could say was, "I suppose it's possible to love them."

"Good." Jacob declared, "it's settled!" He touched her waist, and lightly pushed her toward his waiting family. "Sarah, Rachel, and the girls will take you to the house while the boys and I see to the wagon. He turned away, "You boys want to ride?" He watched proudly while the older boys climbed onto the wagon seat. When the toddler held up his arms begging to go too, Jacob lifted him onto his shoulders and turned to Anna. "You join the rest of the train. Don't worry about a thing. I'll find you in the morning and let you know what arrangements have been made for you."

Stunned by the depravity of what she had just witnessed, Anna watched as Jacob ushered his three wives and five daughters away. As she pushed her cart toward camp, she shivered, wondering what Jacob had in store for her.

Early that evening, as she explored Salt
Lake City's main street with Hattie, Lizzy and John,
Anna tried to put aside what she had learned that
afternoon. They peered into every store window,
walked along boardwalks just being built, and went
into one of the general stores to buy coffee. Anna
was excited about their arrival but troubled too.
Brigham Young was God's oracle, yet from his
mouth came words she could not accept as God's.
Deep in her soul she believed that God wanted a
man to have only one wife. Every time they passed
a man and woman, she wondered how many other
wives he had. When she saw a group of children,
she wondered how many mothers they had. Despite
Brigham Young's assurances, if adultery was a sin
as she suspected, the entire community was sinful.
The participating women were whores, and these
children were bastards.

The next afternoon, while John was with a
surveyor looking at the lot he was given to build his
homestead, Anna and Angel were with Hattie and
Lizzy at their wagon having coffee while they
waited for him to come back.

Anna had not slept that night, – imagining
harems in every house and Satan at every dinner
table. She pictured brothels galore where men went
to shop for wives, herself one of the wretches
among them, and was tormented by what might
become of her. She searched her soul. Was this
God's Kingdom or Hell? She stared at her coffee
longing to talk to Hattie but not wanting to talk
about such things in front of Lizzy. Frustrated and
scared, she was nearly frantic when she looked up
from her coffee and saw Jacob approaching.

Light heartedly and in complete control, he
strode to the fire, picked up John's empty tin cup,

and told Lizzy, "Give me about half." He waited for
Lizzy to pour, took a sip, and turned to Anna.
"Come on, I want to talk to you." Motioning her to
follow him, he led her outside the circle of wagons
and yards into the sagebrush.

Still wary of being alone with him, fearing
her brothel work might begin right there, she
nervously glanced back at Hattie. Making certain he
did not take her out of view, she abruptly stopped
and asked, "What are we doing way out here?"

Amid vivid streams of orange and violet,
the sun was resting behind mountains blue in its
shadow. The air was clear and crisp against her
cheeks. The odor of the sage was wild and earthy.

"I need to tell you something, and I want
us to be alone," Jacob told her, coming
uncomfortably close.

Recoiling, she stepped back. Trying to
avoid whatever it was he wanted to say, she got
right to business. "Do you know where I'm going to
live?" she asked. Angel had followed them and was
now at her feet. She reached down to touch her and
to remind Jacob Angel was there.

Jacob was an adulterer living with at least
three women. He would have raped her back in
Iowa if he had the chance. She wanted no more to
do with him than was absolutely necessary. Her
fingers began to tingle, and the tingling crept up her
arms. She trembled as she waited for his answer.

"I've talked to Brother Brigham. He has
given permission for me to seal my marriage to
Kristina."

Flurries of memories; of Jacob and
Kristina's wedding in Switzerland, of his public
promises to her, and of the ordeals she suffered on
the trail, swirled through Anna's mind as she

listened to him. He was announcing, almost matter-of-factly, the ritual that would ensure Kristina's place in Heaven, as if he was checking off some chore on a duty list, with no more feeling than that.

"There will be a celebration later," he coldly continued. "Right now, I need to take care of you."

With that, he captured Anna's full attention.

His eyes as dark in sunlight as they were in shadow, his soft, luring gaze testament to his intentions, he cleared his throat. He reached for her hand and, before she could protest, drew her close to him. "You are to be mine." Folding his arms around her, he pressed his ready genitals to hers with only cloth between them and kissed her, his thick lips open and his juices running.

Revolted, she pushed him away, knocking off his broad brimmed hat. "What do you think you're doing?" she demanded.

He grinned. "It's all right. I've got permission."

"Permission?"

"Brigham Young's permission. He is allowing me to build onto my house and take a fourth wife. He has agreed that wife will be you."

She was stunned and repulsed. Her mouth dropped open, and she shouted, "What?"

"You are to be my wife," he repeated, beaming. "My beautiful, adorable wife."

The very thought of his flesh against hers was disgusting. She shuddered. Jacob and men like him had more than God on their minds, and she wanted nothing to do with him.

He stepped toward her, and she pushed him away again, quickly retreating when he tried to grab her. "I don't want to be your wife!" she shouted. If there was a time to speak up, it was now. "I don't want to be one of your whores!" She was surprised she had said what she was thinking aloud, sorry she had included Kristina in the remark, but she meant every word.

Oddly enough, Jacob did not seem surprised by her reaction, or even shaken. Unruffled, casually stepping toward her, he continued, "You're a beautiful woman, Sister Anna, and deserve a husband who loves you. I will love you. You're a strong woman, but you need children to fulfill you. You need sister wives to help and care for you."

Her mind was whirling. The very idea was outrageous.

He grabbed her, his hands holding tight as she struggled to get free. "I know all this is new to you, Anna," he told her, his voice soft, his eyes tender, "and that you're not used to sharing a husband. But, you're in a different place now, a place God especially created to prepare His children for Heaven. He has entrusted us with His cause and expects us to follow His instructions. He has commanded that you and the other women marry and bear Him children. By coming here, you have agreed to abide by His command. If you expect to inherit a place in His Kingdom, you must obey."

Anna was grasping for an argument. "But, I can't have children." It was the first time she had said it aloud. Oddly enough, right this minute, she was grateful she could not have children. "That's why Erich and I didn't have any."

"Perhaps in Switzerland you could not," Jacob said, surprisingly undeterred. "This place is blessed by God, and like a seed in His garden, you will flourish. If you do not, if He chooses that you be blessed with the gift of caring for other women's children, you will care for mine."

Sickened by the thought of life in Jacob's harem, Anna's stomach turned. She twisted in his grasp trying to get away from him. Desperate and angry, she struck out, "What makes you think I've got to be gifted with yours? I don't want yours!" She hoped her anger and insults would drive him away, but they did not. As if already prepared for them, he seemed impervious to them.

"You can object if you want,"he told her as he held her firm, "but you'll do what you have to do. You've got no other way to make a living, no one else to take care of you. You have to marry me."

Again, Anna fearfully remembered Jacob dragging her toward the woods on the banks of the river in Iowa and her being helpless against him. Had John not interrupted, she would already be his. She would have no choice but to marry him. A dozen converts from the wagon train were gathering, watching them. They alone, protected her from his taking her now. That knowledge raised her confidence. She knew as well as he did, if these people saw him rape her, they would be witness to his adultery, a sin for which, even here, he could forfeit his life.

She stood straight, her shoulders squared as she faced him and demanded, "Let me go."

He looked toward the gathering converts and released her. "Just remember," he said, "no one else is willing to have you."

"No one else has met me," she snapped.

"It doesn't matter, Anna. Your choice is limited to me. Brigham Young has decided it."

"We'll see about that," she said, as she turned away. "Come on, Angel."

"You know what Jacob's up to?" Anna angrily sputtered, when she returned to Hattie.

"What are you going to do?" Hattie asked, after Anna told her.

Anna's anger was being replaced by doubt. "I don't know." Her heart sank as reality closed in on her. "What if Jacob's right? What if I don't have any choice but him?"

Like a buffer against the storm, Hattie embraced her, assuring her, "He can't be right. They can't possibly force you to marry him. You're young and strong. There's got to be work you can get," Hattie encouraged. "He's just trying to bully you."

"He told me there isn't any work. That I can't make a living without him."

"Do you believe him?"

"I don't believe him about anything."

Hattie nodded and, for a moment, was silent as she protectively lead Anna back to the fire. "There's a little coffee left. Would you like it?" She made certain Anna was comfortable, picked up Anna's tin cup and poured. By the time she handed Anna the coffee, she was smiling. "What if you lived with us for a while? John's a good man. He's sure to let you live with us until you find something. Lizzy adores you, and I'd love to have you."

Anna sighed. For the moment, at least, her troubles were over. Hattie was like a mother to her, Lizzy like a very young sister. She would love being part of their family, if only for a little while. "I promise I'll keep looking until I find something. If I have to dig latrines, I'll pay you back."

"Don't worry about that," Hattie said, grinning. "I'll talk to John tonight."

"No," John said, to Hattie's shock and embarrassment.

The night sky was clear and they were sitting around the fire. Hattie was beside him on one side, Anna and Lizzy were on the other. As John listened to Hattie's proposal, his plate empty in his hand, he was shaking his head.

In anguished disbelief, Hattie and Anna stared at him.

"Can't," he continued. "A woman my age living with me in my house, – and us not being married? It isn't respectable. Even if my own mum's there. I've got to think of Lizzy."

Lizzy clutched Anna's hand. "But, I want her to live with us. I like her."

Looking first at Lizzy then at Anna, John acknowledged, "We all like her. But, just how many rooms do you think we'll have in our house? I'm sorry, Anna, but I've got to think of Lizzy's reputation."

Anna's expectations were shattered, yet she begrudgingly understood. What if she had asked this of an unmarried man in Weiningen? While Lizzy clung to her hand, she quietly waited for the ordeal to be over. Beginning to visualize a life with Jacob, she glumly stared at the ground.

Yet the battle had just begun for Hattie. "Where do you think you are, John? This isn't England, you know." Her jaw was rigid, her voice stern. "There are any number of women living with one man in this place, and nobody seems to care. What's the difference if you have just one?"

"Those other women are wives," John reminded her, "at least as far as the Church and this community are concerned. That's the difference. I'm sorry."

"You can't mean this," Hattie argued. "You know she'll have to marry Jacob, don't you?"

"She doesn't have to marry him or anyone else if she doesn't want to. I'll go into town tomorrow and talk with one of the apostles. He'll know what she can do."

With John so sure, Anna felt a little better. A man was more important to the community than a woman. Maybe he could help her. Yet as the evening continued, her hopes ebbed. Needing reassurance, she kept Hattie talking by the fire most of the night.

More restless with every passing moment, her entire future dependent on what John found out, through the next morning and early afternoon, she and Hattie anxiously waited for his return. By late afternoon, they were both distraught, wondering what had happened to him.

"Well?" Hattie irritably demanded of him, when he did not return until just before supper.

"Looks like we're getting our endowments on Sunday," he announced. Obliviously cheerful, it seemed he had completely forgotten his errand.

Bursting with expectation when she first saw him, Anna closed her eyes. Maybe she had hoped too much, asked too much of him.

"What do you mean?" Hattie asked, even more impatient with him.

He walked to the wagon, brought out the jug, and poured two fingers of mash into a tin cup. "I mean we're gonna be officially initiated into the Church on Sunday."

"What about Anna?"

"Her too." He gulped the mash, wiped the cup with his shirttail, tucked his shirt back into his trousers and approached the fire. "Supper ready?"

"No," Hattie said flatly, her patience growing ever thinner. "Did you even try to find out about Anna's situation?"

For the first time since his return, John's eyes met Hattie's. "I didn't forget." Though Anna was but feet from him, now looking up at him, he did not look at her. "I went to see Brother Brigham's assistant to see if I could find some work for her."

"Well?" Hattie asked, pushing him along. "What did he say?"

John looked away from his mother and at the fire. Taking a deep breath he then faced Anna. "Nothing. There is no work for her."

Hattie touched his arm, searching his eyes. "Not a thing?"

He shook his head. "I talked to a lot of people. They just kept reminding me that there's more women here than men and that many of them are widows with no way to support themselves. They told me the young ones get claimed pretty fast, but older women, not much to look at, have trouble finding husbands. What jobs there are go to them."

Anna's heart pounded against her ribs. A lump caught in her throat.

"Oh, no," Hattie said, her kind gaze on Anna. "Does that mean she has to marry Jacob?"

So depressed she could hardly think, Anna stopped breathing while she waited for John to admit what she already knew. She was confused when she saw in his face the glimmer of a smile.

"Maybe not."

Hattie gripped his arm and squeezed. "Why, John? What have you found out?"

"Since Brother Brigham personally gave Jacob permission to marry Anna," John continued, "I asked Brother Brigham's assistant if she actually had to." Fixed on Anna, John's gaze was steady and deliberate. His voice was soft and caring as he told her, "You don't."

Without giving him a chance to go on, Anna squealed, and Hattie and Lizzy squealed with her. The three embraced.

"Then what am I supposed to do?" Anna asked, suddenly pulling away. The initial moment of joy was gone, and they were all staring at him.

"You still don't have any way of supporting yourself, so you'll have to decide," he said, slightly apprehensively. "You don't have to marry Jacob, but you're strongly encouraged to consider him. Since he's spoken for you and is willing to care for you, the Church won't give you any other help."

"Decide what?" Anna sighed, again discouraged.

"My God, John!" Hattie shouted, as she put her arms around her. "Can't you do anything?"

"If you'll be quiet for a minute, Mum, I will.

"Anna," he said with authority, pulling her away from his mother. He lifted her chin and gently gazed into her eyes. "I said you had a decision to make. Jacob is only one choice. I've asked, and Brother Brigham has consented. If you want, you can marry me instead."

Collectively, Hattie and Lizzy held their breaths while Anna stared at him, dumbfounded. "Are you sure, John?"

There was a pause. Unable to contain herself, Lizzy clapped her hands and blurted, "Oh, do, Anna. Say, yes!"

"Mum and Lizzy love you," he said. "How can I turn my back on you?"

"Well," he asked, when she hesitated, "what do you want to do?"

Chapter Twenty-five

Salt Lake City, Utah
10:35 a.m.
Thursday, April 22

From west-northwest of an archaic sea choked with salt, Delta flight 1890, a Boeing 757-200, rolled across the tarmac at Salt Lake City International Airport to Gate C5. "I'm chasing a story, Herb," Alex had told his editor, Herbert Brown, over the phone in the middle of the night. "There's something going on in Utah that has to do with that killing at The Garden tonight and with a friend of mine who's disappeared. I'm leaving early this morning."

A couple of years earlier, Alex had won a Pulitzer Prize for exposing a twenty-million dollar corruption scandal at the commissioner's office and the NYPD, so Herb usually gave him a free rein. He was discreet with his sources, careful in his investigations, and his exposés predictably shattered their subjects, making the paper's sales soar. Its publishers loved him. Herb usually waited until Alex had already drafted a story before becoming involved, so Alex was surprised when Herb told him, "Fine. Just call me every few days to keep me posted."

Ruffled a little by having to check-in, believing Herb no longer trusted him, Alex reluctantly agreed."

The plane was only half full, and as Alex left first class, he was one of the first to reach security in Terminal 2. "Alex?" he heard a woman call. A tall brunette, her eyes brilliant green with splashes of hazel met him.

"Sharon."

She hardly knew him, but she hugged him anyway. "Thanks for coming." The last twenty-four hours were the loneliest, most frightening of her life.

"So, where from here?" he asked.

"We need a place we can talk about this in private, share what we know with each other, and start looking for them. I've checked you into the room next to mine at a little motel where nobody will find us. We can talk in the car on the way."

There was a sudden commotion. Security guards, watchful but docile, instantly came alive. A squad of them joined those staffing the check stations, formed a line, and abruptly pushed the waiting passengers aside. A well dressed man in his forties with graying, dark hair and eyes like polished walnut passed by them with his entourage.

"Whose that?" Sharon asked.

"The Honorable Senator Kenneth J. Albrecht of Pennsylvania and his staff," Alex said with disdain. He eyed the man's navy blue, silk suit and expensive Italian loafers.

"What's he doing in Utah?"

"He's Mormon. Got his education at Brigham Young University and was key in getting the 2002 Winter Olympics to Utah."

"He wasn't involved in all that nastiness, was he?" Sharon quipped. She was recalling the bribery scandal that rocked the games and tainted the entire Olympic organization, not only in America but internationally. A million dollars or more was directly or indirectly paid to members of the International Olympic Committee to induce them to select Salt Lake City for those games.

"One might say so," Alex told her.

"He wasn't one of the men charged was he?"

"No, only Frank Joklik, the President of the Salt Lake Olympic Committee, and Dave Johnson, the Vice President, were criminally charged."

"What about Senator Albrecht?"

"Seems Albrecht's job was to obtain the funds they used to make the bribes. Got about half the money from the CEO of one of the largest financial institutions in Utah, but neither of them were ever charged."

"So if Albrecht has ties like that to Utah, what's he doing representing Pennsylvania in the United States Senate?" Sharon questioned.

"His family moved to Pennsylvania when he was ten, and he grew up there. His ancestry was German, so he's about as American looking as any man can be and was the perfect candidate for the Church to groom for national office. Takes the part well too, don't your think, with that toothy, pseudo grin of his? I doubt if half the people who voted for him even cared he was Mormon. Didn't know what being Mormon meant for either him or them. But that's what the Church was looking for, someone who could give the appearance he was completely independent of Church influence. The strategy was working until the Church showed itself. When Church leaders summoned him to Utah to help it win the 2002 Winter Olympics bid, Albrecht dropped virtually everything he was doing for Pennsylvania to answer that summons. Now that it's obvious Albrecht is not independent of Church influence, he makes no bones about his affiliation with the Church and comes to Utah three or four times a year. I've covered a couple of his visits myself."

"I thought Salt Lake City was the bidder for the Winter Olympic games."

"Yeah, sure," Alex said, sarcastically. "The Church is Salt Lake City.

"Look at their motive. The 2002 Winter Olympics offered an opportunity unprecedented in Mormon history. Once on air, in a matter of minutes, the Church would be able to send its message to the entire world. What did a little bribery matter?"

"How is it I never heard of any one going to jail for all this?"

Alex laughed. "Don't forget. You're in Mormon country. Albrecht and the other accomplices melted into the woodwork. Only Joklik and Johnson, the president and vice president of the olympic organizing committee, ever came to trial. That is if you can call it a trial.

"The State of Utah, which is mostly Mormon, declined to prosecute Joklik and Johnson at all. When the U.S. Attorney tried to prosecute them, a Mormon judge for Utah's Federal District Court blocked the attempt. He threw the Feds case out before the trial even got started. When the Feds appealed, the appellate court said, 'not so fast,' to the Mormon judge and demanded he does try them. The judge did as he was told but stopped the trail again, halfway through it. He again ruled the government didn't have a case and threw the U.S. Attorney out of his court. He then found Joklik and Johnson 'not guilty' so they could never be tried for the crime again."

"So much for justice in Utah," Sharon said, recalling her experience with the patrolman. "You think the Church has anything to do with what's happened to Wayne and Kim?"

"Don't know. Wayne and I kind of drifted apart after I started criticizing the Church during the Olympics. But then, how could I help it? The Church came out of the bribery scandal completely unscathed. Worse yet, during those games, just as the Church planned, NBC gave prime time to the President of the Mormon Church to broadcast the Mormon message to the world. Every day the Olympics aired after that viewers were subjected to features and interviews swathing the members of the Church in purity. As a reporter, it was like I was in a swarm of mosquitoes and didn't know what to scratch first. My stories couldn't help but hurt Wayne. So, it's no wonder we lost contact."

Chapter Twenty-six

Salt Lake City, Utah
Fall 1854

The sun reflected off the mountains, east and west, north and south, creating in the valley a great cathedral of light as Anna and John, Hattie and Lizzy joined a parade of worshippers bound for the center of the city on Sunday morning. On this day, they were to be confirmed. They would be endowed with the key words and tokens they would need to pass into Heaven and would be prepared to officiate in priesthood ordinances. For the occasion, each carried a special bundle of clothing. Once endowed, Anna and John, as well as many other couples married and to be married, would be celestially sealed together for eternity.

Anna had found romantic love with Erich. She never expected to find that kind of love again. Perhaps, John felt that way too. Hattie had told her how much he loved his wife and how hard he had taken her death. He was bearlike, but he was decent. She respected him and liked him. She had decided that an arrangement with him was all she should expect of a remarriage, – certainly all she wanted. Most appealingly, once she married John, she would become Hattie's daughter-in-law.

A light breeze raised clouds of dust as hundreds stood beside the mammoth, yet unfinished, Temple foundation. They hushed as Brigham Young, successor prophet and savior, came to the podium and removed his boxy, wide brimmed hat. He began by saying in a voice rich with timbre, "From the moment our Prophet, Joseph Smith, first talked with God, Satan has been biting at our heels. In Missouri, he caused us to be driven out by mobs who burned our homes and murdered our people. In Ohio, he created circumstances from which Brother Smith was forced to flee. In Illinois, Satan threatened us with a militia of thousands and sent a mob to murder Brother Smith and his brother. With his lies, Satan has repeatedly corrupted peoples' minds against us. Yet the trials he has put us through prepared us, proved to God that of all His people, only we are worthy to build His Kingdom.

"God led us here, and upon His commandment, we will create Zion. In its infancy, His kingdom of Zion will stretch from the crest of the Rocky Mountains to the crest of the Sierra Nevada, to the exclusion of all other people. The Gentiles among us do not belong in the same land as we, the faithful. Nor will they be invited to join us. Scripture requires that we drive them out." Brigham's eyes narrowed as he stared at them, reciting, "'I will send hornets before thee, which shall drive out the Hivite, the Canaanite, and the Hitite, from before thee.... They shall not dwell in thy land, lest they make thee sin against Me.'" His voice raised in excitement. "We have already settled Fort Limhi on the Salmon in Idaho, Genoa in the Carson Valley of Nevada, San Bernardino in California, Las Vegas in the Nevada Desert, and Fort Bridger on the Overland Trail. We have taken possession of every stream and spring in this valley, and soon, the Gentiles will be gone.

"Let us pray. 'Lord God, your people are gathered and upon this earth shall build a kingdom to serve you, pure and subservient, rich and full, to spread from across the mountains to the Pacific. Give us strength to fulfill your wish. Give us the power and will to drive all evil from this land.'"

Anna held a Book of Mormon over her heart. Believing the kingdom of which Brother Brigham spoke was one of purity and faith, a land where there was and always would be only good, she joined him in prayer. All of the settlers coming west who were not Mormon's were Gentiles. She believed that when Brigham spoke against them, he spoke for God. Gentiles were Satan's tools, so while she prayed with the rest of the congregation, she too prayed that all Gentiles be purged.

"Our work is just beginning," Brother Brigham continued, gesturing toward the mammoth Temple foundation. "We must finish His temple and build a community to defend it. We must strengthen our faith. Harvest will begin soon, and all of you are expected to do your share. We live as a community here, and as with all other things, the good of the community comes first. While the weather is good, you will build your homes in your spare time. When harvest is over, you will resume work on the Temple. Prepare yourselves. The price you will pay for your place in Heaven is high.

"Let us lift our heads and pray. Lord God, we kneel before you. We embrace you. We prostrate ourselves in your service. Our work shall be to your glory. Each of our sacrifices will be as a brick in the road to Heaven, and we willingly offer them. We are your servants. We are your slaves, if you wish. Test us, dear Lord. Let us show you our devotion by passing all trials you put before us. Trust us, for we are obedient."

Invigorating and magnetic, Brigham Young was God's voice. Tingling as she listened to him, Anna accepted without question everything he said. Having passed the ordeals of the trail, she was both weary and confident. Empowered by his words, she was ready to meet anything that might befall her.

After morning services, the congregation joined for a picnic in what would become Temple Square. After the food was eaten, they separated into their original groups of fifty in study groups, keeping their special bundles by their sides as they waited to be called to the Council House for their endowments.

As Anna awaited her turn, she felt an anxiousness growing inside her. She believed in her new faith and thought it wonderful she would be offering her life to the Mormon Church that day. But, when she thought of John, her shoulder muscles tightened. An unrelenting tension in her neck grew into a pounding headache. She had been united with Erich only for their lifetimes. Today, she would be sealed to John forever. That thought had haunted her ever since she agreed to marry John, flooding her heart with sorrow from the very night she said, "Yes." She had not slept since.

Believing Erich's soul was lost at sea, she did not know if she would see him after death. If she did, what then? What would he say? What would she say to him? She would have been sealed to John by God's church and could never again touch Erich or be with him. She could never belong to him again. Even if they were in the same Heaven, God would force them to be strangers. Yet what choice had she? She would not survive if she was not sealed to someone in this place. If she did not live by the Church's rules or expectations, she would not find salvation and would not go to

Heaven. She held her breath, accepted her circumstance and sighed. Better John than Jacob.

By the time her group was called, Anna was neither joyful nor hopeful. She was merely resigned. As she walked to the Counsel House with John and Hattie, among a dozen others called, her bundle of special clothing in hand, she did not touch or even look at John or could she return Hattie's caring, well-wishing gaze.

Chapter Twenty-seven

Present Day Chicago
2:00 p.m.
April 22

The casually elegant Georgian Park was a twenty-story, five star hotel in a suburb some distance west of Chicago. Despite its ten story, terraced atrium, the Georgian Park had a reputation for guarding privacy, and few noticed who came and went.

In a small, windowless conference room on the fourth floor, nine white, middle-aged men sat at an intimate table. Casually dressed so as not to draw attention, they wore dull, anemic colored, designer slacks and expensive, pastel shirts.

Lawrence Wright was the Attorney General for the State of Colorado. Jeffrey Talbot was the Mayor of Las Vegas. William Haversack was Ohio's Secretary of State. Justice Samuel Carter sat on the Supreme Court for the State of New York. Gene Bellamy was the Director of the United States Census Bureau. Albert Matthew's was the Lieutenant Governor of the State of Utah. Bret Baldwin, Regional Commissioner for the Western Region of the United States Internal Revenue Service, was responsible for all thirteen western states. Dr. James Gravner was State Senator, State of California. Also seated at the table was United States Senator Kenneth J. Albrecht of Pennsylvania.

"So, where is he?" Albrecht asked everyone.

"Said he had a call to make. Wanted to check on something," Justice Samuel Carter said. "He'll be here in a few minutes."

"Let's go ahead and take roll," Albrecht decided. "Put your identification on the table and stand."

In response, each man at the table stood, took from around his neck an eighteen karat gold medallion, placed it in the middle of the table amid the others, and identified themselves by code name. "Michael," Senator Albrecht identified himself. "Moroni," Haversack said. "Lion," Matthews continued. "Eagle," Bellamy said. Dr. Gravner was "Bull," and so on, until they were all identified one to the other in code.

"Samson," a voice from the doorway added. A man with chiseled features joined them, overwhelming them with his cologne, an obnoxious blend of pepper, citrus, and leather. He took a gold medallion identical to the others from around his neck, placed it on the table, and then took charge. "Repeat the oath after me," he demanded.

"In the name of Jesus Christ, Son of God, I do solemnly obligate myself to forever regard the Prophet and the First Presidency of the Church of Jesus Christ of Latter-Day Saints the supreme head of the Church on earth. That I will obey them in all things, the same as I obey the supreme God. That I will stand by my brethren in danger or in difficulty and will uphold the Presidency, right or wrong. I will forever conceal and never reveal the secret purposes of this society. Should I ever reveal or attempt to reveal those secrets, I promise to hold my life in forfeiture. Be seated.

"Do you have your census report? No digital copies of any of it had been saved," the man code named Samson asked Gene Bellamy, director of the U.S. Census Bureau, the man the society called "Eagle."

"I'm ready." Bellamy's full report was a fifteen pound tome crammed in a five-inch-thick, white binder. It was on the floor in a locked briefcase leaning against his chair. On the table in front of him was a two page summary of the report.

"The goal of the Church of Jesus Christ of Latter Day Saints both in the present," Bellamy began, "and for all preceding years since our founding has been to fill the earth with our gospel and our people. As you know, Baylor University professor Rodney Stark predicted that the Church would grow as much as fifty percent a decade and would reach as many as 280 million members by 2080. The Church used Stark's prediction to solidify that goal and from 1984 to the year 2000, it not only met expectations but exceeded them. The Church was averaging a growth of fifty-two percent per decade. Several years ago, however, Brother Roger Loomis informed us Church growth was slowing. Unless we did something, it would continue to decrease until projected membership in 2080 was only 30 million members, 250 million short of our goal. We knew we had to do something.

"We have determined that to meet the Church's goal of 280 million members by 2080, its growth has to be exponential. The bigger it gets, the faster it will grow. The rate of growth must meet or exceed fifty percent per decade," Bellamy concluded.

Samson took over. "To achieve and sustain this growth, converts must convert as many people to the Church as our established members convert. The Church is good at baptizing people, especially teenagers, who are willing to go on missions. But the Church is not good at baptizing people who already have a number of children they are willing to raise in the church. Converts don't stay in the Church. The majority go inactive within a year. And our missionaries are getting less effective. We're becoming bloated with undedicated new members.

"We are in crisis! Our strength isn't dependent on numbers, but on the members who are dedicated to our teachings. We gauge that strength by the number of children born into the Church. We need children of active, dedicated families who will not stray from it. Until 1983, births exceeded our goal of fifty percent per decade. After that, births started to decline. Converts tended not to have as many children as traditional Mormon families. We are losing ground. Our births are declining by thirty-four percent. We cannot grow exponentially without cutting deep into the membership of religions competing with us for converts. We'd have to reproduce ourselves in petri-dishes to gain a competitive advantage.

"Yet, we must gain that competitive advantage. If we do not, Mormonism will never be a major world religion. It will dissolve into insignificance." As if Samson sentenced the religion to death, a pall of gloom enveloped the room. For a moment, there was complete silence. He paused, waiting for the gravity of his message to be absorbed and then continued, "Our polygamist colonies are a drain on us because of the scrutiny Gentiles put them under. Our missionaries are of limited effectiveness. We must return to our core." He studied the men at the table, searching for any weakness. "We are in agreement then?" he confirmed. "The project our group has undertaken to get the competitive advantage our Church so desperately needs is for the good and benefit of the Church? No matter what happens to those involved?"

Bellamy took a slow, deep breath. He sighed. With great reluctance, he responded for all of them, "Yes."

"Are those loose ends you told me about tied?" Senator Albrecht asked Samson.

"Not yet. Min has been dispatched and his vessel taken. But, a mistake was made. Min's friend, Henry Blanchard killed one of our men and survived. He's in police custody while they investigate."

"Can they trace the man he killed to us?" Justice Samuel Carter asked, clearly concerned.

"I don't think so. Our man carried no identification, and his partner was able to retrieve his medallion before the police arrived."

"What about Blanchard?" Justice Carter pressed. "Does he know why our men tried to kill him? Has he said anything?"

"Not yet,"Samson told them, "and he won't. I've got someone inside to see he never does. There's more though. Blanchard isn't our only problem. Alex Caldwell, who's a senior reporter for the New York Post, was with Blanchard at the time of the killing. Caldwell didn't witness anything, but it looks like Blanchard told him something about Min. Caldwell called his editor last night and caught a plane to Utah this morning. He would have arrived about the same time Albrecht left Salt Lake to come here."

"Better corral him, and now," Albert Matthews, Lieutenant Governor of the State of Utah, warned. "Caldwell can do damage there."

"Don't worry, we'll take care of him," Samson promised.

Chapter Twenty-eight

Salt Lake City, Utah
Fall 1854

Frightened and ashamed, Anna cringed as rough, weatherworn hands pulled her protective hand away from her naked breasts and caressed them. Standing calf deep in murky water, naked and defenseless, in a room shrouded with cloth, she was at their mercy. She whimpered as the hands caressing her fell away. "No!" she pleaded, as they returned, forcing away the hand protecting her genitals. "Please," she begged, afraid to push them away, "not there!" She closed her eyes as the calloused hands roughly rubbed between her legs. She wept as the water they brought with them ran down her thighs. She had been molested and humiliated. She opened her eyes to see Bellva, a wiry, weathered woman, wring out the washcloth which defiled her and walk away. Thank heavens it was over, Anna sighed, sniffling.

"You are in the presence of God's servants, preparing for His endowment," said a tall, thin woman standing in the corner. She was the officiating high priestess. "You must show you appreciate Him and the rituals He brings you. This is a joyful occasion, and you should be happy. Stop sniveling."

The washing finished, Anna again covered her breasts and genitals with her hands, wondering if she should reach for her clothes. She knew she should not when the priestess stepped toward her carrying a large wooden spoon and a cow's horn.

What next? Anna feared. She stared as the priestess handed the spoon to Bellva. She watched with cautious interest as Bellva held it steady while the priestess tipped the cow horn and poured into the spoon a viscous, green oil. She looked on with dread, as the priestess handed the horn to Bellva and took the spoon. The priestess held it in her right hand, faced Anna, and poured the oil from the spoon into her left hand. Whatever the priestess was going to do with that oil, she was going to do it to her, and Anna instinctively pulled back.

Without losing a drop of the green oil, the priestess rubbed a little on Anna's forehead. She then rubbed a little on Anna's ears, eyes, and mouth, at each stop murmuring a prayer.

Anna froze as the priestess descended her body. Soon she was trembling.

Caressing Anna's hardening breasts with the thick and soothing oil, the priestess continued murmuring, "...her breasts, so that she can nourish the children she will raise with her husband to be." Seductively tracing a line to Anna's belly and circling it with oil, the priestess then oiled the path to Anna's groin, lingering there, cupping her hand around Anna's pubis and slowly descending. Beneath the hair, between her legs, she reached for Anna's vagina.

Anna shuddered. My God! she gulped, trying not to scream out loud.

The priestess' hand was warm, her intrusion carnal as she gently and intimately rubbed the oil on Anna's flesh. The priestess then rested and prayed, "So that she will raise up godly seeds that will be pillars of strength to the upbuilding and strengthening of God's kingdom on earth."

Ashamed, after the blessing, Anna chastised herself. Am I supposed to feel holy? Well, I don't! She had never exposed herself that way to anyone. She had never been touched that way, not even by Erich, – and definitely, not by John. She felt violated and was distraught. Wishing with all her might this humilation would be over, she gave her hand to the priestess and stepped out of the tub.

Letting go of Anna's hand, the priestess stepped away, and Bellva took over.

"After you have earned your place in God's Kingdom through your husband," Bellva gently explained, "you will be called to take your place in His Kingdom on the morning of the resurrection. When you are called on that day, you will be called not by your given name, but by your celestial name. Listen carefully as I tell you what it is." Bellva gently touched Anna's shoulder, leaned forward and whispered, "Your celestial name is 'Rebecca.'"

Rebecca, Anna silently repeated three times. If she forgot it, she would never get into Heaven.

"You will be required to speak your celestial name once today," Bellva told her, "but otherwise, you must never speak it. However, you should often think of it to keep evil spirits away. Now put on your endowment garment."

As quickly as she could to cover the shame of her nakedness, Anna desperately reached for her special bundle of clothing. Tearing at the ties, she released a special undergarment, a robe, an apron, a woman's cap, and a pair of moccasins. The undergarment was a plain, muslin drape with long sleeves and a round, shallow neck, representing that given to Adam when he was found naked in the

Garden of Eden. Anna grabbed it and quickly slid it over her head. Sewn into it were four symbols known as the Marks of the Holy Priesthood. On the right breast was a square, on the left a compass. Over the navel was a small hole, and over the knee was a large hole called the "Stone." As soon as it covered her, Anna felt better.

"As long as you wear this garment, no harm can befall you," Sister Bellva promised in a whisper. "Now put your clothes back on."

Anna hurriedly covered her special undergarment with the clothes she was wearing when she came into the washing. She then rebundled the rest of her endowment garments. In her stocking feet, she stepped outside the curtained room into another, larger room with the other women who had been washed and oiled. She studied their faces. None looked well, some looked a little shattered, yet they stood quietly and calmly without a word said among them.

Hattie was waiting for her next to a curtain wall. Embarrassed by what Bellva and the priestess had done to her, Anna glanced at her then looked away. Hattie would have gone through it too.

When the remaining women joined them, the curtains next to Hattie, marked "A" and "B", were opened. Behind them were the men, only half dressed in their garments and shirts. They too had been washed and oiled. John was in the second row, dour and staring at the floor. Dispirited by her own experience, Anna at first wondered what the priests had done to him. Exposed and unappealing, all of the men acted awkward and embarrassed. Trying to avoid the women's stares, most of the men looked away. Anna then realized she did not want to know what the priests had done to the men during their washing and oiling, but she did not look at John again, and John did not look at her.

The tense few minutes they waited seemed an eternity. Then, from the doorway appeared Brigham Young. "It is time to decide," he told them. "The good and holy things that are to be seen and heard in the House of the Lord are yet to come. If you want to back out, now is the time to do it. Once you go forward, you cannot change your mind. Once you begin, you must finish, for you will be bound to what happens and what you promise forever. If you wish to go forward raise your hands."

The converts had journeyed halfway around the world to see and hear those "good and holy things" Brigham was promising them. They had abandoned almost everything and everyone they knew. Anna had lost everything, even Erich. Despite what happened in the washing just moments before, there could be no doubting now. So with the other converts, she eagerly raised her hand.

"You will hear and see much," Brigham told them. "You will learn things that are too holy even to speak of between yourselves. Be quiet and listen. Once you leave here today, you must never reveal anything you have seen or heard." He glared at them. "If you try to reveal them, your memories will be blighted, and you will be everlastingly damned! Remain where you are and prepare yourselves." He left the way he came.

In a few minutes, there came the sound of voices from an adjoining room, a conversation between the gods Elohim and Jehovah, discussing the creation of the Earth. A series of performances followed, with the converts moving from room to room to witness them. The actors portrayed Michael the Archangel, the Gods Elohim and Jehovah, and Adam and Eve. They reenacted the creation, Adam and Eve's ouster from the Garden of Eden, and the part each of them played in it. During the Garden of Eden reenactment a voice from outside the room scolded Adam. The voice also told him that, until redemption, he would have to wear the special garment to protect him from evil.

Already wearing the special garment, and by then, the green silk apron from their special bundles, the converts put on the caps and moccasins. The women's caps were made from one yard square of Swiss muslin rounded at the corners for ties under the chin. The men's were made like those worn by pastry cooks with a bow on the right side. The moccasins for both the men and women were linen or calico.

When all the converts were dressed, the man portraying Jehovah told them, "You must now learn the grip of the Aaronic Priesthood. Remember, you are not to reveal this grip to anyone. Face the person next to you. Hold the thumb of your right hand over the knuckle of your index finger and clasp your hands together."

John faced the man next to him. Anna faced Hattie, and as instructed, they clasped their hands together.

"Now repeat after me and swear," Jehovah told them, "I will obey the laws of the Mormon Church and all they enjoin in preference to those of the United States."

Like the other converts in the group, all of them from Europe, Anna had no allegiance to the United States and had no qualms about swearing to let the laws of the Mormon Church take precedence.

The laws of United States meant nothing to her. They meant nothing to any of them.

"Remember," Jehovah warned, "you are not to reveal to anyone what you have said or learned here. If you reveal this grip or oath, your throat will be cut from ear to ear, and your tongue will be torn from your mouth. Using his thumb, Jehovah menacingly demonstrated, slowly dragging his thumb across his throat, pressing so hard against it his jugular veins throbbed. He yanked at his tongue, sliced through it with his thumb, and gagged. "Do you swear to so abide?" he demanded when his point was made. At a perfect right angle, he raised his right hand toward Heaven and waited.

In disbelief, Anna's eyes widened, and she stared. Was she really expected to give them permission to kill her? Would they actually torture her like that? She was confused and afraid. Those around her hesitated too.

Jacob was one of the elders watching them. He was especially watching her.

Coming among the converts, the elders stood very close to those who had not yet sworn and poked them. Jacob came toward her.

Afraid, though not yet ready to swear it aloud, Anna raised her right hand and slowly nodded. When the converts were ushered to the next room, she raced ahead of Jacob with Hattie, avoiding his challenging her.

In the third room called the "World," men portraying Christ's apostles Peter, James and John held the keys to Heaven. Additional men joined them, and together they mocked and satirized other religious sects. When the men finished, it was time to receive the secret of the second grip of the Aaronic Priesthood. As instructed, the converts

downed the robe out of their bundle. A straight
piece of cloth, the robe was doubled and gathered at
the shoulder and waist. It was tied around the waist
by a long, narrow sash.

The sacred grip was simple and basic. "Put
your right thumb between the knuckles of your
index and second fingers, then clasp your hands
together," they were instructed, and Anna and
Hattie clasped hands.

His voice harsh and threatening, Peter
warned them, "If you reveal this grip you will be
sawn asunder and your members cast into the sea."
To demonstrate, he drew his hand sharply across the
middle of his body showing the converts exactly
how they would be bisected. Then without taking a
breath, he sinisterly demanded, "Do you so abide?"

Anna could neither utter nor nod. The oath
frightened her, the punishment it allowed frightened
her even more. Trying to avoid notice, she lowered
her head.

An instant later, a sharp, bony finger poked
her hard in the ribs. The tall, thin priestess who had
oiled her was beside her, glaring at her with dark,
piercing eyes from a face rigid as stone. "Swear!"
the priestess hissed.

"I swear!" Anna blurted, her voice
conspicuously alone among those who had already
sworn.

In the ritual that followed the men swore to
be chaste. The women swore not only to be chaste
but to be obedient to their husbands. Peter
explained: "The meaning of chastity for a man is
different from that for a woman. A woman must be
true only to her husband. She must look up to her
husband as her god and be obedient to him. As you
have been told, it is not possible for a woman to go

to Christ except through her husband. A man may take more than one wife because a man is to be exalted in the world to come for having more than one wife. It is not unchaste for him to do so."

Other men came into the room and reenacted Joseph Smith's receipt of the Mormon Gospel from an angel. When the performance was over, Peter told them to shift their robes from the right shoulder to the left. He then revealed the first grip of the Melchizedek Priesthood, the same level of priesthood attained by Christ. "Now, swear," Peter commanded them. "I swear to avenge the death of Joseph Smith, the martyr, on this American Nation, together with that of his brother, Hyrum. And I will teach our children and children's children to do so." He paused until all the converts repeated the vow, then added, "I swear to absolute obedience to the Mormon Priesthood."

With no other choice, the priestess still at her side, Anna raised her hand and mumbled the words, timorously waiting to hear the penalty for breaking these vows. It was disembowelment. Transgressors were to be cut open and peeled, their intestines ripped from the cavity to which they were attached and unraveled. Unable to believe men of god could be so cruel, Anna shuddered.

Shivering with fear and uncertainty, Anna followed as the converts were led to yet another room. It was called the "Prayer Circle Room," where the highest, grandest grip of the Melchizedec Priesthood was revealed to them. In response to the instruction, Anna clasped her hand around Hattie's, the point of her index finger resting on Hattie's wrist, their little fingers entwined.

"This," the man playing Peter said of the place on the wrist where the index finger pointed, "was the place where Christ was first nailed to the cross. But, the Romans did not leave the nail there. They tore it out and nailed Christ to the cross again.

"Move your second finger next to your index finger to mark the spot. This we call the 'Sure Sign of the Nail.' Now raise your hands and swear under penalty of eternal death: 'I swear obedience to the Mormon Priesthood...'" the oath began.

When all had sworn, a circle ritual was held. The men joined hands in front of the altar. Outside the circle, the women stood behind them, their faces veiled.

Although disturbed by the gruesome threats of death against her if she faltered and deeply concerned for Hattie and Lizzy and even John, Anna was committed to earning her way to Heaven through the faith she had chosen. Deep in thought about the meanings of the rituals in which she had taken part, she barely heard when John called her name for the celestial marriage ceremonies and blankly stared at him for a moment before responding.

The time had come when she would forever turn her back on Erich, and as she walked toward John, her feet were like weights. Battered by conscience, when they took their celestial oaths she stood rigid next to him, barely hearing what was said. Though Erich was the only man in her heart, God had chosen John to be her eternal companion. As she was sealed to John forever, she was silent.

Chapter Twenty-nine

Salt Lake City, Utah
Fall 1854

The evening after they were sealed in the Council House, Anna and John joined three other couples to be married in the center of the wagon camp before their group of fifty. The women brought food, and the men brought whiskey. Those who could play brought their instruments, and they danced until midnight.

"A husband and wife should sleep alone on their wedding night," Hattie told Anna and John when the four of them returned to their wagon. There was a twinkle in her eye as she winked at them. "Lizzy and I can sleep by the fire."

Anna danced with John only once that night. Making herself busy among the women, she avoided him at every opportunity. Though she knew it was inevitable, she dreaded the moment John would come to her as her husband. She had tried to prepare herself, tried to persuade herself he deserved his pleasures, but she was not persuaded, and she was definitely not ready. "Wait. Don't go to bed yet," she half pleaded, her hand reaching for Lizzy's. "Stay up awhile longer with us."

Anna was obviously reluctant, but Hattie had none of it. "No, you and John should be alone. Go on to the campfire, Lizzy. I'll be there in a minute." Hattie smiled as Lizzy and Angel settled down beside the fire, then she turned to John. "Would you mind getting Lizzy and I some blankets?" She pointed to the pine chest beneath the wagon. She waited until he was dragging the chest out from under then took Anna's hand and quietly, yet firmly told her, "I know you loved Erich and that you miss him, but you've got to lock away those memories. You'll never forget what that love meant to you, but you have to leave it behind. John is your life now. As his wife, you have to do everything you can to make him happy."

Hattie's gaze was as unwavering as it was kind, and Anna understood. This was one of the trials God had put before her. God was guiding her and had selected John to take her through. Being with him was her duty. It would someday be her salvation, – something Erich had wanted for both of them.

"Coming?" John smiled, as he gave Lizzy the four, wool blankets.

When he and Anna got back to the wagon, he gently cupped Anna's hand between his own. Hattie was with Lizzy. "You all right?" he whispered.

Her conscience continuing its battle between survival and love, Anna was pale and distant. She nodded unconvincingly. She could barely see John through her fog, but she went with him, reluctantly yet compliantly, into the wagon.

Hattie had prepared their wedding bed. Anticipating the ultimate happiness of their union and her desire each of them be made whole, she had spread out for them her own wedding quilt, a warm, thick, patchwork of greens and violets. She had covered a wooden box with a blue checkered napkin and placed on the makeshift table a single, lighted candle, a full jug of mash, and two tin cups.

John grinned. "Guess she thought of everything." He reached for the jug. He was handsome in the candlelight even with his full, dark beard. His deep, blue eyes were soft and gentle. His hands shook a little as he poured, and he looked quite vulnerable – nervous almost. "I haven't been with a woman since my wife died," he apologized, the mash sloshing in the cup as he handed it to her. "I haven't wanted to be." His breathing hurried, he paused and took a deep breath. "I'm a little welled up inside – a little anxious maybe." He poured mash into the second cup and gulped it down. "Do you understand what I'm saying?"

Anna never considered that a man might get scared about something like this, much less that he would admit his fears to a woman. She was shocked, but realizing how hard the admission must have been for him she did not show her surprise. "I think I do."

As if a great weight had been cast from him, he sighed. "Then let's drink to the adventure, however it turns out." He refilled his cup, clicked it against hers, and drank until it was empty.

Never having liked whiskey, Anna took but a tiny sip. It burned at first, but the recipe wasn't bad. Flowing through her, the mash relaxed her, and she felt better. "Let's have another," she urged. Maybe what was to happen would not be as nasty if she was drunk.

John poured her another, then turned his back to her. "I'll let you get dressed," he said. "Or do you want me to go outside?"

Having gulped the second mash, Anna did not care. "Just stay where you are. I'll be back in a minute." She took the nightgown Hattie had put under the pillow for her, slipped beneath the quilt and stripped. Unaware she had put the nightgown on backwards, she peeked over the edge of the quilt, and asked, "How about another one?"

John grinned and poured two more. Blowing out the candle, they drank, and he joined her beneath the quilt.

For weeks, the entire community worked the harvest from dawn to dusk. On a day like any other in those weeks, at noon, in the center of what would become Temple Square, the women got dinner. Long tables were set with mounds of food: biscuits, beans, carrots, potatoes, stewed chicken, and gravy. When everything was ready, a bugle summoned the men from the fields.

As the women waited for them in the hot sun, a dry, dusty wind buffeted their bonnets. Jeremy Gibbs' third wife, Clara, was standing next to Anna and asked her, "Have you ever seen the locket Brother Jeremy gave me on our wedding night?" Clara was a petite woman a few years older than Anna. Although she was generally shy, she had warmed to Anna in the last few days and was making an effort to get to know her. Sweet and generous, she had, just the night before, brought Anna and her family fresh baked rolls from an iron oven Jeremy had specially shipped from Chicago. Clara had once been beautiful, but the dry, dusty winds and powder-like dirt in the valley had taken their toll. After working three years in it, her skin was dark and leathery and creased with deep wrinkles. The sun had bleached her dark hair, and wisps of blond stuck out from beneath her bonnet. "It's something very special." She unfastened the clasp, cupped the locket in her palm, and opened it. A lock of brown hair was inside. "It was Joseph Smith's," she whispered with pride.

Respectfully impressed by its importance, Anna studied the lock. "Where did Brother Jeremy get it?"

"From his brother," Clara told her. "Jeremy's brother was one of the men who claimed the Prophet's body after the murder."

Giving the woman's relic the reverence it deserved, Anna praised her for the thoughtfulness of her husband's gift and enviously observed, "Having it must give you peace."

The next day, predawn fog hung thick over the valley as Hattie walked down a wide street to Temple Square, hatchet in hand. The city was waking, and as the sun dawned on the horizon, other women with hatchets joined her. Their job that morning was to split wood for the harvest cooking fires that day.

Everything was peaceful but for a low, convulsive noise coming from the Square. Alarmed, the women ran toward it. The atmosphere was warming, the fog fading, as they saw when they got there, a young man strapped to a post, the convulsive sound coming from him. With big, deep breaths, he was sobbing. It was young Jed Pitker. Hattie recognized him from Sunday meetings. Beside him was Elder Jeremy and Brigham Young's blacksmith, Brother Hefner. One of the other elders was talking to him, scolding him.

"What has he done?" Hattie asked the woman next to her.

The woman looked down at her feet. As if she shared some of the guilt, she sheepishly told her, "Adultery."

"Adultery! Oh, no," Hattie quickly reviewed in her mind the various punishments for sins but couldn't think of the one for adultery. Then suddenly she realized. "They're not going to kill him?" she blurted.

The woman continued to stare at her feet. "I don't know."

Horrified, Hattie stewed for only a second before she acted. Racing to the post where the young man was tied, she raised her hatchet, slammed it against the post, and severed the straps that held him. "What are you doing?" she demanded of the elder standing dumbfounded next to her. "You can't kill this boy. He's done nothing to deserve this."

The other women stayed back, unwilling to get involved. It was Brother Jeremy who came forward. "We're not going to kill him, Sister Hattie. Now move aside. This is none of your business," Jeremy nodded to Hefner and the blacksmith came forward with new straps. Young Pitker was still sobbing.

"Go on over to the other women and take your place there," Jeremy told her. "This man is an adulterer, but he is very young and we are being lenient. It was a Gentile woman who, with Satan's help, lured him to her, and he was not able to resist. Now stand back. We will all learn from his punishment."

Relieved the boy would not be killed, Hattie joined the group of women and waited.

Once again strapped to the post, Pitker stopped sobbing and watched as Brother Hefner approached him with a whip. "I'm gonna do ya a favor by leavin' on that shirt," he said.

"Thanks," Pitker told him, without realizing the shirt would shred, catch in his cuts and stick there. Peeling it off after the blood dried would be excruciating.

Eight paces away, Hefner turned back to him, cracked the whip, and struck.

"Aaagghhh!" Pitker screamed, as the whip opened his back. "Oh no, no more!" he pleaded, as Hefner snapped the whip and hit him again. Again and again Hefner struck him and each time Pitker screamed.

Hattie was disgusted. When it was over, Hefner cut Pitker down, and she and two other women went over to help.

"We'll see he gets home," Brother Jeremy told them. "You women get back to your chores. You have better things to do.

That night, when John came back to the wagon for supper, he walked into the torrent of Hattie's anger. "What kind of justice lays open a boy's back for being human?" she demanded. There was fire in her eyes.

John did not have to guess to know what she was talking about, and without hesitation, he answered her, "The man committed adultery, Mum."

Anna handed John a wash bowl with fresh water, a well used bar of soap and a towel. He took them to the back of the wagon. He had been digging potatoes all day. The last thing he wanted was to argue.

Hattie followed him. "Who decided his punishment, anyway? Some slave master?"

"You know as well as I do the Bishop's Council decided." John was bone tired and did not want to concern himself with matters that were none of his business.

"But, seventeen?" she argued. "If they had to flog him, wouldn't five or ten lashes have been enough? Eighteen could have killed him."

John sloshed the water on his face, rolled the soap in his hands to get a lather, and washed.

"You're right, Mum. They could've given him less, but they didn't. They didn't kill him, either. He's just real sore."

"What do you mean 'sore'?" Hattie challenged, standing beside him at his elbow. "His back was shredded!"

John finished washing his hands and forearms, then dried them. "It's what the bishops thought he deserved."

"That's what's so terrible. They don't even know it's wrong! You should do something, John, so nothing like that happens again."

He finally turned toward her. "Mum," he sighed, exhausted, "this is the priests' business. It's their duty to decide what punishment fits each man's sin. There's nothing I can do. Besides, from what I've been hearing, he got off easy."

"What about the girl? What are they going to do to her?"

John threw the dirty water into a bucket of dirty water they would reuse, then wiped out the bowl. "They're not doing anything to her," he said, as he walked back to the fire.

Anna and Lizzy were waiting with supper. As they served him at the split wood table he made when they first arrived, Hattie continued, "How do you know they're not going to do anything?"

"She's a Gentile, Mum. The priests don't have any authority over her."

"I can't believe they're just going to let her go," Anna observed. "I thought adultery was a sin for both the man and woman."

"Don't think the bishops cared much about her sinnin'," John observed. "She can go to Hell for all they care. She's going there, anyway. The priests just want her and her family out of town. Jacob told me they were going to force them out."

"Why punish the whole family?" Hattie asked.

"Because they're Gentiles, and the Church wants them out."

The next morning, scores of men with scythes and sickles cut through dense rows of corn in large fields. Behind them, at the edge of the fields, women sat on stools and in rockers tying the corn the men harvested into bunches. The day was temperate, and as usual, a soft wind stirred the dust.

Coming from what would become Temple Square, Hattie and Anna were hurrying into the fields with a number of other women. Having already chopped wood for the women who were preparing dinner, they were arriving well after the field work had begun. Hattie and Anna headed for one of the circles made up of women in their group of fifty and sat next to Sister Clara, Elder Jeremy's wife. Always friendly, Clara smiled.

"So," a blond woman stringing in the circle asked, "is young Brother Pitker able to get around yet?" Sister Lucinda's long hair was parted on the side and pulled away from her face in a pony tail. Her face was one of horizontal lines, dominated by a flat, brow ridge that left only a tiny bit of space between her thick, dark eyebrows. She had a flat and rigid, thin-lipped mouth, and she was hardly ever caught in a smile.

"I heard they made young Pitker get up this morning and go into the fields," Sister Margaret said. Her head was shaped like a thumb. Her long, bulbous forehead was prominent even beneath her bonnet. She was sitting directly across the circle

from Lucinda, her brown eyes expressionless.
"They said he didn't deserve a rest."

"That girl's gettin' a rest," Naomi added in
disgust. Naomi was big and brawny, long and
broad. Her nose was generously proportionate to her
face. Her plump cheeks were ruddy. Her mouth was
downturned. People often said she looked like one
of the bouncers at a saloon in town. Her size
intimidating, the women did not mess with her.
"Imagine lettin' that little trollop get away with it.
They shoulda' bloodied her, too."

The women were talking about young Jed
Pitker's forbidden relationship with the Gentile girl,
the same matter that upset Hattie last night. When
Anna surreptitiously glanced at her, she could see
Hattie was fuming.

"That boy is only seventeen years old,"
Hattie reminded them. "What are they doing
publicly flogging him?"

Naomi was unsympathetic. "He's old
enough to know better," she responded, her
formidable body postured for battle. "Old enough to
have a wife and old enough to suffer the
consequences when he disobeys our teachings."

"Either way, it doesn't matter," Lucinda
said. "What's done is done. It was for the elders to
decide how Brother Pitker was to be punished. It is
not for us to question them. They gave him the
same punishment they would have given any other
Saint, and they are done with it. We should be done
with it too."

Hattie flushed. Her eyes narrowed. She
was just about to argue, when Sister Clara put a
hand on Hattie's arm.

"You'd better stop," she whispered,
"before you get into trouble and get punished

yourself. We're never to criticize the priests, no matter what they do."

Hattie and Anna stared at her in disbelief. This was not a casual warning, for there was actually fear in Clara's eyes.

Anna thought back to their endowments only a few days ago. They vowed to be disemboweled if they were not absolutely obedient to the priests. Could it really happen? Despite the warning not to do so, when John was not home, she and Hattie secretly discussed the meaning of the vows they took that day. No matter how awful the punishments of torture and death sounded, they could not believe the Church would actually harm them and decided not to take the threats too seriously. "Do what Clara says, Hattie," she whispered, beginning to change her mind. "Don't argue. It's not that important."

Hattie must have doubted their decision, too. "You may be right," she whispered. "Guess it's none of my business anyway." Sitting back, removing herself from the discussion, Hattie went back to tying together the corn in her lap and listening.

"That girl wouldn't have gotten off so easy if she was one of us," Maggie observed. Maggie was twenty-two but looked like thirty. Yet, still, she was beautiful. Her wavy, blond-red hair was braided and pinned like a halo around her head. Her skin was not as leathery as the older women's, and though worn, her clear, blue eyes were bright and friendly.

"She wouldn't have even done it if she was one of us," Lucinda added. "That Gentile girl seduced young Pitker into adultery! Yet, he's the one that's punished. It's unfair."

Margaret's brown eyes began to reflect a keener interest in the subject. "Maybe it's unfair, but whether the girl was punished or not doesn't matter. Jed Pitker sinned, and it was right he be punished. Her soul is lost, but his soul will be saved because he *was* punished."

Most of the women nodded in agreement. "It isn't Brother Pitker's back that matters," Margaret added. "It's his soul. That Gentile girl doesn't matter at all."

"Did you hear what some of the elders did last night?" Sister Clara asked, changing the subject.

She glowed with pride. "With God's help my husband, Jeremy, and two others saved the little Miller boy."

"What was wrong with him?" Anna asked, grateful for the change.

"He had the fever. Fever so bad he was seeing things that weren't there."

"What'd they do?"

"They prayed. Called God to the boy and laid their hands on him."

"Praise God," Naomi said.

Anna was about to ask how that worked when Sister Lucinda startled them all by shouting, "Arri ba la jahidra! Ka lava di modiva...." As if struck by some malady, Lucinda's thick, flat brow got red and wrinkled. Her eyes bulged and looked as if they might burst. She trembled and started pulling at her hair.

"He's come to her!" Naomi announced excitedly. "What's He saying?"

"We don't know," Clara told her.

"Maggie, get Sister Sarah!"

Jacob Tuttle's oldest wife, Sarah, was at another circle of women about half an acre away. While Maggie went to get her, the women protectively closed their circle around Lucinda. Clearly possessed, Lucinda babbled on unintelligibly as Sister Sarah, Maggie and all the women in the second circle hurried toward them.

"She's talking about the harvest," Sarah interpreted, when she got close enough to hear. "Praise be! The Holy Ghost is speaking to us through Lucinda. He's telling us the harvest will be good, but warns us to be careful handling what we have reaped. We are not to be wasteful. He reminds us that He has been good to us this year and tells us we must appreciate what He has given us."

Seemingly distancing herself from them, Lucinda closed her eyes and breathed deeply. With all the women's attention riveted on her, she opened her eyes and returned to them as if nothing had happened. "What's wrong? What's happened?" she asked, looking around her in amazement. "Why are you all staring at me?"

Believing Lucinda had been truly visited, the small crowd of women laughed and then cheered. It was as if all had shared her communication with the Holy Ghost.

Anna was stunned. She had heard that some of the women occasionally became possessed by God's spirit, but she had never witnessed it. Her faith, a fledgling's trust in the Church, told her she must believe the Holy Ghost had come. She was disappointed in herself when all she felt was doubt. It was too hard to accept the strange tongue that came out of Lucinda was God's. Anna tried to reason. Maybe Lucinda was just exhausted because of the harvest. Maybe she had gotten too much sun.

But then, what about Sarah? She seemed to understand the tongue?

Hattie leaned toward Margaret, who was beside her. "How did Sarah know what Sister Lucinda was saying?" she quietly asked.

"Sister Sarah is often chosen by the Holy Ghost to speak for Him in strange tongues," Margaret patiently explained. "Through her own experiences, she has learned to understand Him, no matter what tongue He uses. We often look to her for translation."

"I see," Hattie said.

Yet, Anna saw disbelief in Hattie's eyes. How can these women who are no different from Hattie and me talk for God? Annie silently questioned.

"His spirit is among us," Sarah explained. "If we are still and pray, perhaps He will come to someone else. Look to the sky, Sisters, and ask Him." Like small children, the women folded their hands and eagerly looked skyward.

Long moments later, Clara burst into tongue. "Ji ba ri ga ditra! Di tow kri bala!" Biting them off in anger, her syllables were short and choppy.

God was clearly upset, but why?

"What's happened, Sarah?" Maggie anxiously asked. "Did we do something wrong?"

Clara's unintelligible tongue lashing continued, "Bu ji di dahhhh! Wah kah da!"

"God's talking about young Jed Pitker," Sarah translated. "He says eighteen lashes were too many, and He is very angry with us. He says young Jed was lured into sin by a sinful woman and that she was the one who should have been punished. She is a nonbeliever, and since she is not one of the chosen people, we are not to touch her body. But still, she must be punished! She is a heathen, a temptress, and should be driven from the city. The valley must be cleansed of her and her people. We are to snub her, to ostracize her parents' store, and drive them all away. As long as we allow her and her kind to live here, God will be angry with us."

"And if we do that," Sarah asked Clara, "will God no longer be angry?"

"No," Clara growled in her tongue. "There is something else, something that will anger Him still."

"What?" Sarah implored. "What can we do to appease Him?"

"Punish her."

"The Gentile girl?" Sarah asked.

"No. The old woman who tried to stop young Pitker's punishment. The old woman who interfered with the bishops' orders."

Sarah translated, and at once, all the women turned and stared at Hattie. "What are we to do with her?" Sarah asked Clara, her eyes fixed on Hattie.

Frightened, Anna stood. There to defend her, she rested her hand on Hattie's shoulder.

A moment passed, and there was silence. Another moment passed, and in the Holy Ghost's strange tongue, Clara handed down God's verdict.

Chapter Thirty

Salt Lake City, Utah
Fall 1854

It was late in the afternoon. Anna and Hattie were alone at their campsite preparing supper. At her own fire only a few feet away, Hattie was cleaning the fish she had caught for her own supper. "What do you think?" Anna asked, as Hattie ventured to join her.

"You're not supposed to talk to me," Hattie reminded her. "You'll get us both in trouble." Hattie's punishment for her interference in young Pitker's flogging was for Hattie to be shunned. No one was to speak to her or care for her for four days. To show their neighbors they were abiding by the punishment, Hattie had made a bed for herself in the sagebrush near her fire from discarded cornhusks. No one was to help her.

At nearby campsites, other women were busy. "No one will know. No one will hear us here," Anna assured her. "They'll think you're doing chores for John." Lizzy was getting water from the river. John was still in the fields. "Do you think the Holy Ghost really came to them?" Hattie was always practical, not given to fantasy. If she believed it, Anna would believe it.

"I can see why it bothered you," Hattie observed.

"Do you think they made the whole thing up?"

"I don't know," Hattie told her. "It was very odd."

"Why?"

"It was the message," Hattie explained. "I just know it was the Priesthood who wanted me punished, not God. They were telling us to drive those Gentiles away, too."

"What do you mean?"

"Didn't John tell us the other day the priests wanted to force the Gentiles out of the valley. Doesn't it seem odd that Clara and Sarah would bring us the very same message? Their husbands both priests and all."

"Remember when we first came here, when Brigham Young told us God's instructions would come through the Church and the Priesthood?" Anna asked. "Maybe this is how it happens. God comes to the priests, and they speak to the men for Him. If He wants the women to hear, he speaks through the priests' wives. Isn't that possible? Then again, maybe we shouldn't even be talking about it?"

Questioning God's message might not only be wrong, but unwise. Their lives and their futures depended on the faith that brought them there. Didn't they have to believe God was near them? "Maybe we should just believe God talked to us," Anna pressed, " and not worry about it."

Hattie nodded, but said nothing. Carrying an iron pot of stew to the fire, she nestled it in hot coals.

The harvest dance was at the end of October, and Anna, Hattie and Lizzy got all dressed up. Their gingham gowns and white stockings were faded and darned, but it did not matter, – so were many of the other women's. The harvest had been much better than expected. They had all worked hard, Hattie had been accepted back into the fold as if nothing had happened, and it was time to celebrate.

Despite the merriment, Erich was much in Anna's heart and mind that evening, and she yearned for him. She missed him as she walked with her new family to the square. He nearly absorbed her, until she danced with John. Light of foot and in perfect rhythm, John flung her to the side then around him in a square dance. He put his arm around her waist and sashayed with her around the circle. His arms enfolding her, his hands strong and sure, he repeatedly whirled her away and twirled her back to him. She laughed. Breathless in her mirth, all thought of Erich went out of her. Her feelings for John were growing. As she danced with him, her cheeks began to burn and her heart reach out to him.

"Look what Jacob gave me," Kristina said. John and Anna had taken a break. She and Kristina were filling cups at the cider bowl. Kristina lifted a silver locket from her chest and opened it. "See," she said proudly. "Isn't it wonderful? It was Joseph Smith's."

By then, Anna had seen at least a dozen locket's containing a lock of Joseph Smith's hair. She doubted any of them were genuine and was unimpressed. She tried to be reverent but did not feel like it. "That's nice," she observed, as she turned and looked for John.

"Jacob surprised me with it last night," Kristina continued, apparently failing to recognize Anna's disinterest. "We're having another baby, you know. Due in the spring." Her eyes were dancing, just as they had before the birth of her first baby.

"That's wonderful," Anna told her. She had been afraid Kristina would never get over the death of her baby, but in the last weeks, Kristina was better, happier. This must have been the reason. She put her arm around Kristina's waist and hugged her. "Let me know if I can do anything for you."

Kristina beamed. "Thank you, Anna, but my Sister wives, Sarah and Rachel, are so good to me, I'm sure I'll have everything I need. Did you know Sarah is having a baby, too?"

"You don't mind, then, – Jacob having other wives?" Anna had yet to understand how a woman could sleep with a man who slept with other women.

Kristina must have felt Anna's disapproval because she immediately sobered. "You mustn't feel bad for me, Anna. Sarah and Rachel are good women, and I depend on them. If they weren't there to help me, I don't know what I'd do." As if working through an unpleasantry, Kristina paused. "I try not to think about other things. I'll see you tomorrow," she said, walking back to Sarah and Rachel with three cups of cider. Off in a far corner having a drink with two other elders, Jacob was nowhere near his wives.

I guess it's all right, Anna thought to herself. Kristina seems a lot more accepting of her life with Jacob, and he does seem to be good to her.

A few weeks after their arrival, just as he had promised, Jacob arranged a baptism for Kristina's dead baby. It was performed in full view of the congregation with an apostle conducting the ceremony, and little Joseph's substitute was personally blessed by Brigham Young. As a memento of the occasion, Kristina was given the substitute baby's baptismal dress. A small, granite marker was erected in the cemetery on Jacob's plot, and a funeral was held to which every person in the wagon train came.

Kristina had told Anna at the time that the holiness of the occasion and her baby having been given the sacraments of the Church convinced her that her baby had found reward in Heaven. Her dream for him had been fulfilled, and she could finally release him to God. With no reason to fight the rules anymore, Kristina was satisfied simply to do what she was told. Bonding with Jacob's other wives, sister to sister, she had found love in his home and was apparently at peace.

The moon was full and clear in a star bright sky, the mountains bathing in its glow, as people started leaving the dance. Jacob had sent his wives home without him and was walking down the middle of the dimly lit street with two other men. John, Anna, Hattie and Lizzy were about twenty paces behind them. Only a few people had headed their way, so the street was nearly empty. Walking ahead of Jacob were two young women, whose shapely figures, framed by the moonlight, were attracting him. He called to them,"You ladies need an escort?"

As they turned, Anna could see how good looking the young women were and wondered why they were out alone.

"No thank you, Brother Jacob." They seemed to know him, yet were perfectly content to walk by themselves.

A young private in the U.S. Army was standing at the corner beside a picket fence, a sergeant beside him. Both were off duty but in uniform. "I'll give ya an escort," the private offered.

"What do ya think yer doin'?" Jacob shouted. "Scum don't have nothin' to do with our women!"

"Who you callin' scum?" the sergeant challenged, his shoulders rounded, his fists clenched.

"You Mormon boys better take it easy," the private added, his feet braced. He must have been all of seventeen.

"Who you callin' boys?" Jacob shouted. He and his companions suddenly rushed the two soldiers, pushing the private's head through the fence, breaking one of the pickets. His head lodged in the opening, the private fell unconscious.

The sergeant kicked one of the Mormons in the groin, and as the man bent double with pain, the sergeant jumped on Jacob. Soldiers from down the block came running. Mormons came rushing out of nowhere, and the squabble turned into a brawl.

"Take Mum and Lizzy home!" John told Anna, making a move to join it.

Anna took his arm. "Don't John. Come with us." She could feel that his taut forearms and flexed biceps were ready to fight, but she would have none of it. Looking him straight in the eye, she drew closer to him. "That young soldier wasn't doing anything Jacob wasn't doing. I don't want you getting hurt over that."

John looked back at the row, to his mother and daughter, and then to Anna. His combativeness dissolved. Something between he and Anna was changing. Putting his hand on Anna's, his blue eyes deep and caring, he smiled. "You're right, let's go."

Suddenly and without warning, someone grabbed him, and he was torn away from her. Jeremy was dragging him into the brawl. He threw

John to the ground and rolled him straight into the fight between the sergeant and Jacob.

Rolling away, Jacob escaped. As John and the sargeant wrestled for domination, Jacob drew a knife from the sheath he wore around his waist and circled them. His grip tight, his teeth clenched, he continued to circle them, – waiting.

John, the larger of the two men, got his arm around the sergeant's neck, turned him on his back, and rolled on top of him. Pinning him with one hand, balling the fist of his other, he knocked him senseless. The sergeant was helpless. Releasing his grip, still astride the sergeant, John relaxed, and Jacob struck. Predator swift, not inches from John's exposed back, Jacob dove knife first for the kill.

Chapter Thirty-one

Salt Lake City, Utah
Winter 1855-1856

A year later, the harvest dance was a great
deal smaller, for by the fall of 1855, there was not
much to celebrate. That summer, clouds of locust
swarmed out of the Wasatch Mountains into the
valley devastating the crops. When the food in the
fields was gone, the locusts died. Millions of insect
bodies washed up four feet deep on the shores of the
Great Salt Lake. Drought came, then an early
winter. By mid November, the valley was deep in
snow. The below freezing temperatures were taking
a toll. Almost sixteen hundred cattle out of the
Church's herd of two thousand died. Half the cattle
in the territory froze or starved to death, and a day
of fasting each month was initiated.

For months, the army searched among the
Mormons for the man who murdered the sergeant,
but no one would talk. Few knew who did it and
those who did, including John, said nothing.
Soldiers had seen John fighting with the sergeant,
but there was no evidence to charge him. No one
had seen a knife, and there was no blood on John's
hands. He was free, but the army was still
watching, waiting for him to make a mistake. Jacob
had gotten away with it.

A source of little heat, the sun was, at best,
a light in the sky one afternoon late in January 1856
as John brushed snow from his shoulders and
opened the door to their house. They had built the
house before the last winter out of adobe. There

were two windows and a single door. It was only one room, but palatial compared to their wagon. "Looks like we're in for a big one."

From her place by the fire, Angel got up and greeted him, tail wagging. "Good girl," he said, kneeling down and petting her. She took several months to completely warm to him, but once she did, she was as devoted to him as she was to the rest of the family.

The women were crowded near the fire. Lizzy was tending it. Anna was sitting on a stool mending a work dress, and Hattie was kneeling next to the coals stirring the contents of their cast iron pot. Supper for the five of them, Angel included, was a thin, root soup. The only reasonably filling meal they allowed themselves was at midday. Breakfast was a couple handfuls of bran or dried corn. If they did not seriously ration their food now, they would not survive until the first crop was harvested late next spring.

"Did you see Brother Jeremy about getting our chicken back?" Hattie asked.

John nodded. "Says a coyote got her."

"How many of his did the coyote get?" Anna asked, suspiciously. The loss of even one chicken was devastating.

"None. Just ours." John was calm, too calm.

"Then he can give us one of his," Hattie presumed.

"Says he needs all of them for his family."

"What about our family?" Hattie snapped. "That hen was the best producer we had. She could have kept us in eggs all winter."

As if to put her off, John turned his back to her. Removing his thawing coat and hat he hung them on a wall peg beside the door creating a puddle. With Angel following him, he ambled to the rocking chair and sat down.

"That fart son of his stole her," Hattie accused, before John's rump hit wood. "They owe us."

John stared at the fire, rocking, his hand casually resting on Angel's head.

"I think they ate her," Lizzy said, softly. "I heard his little girl, Beth, bragging about how they had chicken for dinner last Sunday." Anger suddenly erupting, she exclaimed, "Bet that chicken was our Rosy!"

"You shouldn't bet," Hattie told her, "but I'd take that bet." Hattie stood, looked at John with her hands on her hips, and puffed, "What are you going to do about it?"

As he continued to stare at the fire, clenching and unclenching his teeth, John's jaw loudly popped. He took a deep, controlling breath, then told her, "I already asked Elder Ira to do something about the chicken. He wouldn't. He told me to let the matter go and not stir up trouble. That if we want our chickens, we'd better keep an eye on them." The veins at John's temples were bulging, his face crimson. He clenched the rocker. The calm he had feigned when he came in was gone.

"Why don't we just take one of theirs?" Lizzy suggested. "That's what they'd do to us."

"That isn't right, either," Anna told her.

Unable to sit any longer, John stood and reached for his pipe, seething, "Best just forget it."

"There isn't anything we can do?" Anna asked.

"I say, take that kid out to the wood shed and his father back a' the barn and teach them some regard," Hattie declared. "At least they'd think twice before they stole from us again. Food's scarce around here. Something like that could mean our lives."

"Getting back at them won't make the stealing stop," John said. "There'd just be others taking their place. I can't fight them all." Thinking out loud, he reasoned, "If they steal our oxen, the Church'll get after them. So I'm sure they'll be safe in the barn. The pig and chickens are something else. They'll have to come inside."

Anna and Hattie exchanged troubled glances.

"They're filthy," Hattie argued. "Before long this house'll be filthy too. After a day or two, we won't even be able to breathe in here."

Better that than starving," John said, putting his hat and coat back on.

"That sow'll destroy everything she can get her snout on," Anna protested. Though stock lived in her house in Switzerland, they were in fresh, clean stalls.

"I'll tie her tonight and build some kind of pen for her in the morning," John promised, as he opened the door to go outside and fetch her. "You and Mum'll just have to learn to live with her." The pig was the last of three, the two chickens the last of twenty. "I'll talk to Brother Pietz tomorrow and see if he won't let us breed her to his boar."

Supper that night was sheer havoc. Tied to the door, their hundred pound sow was squealing and struggling. With nothing tethering them, the two chickens were everywhere, fluttering and squawking up and over beds, under stools, in and out of every corner, with Angel right behind them, incessantly barking as she tried to herd them outside.

"Nice," Hattie remarked sarcastically. She slipped a short rope around Angel's neck and made her stay put. But it did not help. Angel leaped at a chicken that came too close and the chicken took flight, landing on the table, nearly spilling Lizzy's soup.

"Stop that!" Anna yelled at Angel. "Sit!" Angel obediently sat but, worrying about the intruders in her den, continued to watch them.

Knowing better than to laugh, John was grinning. "Don't worry. They'll settle down in a minute." He was at least partly right. By bedtime, the various occupants of the little, one room house, crowded like sausages in a can, had become resigned to one another, and everything was peaceful. There was only one sound to be heard, the pig's snoring, building with each slow breath like the roll of thunder. She was their breeding sow, a member of the family they would butcher only if things got dire.

As Anna lay in bed beside John, she giggled, and everyone else began to laugh.

"Okay," John said, without waiting for Anna to ask, "I'll take care of her." His long johns were stretched and sagging at the knees and buttocks as he put on his boots and walked to the door. Kneeling next to her, he cooed at her and coaxed the sow to roll over. She snorted, grumbled and grunted, and did what he asked, but before he got back to the bed, she was snoring again. He looked at Anna and shrugged his shoulders. "At least Brother Jeremy's not going to get her."

John slid into bed but was unable to sleep. His hands behind his head, he and Anna listened as the sow's snoring fell into a baritone rhythm. Soon, Hattie began to snore. In the light of the smoldering fire, they could see that Lizzy was sleeping too. He looked at Anna, and Anna looked at John. Like two children, they quietly giggled. The moment shared, he put his arms around her, and Anna let her knee brush against his thigh.

His touch surprisingly electrifying, she was unable to take her knee away. He was warm and magnetic. His flesh was irresistible to her. Unable and unwilling to stop, without fighting it, she wrapped her leg around his and rolled over to face him.

His breathing was short and erratic, and he was trembling. He put his arms around her, tenderly drew his hand down her back to her buttocks, and kissed her.

John was whistling as he dressed the next morning as Anna was unable to take her eyes from him. That night and each night thereafter, he needed only to touch her, to draw the breath from her with a kiss, and she was his. For her, he soon shaved off his beard, and she saw him for the first time. His jaw line was strong and square with cavernous dimples. There was a tiny scar under his lip, and without an unforgiving framework of beard to encase them, his blue eyes sparkled. She was deeply in love with him.

It was a cold, sunny morning in mid February. The sky was a brilliant blue. The trees and bushes were thick with white, frozen crystals.

John had taken the ox fifteen miles east to Little Cottonwood Canyon, a "U" shaped trough carved by a glacier during the ice age, to help haul stones for the Temple. Anna and Hattie planned to spend the day cleaning the barn. Lizzy was not yet up. Too tired to do anything but read, she had spent the last three days in bed.

"You need to sleep today, too?" Hattie asked, her brow creased with worry. "Better get up and let us check you." For months their food rations consisted mostly of dried beans and grain, with no greens and few vegetables. Despite Hattie and Anna each having given Lizzy half of their portion of the food, Lizzy had lost a good ten pounds in the last month, and they were worried about her. Hattie helped her to the fire. "Let's get your nightgown off. We're going to find out what's wrong with you if it takes all day." They wrapped her in a blanket, and while Hattie checked for fever and ticks, Anna looked for rashes.

Lizzy could barely stand. "I'm tired. Can't I please go back to bed?"

"Sit here," Hattie offered, bringing the rocker to the hearth. While Anna finished inspecting for bites, Hattie examined Lizzy's mouth. Lizzy's gums were swollen and bleeding. Quickly checking her fingernails, Hattie found blood beneath them. "Get Mrs. Tork," she told Anna.

Mrs. Tork confirmed Hattie's suspicions. "Black canker all right. Scurvy." She took Hattie and Anna aside. "If she doesn't get better soon, she'll die. If Lizzy's got canker, other children do. We've got to gather the women and go into North Canyon. We'll need all the spruce we can carry."

Within an hour, Anna had thirty volunteers. Within two hours, they were on the trail to North Canyon with three wagons: fifteen women in each of the first two, the last wagon empty, the only oxen left in town pulling them through knee deep snow. Hours after nightfall, they returned with a wagon piled high with bows.

Mrs. Tork gave them instructions, and the spruce was divided among the women to take to their own children and others'. Anna brought home two bushels full, and with the needles, Mrs. Tork made tea. "Lizzy needs to drink a lot of this," she told them. "It's impossible to give her too much."

Lizzy had become so weak she would eat or drink nothing voluntarily. Anna helped her sit while Hattie forced her to drink the tea.

Beside himself with worry, John stayed at home the next day, pacing nervously. Though he had given his daily ration to Lizzy, she still refused to eat. The only thing they could get down her was the tea, one cup after the other forced down her until she threw up.

"I remember women talking about elders healing the little Miller boy by laying hands on him," Anna told John. "I think you should get Brother Jacob."

His eyes restive with fear, John looked at her and then at Hattie. "What do you think, Mum?"

"We need God's help. If Jacob can get Him to come, let's ask him. We've got to do everything we can for her." Lizzy last threw up half an hour ago, and Hattie was about to give her another cup of spruce tea. "Go on now. It'll be dark soon."

A little after sunset, John came back with Brothers Jacob and Jeremy. Kristina and Clara came with them, each with a small pot of potato soup. "How is she?" Kristina asked.

"Not very good." Looking around for someone else, Anna took their coats and set the soup on the hearth near the flame. "I thought you were going to bring an apostle to lay hands on her.

Jacob reached into his buffalo coat, took a flask from the pocket, and handed the coat to Hattie. "None could come, so they endowed Brother Jeremy and myself with the power of healing. See that there's quiet."

Jeremy was tall and lanky, his head barely clearing the ceiling as he draped his heavy coat over the rocker. "Got the oil?" he asked Jacob.

Jacob showed him the flask and nodded.

"How you doing?" Jeremy asked Lizzy, as they approached her. Everyone else was by the fire, respectfully, yet nervously watching. Jeremy gently touched Lizzy's brow, lifted her eyelids, and said, "Get up child." He pulled back the corner of her blanket and uncovered her. "Get on your knees and pray with us."

Lizzy was as weak as boiled spinach and could barely lift her head.

"Come child," Jeremy encouraged, his voice losing its gentleness. "God does not help those who do not come willingly to Him. Follow Christ's example and rise."

"She's too weak," Hattie told him. "Let me help her."

"Stay where you are," Jacob ordered. "Brother Jeremy can do God's work."

"Get up, Lizzy," Jeremy demanded, with no gentleness left in his voice. He propped her on one elbow, slowly drew her knees to her waist, and dropped her stockinged feet to the floor. Her drooping body forced to sit, he pushed her to the edge, and slid her off the bed. Turning her to face it, making her kneel, her head and shoulders drooping across the mattress, he knelt beside her.

Anna stepped forward to defend her, but Jacob held her back, whispering "Leave him alone."

John's fists were tightening. His face was afire with anger.

"Raise yourself, look to the sky, and pray," Jeremy commanded, standing. With the Book of Mormon open in his hands, he read, forcing her to repeat every word.

Jacob stepped to John's side. "If we can force her to find strength enough to pray, she might find strength enough to live. If she just lays there, she'll die."

Half an hour past while Jeremy prayed with Lizzy, her voice getting stronger at first then fading. "Get her to stand," Jacob suggested, "and we'll sing." He and Jeremy took Lizzy by the arms and lifted her. She could not stand alone.

Jeremy's deep, bass voice lead out as he sang, "Come, come ye saints, no toil nor labor fear, but with joy wend your way." The adults joined him. "All is well! All is well!"

At song's end, Lizzy collapsed. While Jacob held John back, Jeremy lifted her into bed. Anointing her with oil, they laid their hands upon her, blessed her, and restored her blanket. Holding her limp hand, Jeremy said, "Let us pray.

Chapter Thirty-two

Provo, Utah
2:00 p.m.
April 22

The Rest-A-While Inn on Highway 89 was old but well kept and immaculate. Its adobe finish, shake, dormer roof and large windows, though nothing like Sharon's usual travel accommodations, had been the nearest safe harbor for her. It was a welcome haven after the State Patrolman roughed her up the previous day. "You're in here," she told Alex, as they approached the outside entry to room 215, up the exterior stairs and on the back side of the two-story motel. "This one's mine," she said, referring to the room on the right, number 216.

"I've seen worse," he said, noticing the bedspread's faded colors and the path worn in the rug between the two queen-sized beds and the bathroom.

"Go ahead, put your things in here while I get us something cold to drink," Sharon told him. With his key, she unlocked the first of two doors dividing the two rooms. With hers, she unlocked the second.

"Bottled water all right?" she asked.

"Sure. Got anything to eat?"

"Just an orange."

"Never mind. I'll wait."

They had talked all fifty-five miles from the airport. He told her what happened in New York and Hank Blanchard's arrest for murder. She told him about Wayne and Kim's disappearance.

"Here," Alex said, digging into his wallet. He handed her a single piece of crumpled paper. "This is what I got out of Hank's wastebasket."

Though grease spotted and wrinkle worn, the columns on which the numbers and letters appeared were quite legible. The sheet was entitled "Project Samson." The information included was identified as "Inventory – Status as of April 5." There were two columns which appeared to identify "vessels" of some kind. Each vessel was first identified by a five digit number. The location of the vessel was a four letter code. The next two columns were two digit numbers, the first identified as "t.imp," the second as "s.b." The last column, seemingly describing the vessel's condition, was "dd," a "P" followed by a number, or an "NP". The word "Min" appeared in the upper right had corner.

The "vessel" numbers were in series, and there appeared to be two locations: "UTVR" and "AZPG". There seemed to be no correlation among the rest of the numbers.

"I remember, now," Sharon said. "There was an ancient looking Egyptian urn in Kim's living room. When I asked her about it, she told me one of the figures on it was the Beekeeper." She paused. "They called the Beekeeper 'Min.' The urn was gone when I came back to the house and discovered she and Wayne missing."

Alex took her forearm and squeezed. "That fits with what Hank told me Wayne said: that this was 'all about the bees.' Can you think of anything else?"

Sharon shook her head. "No, but I think it tells us what this inventory is. The vessels are antiques like Wayne's urn. The locations are probably storage facilities of some kind.

"Like that tithing storage where they took Wayne and Kim's belongings?" Alex asked.

"Exactly, but I wish I knew what the rest of the descriptions mean. For example, I've never seen the condition of artifacts described that way, – 'dd', 'NP', and 'P' with a number. I don't know those designations."

"Even more critical to our finding Wayne and Kim," Alex suggested, "is knowing why this inventory is so important."

"Maybe Wayne was involved in a black market for antiques, and all these vessels are stolen," she said.

"That medallion of Wayne's has something to do with whatever he was involved in too. Otherwise he wouldn't have been so upset by Kim's discovering it. Where'd you say the tithing storage facility was?"

While Sharon and Alex talked, two men in dress slacks; starched, white shirts; and narrow, dark ties; with holsters hanging from their belts bulging with handguns, were in the motel office asking the desk clerk about a man and woman of their description. The man asking the questions was freckle-faced, tall and stocky. His hair was red, his face chiseled, and he repeatedly clenched his jaw. His companion was middle-aged and balding, his skin pale and seemingly hairless. From his thick neck and tight shirt, it was obvious he was a body builder. While the redhead dealt with the desk clerk, he was examining the guest book the manager had voluntarily provided them. He found what he was looking for, "Where's 215?"

The manager pointed. "Up those stairs and around back. She's next door."

At the Formica table in room 216, Sharon was sketching for Alex an outline of the storage facility where Wayne and Kim's possessions were taken. She was describing the security she saw there.

The door to the room next door suddenly exploded with a well placed kick, tearing it open and breaking it apart.

"Sh-h-h," Sharon said. Alex had relocked the adjoining door, and she quickly locked hers. There was a flurry of activity on the other side. "They're searching your room."

"That's my bag," Alex said, as the flexible nylon and plastic suitcase he brought hit the wall. "They're robbing me!" Instantly, the fury of the search abated, and there was nothing.

"He must be in her room," one intruder whispered to another. "Make sure they don't get out the front."

"It's not your things they're after," Sharon realized. "They're after us!"

"Go!" Alex mouthed, his hand pushing her toward the outside door.

As his side of the adjoining doors crashed open behind them, cracking the door on her side too, he raced past the table and grabbed the inventory and tablet. Rushing, shoulder first out the door, Sharon charged, knocking off his feet the chisel faced intruder waiting for her.

"Run!" Alex shouted, following her. They hurried along the railing and down the stairs, past vending machines and to her car. Speeding out the drive, they headed north into town, their pursuers in a white Impala, right behind them.

Chapter Thirty-three

Salt Lake City, Utah
1856

There were only whispers that night as Anna, Hattie and John kept vigil over Lizzy. John was in the rocker staring at the fire, occasionally pacing. Anna and Hattie were feeding the fire, boiling water, brewing exorbitant amounts of spruce tea, and taking turns forcing Lizzy to drink it. Angel was laying protectively at the head of Lizzy's bed. The chickens were quietly roosting in the corner, and the sow was in a small pen John had made out of skinned branches.

"I'd better get the pig and chickens outside and feed them," Anna said at dawn.

Preparing to boil more tea, Hattie stoked the fire.

"Feed me, too. I'm hungry," Lizzy said. Her head was propped on her hand, and she was smiling at them. "Hi, Angel," she said, as Angel laid her head next to her pillow. "Come on," she encouraged, and Angel jumped on the bed beside her. "So how about some food? We got anything?"

Fairly bursting, John smiled, rushed to her and helped her sit up. "So what do you want? Rabbit? Deer? Elk?" he asked, as he put on his coat.

"Anything that's big," she grinned.

He hurried back to her and kissed her on the forehead. "Be back before dark," he promised, excitedly. Taking the rifle that hung next to the door, he went out into the snow. The valley had been hunted out that winter, but it didn't matter. John would bring back something.

Lizzy looked pitifully at Anna. "I thought we already had food."

Anna laughed. "Don't worry. We'll find enough to hold you until he gets back."

Hattie made more tea and enthusiastically handed a cup to Lizzy. "Drink this while we fix your breakfast."

"Not more of this?" Lizzy whined. "I hate this!"

"I don't care," Hattie told her in her don't-mess-with-me voice. "'This' helped save your life. You'll drink it 'til I tell you to stop."

Sulking, Lizzy took the cup Hattie offered, curled her lip, and sipped.

The high ranking elders' of the Church lived in one of the established and better neighborhoods of the city. Their houses had multiple rooms and were clapboard, not adobe. Elder Ira Blake's house had two stories and a covered front porch and was only a block away from Brigham Young's new, twelve apartment mansion. It had five bedrooms, a living room, a den, and a huge kitchen where Ira's family ate in shifts. With an apartment out back, there was plenty of room for his five wives and fourteen children. It was March 1856, and Elder Ira had called a meeting there.

Without being given an explanation, and to his surprise, John was invited. On his arrival, he was shown to the den. When he entered, the door was closed behind him.

Elders Jacob and Jeremy, Ned Haight, the wagon master, and two other elders were already seated in overstuffed leather chairs facing an elegant, walnut desk. All were smoking cigars. As John came into the smoke choked room, they hardly acknowledged him.

Brother Ira, who ranked higher than anyone else there, was sitting behind the desk in a high-backed, leather armchair. A half burned, hard chewed stogie was in his hand. Ira's eighteen year old son, the oldest of six, was standing at Ira's right near the bookcase. "Have a cigar, Brother John?" Ira greeted, holding out a box that was half full.

"No thanks, I have my pipe." John did not like the smell of cigars and found the smoke in the room almost unbearable.

"Suit yourself." Ira's eyes were small and dark, nearly hidden behind his corpulent cheeks. A long, gray beard covered his lips and jowls, dominating his face. His expensive, three-piece suit, tailored back East for him a few years ago, was now too tight, and strained across his ample girth.

John did not want to be a leader in the Church and did not care about Church politics. He had never attended a meeting like this. As a result, he was not a favorite among the men there and had not risen in their hierarchy. Not having much feel for them, he did not realize refusing to take a cigar conveyed to them he might be too independent to become one of them. He stepped to the window, a fancy, glass window with panes, reached for his pipe, tapped it on the back of his hand, filled and lit it. Only he and Ira's teenage son had not been asked to sit.

Just as John's worn, rustic clothing and low rank set him apart from the other men Ira had summoned, Ira's fancy suit and lord like posturing set John even deeper at the bottom of their strata. So obvious were the dynamics of the situation, even

John understood them, and he was very uncomfortable. He had never been invited to one of the elders' houses and had no idea what they were like inside. He did know, however, that the richness of Ira's house, together with the other men's attitudes, were intended to make him feel a lesser man, and he did not like it. In a subtle act of defiance, he looped a thumb around one of the straps of his dilapidated suspenders, pulled the brace away from his homespun shirt, and snapped it. That should show them he was not impressed or intimidated by them.

Ira's fancy desk chair rocked and swiveled. As he leaned back in it, he put his hands behind his head and swiveled to face John. "You know James Walters and William Westfall, don't you, Brother John?"

"Yes, they've got a trading post about ten miles southeast of here. Do a lot of trading with the Shoshone."

"How well do you know them?"

"Not well. I stop there once in a while when I'm working in Little Cottonwood. Seem like nice enough fellas."

"They ever criticize the Church in front of you or ask you questions about us?"

"Not really. They ask after my wife and family, but that's all."

"Ever ask you how many wives you have?"

"Once."

"Ever seen any Federal officials out there?"

"I met an Indian agent there once. He stopped to see them on his way south."

"What were they talking about?"

"Don't know. He was headed out just as I was coming in."

"Thank you, John," Ira put his hands down, leaned forward, and turned back to the other men. "Brother Brigham has asked me to take care of something for him. I'd like you men to help me.

"John has just confirmed that Walters and Westfall are curious about our plural marriages and are in direct contact with Federal agents. "Brother Jeremy, you know anyone else that goes there?"

"Nope."

"Then we'll have to make our decision based on what we already know, Brother John being our only witness. Is that all right with you, Brothers?"

Everyone agreed except John. "Make a decision about what?"

"About what to do with these men."

"Why? What have they done?"

Folding his hands on the desk, slowly and deliberately tapping his thumbs together, Ira told them, "William Westfall was a member of the Church but left us about a year ago. We didn't think he'd be a problem then, so we let him go, reminding him of course, of the oath's he had taken and that he'd lost his place in God's Kingdom. "A few days ago, Brother Brigham received a joint letter from several of our missionaries in Washington D.C. The missionaries informed him that Westfall and Walters are sending letters to the United States Government, in particular, to the Department of the Interior and to the President, accusing us of grooming the Indians to fight for us in case there's trouble with the Gentiles. Westfall and Walters also questioned the morality of our women. Gentiles here have supported their accusations and are accusing us of harassing and intimidating Federal officials and of interfering with their work. The authorities in Washington believe them, and there's trouble."

John knew, as did everyone else in the community and in this room, that Westfall and Walters' claims were true. The Mormons did establish Indian missions to make the natives allies against the Gentiles and knew that their forcing Gentiles out of the territory might make trouble. The Mormons harassed federal judges. Justice Stiles' official records were stolen and burned, and he had been intimidated in his own courtroom. Justice Drummond retreated back East and resigned because his court records were destroyed with the knowledge and approval of Brigham Young. Federal officials of all kinds were constantly insulted and harassed. It was the Church's policy to force them back to Washington D.C. to resign. That policy was not, however, intended to become general knowledge back East.

"Brother Brigham wants Westfall and Walters stopped from spreading these tales," Ira continued. "Our job is to decide how."

"Wish Porter Rockwell was back," Jacob said. "He'd do what he did to that puke governor in Missouri."

John had heard several murderous rumors about Porter Rockwell. Until that moment, he thought they were untrue. It was said that after the Mormons were forced out of Missouri, Porter Rockwell was sent back to assassinate the governor, and that the Church called the murder "holy." The assassination attempt failed.

"Where is Brother Rockwell?" Jeremy asked. Neither Jeremy nor anyone else seemed troubled by the mention of Rockwell's name.

"Brother Brigham sent him south to quell some trouble down there," Jacob said.

"Who then among us can do what is required?" Ira asked, looking directly at Ned Haight.

Obviously flattered by his selection, bathing in self-importance, Ned leaned back in his chair, puffed on his cigar, and talked of his qualifications. "When I was a lot younger, I joined the Whistlin' and Whittlin' Band," he recalled for them proudly. "Our job was ta protect the Prophet's life, keepin' watch fer anyone wantin' ta take it. We called the troublemakers 'Black Ducks,' and every once't in awhile, we'd have ta whittle one of 'em down a bit and send him 'cross the great river.' We'd get 'em whenever they was seen 'round Joseph Smith's home late at night, – or when they was askin' 'bout things that was none a' their business. Caught more than a few of 'em myself. We'd whittle us a three cornered rail, makin' the top corner r-e-a-l sharp, then whistle whilst we carried the puke off on it. That was some few years back, but I reckon I can still do whatever you need me to do."

Ned Haight's references were veiled, and though everyone else seemed to know what Ned and his band did with the Black Ducks they carried off, John did not.

"Good," Ira said, turning back to the others. "So, what are we to do with James Walters and William Westfall? Are they equally guilty, or should we treat them differently?"

"They both signed the letters, didn't they?" Jacob confirmed.

"Yes," Ira said, "but Westfall perhaps owes us more, having been one of us."

"Shouldn't matter," Jeremy argued. "The harm each of them caused is equal. Their treatment should be equal."

"Is everyone in agreement?" Ira asked.

Everyone but John said, "Yes." Ira did not ask for his vote.

"Very well," Ira said. "Ned, your mission is to 'save them.'"

Afraid to believe the rumors of murder were true, still loyal to the Church, John did not want to believe these men might do serious harm to the two traders. He wanted to ignore the possibility, but could not, as while he listened, that same fear pricked at the edges of his mind.

Before he gave in to it, he had to hear more. He had to be certain. Yet, before he heard any of the details, Ira abruptly dismissed him.

"Thank you for coming, Brother John," Ira said. He stepped from behind his desk and ushered John to the door. While the other men remained seated, Ira leaned toward him, putting his arm around his shoulders. "When you have considered and made known your desire to become acquainted with all of the Church secrets," Ira whispered, "when you have proven yourself, you will be invited to stay."

John was very afraid. If they did not intend to murder Walters and Westfall, why didn't they let him stay? He imagined the worst. When he got home, he was too disturbed by what happened at the meeting to talk about it. He could not sleep that night, and though he worked side by side with Jacob the next day with nothing said about the punishment, he could not help but be troubled.

A week went by. He heard nothing and said nothing. Time dulling his memory of exactly what was said at the meeting, lulling him into thinking he was mistaken, he became convinced he was imagining it. He relaxed, and one day, while Lizzy was outside doing chores, he told Hattie and Anna about the meeting.

"What do you think they're going to do?" Anna asked.

"I don't know," he told them, his recitation of the events again stirring his conscience.

"They were talking about murders and riding men out of town on rails," Anna observed. "It has to mean some kind of violence."

"How could they mean to kill them?" Hattie asked. "The elders are men of God. Look what Jacob and Jeremy did for Lizzy. God wouldn't have given them the power to heal her, if they were evil."

"Maybe so," Anna said, "but I know one thing, God didn't have anything to do with whatever Jacob and the others decided to do. I don't like this, John. Has anyone seen Westfall or Walters since the meeting?"

"I don't know. I've been afraid to ask."

"Could you ask Elder Ira?" Hattie suggested.

"I think if Elder Ira wanted me to know what was going to happen, he would have let me stay. But, maybe we can find out on our own. I've got to work at the quarry in Little Cottonwood tomorrow. I'll try to get away and go to the trading post to see for myself."

"They'll know, if you do that. You'll be gone too long," Anna warned him. "We don't want you getting into trouble. What if I go," she suggested. "You can tell everyone that one of the oxen is lame and leave him here. He can take me."

"I don't like it," John said. "What happens if you do find something at the trading post? What happens if you're discovered?"

"But I have to go, John. You can't. If you leave your work party in the middle of the day, the elders will want to know why? You might even be followed."

"I guess we don't have a choice. We can't very well ignore it. I'll let you go, but only if Mum goes with you."

"What about Lizzy?" Hattie asked. "We can't leave her alone."

"Sister Rachel's been asking if Lizzy can come to one of her prayer days," Anna told them. "There's one tomorrow."

"Good," John said, "but I want you two to be careful. If something's going on when you get there, leave. Don't let anybody see you, – and don't take any chances."

Chapter Thirty-four

Utah 1856

Snow crunched under the wagon wheels as Hattie and Anna left the main trail to Little Cottonwood Canyon and turned onto the three mile trail to Westfall and Walters' trading post. They wore thick shawls over their wool coats and wool scarves over big brimmed bonnets tied at their chins. Only their bare faces were cold. Their cheeks and noses crimson, their breaths long clouds of vapor, they traveled cautiously between magnificent spruce and fir trees, slowly approaching the trading post. The trail up to the post compound was deathly still. There were fresh wheel tracks and, beside the trail, tracks left by several shod horses. Wagons and horsemen must have gone in ahead of them. Deciding not to take the wagon inside, wanting to be able to get away quickly, Anna turned it around to face the direction from which they came. They left it ten yards from the front gate.

There were horse, boot and wagon tracks everywhere, but there was no sound. They approached the compound cautiously, opened the gate and peered inside.

Something was wrong. The door to the nearby store was open, the inside trashed and emptied. The men, wagons and horses that had made the tracks outside were nowhere to be seen. Refuse was scattered inside and out, and no one was around. They walked through the store, checked the empty storage room, and went out back. "Mr. Walters," they called. "Mr. Westfall." No one answered. The smokehouse behind the store was stripped of meat. The resident horses were gone.

Spooked by the silence, increasingly afraid they would discover the worst, they searched in and around the post, then outside the walls through the sagebrush, repeatedly calling, almost frantic in their search. Yards in back of the compound and in the trees, they stumbled on what they feared they would find, two corpses, face down, frozen, and covered by an inch of snow.

"Oh my," Hattie sighed, as Anna turned away.

Avoiding the bodies, they studied the boot tracks around them. "Same as some of the boot tracks outside the compound," Hattie observed. "They're filled with an inch of snow. It hasn't snowed since the day before yesterday, so they must have been killed before then."

There were three sets of tracks leading to the bodies. Only one set, made with heavy boots, led back to the compound. "You think he's still here?" Anna asked, anxiously looking around.

"No. If he was we'd have seen him by now. He did whatever he came to do and left."

"Who do you think took everything?"

"Whoever was in those wagons must have come after he killed them."

"How do you know that?"

"There's no snow in the wagon tracks."

Anna forced herself to look back at the bodies. She was grateful the snow had covered most of the blood and that the bodies were frozen. They were as they fell and without bloat or rigor mortis. "What do we do?"

"Bury them."

"What if he comes back?" Anna asked about the murderer. "What if he forgot something? What if he sees our trail?" She was scared and wanted to get out of there.

"He won't be back. He's already made his escape."

As confident as Hattie sounded, Anna did not believe her. Hattie knew as well as she did, there was absolutely no proof here that the killer would not be back. Yet, Hattie was right about something.

"These men deserve a decent burial," she said, demanding Anna not be afraid,"and we're going to see they get one. We can't let the wolves get them. We should feel lucky they haven't gotten to them already."

Listening intently to the forest for the snap of a twig or the cry of an animal, anything that might signal a predator, Anna shuddered. Wolves and cougar were all over the canyon.

"Let's get to it," Hattie insisted as she reached for the nearest corpse.

Cold and revolting, the corpse was like soft wood, with just enough give to remind them it was human. They dragged it several feet to level ground, where marsh grass stuck through the snow, then dragged the other one over, placing it next to the him. With an ax and shovel from the wagon, they dug a grave four feet deep in the wet soil.

"How are we going to get them into the hole? We didn't bring a rope, and we're not strong enough to lower them," Anna asked.

"We'll have to push them in, – and hope God forgives us."

The bodies smelled like spoiled meat and were like logs with intractable branches. Anna and

Hattie had to lift them to get them to roll, and when they tumbled into the grave, they did not fit. One of the arms was outstretched. The hand was above ground level and would be exposed.

"Oh, Hattie!" Anna exclaimed. "We can't bury them like that."

"Can't get the hole any deeper, either," Hattie observed. "We'll have to go wider."

Starting three feet from the graveside, they dug toward the bodies. They did not finish until late afternoon.

"Now, roll him," Hattie said, finally satisfied with the hole.

Anna was inside the grave, her hand on the arm that was raised, doing everything she could to avoid the cold, blank face that was only inches from hers. She pulled. Giving way, the body tumbled and fell against her. "Get me out of here!" she cried.

Hattie gave her the blade of a shovel and pulled.

"Let's cover them and go home." Anna urged.

On two rough pieces of wood they scratched the names "William Westfall" and "James Walters," then pounded the wood into the ground as markers. "May God bless you both," Hattie said over the grave.

As Anna and Hattie drove the wagon onto the main trail toward home, a light snow fluttered without sticking. The air was crisp, the trees fragrant. From either side, long shadows crossed the road.

"Do you think it was Ned Haight that killed them?" Anna asked, unable to decide for herself.

"Hard to tell. Could have been anybody. A trapper. An Indian. Somebody who wanted to rob them. Maybe the murderer was in cahoots with whoever was in the wagons."

"Just one Indian?" Anna questioned, remembering there was only one set of footprints away from the bodies. "Indians don't do something like that alone, and they wouldn't have been wearing boots, either. There would have been a raiding party. They wouldn't have had a wagon. A trapper wouldn't have had a wagon that big. He couldn't take all those supplies with him. Robbery's the only other thing that makes sense. But, who? Everyone we know keeps a good eye out for strangers. It must have been Haight!" Anna paused. "Do you think we could have stopped it from happening if we'd come three days ago?"

"Maybe," Hattie said softly.

"What do you think we should do?"

"Tell John what we found."

Too tired and upset to make supper that night, Anna and Hattie helped with the fire, and Lizzy cooked. John got home late. Though they were eager to tell him what happened to Westfall and Walters, they waited until Lizzy had gone to bed and was asleep.

"I'm so sorry you had to deal with that," he said, his first words for them. "I should have been the one to go. Are you all right?"

"Yes, John," Hattie assured him.

"Well, I'm not." Anna said. "However frozen, however much they looked and smelled like spoiled beef, those men were not beef. Touching their bodies gave me the willies, and I'll not soon forget it." Believing the Church might be responsible for the murders made it worse and scared her. "What if it was the Church, John? What if Ned Haight did kill them?"

"We don't know that," Hattie argued, "and it's too important to guess. That's rough country out there. Anything could have happened to them."

"You're right," John said. "It is rough country, but that's not what killed them, is it? They weren't killed by a stranger but by one of us. I should have done something."

"Like what?" Hattie challenged, refusing to let her son blame himself. "Who could you have told? A Gentile? A federal agent? What would you have said to them? You didn't have any proof. All you heard was that Ned Haight was going to 'save them.'"

"Maybe, but I should have known what that meant. I should have known they were going to kill them, and I could have warned them.

"I was duped! Like a fool, I was their accomplice, and my foolishness cost Westfall and Walters their lives."

The next day, John brought all four oxen to the quarry in Little Cottonwood and, at noon, slipped away to the trading post to see for himself. He no longer cared if his absence was noticed and was gone for over three hours.

"Where you been?" Jacob demanded, on John's return. Jacob had been waiting for him.

"I went to the trading post." Even though John had found nothing to link Ned Haight or anyone else to Westfall and Walters' murders, he was ready to confront Jacob as one of the men he held responsible.

"Then you saw?"

John nodded. His face was flushed, his stare accusing.

Jacob's eyes were cold and threatening. "You understand, don't you, John? Because of Westfall and Walters, President Buchanan is talking about an investigation, threatening to send an army against us. We couldn't let them continue to spread lies and raise suspicions about us. Now could we?"

"Why didn't you just run them out of the valley?"

"If we'd done that, we'd only given them better reason and opportunity to talk against us." Jacob took John's arm, his strong fingers crimping John's coat. "We elders are responsible for the safety of thousands of our people. When they're in danger, God sometimes calls on us to take someone's life. We take that life in God's name and for God's purposes. We can tolerate no interference. You understand, don't you, John?" Jacob threateningly repeated.

John reluctantly conceded, "Yes, I understand."

In the late afternoon, the trail was dark in shadows. A light snow fell as multiple teams of oxen combined to pull, on skids, through the canyon and back to the city, each of six huge stones quarried that day. John walked beside his team of oxen and one other team, there to drive them if they stalled, but his mind was on something else. He had been inadvertently part of a double murder, and he had to decide what to do.

To go to the federal marshal he must have proof Jacob and the others murdered Westfall and Walters, and there was none. There were only his suspicions. Given that, all he could do was make trouble, trouble worse than that caused by the men the Elders murdered, with accusations far more serious. Talking about the murders would serve only to get himself, maybe his family, killed. John considered going to Brother Brigham or one of the apostles but thought better of it. According to Elder Ira, the authority to murder the traders had come from Brigham Young. He thought about the meeting. Why were so many elders there if the decision had already been made? They must have been invited to spread the responsibility for the decision, to make them believe they had a part in it. Ned was the only one required because he had already been chosen to be the murderer. The others would be witnesses against him if anything went wrong.

John stopped, and the oxen walked on. It finally hit him. It wasn't Ned Haight who would be blamed for the murders if there was trouble. It would be him! That's why he was invited to the meeting. He was to assume the entire responsibility. He cursed his stupidity. He walked for miles, fuming, wondering what he was going to do about it.

Only after he cooled down, did he think back on what Jacob told him. "We're responsible for the safety of thousands of our people. When they're in danger, God sometimes calls on us to take someone's life." What if William Westfall and James Walters did cause serious trouble for us? What if they did endanger the thousands of Mormons who lived here? Maybe the elders had no other choice. John's part, his duty to the Church, was to protect the elders, defend them for what they did by sacrificing himself. The lowest in rank, he was the only one expendable.

The realization distressed him more, and John sighed. Troubles are sometimes greater than one man can understand or handle. Maybe this was that kind of trouble. He felt guilty about the murders, but he realized he was neither strong enough nor clever enough to deal with the matter himself. Though he tried to make sense of it all, it was easier in the long run to put his trust in the Priesthood. Reasoning his anger away, he tried to put his guilt and thoughts of betrayal behind him.

That night, Anna and Hattie were waiting for John at the door. He put the oxen in the barn, brushed and fed them, then came inside.

"Better go get the chickens," Hattie told Lizzy, after they greeted him. "Well?" she impatiently asked him, when Lizzy was out the door.

"We should stay out of it," John told her. "I talked to Jacob, and he told me the elders were only protecting us. Westfall and Walters were raising such a row with their lies, the United States is threatening to attack us. They had to be stopped."

"But, John," Hattie argued, "taking someone's life is a sin."

"Unless God sanctions it," he told her. He sighed and added, "I don't understand it all either, Mum, but since God trusts the priests, shouldn't we trust them, too?"

The door opened, and conversation stopped as Lizzy came inside with a chicken under her arm. They waited until she put the hen in its crate and, without resuming, watched as she went back outside for the other one.

"I suppose there's nothing we can do about the murders now, anyway," Anna said, still troubled about them. "Maybe this is just another test of our faith. If God ordered it through our priests, who are we to deny Him?"

"I suppose the elders do know best," Hattie sighed. "Certainly they knew more about the danger than we did. We could have all been killed if Westfall and Walters had brought an army against us."

Having been part of the conspiracy of murder, however justified, they shared in the responsibility, and though they now had reason on their side, they found little comfort in it. As John sat in the rocker by the fire, Anna handed him a cup of arrowroot tea. A quiet sadness lingered in the room, and they said nothing further. When Lizzy came back with the second chicken, she seemed to sense something was wrong, and when it was safely in its crate with the first one, she quietly sat at John's feet with Angel. Supper would wait.

When the silence became unbearable, Hattie inattentively poked at the flames and softy hummed a sea chantey she learned as a child. Melancholily, John started singing with her, and while Anna listened, Hattie and Lizzy joined him.

Call all hands to man the capstan
See the cable run down clear
Heave away and with a will boys
For old England we will steer
And we'll sing in joyful chorus
In the watches of the night
And we'll sight the shores of England
When the gray dawn brings the light.
Rolling home, rolling home, rolling home across the sea
Rolling home to dear old England
Rolling home, dear land to thee....

Chapter Thirty-five

Atlanta, Georgia
4:00 p.m.
April 22

At a small kitchen table, scissors in hand, a stack of bright colored construction paper to her right, the outline of an apple on the red sheet of paper in front of her, twenty-four year old Emily Brighten began to cut. The kids'll love this, she thought of the composition she was making to go on her bulletin board. Each piece of fruit would hold the name of one of the children in her first grade class. On the last day of school, the children would write on their fruit the best thing that happened during the school year and keep it as a remembrance.

A devout Methodist, Emily enjoyed teaching in the parochial school. She loved being in the company of children and eagerly looked forward to the day she and Mark would have children of their own. After cutting out four paper apples, she reached for the outline of a banana and, with three sheets of yellow construction paper, cut those out. Mark's shift did not end until eight tonight, so dinner would be late.

Washed dishes were air drying on the rack. The tuna casserole she made for dinner was covered and on the stove ready to go into the oven. The radio was on her favorite oldies rock station playing "A Horse With No Name."

When she was not cooking, the kitchen doubled as her office. Her laptop was on the counter next to the mouse-shaped cookie jar full of Mark's favorite oatmeal raisin cookies. An upright organizer with bills, letters, coupons, and mail yet unsorted, and a stack of green folders in which Emily kept her genealogy research was on the refrigerator. Attempting for years to trace one of her paternal great-grandmothers, she had registered with "WhoWereMyGrandparents.com," a major search tool for people seeking to find out more about their ancestry. These green folders contained everything she had learned.

Emily's father never talked much about his parents, just telling her they died when he was little. Raised by his maternal grandparents and never meeting his paternal grandparents, her father knew nothing about them or their families. Content to leave things the way they were, he never tried.

Emily, however, was not content to lose her paternal ancestry. A piece of her past was missing, and she was driven to find out all she could about her father's side of the family. "WhoWereMyGrandparents.com" out of St. George, Utah had been the answer. It helped trace her father's family back eight generations, all the way to Scotland in the early 1840s. His ancestors migrated to Illinois in the 1850s and moved to Georgia in 1905. She finally knew how she got her red hair and green eyes. The branches of her family tree were filled, and she could pass her heritage down to her children.

Emily and Mark's apartment was on the fourth story of a brick building in the old part of Atlanta, gentrified for younger, middle class renters. The grade school in which she taught and intended to send her children someday was in walking distance. Across the street was a playground where she felt safe even if she was alone.

So when a knock came at the door and through the peephole she saw two, clean cut, young men dressed in white shirts and ties, she opened the door without fear and greeted them. "Hi, what can I do for you?"

Twenty-four hours later, she was a statistic, the subject of an intense search. She was missing. Mark and her parents were desperate to find her, and he was under suspicion for murder.

Chapter Thirty-six

Salt Lake City, Utah
1856

The drought and severe winter had devastated Church stores and food supplies. By June, supplies were running short, draft animals were dying. There was very little money with which to bring to Utah the hundreds of European converts waiting in Iowa. In Utah, a clash between the Mormons and local Gentiles was inevitable. A run-in with the United States Government over territory the Church was claiming as its own was certain. With threats of invasion building, the Mormons needed to populate Zion quickly to strengthen its forces. The most expedient way to do that was to bring the new converts west.

The immigrants in Iowa were some of the poorest people the Mormons had ever brought out of Europe. Many of them were sick. Most were unable to pay for the journey themselves. There were more children than adults and, as usual, more women than men. There had to be some way to get them to Utah.

"Let's bring them out by handcart," Elder Jacob proposed, at a meeting held to come up with an idea.

"Do without wagons?" Elder Ira confirmed.

"All but a few." Jacob was excited about the notion. "Just think. Carts require less than half the wood wagons require, and only a few oxen will be needed for the wagons that will go. Less feed.

Less water. Our costs will be nothing compared to what they've been in the past."

"We can send word immediately," Elder Jeremy added. "The first train can leave in a month and be here by September." To make an impression on their superiors, he and Jacob had worked the plan out in advance.

"Will these people be able to push handcarts?" Ira asked. "I understand they're quite frail."

"We've used the carts before," Jacob told him. "We've given them to lone women, and they've made it. I know they can."

Intrigued, Ira asked, "How many converts do you think you can get here by cart?"

"Most of them. The rest by wagon. They'll be here before winter."

"They better be," Ira reminded him, interjecting a harsh reality. "If they're not, they'll die out there."

"Don't worry," Jacob assured him. "They'll be here in plenty of time. That's the beauty of handcarts. They're light and can travel faster."

"I'll take your idea up with Brother Brigham."

If Jacob and Jeremy's scheme was successful, they could advance in the Church. They might even become apostles someday.

It was late June 1856. The leaves on birch and other deciduous trees in the mountains were a rich, light green, the evergreens a contrastingly darker green. In the Great Salt Lake Valley the sage covered desert was muted with dusty grays and browns. For nearly two years, hunger and hardship had been the rule for the Mormons who had settled there, and they were restless. Their community was steeped in unhappiness. Members were defecting, and Brigham Young was desperate. The Church was in crisis, its very survival in jeopardy. The situation was as critical as it was in 1838 when Joseph Smith loosed his henchmen, the murderous Sons of Dan, against Church members who refused to surrender their property to him. So just as Joseph Smith had done twenty years earlier, Brigham Young and his Presidency turned against their own.

That Sunday in June seemed pleasant enough on the surface. The sun was out and the temperature was approaching seventy. As usual on a Sunday morning, with hundreds of others, Anna and her family walked toward the Temple grounds. Most of them were near giving up, and as had become the norm, there was no joy or hope in the parade. The threads of their faith were unraveling. Their will to persevere was but a dull, distant memory, and the temptation to follow those deserting was almost overwhelming.

Anna took a deep breath of air that was as pure as the Wasatch Mountain's water. Her hair was graying at the temples. Her hands were brown and scabbed, withered and wrinkled, and there were heavy calluses on the pads of her palms and fingertips. She looked and felt a good ten years older than she did two years ago when she came here.

Walking beside her, Hattie was twenty pounds thinner. The leathery skin around her mouth and eyes was cut by deep, dry crevasses. From having given most of their own food shares to Lizzy and John, both women were grossly undernourished.

Wishing she was home, imagining she and her new family were cradled in the Alps, Anna mentally transported them there. She might have been lost in that dream had she not been suddenly jerked back to reality by a scream, – a man's scream, – coming from the Tabernacle grounds. Eager to help, she and everyone around her ran toward the sound, unprepared for what they would see.

Arms wrapped around a twelve-inch-thick post, his wrists bound to it, Brother Heffner, the blacksmith who had whipped the Pitker boy, was stripped to the waist. His garments, shirt and suspenders hung from his hips. Blood dripped inexhaustibly from deep wounds crisscrossing his back.

"Fifteen! – Sixteen! – Seventeen!" Elder Yost, a man as big as Heffner, counted, each time drawing back a bullwhip and slashing Heffner's back. "Eighteen! – Nineteen! – Twenty!"

Rigid against the post, his body in shock from the beating, Brother Heffner whimpered.

"Twenty-one! – Twenty-two!"

Heffner's pants were soaked with urine. His legs were trembling.

"Twenty-three! – Twenty-four!" Yost shouted.

Finally resting the whip, Yost nodded to a man with a bucket nearby, who then dumped its contents of thick saltwater on the remaining shreds of Heffner's back. Ignoring Heffner's screams, the man then walked away.

Standing at the meeting place on the grass nearby, seemingly in charge of Heffner's beating, Brother Jacob bellowed, "Let no one give this man aid. His punishment is just, and you will not help him. His gaze found Hattie, and he glared at her.

"Look at him as you come to worship. Remember what you have seen and be mindful."

Blocking Lizzy's view with her hand, rushing her passed the man still tied to the post, alone in his suffering, his back in bloody tatters, Anna kept their gaze forward and away from him. Neither she nor Lizzy need look at his back anymore to remember.

She glanced at the big stage built on the lawn just ahead of them. Brigham Young was sitting in a wooden chair. His square beard, his dark hair and side burns framed the anger in his red, scowling face. Standing behind the podium, waiting for all to be seated on wood benches set out on the grass, was Heber Kimball, apostle and First Counselor to Brigham Young. His narrow eyes were spitting fire.

Not knowing what they had done to anger their leaders, knowing only that the hammer of God was about to strike, over two-thousand people in single files walked between the rows of benches and took their seats in silence.

Waiting until everyone was seated and there was silence, Kimball addressed them. "The Apostle Peter confessed to Joseph Smith that Peter had hung Judas for his betrayal of Christ, – and that, as he died, Judas' bowels gushed out. Judas was like salt that had lost its saving principle, good for nothing but to be cast out and trodden under foot." Kimball's voice was low and sinister as he threatened them, "You, too, are like salt, and one day you will turn against the elders and break the covenants you have made. When you do," he vowed, "you will be destroyed just as Judas was destroyed. If you do not believe me, hear it from God's Prophet on Earth, Brigham Young."

Ceremoniously standing, his portly figure imposing, Brigham Young deliberately studied the congregation. His gaze passing from face to face, he silently judged them, accusing them, making each man worry that his gaze would soon fall on him. When he finally spoke, Brigham's voice was cold, his manner menacing. "There are sins that men commit for which they cannot receive forgiveness in this world or in that which is to come. If only they had their eyes open to see their true condition, they would be perfectly willing to have their blood spilt upon the ground, – spilt so that the smoke thereof might ascend to Heaven as an offering to God to atone for their sins. If their blood is not spilt, there will be no atonement. Their sins will stick to them and remain upon them in the spirit world.

"I know there are transgressors who would beg their brethren to shed their blood. I have had men come to me and offer their lives to atone for their sins, for to shed their blood is to save them, not destroy them."

Anna gripped Lizzy's hand and squeezed. She was terrified. My God, she thought, he wants to murder us! John told us those were the very words Elder Ira used to describe what they were going to do to Westfall and Walters. They were going to "save them!"

"Remember this when you are told to save a sinner," Brother Brigham continued. "When God demands his salvation, your duty is clear. The sinner has committed a transgression too grave to otherwise be forgiven, so he must atone with his blood.

"You, all of you, know what those sins are: Murder, for anyone who murders should have his head cut off. Adultery and immorality. If you find your brother in bed with your wife, put a javelin through both of them. You will be justified. They will atone for their sin with blood and be received in God's Kingdom. Every man or woman who violates the marriage covenants made to God must pay this debt. If I am guilty of seducing any man's wife or any woman in God's world, then sever my head from my body. Females who are not clean shall not only be wiped from our midst but out of existence. Help us, God, to wipe such persons out and know that this is Your will.

Continuing the list for which blood must be spilled, Brigham listed, "Stealing. I should be perfectly willing to see thieves have their throats cut. I would rather die by the hands of the meanest of all men, false brethren, than to live among thieves. If you want to know what to do with the thief that you find stealing, kill him on the spot and never suffer him to commit another iniquity. As to the law in regard to the African race, if the white man who belongs to the chosen seed mixes his blood with the seed of Cain, the penalty, under the law of God is death on the spot. Cut off his head, kill the woman, and take the lives of their children. This shall always be so. Cut off the head or slit the throat of any man who uses the name of the Lord in vain, who lies, – counterfeits, – or who condemned Joseph Smith or consented to his death.

"A man may live here with us, but he must not blaspheme the God of Israel or damn old Joe Smith or his religion, for we will salt him down in the lake. Those who lie and steal and follow Israel will have their heads cut off, for that is the law of God, and God's law should be executed."

Shivering with fright, Anna sought reassurance, and her right hand found Hattie's. She hoped Brigham would stop, but he did not.

"Let those who break their covenants or turn their backs on the faith die! Let God and our brethren unsheathe their swords and let their blood be spilled! All mankind would gladly have their blood shed for these principles. Hundreds who have not sacrificed their blood to the Almighty are now angels of the devil because they left the Church.

"Will you love your brothers and sisters enough to help them atone for their sins and find eternal exultation? Will you love that man or woman well enough to shed their blood? If you say you can and this is right, raise your hands and call on the Lord to assist us!"

Anna felt the charge of excitement, the energy around her. Rather than terrify the crowd, Brigham Young aroused them, inspired them to help their brethren to Heaven, to save by murder those among them who faltered. Hundreds cheered him. Raising their hands, they shouted, "Go it! Go it!"

Their prophets and apostles, God's oracles on earth, were committed to fighting the corrupted among them, and their people were joining them. Zealots by the score raised their voices, inciting the crowd to a frenzy. Their zeal was as terrifying as their promise. Believing they were appointed by God to shed the blood of anyone who stood in their way, they punched at the sky, their voices thundering, shouting, "Go it! Go it!

Red faced, brows sweaty, searching for the corrupted among them, Jacob, Jeremy and all the other priests and enforcers watched those they already suspected. Jacob stared at John, but it did not matter. John had already raised his hand and was cheering.

Petrified by the murderous cacophony, especially disturbed by John's joining in it, Anna could not utter the cheer and only mouthed it as she held tight to Lizzy and Hattie's hands. God's ways were getting harder and harder to understand. She tried to reason, to turn her back on fear, thinking she might be wrong. These people were good people, God fearing people. How could they be wrong?Brigham Young's message was very troubling. Yet, who else among them could explain what God wanted? Visualizing the course they were about to take, she prayed for them all.

Fervor aroused, loyalty now a matter of life or death, all eyes were on Brigham. When he raised his hands for quiet, shouting pitched to the sky suddenly dropped to the ground and was silenced.

"Brothers and Sisters," he began, "as you came to service this morning, many of you saw Brother Heffner staked out in the yard, his back in receipt of twenty-four lashes. As you passed, you must have asked yourselves what he did to deserve that punishment. Two months ago, Elder Ira Blake, a good man with many wives and children, asked for the hand of a girl from Manti. The girl was a good choice for him. Her hips were shaped and slanted for easy child bearing, and her breasts were ample enough to keep the babies about her from starving.

"Elder Ira asked her to marry him because that was the will of God. This girl was honored by his request, as well she should have been, but refused him for love of a boy. She told Brother Ira she was 'already engaged.' The boy she supposedly loved was Brother Heffner's son.

"When Elder Ira told her it was God's will that she marry him and not this boy, she still refused. Wishing only to do God's work, Elder Ira sent emissaries to Brother Heffner's son asking him to give up the girl. The boy not only refused, he told the emissaries he would rather die than give her up to any other.

"Elder Ira must achieve God's purpose by whatever means he can. The couple left him no choice but to use force. Ira sent Avenging Angels to give the boy one more chance." Brother Brigham nodded to Jeremy, who was sitting on a nearby bench, then continued, "When the boy refused to give the girl up, the Angels were forced to take these from him."

Jeremy took from beneath the bench a stained leather pouch. He opened the pouch, emptied it, and stood on the bench displaying the objects to the crowd. The blood dried, the boy's cut and ragged bollocks dangled from Jeremy's hand.

"Hang them from the pole," Brigham ordered, pointing to a ten-foot pole at the edge of the stage. "They are to rot there," he ordered. "When this boy refused Elder Ira, he refused God."

There was a scream from the yard, a long, hideous cry that twisted Anna's stomach. Yet, undisturbed, Brigham continued.

"Brother Heffner made matters worse by pleading for his son, by trying to make trouble for Ira by coming to me. For this discourtesy, he was flogged. For arguing with an Elder's decision and the Priesthood Ira represents, Brother Heffner invited himself to share his son's fate." Brigham waved, and Elder Yost walked toward them carrying a second pole. Brother Heffner's bollocks, fresh and bloody, were nailed to it. "Hang them beside his son's and release him," Brigham ordered.

"Think this is harsh?" he threatened, turning back to the stunned and frightened crowd. "I say, the day will come when thousands will be made eunuchs in order to be saved in the Kingdom of God. Let every Gentile who courts a Mormon girl and every Mormon who disobeys or challenges the Priesthood be castrated. If by chance any of you have done so, consider yourself lucky, for your brother has cleansed you of your sin."

Anna had embraced Lizzy and turned her away the instant she saw the boy's organs. "Don't look," she reinforced, as the boy's father's were paraded before them. Old moralities were blurring, and she was tumbling over the edge of reason.

After supper, several weeks after the horror of that day, there was knock at the door. John opened it.

There was no moon, and the thick clouds that roamed the sky were threatening rain. Standing in the doorway in the dim light of the only oil lamp were three men, Jacob and two others. Dressed in their Sunday best, the family nervously waited as John asked the men to come inside. Jacob had told John that morning they were coming. "Sit here, won't you?" John invited, showing them three chairs at the table.

Tribunal style, the men arranged the chairs on one side of the table and then sat down. "We'll begin with Brother John," Jacob announced. "John, stand before us."

Standing across the table from them, John put his hands behind his back and expectantly glanced at the two men who came with Jacob. He did not recognize either of them, and Jacob did not introduce them.

"Brother John," Jacob very formally began, "how often do you pray to God?"

Mistrust was rampant through the Church. The Presidency was requiring every member to prove his loyalty to it, to pass the test of an inquisition and to be rebaptized. Failure meant death or castration. Beads of sweat appeared on John's forehead and chin. What was he going to say?

He believed in God but hardly ever spoke to Him. John spent his time working, trying to keep his family alive, but that wasn't going to be enough. Yet, he dare not lie. "God's hand helps me plant and harvest. He is in my heart every day. My every deed is a prayer to Him."

As if he was about to challenge John, Jacob inhaled but then only glared at him and continued the interrogation. "Who is the Prophet, and when was he murdered?"

"Joseph Smith. In 1844."

"Who killed him?"

"Gentiles."

"Who is God's cursed?"

"Gentiles." The answers to Jacob's questions had been drilled into every Church member for weeks. John knew that to forget the answers or get them wrong would instantly signal a lack of commitment and faith.

"Would you give your life to God?"

"Yes, I would give my life to God."

"Would you give your life for the Church?"

John's answer had been rehearsed a hundred times. The Gentiles may be coming in force against them. Every member of the Church was being instilled with a resolve for war. "I would give my life for the Church."

"Have you stolen from your neighbor?"

"No."

"Have you lusted after your neighbor's wife?"

"No."

"Have you spoken against any part of the Book of Mormon or the Doctrines and Covenants?"

"No." An affirmative answer to any one of those questions would have meant John's death. If he lied, that also would have meant death.

"Do you regularly teach the Gospel of Salvation to your family?"

John fidgeted. He always let Hattie handle the lessons. "We sit together to learn the Gospel twice a week, every Tuesday and Friday after supper." Though John might not have listened as intently as he should have to the lessons, he was usually present. Hoping his inquisitors would not challenge him, he looked at them doe-eyed.

His breathing slow, his voice deliberate, Jacob then asked John, "Do you believe in blood atonement, that one man can help another to salvation by shedding his blood?" There was an evilness in Jacob's stare, like a predator set for a kill.

If John was not to become Jacob's victim, he must respond only one way. "Yes, I believe I can help a man to salvation by shedding his blood."

"Are you ready to be a man with the power to save another through blood atonement?"

John's eyes glazed. His throat constricted as he pictured his hand poised to kill another. He swallowed, and thick phlegm lodged in his throat.

Could he really take a man's life? He glanced at Anna, and she stared back.

The Heffner beatings and castrations and their aftermath had left her lost and uncertain, her faith fragile with doubt. It was a dangerous way to be. Working to draw her back to the faith, to remind her how close Brigham was to God, John had been working to calm her. He tentatively got her to agree, though reluctantly, that blood atonement might actually be for the benefit of the sufferer. If nothing else, they both believed that if anyone knew God's wishes, Brigham Young did, and Brigham was in favor of it. Whether Anna agreed or not, for her sake and for the sake of the rest of his family, John had no choice. "I am ready to help a man to salvation."

Following John's gaze to Anna, Jacob must have perceived trouble between them. His expression betraying a satisfaction that went beyond the inquisition, his eyes squinted, and a light shown deep inside them. He pressed John further, "Why must you shed the blood of a sinner?"

"Because saving a sinner is my duty to God."

"Good!" Jacob shouted, triumphantly. "You are excused.

"Sister Anna."

Jacob repeated many of the questions he had asked John, the two men beside him all the while silent. After Anna had responded favorably to the simple questions he asked her, he challenged her with the question foremost at issue. "Do you believe in blood atonement, Sister Anna? Do you believe that a man has a duty to help a sinner to salvation by shedding the sinner's blood?"

Anna blankly stared at him, hesitating, silently arguing, "Thou shalt not kill," was God's commandment. Wasn't blood atonement murder? If a man is worthy of salvation, why does God need our help to save him? Why doesn't God shed his blood if that's necessary? Anna didn't know what was right anymore. Yet, if she had learned nothing else here, she had learned that when God commands they do something through His oracle, Brigham Young, their duty was to obey. If John did not obey, he would atone for that sin with his own blood. Would he also atone if she did not obey? She was terrified.

"Yes, I believe!" she blurted, suddenly and with clarity, taking Jacob and everyone else by surprise.

Jacob smiled. "Then let me ask you something else," he pressed.

"Do you believe the Church is God's word in everything? Even in marriage?" he probed.

She knew he was referring to polygamy. Knowing she would be in serious trouble if she told him the truth, she simmered with dread. She would be considered disloyal, be held in suspicion, and never be rebaptized. Then, what would happen to her? What would happen to John? She tried to be evasive. "I believe that John and I have been forever sealed by God and that, without the Church, there would have been no union. I believe, as the Church teaches, that our marriage is sacred."

"Just your marriage or all marriages?" Jacob pursued.

"I believe that every marriage is sanctified."

She was walking a narrow line, and Jacob appeared to be trying to knock her off of it. "Do you believe in the doctrine of plural marriages?"

She paused. "As a loyal member of the Church, I have accepted all its doctrines."

Jacob gave her a smirking, self-satisfied smile, then said, "Congratulations, Sister Anna, you have satisfactorily answered our questions."

He did not seem to care what Hattie and Lizzy thought about polygamy or blood atonement. He only asked brief and basic questions they had answered numerous times before. When they had answered them without fault, he said, "Well done." Quickly and quietly conferring with the two men who had come with him, he announced, "We have found you to be loyal and righteous members of the Church. Therefore, you will all be rebaptized. "Congratulations."

Chapter Thirty-seven

Utah 1856

In the next several weeks, thousands were interrogated in the Church inquisition. The loyalty of every member of the Church was scrutinized. Only after satisfactorily proving themselves to the elders were the members rebaptized. Only after they had been told over and over that God demanded they do whatever the priests told them to do, raising in them a new religious conscience, were they acceptable. More pledges of loyalty were required. Oaths to the Church were burned in their hearts. Meetings were called for public confessions. No sin or secret would be tolerated or would escape the Church. No man or woman would get away with any transgression, and all would be pure.

One afternoon in mid July, Anna and John, with a group of fifty, met in the Temple yard where benches were arranged for them in neat order. Bishop Jasper was on the stage presiding.

Jasper's dark sideburns, thick and showy, extended three inches across his cheeks, nearly touching his nose. Treated with a concoction of bear grease and sap, they were stiff and oily. His lips, unnaturally full, were stained red with the berries he had for lunch. Clearing his throat, he spat on the stage and began, "Through Joseph Smith and the Holy Ghost, God has anointed the Priesthood with the power to speak for Him. Your duty is to obey the Priesthood. Because we, his priests, represent God, and because we are charged with the duty to build His Kingdom on earth, we must be in control of your every act. You are here to serve God. Mistakes you make, sins you commit, can only frustrate His cause and compromise the purity of His Kingdom. To disobey any order given by a priest or keep from the Priesthood any transgression by your brethren is an unforgivable sin. And," he paused for effect, "there will be no sinners here.

"If you have committed a sin or know of someone else who has sinned and haven't told, this is your chance to confess. You will be forgiven, readmitted into the church and rebaptized if you fully disclose your sins and repent. You will not be forgiven if you hold anything back. If your brethren knows you have sinned and does not tell, he is equally guilty of it. The only means to salvation will be atonement in blood for you both.

"When I call your name, you are to stand and publicly confess your sins. Brother Paul Jergens."

A thin, sapling of a man, barely nineteen, stood, hanging his head. His buttocks was trembling. He looked terrified as he admitted, "I didn't want to help cut logs for Bishop Carter's new house, so I told him I had to do a chore for Elder Ira. Then, I went fishing."

Though Anna knew the boy's confession was probably not what Brother Jasper was looking for, a lesson in obedience was never wasted. She wondered if the boy would be flogged or worse.

Solemnly nodding, Jasper told him, "You lied and disobeyed an order from one of God's priests. By your acts, you have committed two sins. Had you kept your sins from us, you would have atoned for them in blood, but you have confessed. Because you have confessed, you have found your way back into the Church, and you will be rebaptized.

Relieved, Anna sighed.

"Brother Gilbert Johansen," Jasper called.

Brother Gilbert, a stout man with curly red hair and beard, stood. His face was ghostlike, as ashen as a long spent fire, betraying he had sinned even before he spoke. His younger two wives sat to his left. His wife of six years, a woman slightly older than him and close to fifty, sat to his right. The corners of her mouth were drooped in a frown.

She was a plain woman, an obedient servant to her husband and to God, and she had born twelve children. Widowed one day when her first husband dropped dead in the fields, she was then married to Brother Gilbert. She became his third wife, bringing into their marriage two daughters not yet grown. The older daughter, Rebecca, was sitting to her right, sheet white and trembling.

Rebecca was a well endowed girl of fifteen. Her face quite comely, she was ripe for the picking.

"What have you to say to us?" Bishop Jasper spurred, anger erupting in his voice.

"I have committed adultery," Gilbert began, his voice stumbling. "I sinfully fornicated with my wife's daughter, Rebecca."

Oddly enough, in a society where a man could have as many women as he wanted in marriage and whose founder was notorious for his fornications, adultery was the deadliest of all sins. Gilbert had already been charged and was making the adultery public.

"I have been fornicating with Rebecca for months," he told them, "and I have refused for her every offer of marriage, more especially, the offer from Bishop Jasper."

Jasper glared at her. "Sister Rebecca, what have you to say?"

Clearly frightened, she stood, her hands trembling. Her voice shaking, she admitted, "I gave myself to my mother's husband outside of marriage, hoping I would be his wife one day."

A full confession, as humiliating as possible to the transgressor, was a must. When did the intercourse begin?" Jasper questioned her. "How many times did you fornicate? Where, and at what times, did sex occur?" He unmercifully delved into every detail. "How many times did Brother Gilbert plunge into you? Was your mother watching? Did she know?" The bishop seemed to be getting a vicarious, almost lustful, pleasure out of hearing the specifics.

Rebecca was in tears.

When Jasper was finally satisfied, he demanded each of them enter into a covenant. "Do you promise never to fornicate out of wedlock again?"

"Yes," Rebecca promised. "We will wait until we are married."

Less than two weeks later, after supper and just before sunset, Bishop Jasper came knocking at John and Anna's door. He brought with him a tall, bruiser of a man known to them only as Brother Hector. "We need to speak to you outside?" Jasper told John. When John stepped with them into the yard, Jasper confided, "New charges of adultery have been brought against Brother Gilbert."

"With Sister Rebecca?" John asked, incredulous they could be so stupid.

"Yes."

"Have they confessed to the new charges?"

"No, the testimony of the saint who brought the charges is enough," Jasper told him.

"I have already met with my two counselors. After reviewing the evidence, we have determined that Brother Gilbert and Sister Rebecca are guilty. They have broken their covenants." Threads of anger wound through Jasper's voice. "After promising before the Priesthood they would never fornicate again, after being rebaptized and accepted back into the Church, knowing the consequences, they deliberately sinned! The only way they can atone for that sin is by shedding Brother Gilbert's blood." He stretched out his hand and gripped John's shoulder. "You have been chosen, Brother John, to help us."

Stunned, John said nothing. It was not a request. It was an order. If he had any doubts, he could not show them. "What do you want me to do?"

"Get a shovel and come with us."

Anna and Hattie watched from the window as John went to the barn, got his favorite shovel, and mounted the horse Brother Hector brought for him. "They must be organizing a work detail," Anna observed, as the three men rode away.

Gilbert Johansen's small house was claustrophobic with his three wives and their children. When their visitors arrived, Bishop Jasper brushed all but Gilbert, Rebecca and her mother outside into the darkness. So the family could not return and interrupt what was to happen, John and Hector stood guard inside the doorway.

Rebecca and her mother sat on a thin, worn sofa, its once gold fabric a dull brown. Gilbert stood beside them against the wall. Unprepared for what

Jasper was about to say, they anxiously watched him sit in the rocker next to the fire.

"Brother Gilbert," Jasper did not mince words, "the Bishops' Council has found you guilty of breaking your covenant with the Church not to again commit adultery. To atone for your sin, your blood must be shed," he condemned, coldly and without pausing. "So you will know what to expect, salvation requires that the blood run. Your throat will be cut."

"No!" Rebecca cried, running into Gilbert's arms and embracing him. "Please no! Let him marry me instead."

"Too late for that," Jasper said cooly. Once all this was over, she would be available to marry, maybe even to Jasper. "The decision has been made. Go sit with your mother."

Rebecca's mother was grave and silent. When Gilbert died, she along with his other wives and children would be separated, divvied up among men in the community willing to take them. Once again in her life, she would become the property of a stranger. Obviously pitying the daughter who was so easily seduced, suffering with her the pain of her heartbreak, she comforted Rebecca when she came to her.

Without giving the women any time to grieve, Jasper ignored Rebecca and told her mother, "You are to prepare clean clothing in which Brother Gildbert will be buried. If anyone asks about him, you will tell them he has gone to California."

Addressing Gilbert, Jasper said, "Talk with God and to your children. Prepare yourself. Let no one but you three know what is to happen tonight. We will be back for you about midnight."

John and Hector rode with Jasper to his farm and picked up his buckboard. With John and Hector following on horseback, Jasper drove the wagon south and into the desert. Some distance out of the city and out of view, the three dug a four-by-six by six-foot grave and went back for Gilbert. Though they arrived a few minutes early, Gilbert was waiting for them outside the fence. His best boots and a bundle of clean clothes were under his arm.

Brother Gilbert was a staunch believer in the Church and its tenets, in Brigham Young and in the Priesthood. He could not keep his hands off Rebecca, so the only way he could find salvation was through his atonement in blood. He had said goodbye to Rebecca and her mother and told his other wives and all his children that he was going to find a fortune for them in California. He was ready.

Offering his hand to each of the men who took him into the desert to his grave, he thanked them for saving him. As he knelt beside his grave, he closed his eyes and prayed, his voice steeped in fear. It broke when John leaned him over his grave and held him. When Jasper cut him from ear to ear his voice stilled, and his blood flowed into the earth. His essence rising to Heaven, he seemed at peace.

It was an hour before dawn. Everyone else was still sleeping. The energy of righteousness all about him, John was as he had never been before. "Gilbert died so calmly I felt God's breath on us – soothing us – rewarding us for our devotion," he told Anna, when he described what he did that night. "Brother Gilbert knew his salvation was assured, and he smiled as he died. And Anna, I not only got to witness his salvation, I helped save him."

Anna did not understand what John thought he witnessed, but she was not sorry Gilbert was dead. He deserved to die for fornicating with his wife's fifteen year old daughter. Yet, something about killing a man to save him still bothered her. More troubling even than that was John's enthusiasm for it.

Chapter Thirty-eight

Salt Lake City, Utah
Fall 1856

It was a Sunday afternoon in early August. The temperature was over one hundred. The thin grass on Elder Ira's front yard was brown and sun scorched. With their group of fifty, unprotected from the hot sun, Anna and her family stretched wool blankets on the ground, sat down, and waited. On nearby tables, biscuits, beef, potatoes and pies were beset by flies roaming over the crowd and sticking to sweaty faces.

Standing before them, lifting his hands, Elder Ira directed the fifty to stand. "Let us pray," he invited. "Dear God, come to us as we share our thoughts today. Strengthen us against the Gentiles. Show us your will. Help us recognize the evil that threatens us, and prepare us to face it."

An old man with tears already in his eyes stepped forward. Bowing his head, he told them, "My son was only seventeen." In the last few months, the old man had told his story thirty times or more. Many of those present had heard him at least twice but with the Gentile threat so near, his recital had not lost its poignancy. He told them his son was just minding his own business, walking down the street with his girl, when Gentile thugs started throwing rocks at them, "aimin' to kill 'em! Rocks was chippin' out hunks a' their skin, but they had no place ta run." By the time the Gentiles were finished with them, his son was brain injured and left a "zombie." His girl was blinded.

There was a mentally diminished, severely scarred man in his late twenties sitting nearby. The old man helped him up, faced him toward the crowd, and displayed him. "My son ain't been the same since. Can't feed hisself. Can't even tie his own shoes. Just stands 'round all day, starin' at me. The old man gently patted his son on the back, and turned him. As everyone watched and pitied them, he guided him back to his blanket, turned him away from the crowd and helped him sit down.

"Them Gentiles should'a been hung!" an elder shouted from the crowd, as the old man sat down next to his son. "Should'a strung the whole lot from the nearest tree."

Just feet away, Elder Ira stepped forward. "We are purity in a world of sin," he told them. "Like doe in a forest inhabited by wolves, we are unmercifully hunted. Thousands of Gentiles are bent on destroying us. Their government threatens to drive us from our homes. In their world, one man murders another for the fun of it. Ruffians burn family homes out of spite." Ira gestured toward the young man. "Bullies make strong, young men idiots.

"The heathen Gentiles hate us and will do everything they can to annihilate us. We must unite against them. We must drive them off our lands and defend our territory against them. Pray God give us strength."

All of that summer and into fall, at services and meetings, at social gatherings and in work parties, stories of the Gentiles' persecution and murder of the Mormons were told and retold, stirring up old wounds and fomenting hatred. The zeal to avenge Joseph Smith's murder and vindicate the persecution suffered by the Mormons in

Missouri and Illinois was rekindled, and just as Brigham Young planned, the saints came out fighting. The intimidation of Federal officials in Utah grew more aggressive. Public denunciation of them turned vicious. All that was Gentile was boycotted, and Gentiles were forced to leave. The Mormons were at war.

By October, emotions were running high on both sides, and from the depths of righteousness, came the Mormons' resolve. "At all cost, these lands will be ours!"

Though John's, Anna's, and Hattie's taste for revenge could never be as great as those who had personally suffered Gentile persecution, and though they had not personally known Joseph Smith, they too were swept up in the swelling wave of religious zealotry. If called upon, they were ready to pay any cost to defend Zion against its enemies. Now convinced the murders of James Walters and William Westfall were justified for the security of Zion, their consciences were clear. Their belief in the faith that had brought them to Utah and the men who led them was reaffirmed. Lost in spiritual renewal, they were ready to die for it.

The bright crimson and gold of fall had faded, and the mountains were cloaked with snow. After months of propaganda against the Gentiles, the saints were a well indoctrinated army, sure of its cause and ready for anything that might come its way. Anxious for reinforcements, the Mormons were expecting, any day, the arrival of the first group of converts coming west by handcart.

Late in the first week of October 1856, a Church conference began. The crowd crackled with excitement as Brigham Young rose but became mute the instant he spoke. "We have trouble," he began, his voice nearly inaudible.

Oh no, the moment is here, Anna thought. The Gentiles are coming. She took John's hand and squeezed.

"It is a tragedy," Brother Brigham continued. "Our brothers and sisters on the trail need our help." He paused. "Winter has caught them up, and they are in the grips of it."

Almost in unison, the congregation cried out for them.

"The green wood from which the handcarts were built dried and changed shape," Brigham explained. "Many of the carts fell apart and had to be abandoned on the trail. The converts abandoned their stores and belongings and walked. Now the sick and weak are not able to keep pace, and the trains have slowed to a crawl." As if railing against nature herself, he shouted in anger and desperation, "Four hundred have died!"

Amid the shock and sorrow, a solitary voice in the crowd prayed, "God bless them."

"There are a thousand more on foot," Brigham continued. "Behind them, nearly four hundred wagons, strung out for miles on the other side of Fort Bridger. Our people are wallowing in the snow," he cried. "They are starving!"

As if to harness his frustration, he paused. Mute with grief, the members waited. When again able to speak, he calmed and took control. "Hundreds more will die if we do not send rescue parties. We need immediately sixty teams of mules and horses, fifteen wagons, and forty men to drive them. We require twelve tons of flour, clothing of all kinds, and your prayers."

There was no hesitation. Scores of people stood and pledged everything they could. John pledged his wagon, volunteering to drive. Jacob pledged the four horses John would need to pull the wagon but did not volunteer to go himself. Two days later, John left with the first rescue party, leaving Anna and Hattie to take his place in the harvest.

The wind was brisk and carried light snow flakes as Anna walked back to the house one evening after working in the fields. Hattie was too old for hard labor, so while Anna worked the harvest, she and Lizzy shared the women's work and work around the cabin. They were dead tired as Lizzy served them the supper of beans and cornbread she had prepared herself.

After dinner, as Anna and Hattie rested in front of the fire and Lizzy scraped the dishes, giving the few scraps there were to Angel, someone knocked at the door. "Go see who it is, will you, Lizzy?" Anna asked from the rocker. "I'm too tired to get up." She yawned. "I hope no one's come to visit."

Outside, Brothers Jacob and Jeremy were waiting, their black hats powdered with snow, their buffalo coats making them bear-like. As Lizzy opened the door, they kicked the snow off their boots and, without waiting for an invitation, came inside.

Anna sighed, forcing herself to stand. Hattie remained seated. Without a word, she nodded and smiled.

"Good evening, Brothers," Anna greeted. She wished John was there so she did not have to talk to them. "John is with the rescue party," she reminded them, assuming they had forgotten, believing their business was with him. Expecting them to leave without accepting, she offered them tea.

"Thank you, no," Jeremy said. To her surprise, he handed his coat to Lizzy, "Hang it up for me."

"Mine, too," Jacob added.

Hattie rolled her eyes as the two men made themselves at home, warming their hands over the fire with their backs to the women. When their front sides were sufficiently warmed, they turned their backs to the fire, warmed their backsides, and took over. "Sit down, Sister Anna," Jacob said. "We're here to talk to you about something."

Sitting deep in the rocker, Anna cradled herself in it, hoping to garner strength. What could they possibly want? Why did they wait until John was gone to come? Certainly, whatever they needed to say could have been said before he left or waited until his return. A visit like this while he was away could only mean trouble.

Jeremy fixed his attention on Lizzy, "How are you feeling?"

Lizzy had hung their coats on the rack next to the door and was standing beside Hattie.

"Ever get over that sickness?"

She did not answer him. Jeremy had seen her on at least two dozen occasions since she was sick. He could see her now. He knew perfectly well she was just fine.

Her silence did not seem to bother him, "You're growing into a handsome young woman. Thirteen, aren't you?"

Lizzy sheepishly nodded, but still said nothing.

"Why, you'll be a wife in no time."

Hattie should have been pleased, a priest taking an interest in Lizzy when she was just thirteen. But, Hattie was clearly not pleased. She stood, folded her arms and, looking like a fortress, stepped between them.

Anna was not only guarded, but determined. No child would be taken from this house into a brothel, whether Jeremy's or not! "What can I do for you?" she asked, trying to divert his attention away from Lizzy.

"We've come to see you about a matter of interest to all of you," Jeremy began, "in particular, to you and Brother John." He cleared his throat, lit a pipe, and took several puffs before continuing. "When the new converts arrive, they will bring into the valley a number of single women and widows. Those women will need to be supported."

Jeremy looked through a doorway into the small room John finished building a month ago. "I see you've added a bedroom." He acted like he had just discovered it, but Jeremy already knew they had added a room. Jeremy sold John the lumber.

He was making Anna nervous.

"Brother Brigham has suggested that men with only one wife consider taking on another. We have already talked to John about it."

Anna and Hattie stilled, then Hattie inquired, her voice cracking but calm, "What did John say?"

"He was quite accepting and said he'd think about it while he was gone."

Anna was hurt and stunned. How could John even consider taking a second wife? Why hadn't he said something?

Jacob fidgeted. He could wait no longer. The lingering humiliation of Anna's rejection of him suddenly burst into the open, and he blurted, "We've come to ask you not hinder him."

Not caring what he or Jeremy might think, an angry challenge rolled off Anna's tongue. "Hinder?"

Jeremy ignored it. "You and Brother John have been married two years. Yet, there are no children."

"They have me," Lizzy argued, attempting to come to Anna's aid.

Jacob was blunt. "You serve only as proof that Sister Anna is to blame for their barrenness."

The vengefully smug look on Jacob's face compounded Anna's anger. Her ears and cheeks burned, yet she said nothing while Jacob chastised her.

"As John's wife, your duty is to bear him children. As one of the faithful, your primary obligation to God is to populate His Kingdom. If John takes a second wife and you accept her, you'll share in all the products of their union and, in that way, contribute to the glory of God. If you do not, you will not contribute to His glory. We ask that you consider the idea. We ask that you put aside your selfish prejudice and make the sacrifice God requires of you. Remember, a place will be reserved for you in Heaven only if you obey Him." Jacob paused, then, as if to mount the fatal blow, added, "You must agree, Sister Anna. It is expected. Remember, Brigham Young forewarned you. 'Any woman with the power to consent who denies her husband another wife will be destroyed!'"

Jacob's proclamation of death hit hard and terrified her. Brigham Young had indeed made that threat. Her heart was pounding as Jeremy abruptly ordered, "Prepare your home and yourselves to welcome another woman. When Brother John returns with the woman he has chosen, you will be ready."

Anna and Hattie stared at one another. Jacob and Jeremy put on their coats and hats and left. "Good evening, Sisters," Jeremy said, as he closed the door behind them.

"What are you going to do, Anna?" Hattie asked.

Anna's mouth opened, but she could not speak.

That night, as she gazed at the fire trying to imagine her life sharing John with another woman, her chest was as taut as a clenched fist. Unable to sleep, she repeatedly pictured the woman he might choose making love to him in the same bed he shared with Anna, – sometimes while she was lying next to them. Fear and revulsion blew through her like a powerful gale. Tears enveloped her eyes, and she sobbed.

It was early afternoon, after dinner. Jacob's new, single story, frame house was three blocks from the Temple site. It had a peaked roof and full, covered porch; two bedrooms in the basement; a multi-bed attic; and six rooms. His old, sod house, with only four rooms, was out back and was used for storage. The harvest was good that year, and the old house was filled to capacity with carrots, potatoes, beans, turnips, wheat, oats and corn. Anna was very uncomfortable about knocking at the front door of his fancy house, so she went to the back door.

"Sister Anna?" Kristina greeted warmly. "Come in. We're just cleaning up." From the back door, she led Anna through a small, well stocked pantry and into a large kitchen dominated by a heavy, knotted pine table. It was big enough to seat ten, plenty of room to feed, in two shifts, Jacob's rapidly expanding family. The kitchen floor was pine too, and there were painted cupboards everywhere. At the far end of the table, Sister Sarah and her oldest daughter were doing dishes in the wash tub.

"You've come for a visit," Sarah observed, clearly not expecting her.

"I brought you some bread as a house warming." Anna handed Kristina two, plump loaves that smelled of cinnamon and sugar.

"The children will love these," Sarah told her. "Thank you."

Confident she was welcome, Anna smiled. "What a wonderful kitchen."

Sarah and Kristina beamed. "Why, thank you, we are very proud of it," Sarah replied. "Will you sit with us awhile?"

"I'd love to, but could I help with the dishes?"

"No, Margaret can finish up. Can't you dear?" Sarah's daughter was sixteen and soon to be the first wife of Ira's eldest son.

"I don't mind." Without objection, Margaret put her towel aside and submerged her hands in the wash tub. They would not ask her to leave if she was doing chores.

"What brings you here?" Kristina asked, after tea was made and the three were seated. "This is the first time you've ever come to see us."

"Yes, and I owe you an apology."

"It's good to see you."

Sarah and Kristina smiled and waited. Anna was not the visiting type. She had come for a reason.

Cautious about conveying her true feelings, too afraid her negative attitude would get back to Jacob, Anna hesitated. It might mean her life. She paused. When that became awkward, she abruptly asked, "With Margaret about to be married, do you think Brother Jacob will take another wife?" Starting with small talk, easing into the subject, to first wind her way through a maze of subjects that mattered to no one, might have been better. But, she did not. The matter was too pressing and immediate. "Looks like there's plenty of room for another wife."

"Jacob has already asked our permission," Sarah told her, "and we have given our consent. He will take a wife from the new converts."

"Doesn't that bother you? You won't even know her."

Devout and obedient, Sarah responded as she had been trained to respond. "His new wife will come into our home a sister, whoever she is, and we will accept her as a sister. She will be family."

"Is...is it hard to accept someone like that?"

Having already received two women into her home and marriage, Sarah had long ago given up any exclusive claim to Jacob. "You get used to others joining the family," she sighed. "I admit there was a little confusion when Sister Rachael first came. But, all that's over now." She paused, looked fondly at Kristina, and smiled. "When Kristina came, I felt like I was getting another daughter."

Unable to believe what Sarah said was possible, Anna gently challenged her. "But Kristina is not your daughter, you share a husband. How can you love him and still love each other?"

"Jacob is our provider and brother. He is father to our children. Of course we love him. He marries us, and together we bear and raise children for God and the Church." Though there was conviction, even feeling in Sarah's words, there didn't seem to be any passion for him.

Then how could there be passion? Anna thought. How could any woman sustain love for a man who cheats on her in her own house? "How do you feel, Kristina?" she asked, still searching for the truth.

Kristina smiled. "I'll admit I was confused at first, but then things started to make sense. The more wives Jacob has, the more children he can contribute to our family of saints. The stronger we'll all be. Not wanting to help him would be selfish, would jeopardize his glory, – and that would be sinful. Jacob is a man of faith, and if we all work hard enough to do our duty to God, he will become a god someday."

Kristina took Sarah's hand and squeezed. "I love him because he gave us each other."

Anna stared at her. Betrayed by him and melancholy, Kristina had stopped loving Jacob on the trail. She obviously had no romantic feelings for him now. Her life, her love, revolved around the women with whom she shared him, all of them bonded to him only by their faith. Kristina's situation was nothing like hers, Anna realized. I love John. She refused to compare these women to herself any longer. Feeling no better than when she had come, Anna abruptly made her excuses. "I better go help Sister Hattie. She and Lizzy are cleaning the barn today.

"Thank you for the tea." Anna hugged each of them, turned her back and hurried away.

That night, as Anna slept with John's blanket around her, he came to her in a dream. Strong and pleasuring, he carried her into a sparkling, mountain pool, where they began to make love.

Caught in the dream, her defenses down, she was unprepared when the water instantly turned dark. A tempest blew. Currents churned about her. Something brushed her leg, and as she peered into the water, other women swarmed about them, feeling him, caressing him, tainting him with sin. She slapped the water but could not beat them away. She dove, but they had disappeared. Breaching, desperate for his love, she looked for John but could not find him.

As she treaded alone, searching for him, angry currents tugged at her, pulled at her. She was forced in circles as the pond drained and disappeared. She was left in mud, a soft, sensuous medium for lust, when John appeared an arm's length away. She reached for him, her passions afire, but he pulled away. Sirens fell upon him, – tempting and teasing him. Forcing him to come to life, they fed on him in frenzied copulation.

Her body flailed as Anna struggled to save him. The mud sucked her under. She tried to free herself but could not.

Chapter Thirty-nine

Provo, Utah
2:35 p.m.
April 22

Weaving, rolling from one side of the street to the other, drifting on worn suspension, the white Impala chasing Alex and Sharon closed, its bumper inches from Sharon's convertible. "Turn here!" Alex shouted. Before Sharon could react, he grabbed the wheel and turned it sharply right.

"Don't do that!" Sharon disciplined, slapping his hand and reclaiming the wheel.

Alex had sent them into a narrow alley, a turn too sharp and sudden for the big Impala. Gaining seconds while the Impala illegally "U" turned, they were out of the alley and at the intersection a block away headed north by the time the Impala came after them.

"Left!" Alex shouted, though she was only a foot away from him. "Go back in the direction we just came. Hurry!"

Flooring the turbocharged accelerator, going seventy on two lane streets limited to thirty-five, Sharon passed two cars on her right. Both lanes full, she jumped the curb and passed the next cars from the sidewalk, grateful there were no poles or pedestrians.

She barreled down the street that went past their motel and through the intersection. Half a block further, she turned into an uncovered, street level parking lot between two single-story, wood structures, drove out the other side and onto the adjacent street.

Outside the alley, the Impala circled like a dog that lost its scent, its occupants studying every possible exit.

Two blocks to the right, another to the left, then right again, Sharon sped to the end of town. They were miles from the hotel when she came back onto the highway from which they started. Nervously checking the rear view mirrors for the Impala, she and Alex traveled south. "Think we lost them?" she asked.

"For now, but I don't think we dare go back to the motel. Do you have anything there you can't do without?"

Sharon patted the seal brown, Gucci purse she kept on the console between them. "No, I've got everything I need right here."

"Then let's get to that storage facility and find Wayne's medallion."

On a brush covered hill, on undeveloped land, Sharon and Alex knelt in the dirt, peering across the highway at the storage facility where Wayne and Kim's belongings were taken. The entrance was about a thousand feet from them. A mile north of there they had turned off the highway onto a gravel road and followed it west for at lease two miles. They backtracked on a branching dirt road that led them to the back of this hill where they hid the car among a forest of scrub oak and sagebrush.

As they studied the facility, scrub oak all around them, Alex impatiently observed, "I can't see any detail from here."

"If we get any closer, they'll see us."

"We need binoculars," he muttered, knowing there were none. Resigning himself to the conditions, he sighed. "So which unit do you think their things are in?"

Sharon pointed, inviting his gaze to follow her finger. "See the gate and entrance road?"

"Yeah."

"See where the access road ends in a 'T' in front of the buildings running north and south? Now look south about seventy feet. I'm almost certain their belongings are in one of those two units."

"How many guards did you say there were?"

"Two."

"Any dogs?"

"I didn't see any."

"Any geese?"

"Geese?" she asked, skeptically.

"They raise a hell of a racket when strangers come near and make for cheap alarm systems. They'd be perfect in an area like this."

"I didn't see any."

"Good. Were the guards armed?"

"Yes, they had handguns. Couldn't tell if they had any rifles or shotguns."

"You say those rolls of wire on top of the fence are concertina? Razor wire?"

"Afraid so."

"Go-oo-oo-d," he said, sarcastically. "What do we do 'til dark? Buy bandages?"

"We go to a hardware store."

The moon was but a silver trace in the sky. At the farthest point away from the guardhouse, the southeast corner of the storage facility, Sharon and Alex knelt in powdery dirt next to the chain link fence. A million stars were their source of light.

"Ready?" Alex whispered. With gardening gloves, so there would be no finger prints, he used a pair of heavy, twenty-four-inch bolt cutters to snip a hole through the fence. They wriggled through it on their bellies. "You know these are the only clothes we have?" he mentioned, watching them collect dust.

"Don't worry," she told him. "When we're finished, I'll take you back to that general store and get you a pair of their nice, canvas overalls."

Grinning, he extended his hand to help her to her feet. "Just let's get this over with quickly," he said. Stealthily moving along the south end of the rows of buildings, he and Sharon were unaware they had already been detected by the silent alarm, a red light that was steadily blinking inside the guard house.

"Hey, Bud, ya' got any mustard?" Jack Hansen, one of the night guards, asked of his partner. "I keep tellin' my wife I like mustard, and she keeps forgettin'."

"Guess you'd better trade her in," Bud teased, digging a small package of it out of his lunch pail.

They weren't in the guard house. They were next to the gate having dinner, sitting on folding chairs. The silent, blinking red light would have gone unheeded but for their other partner. Sitting beside them at the gate, her nose in the air, Bud's Doberman sniffed.

"Try this unit first," Sharon said, as they got to the first of the two she thought housed Wayne and Kim's belongings.

Alex quickly cut the "U" shaped bar on the padlock, lifted the garage style door, and peered inside. "Recognize anything?" he asked. The room was packed floor to ceiling with furniture and boxes.

"Yes, that's Kim's vanity," she said of a birch piece with scrolled wood holding a large, gilded-edged mirror.

"So where do we start?"

"Wayne would probably have kept any secrets papers he had in the furniture from his study."

"Do you see any of it?"

Sharon carefully looked through the darkness at the tangle of belongings that only days earlier made Kim's house a home. "That's his desk on the left. His credenza's just underneath."

"See his file cabinet?"

"Must be further back."

Out at the gate, the Doberman was getting restless. "Just go pee over there," Bud told her, not wanting to be bothered. He had tied a loop in her leather leash to shorten it. He untied the loop to appease her. She bound to the end of the leash and pulled. She started pawing. Frustrated, she looked at him, "Maybe I'd better take her."

"Go outside the fence for a change," Jack said. "I get tired of picking up that shit."

"All right. Come on, Sheila, let's take a walk down the road." The dog paused, resisted his pull on the leash, then reluctantly came with him, always obedient to her master.

In the middle of the facility, fully exposed to anyone who might look back there, Sharon and Alex pulled from the unit boxes and chairs, cabinets, lamps and toys. When they reached Wayne's desk they searched the drawers and the veneer, the back and the bottom and found nothing. They moved half a dozen other pieces of furniture and boxes to free the credenza.

"Here!" Sharon said, trying to quiet her excitement. There was something jutting from a narrow crevice carved in the back left corner, half-an-inch wide, two-inch-long links of a fine, gold chain. Sharon pulled on them and the entire chain fell out of the crevice, along with Wayne's gold medallion.

"Let's get out of here," Alex urged, barely acknowledging her find.

Outside the facility's chain link fence, Bud was being dragged south along the fence line by Sheila. "Where you goin', girl?" he asked the powerful Doberman. She started running, and he knew. "Somebody out there?" he asked through the darkness, finally alert. "Jack!" he yelled. "Intruders!" Trying to keep up, he ran as the Doberman dragged him to a two-foot-square hole in the fence and squeezed through it. Unable to easily get himself through, he turned her loose and off she went. Following Alex and Sharon's scents, racing down and around the buildings, she was soon out of sight.

An instant later, as Bud crawled through the hole after her, shots were fired.

Chapter Forty
Wasatch Mountains
Late October 1856

Following two weeks of struggling through treacherous, snow choked, mountain passes and harsh winter storms, the rescuers from Salt Lake City found the first company of handcart immigrants, sick and starving. So many of the immigrants were in such critical need of help the rescuers could spare only a few men to look for stragglers and the hundreds of immigrants behind them. The dangers and hardships of going further into the mountains were obvious, and only John and four other men volunteered.

After days of traveling through miles of snow in country covered with sagebrush and roaming wolves, John and the four, with only one wagon of supplies with them, discovered a second large party of converts. That party was worse off than the first. With little food, their bodies had almost wasted away. They had trudged for days through mud and snow with no fire to warm them. Fifty of them had died, and the survivors could barely move.

John and the other rescuers eagerly handed out quilts and blankets, buffalo robes and food, but the supplies they carried were no more than a few sandbags to a river overflowing, not nearly enough. Even so, to the immigrants, John and the other men were saviors. While the converts huddled together beneath scant covers, the five rescuers went searching for fuel, gathering anything that would burn to make fires. It was dark before campfires, big as bonfires, lit the mountain skies. It was a few hours longer before the rescuers could feed the starving hot food.

The beef, potatoes, onions and biscuits for that meal were half the food supplies they brought. Without more food and dry clothing, the immigrants could not walk much further. Those with carts would not be able to push them. Additional wagons and supplies were on their way from Salt Lake City, but that help would not reach them in time. More converts would die.

John could carry only a dozen people in his wagon, but nearly forty of them were too weak to walk. He knew they could not save all of them, and he was heartsick. He considered taking one of the horses and riding back down the trail to see if he could hurry the rescuers behind them, but the rescuers were too far away and the trail much too dangerous for him to travel it by himself. Besides, he already knew the rescue teams were coming as fast as they could. The immigrants needed rest, yet if they tarried too long they would die. They would have to risk losing the very weak and move out tomorrow.

He threw more brush on one of the fires. As he turned away a small, frail hand touched his arm.

"Excuse me," a gaunt, exhausted woman stood beside him, her eyes dark and hollow from weeks of hunger. "Has anyone told you that there's a family back there?"

"Back where?" John asked.

So weak she could barely lift her hand, she pointed vaguely in the direction of the trail. "We left them about two days ago. A nice family with a sweet little girl and a very sick baby." A tear fell to her cheek. "We had to leave them. They couldn't keep up with us. We told them we'd send them help if any came. Has anyone told you?" She seemed frantic, almost desperate that they had been forgotten.

John sensed she was too weak to hear that no one had said anything about them, so he told her,"Yes, I'm going back for them first thing in the morning. You wouldn't happen to know how far back they are, would you?"

Looking confused, starvation having taken it's toll, she shook her head. "Five miles? Ten? I don't know!" she cried. "Maybe you should ask someone else."

"Thank you," John said, "I will. Now, don't you worry about them. I'll find them."

She smiled, nodded as she put her total faith in him, and turned away.

Walking out of the firelight and to the trail, John stared east, into the hostile winter darkness. Into that country, where wolves and weather had already taken so many lives, he would have to go alone.

The sun was an icy blur above the trail east as John rode out of camp the next morning. His wagon, filled to capacity with survivors, was to go in the opposite direction to Salt Lake City. The bay horse he rode belonged to the man who would drive it. Packed in the bay's saddle bags were only the absolute necessities: a small sack of hardtack and jerky, a tin of coffee, a few stick matches, a tin cup, a blanket roll, a hand ax, and some extra ammunition. A loaded rifle was in the saddle holster. A canteen wrapped in cow hide hung from the saddle horn.

Behind John were campfires, haloed in the heavy air, burning as if beacons for his return. Yet those fires would be put out soon, and there would be no beacon. The converts could not wait for him.

For the sake of the sick and weary, John hoped the trail ahead of them would be easier and that not many more of the immigrants would die. He also hoped they would not get too far ahead of him. A lump stuck in his throat as he thought of Anna, Lizzy, and his mother. If he was alone in this wilderness too long, he would die. He looked to see if the campfires were still there but could no longer see them. A bitter cold wind stung his cheeks, and he put up his collar. Confronting the snow storm that was about to engulf him, he hunched his shoulders, tucked his chin, and rode onward.

Half an hour later, when the storm lifted, the well worn trail became a narrow, white ribbon between scattered brush. Steadily rising, it followed a frozen stream that suddenly became a drift several feet deep. John could have gone around, but going around would take him several miles out of his way. He could easily get lost. Preferring the security of the trail, he studied the drift. It did not look too deep. Maybe he could just ride through it.

He kicked the reluctant horse forward. The bay lunged and plunged deep into soft snow, getting stuck up to its shoulders. Whinnying and thrashing, trying to free herself, the bay panicked and, while futilely struggling, built up a sweat. Fearing he would lose his mount to pneumonia or injury, John got off and immediately sunk waist deep in the snow. Tiring, the horse calmed. The only way out was for John to dig them out.

Scooping the snow out by hand, he dug a trench around and in front of the horse's shoulders wide enough for both of them. Once the trench was deep enough, he tugged on the reins and pulled, and the horse crashed through the snow behind him. Sinking to her thighs every time she lunged, moving only a foot at a time, as John scrambled to get out of her way, she followed him to freedom. Lathered, trembling from the exertion she expended to get out of the drift, the bay stumbled and fell on the trail. Afraid she would freeze up, leaving John stranded, he urged her to stand, pushed her to her feet, then dried her neck with his coat sleeve. Continuing on foot, he lead her.

It was nearly dark when the stream and trail bent north through a grove of cottonwoods. Snow frozen to his legs, his feet like ice blocks, John finally stumbled and fell too. If they did not stop now, the wilderness would claim them. He peered up the trail on the off chance he would see the family for which he searched. Bleak and dismal, the trail up ahead held nothing, portended nothing but death. If he did not find them soon, he would have to turn back.

"Guess they'll be just you and me tonight," he told the horse. Disheartened, he wondered how much farther they could go and still get back. He wondered if they could go any further at all. They were exhausted. He led the horse to a clearing about twenty feet off the road, tied her to a tree, and started kicking snow to clear enough ground to make a fire. He was lucky. The snow was shallow beneath the trees, and in the trees there were plenty of dead branches. He would not have to hunt for fuel.

The fire crackled as John decided whether to leave the saddle and blankets on the horse or take them off. If he made the wrong choice, she could die from pneumonia. Deciding she would be warmer without the wet blankets, as long as she stayed near the fire, he tied her to log a few feet away. As he reached for the blanket roll, he saw through the firelight a wagon frame blanketed in snow. It was lame, the wheel broken, and it was a handcart!

"My God," he said under his breath as he ran to it. Frantically searching for survivors, he pawed through the snow, but the wagon was empty. Looking in the shadows, he saw a snow covered blanket at the base of a tree. Something moved underneath it. "Hey!" he yelled, running for it. "Anybody there?"

"Help," a feeble voice whispered.

Throwing off the snow, he lifted a corner of the blanket. Beneath it was a weak, emaciated, young woman.

"Help us, please." In her arms, was a very still, red haired child of about four. Beside her was a man, his hat pulled low over his face, his body wrapped about her like a quilt. Neither of them moved. Their situation was desperate.

"Don't worry, I'll get you warm," he promised. I'll get another blanket and be right back." He hurried through the snow, fetched the blanket and returned. If only he could have brought one more.

For six feet around, he kicked a clearing in the snow. Cutting down a likely branch, he quickly split kindling. He forgot his own fatigue and had a second fire started and snow melting for hot water in no time. "I'll have coffee for you before you know it," he promised the woman when he again peered beneath the blankets. Counting his blanket, there were only three: two blankets on top of them and one beneath them. No wonder they were freezing. He hung the top blankets over a nearby branch and began to untangle the survivors.

"Please don't move him," the woman pleaded, when John reached for her husband's arm. "He died this afternoon but still stayed with us, covering us, protecting us." Her tears had frozen in her eyes, and she could no longer cry.

"What about her?" John asked, fearfully gesturing toward the child.

"Maybella," the woman whispered, "wake up." Panicking, she forcefully prodded her, shouting, "Maybella!"

"Let me," John said, as he knelt in the snow. "Maybella!" he yelled, firmly patting her cheek.

Slowly and haltingly, the little girl opened her hazel green eyes then closed them again. She was nearly frozen, but she was alive.

Gently cradling her in his arms, John took her to the fire, sat her on a heavy tree branch nearby and awakened her. Making sure she was strong enough to sit up by herself for a moment, he fetched the only dry blanket and wrapped it around her. "You stay awake," he ordered her, making his voice stern so she would mind him. "I've got to get your mother."

When John had both of them sitting on the branch next to the fire, both wrapped in the blanket, he went for the horse. Closing the first campsite, he covered the fire with snow. He would reclaim the fuel after the embers cooled.

The woman had warmed and was softly crying when he returned. Motioning toward the cart, through thawing tears, she mumbled, "My baby."

John had forgotten the old woman told him there was baby, but from its mother's expression, he knew he had come too late.

In the bed of the cart, covered with several inches of snow and swathed in a white linen petticoat, was a three month old baby, thin and frozen. It was so small he had missed it the first time he searched through the cart. John uncovered it, stroked its frozen head, and said a prayer. He walked back to the fire without it. "I'm sorry. Do you want to hold him while I make you and Maybella something to eat?"

Her face cast in an internal shadow, the woman looked longingly at the cart and then at her dead husband. Looking away, she wrapped her arms around Maybella.

John did not push her. He waited, but she did not answer him. When he realized she was not going to respond, he asked her, "How about a cup of coffee?"

"Yes, thank you, please."

"My name's John," he said, as he poured. "The party you were traveling with is being taken care of and is up ahead." There was no need to tell her people in it had died and were dying. She had enough to deal with here. "They sent me to find you."

In her dull eyes and faint smile was heartache as she put the cup to Maybella's lips and let her sip. "I'm Opal."

The moonless night was crowded with brilliant stars as John wrapped one of the man's spare shirts around an arms-length branch and set the cloth on fire for a torch. Behind a cluster of trees about fifty feet from the fire, he balanced the torch between two small boulders and went back for the bodies.

The ground was frozen solid, too hard to dig, so he laid the baby and his father on the ground and covered them by hand with several feet of snow. The grave would not keep the bodies from the wolves but would spare them long enough for John to get Opal and Maybella out of sight before the wolves came. It was something John vowed never to tell them.

Opal and Maybella were not able to travel until mid morning. When they were ready to go, John put both of them on the horse, Maybella in front of Opal, so she could hold on to her. John was again on foot, leading them.

During the night, several inches of fresh snow had fallen, then frozen. The trail John and his mount had left in coming was no help in going back. Often they had to crunch through knee deep snow. When they reached the drift that nearly swallowed them the day before, drifting snow had filled the path he and the bay had broken. It was now but a shallow depression. There was no choice but to dig it out again.

The sky was turning gray, and it was getting colder. John glanced at Opal, Maybella, and the brave, exhausted horse that carried them. Wondering if any of them would survive, he turned back to the snow drift and began to paw through it.

Chapter Forty-one

Wasatch Mountains
Late October 1856

In the second week of November, riders came galloping into Salt Lake City announcing the imminent return of the first group of rescuers, John's group. Expecting to see him, Hattie and Lizzy rushed to the Temple site.

At the edge of town, Anna waited with scores of other women, ready with meats, bread, vegetables, medicinal herbs, and bandages for the new converts. Imagining John's arms about her, strong and caring, and the passion she would share with him that night, Anna's eyes searched in the distance for him. She could barely contain herself when she saw the first wagons crossing the flat toward town.

Weighted down by the individual tragedies inside them, the wagons strung out for miles. The converts had lost sons, husbands, fathers, wives and daughters. Those who survived were nearly starved. Most suffered from frostbite. Many had lost a finger, foot, or hand. Some would make the journey into the city only to die there. Overloaded with gaunt, fragile souls, the wagons lumbered into town. The few handcarts that made it were interspersed between them. Frail, exhausted men and women who had wagered against death, unwilling to leave their few possessions behind, pushed them.

Women like Anna, Hattie, and Lizzy who waited anxiously for loved ones who had gone into the wilderness to rescue them, received the converts into their capable hands. It took hours for the entire train to reach them.

At long last, at sunset, John arrived, thin and exhausted. He was with the last of the converts, walking beside his overloaded wagon. Burned raw by the winter sun, his face was peeling. His lips were cracked and bleeding. Though his dark beard, curly and thick, was nearly two inches long, he looked wonderful to Anna.

She ran to him, with Hattie and Lizzy behind her. Wrapping her arms around his neck, she squeezed.

"Why, you're nothing but a skeleton," Hattie observed, when she crowded Anna aside and hugged him. As Lizzy took her turn with him, Hattie looked into his wagon and sighed. The wagon reeked of cold, rotting meat and of dying. Inside, were a dozen men, women, and children who could barely move. "Go home, John, we'll take care of them from here." She pecked him on the cheek and was off, yelling to the nearly two dozen other Church women scurrying toward her, "I need help over here."

"Welcome home," Anna whispered to John. "What can I get for you?" As she stood in front of him, her heart was exposed, her body ready for him. Yet, he did not care.

His blue eyes were cold and distant, and he did not look at her. He was looking back toward the mountains where hundreds more converts were struggling.

"John?" Anna interrupted. "Can I get you anything?"

"No, nothing. Not now," he said brusquely. "I've gotta' help with the stock."

There was something far more important going on than her feelings. Anna understood, but was crushed.

"Let some of the other men get the stock. The ones that didn't go," Hattie told him. She had come back to check on him. "You need food and rest."

He smiled at her protectiveness, though only faintly. "Don't worry, Mum, it won't take long. Do what you can to help these people. When you're finished, we'll all go home together." He glanced fleetingly at Anna. "I want to say goodbye to someone." Turning away from her, he walked to the front of the wagon and climbed inside.

Hurt that John had discarded her, Anna watched for his return, wondering who could be so important to him in the wagon. Her hands idle, she was handed a three or four month old baby, so cold its lips were blue. John would have to wait. "I'd better get you inside," she told the baby, heading for one of the stake houses in which the converts were being cared for.

A woman peered out of the back of John's wagon, looking for help to get down. Her hands were black from frostbite. Hattie immediately responded. Emaciated, the woman was so light Hattie lifted her out of the wagon by herself. Putting her arm around her to steady her, Hattie walked her toward help.

"John," she yelled, as she walked away. "Come with me to the stake house. Get something to eat. If it gets too late, go on home without us. No use you hangin' around here."

John responded from inside the wagon, "Yes, Mum."

It was hours later and near midnight. John restlessly waited for his family outside the stake house, yet his impatience was not with them. Obsessed with what he had not finished, he stared through the darkness at the shadowy reflection of the moonlit mountains. The converts still up there were dying, and he could do nothing to help them.

Inside the stake house, Anna hurried, eager to be with him. While other women bathed and bandaged the rescued converts, saw to their ailments, and got them into clean clothes, she, Hattie and Lizzy helped feed them and make up blanket beds for them on the benches and floor. The iron stove was stoked with as much fuel as its belly could handle, and the room was suffocatingly hot.

"Let the women who are fresher get them settled," Annie told Hattie and Lizzy as they finished. "We've got to get John home."

Though Anna wanted desperately to tell him how much she loved him, she would not get the chance, at least not right away. Once home, Hattie gave him a plate of cold beans and bread to tide him over while he rested and she made stew. For Anna, minutes dragged into hours, her impatience simmering with the stew. John was so tired he slept. Hattie and Lizzy were so happy he was home, they made no effort to give Anna time alone with him. When the stew was ready, Hattie woke John to eat with them. It was nearly daylight.

His appetite dampened by the food Hattie gave him and by utter exhaustion, John was oblivious to the sensual frustration flaring in Anna. He quietly ate his stew, went back to bed and slept until well after dark. Sitting in the rocker, smoking his pipe after supper, he stared blankly at the fire.

Lizzy was sitting on the stool next to him. holding his hand. "What was it like out there?"

Thoughtful, hesitant at first to talk about it, then seemingly relieved he could finally share the burden he carried, John took a deep breath and exhaled. "I've never seen a place on land so cold and deadly." His eyes widened. "Wind scooped up rocks of ice and drove them at us, stinging us like the bejesus. The snow was waist deep in places. Sometimes it came up as high as our chins, burying nearly everything around."

Thinking back to the days he was alone with Opal and Maybella, out of matches, trying to catch the rescuers ahead of them, he told Lizzy, "There was no way to get warm or dry, and our clothes froze to us. Our feet got numb, and our fingers burned. Those poor souls who spent weeks out there before we found them, were..." His voice trailed off. For a moment he left his family, his mind and heart venturing again into the mountains. Talking, though not necessarily to them, he continued, "...were nothing but frozen shadows. Spirits pushed carts loaded with the sick and dying through blizzards and ice, – only to drop dead when they stopped. Children, three and four years old, plodded through snow and mud up to their knees, and felt it freeze on them at night. Before we reached them, a little girl woke up screaming one night to find her brother eating her fingers. When they pulled her away from him, he started eating his own fingers and died before morning."

John covered his tormented eyes with his hands. "It was awful."

Feeling his pain, Anna yearned to hold him but knew he was still in the mountains with those struggling there. He was not thinking of her.

"So many of them have suffered and died," he continued. "So many more of them are in pain and have lost everything they have. Some have nothing and no one left." He looked imploringly at Anna, his deep, blue eyes a well of empathy. "I want us to help."

Powerfully moved and distressed by his story, Anna listened, eager to do for them, share with them almost anything. Yet, she was caught off guard when he announced, "There's someone I want you to meet."

He paused as Anna's expression changed, as her eager eyes turned cold. When he continued, he spoke very softly. "She's lost everyone and everything she knows, and I'd like her to become part our family."

He might just as well have punched Anna in the chest. Jason and Jeremy were right. Another woman had stolen John's fancy, taken her place in his heart. That was why he had ignored her. In pain, she cringed. She knew she had no right to cry, yet tears welled in her eyes. Bravely containing her grief, hating the question she must ask, she forced a smile. "Who is she?"

Hattie, too, guessed what John was up to, and she challenged him. "If you think I'm going to sit back and let you bring another wife into this house, you're sadly mistaken."

"Another wife?" he asked, a sudden confusion in his eyes. He paused, then broke out laughing. "Have Jacob and Jeremy been here?"

"Yes," Hattie said, "they came a few days after you left and told us you were thinking about taking a second wife."

John chuckled. "I gotta admit I told them I'd think about the idea, but that was only to stall them. I had to give myself time to figure out how I was gonna say, 'no.' I don't want any part of that business." He looked at Anna. "You didn't take them seriously, did you?"

She felt a rush of relief, and without her being able to stop them, the tears that filled her eyes rolled down her cheeks. Sheepishly laughing, she told him, "I guess I did."

He came over and knelt beside her, putting his arm around her.

"She was worried sick," Hattie told him. "Thought she was gonna get the apoplexy. Why didn't you warn us?"

His eyes were as soft as a newborn calf's as he gazed at Anna. "You were worried?"

She lowered her eyes and bashfully nodded. "All of us were."

He stood, reached for her hand, and drew her up to him. "I'm sorry," he gently told her, brushing back her hair.

Her heart melting with his touch, she put her arms around his neck and embraced him. "Welcome home," she whispered, kissing him.

The mood quickly turned joyous. But as Hattie buzzed about trying to get tea for everyone, Lizzy brought them back to the subject, "Then, who is this woman you want us to meet?"

His arm securely around Anna's waist, John grinned. "No woman at all. She's a very little girl, about this high." He flattened his palm and held it thigh high. She was orphaned on the trail."

"What's her name?"

"Maybella."

He somberly told them about Opal and Maybella. "Opal seemed to doing fine," he continued, after he told about finding them, "but I was really worried about Maybella. By the time we reached the other converts in her party, she was in such a sound sleep her mother and I could hardly wake her. I didn't think she'd live through the night." John turned to the fire, relit his pipe, and returned to stand beside Anna. "We must have woke Maybella a dozen times that night, giving her a little broth any time she'd take some. Opal was exhausted but wouldn't sleep until she knew Maybella was all right. By morning, she was almost as bad as Maybella.

"The food was short, and the weather was getting worse. We could see a storm coming in, but the train had to move. I put Opal and Maybella in our wagon with the other converts, and we headed off. We were trying to get beyond the storm, hoping we'd meet up with the supply wagons coming from Salt Lake, but the going was real slow. It snowed and blowed so hard we couldn't see the trail. We didn't make three miles that day and took cover as best we could on the trail.

"Maybella woke up on her own, but she wasn't very talkative. She took a little biscuit with broth, and while she rested, I got Opal to sleep. Everything might have been fine if a little boy hadn't died that night.

"We didn't know it, but Opal followed us out into the woods to watch us bury him. She saw us put him in the snow and was listening. She heard one of the men telling us about a man he'd found off the trail a few miles behind of us. He'd been buried in the snow then dug up by wolves. His body was torn in chunks and half eaten. We talked about the same thing happening to that boy we was burying. We didn't know Opal was listening until we turned back toward camp and saw her there, her eyes kinda' wild.

"I took her back to the wagon and tried to convince her the wolves wouldn't get her husband and baby, but she didn't believe me. She wasn't the same after that. She cried all the next day, and when she stopped, she wouldn't talk to me. I couldn't get her to eat or sleep. – Or even take care of Maybella. She just stared back at the trail, back to where we left them."

John's gaze fixed on the floor as he recalled, "I should have stayed up with her that night, but I was so tired I couldn't.

"She was gone by morning. Picked up and left. Put her blanket and coat around Maybella and took off back down the trail toward where I found her. I tried to follow, but her trail disappeared in the drifts. I searched for her for days. Even went back to the graves she must have been looking for, but I never found her. Probably wondered off the trail somewhere, got lost, and froze to death. Doubt if she got more than a mile." He paused. "Maybe if I'd...." He seemed to be going over in his mind all the things he might have done but did not, blaming himself for her loss.

"When you found the graves," Lizzy asked, "had the wolves been there?"

His brow creased as he slowly looked up at her, the trauma of the discovery in his eyes. "Best for all of us not to think about that," he told her. "Best just think of Maybella."

"Where is she?" Anna asked.

"At Elder Ira's with the family that cared for her after her mother died. They wanted to adopt her but can't. The father died before we got here, and they have nothing."

Anna's heart overflowed with love for John and the little girl he saved. "Don't you worry about Maybella," she promised. "We'll take her."

The next morning, in Elder Ira's parlor, while a dozen women and children stared at them from a few feet away, Anna and John sat on a fancy sofa nervously watching the stairs. Ira's youngest wife, a girl of seventeen, was standing next to them holding a ceramic, rose patterned pot. "More tea?" she offered.

"No, thank you. We've had plenty," Anna said. She took John's matching cup and saucer and set it beside her own on the polished walnut table to her left.

What seemed like hours later, a woman came down the stairs with a little girl about four, whose red hair was tied back in a faded blue ribbon. She was only a little more than three feet tall and looked pale and very thin. Her every step was tentative, and she clung to the woman's hand. She had been scrubbed and fed, then dressed in an old, blue dress that had belonged to one of Ira's daughters. It hung on her like a sack. The only thing that belonged to her was her shoes, ragged pieces of leather that looked like they had been chewed by a dog.

Seemingly reluctant to see what was ahead of her, the little girl did not look until she heard John's familiar voice. "Hello, Maybella." Instantly recognizing him, she brightened, let go of the woman's hand and ran to him.

"How's my girl?" he asked, scooping her into his arms.

She wrapped her legs and arms around him, held him tight, and beamed.

"This is my wife, Anna," he said.

Peering out of the corner of her eye, Maybella ventured a look.

Anna felt awkward. Trying to make Maybella feel at ease, she approached her slowly and gently patted her back. "We've come to take you home."

Her short life a tangle of tragedy, all Maybella wanted was love and security. Her dull, hazel eyes searched for it in Anna.

"You're going to come live with us and be our daughter," Anna promised, smiling. "You'll have an older sister and a grandma, too. Have you ever had a grandma?"

Maybella's eyes got bigger, and she nodded, the trace of a smile on her lips.

"She's making you pie for dinner."

Maybella's grip relaxed, and John put her down. While she still held his hand, Anna gently helped her with the coat one of Ira's wives had given her.

"We have a little party planned," Anna told her. "Do you like dogs?"

Maybella's smile broadened, and when Anna offered her hand, she accepted it. Their hands linked, their lives forever entwined, Maybella grinned as the three of them
 left the house.

Chapter Forty-two

The Storage Facility
Provo, Utah
12:10 a.m.
Friday, April 23

Heart pounding, gun drawn, Bud ran west, then north, along the north-south buildings, following the sound of shots. Outside the storage unit Sharon and Alex had searched, Jack, the second security guard, was kneeling, his hand resting on the chest of a body. "Good thing I missed her," Jack said of Sheila, Bud's Doberman. Sheila was on her back, exposing her stomach, submissive to the man who had nearly killed her. "I thought she was the intruder," he told Bud.

Seconds before the Doberman found the first hole Alex had cut in the perimeter fence, Alex was cutting a second on the north side, through which he and Sharon escaped. By the time he and Sharon heard the guard's shots, they were across the road and hundreds of feet away. Momentarily safe in the darkness, they ran south toward the car.

Later, in a grimy, roadside diner, miles from the storage unit, Alex held Wayne's gold medallion between his fingers while he and Sharon examined it. "Quite a coin ya got there," a big man, waiter, host and cook, observed as he peered over Alex's shoulder. The man's big forearms, covered with old and fuzzy tattoos, were bared. His hands were paw like. "Where'd you get it?"

"Belonged to my brother," Alex offered.

"Is it gold?"

"Nah, just cheap plate," Alex told him, trying to sound local. "Keepin' it as a memento."

Immediately losing interest in the object, the big man plopped two, one page-two sided, plastic covered menus on the table. "Let me know when you're ready to order."

It was four o'clock in the morning. They were somewhere north of Provo on a back road that was supposed to take them through American Fork on their way to Salt Lake City. The diner was the only place open for miles. Open twenty-four hours a day, every day, it specialized in grease that found its way into every corner and in pies kept unrefrigerated on open shelves. It was the perfect spot to talk, for they were the only customers.

"Breakfast or dinner?" Alex asked, flipping the menu over, remembering he had not eaten for nearly a day.

Trying to ignore the filthy floor, purposely not thinking about the kitchen, Sharon looked critically at the window sill, its corners packed with aged crescents of grime. It didn't matter, she was starved. "Dinner," she said, turning the menu over and calling the big man over. "A club house sandwich," she ordered, when he came back.

"Cheeseburger," Alex said.

Not to be insulting, Sharon delayed until the waiter was in the kitchen cooking before taking from her purse a two ounce bottle of hand sanitizer. Liberally spreading the gel over the window sill and table, she wiped them acceptably clean with the handful of cheap paper napkins she took from the metal dispenser next to the salt. After wiping down the shakers and ketchup bottle, she sat back, satisfied and ready to talk. "Have you ever seen anything like that?" she asked Alex of the medallion.

The head of the medallion was an eagle, wings outstretched, head down, as if circling in search of prey. Tiny characters, in what appeared to be Hebrew, were engraved just under the claws. "I've seen this symbol before, at a museum when I was doing research in Israel," he told her. "The twelve tribes of Israel were divided into four brigades, and each brigade had a banner. This particular eagle was on the "Dan Brigade's" banner. Even the writing looks the same."

"Why would Wayne be wearing something like that?" Sharon asked. "Are you telling me that he belongs to the tribe of Dan and that the Mormons are Jews?"

"Not at all. Mormons consider Jews Gentiles and heretics just like the rest of us."

"Does it have something to do with Utah? Isn't there an eagle on the State's seal?" Sharon recalled.

"Yes, as a matter of fact, the eagle on Utah's seal is probably the same symbol that's on Wayne's medallion, except that it's in a different pose. It's the same pose taken by the eagle on the American Coat of Arms." Alex turned the medallion over. "You say the relief of the man on this side is 'Min'?"

"Yes, it's the same figure I saw on Wayne's urn." For the first time, Sharon looked at the figure in detail. "Is that a penis?" she asked.

Alex checked it out and grinned. "Yeah, a rather impressive one, I'd say."

Min's long penis was erect. In his left hand he carried the red crown and in his right hand, behind him, he carried a flail.

"Kim told me Min was the Beekeeper and that the Egyptians called the red crown, 'Deseret.'"

"Tell me again what Kim said about the 'Cult of the Bee,'" Alex asked.

"She told me the red crown represented the bee and that the bee bestowed on the Pharaoh the secret of reincarnation, the power over death. When Adam and Eve were expelled from the Garden of Eden, the honey they brought with them was food for their new world. "What do you think this bee cult has to do with the tribe of Dan? Or, Wayne, for that matter?"

"Beats me, but I think I know who can tell us. A professor friend of mine at Berkeley has his Ph.D. in ancient mythology. Wrote a not so best seller a few years ago entitled 'Ancient Myths in Recent History.'"

"Good, let's give him a call." Sharon reached for her smart phone and handed it to him.

"At four o'clock in the morning?" Alex questioned. "I want him to help us, not kill us. Besides, we should gather as much information as we can before we talk to him. No use going to him with bits and pieces. Maybe somebody at Wayne's lab knows something."

The George S. Eccles and Dolores Dore Eccles Institute of Human Genetics and the Eccles Program in Human Molecular Biology and Genetics were part of the University of Utah's Health Science Center, modern facilities at the heart of Utah's medical care. At 7:35 a.m, in search of Wayne's laboratory, Alex and Sharon descended stairs to the subbasement. Halfway down, they met a student in his late twenties, not so fresh from pulling an all nighter.

"Can you tell us where Doctor Wayne Hoffel's laboratory is?" Sharon asked.

"His lab was down there," the young man told them, rather wistfully. "But they packed his stuff up yesterday. Said he was taking his research to Guatemala."

"Did you know Dr. Hoffel?" Alex asked.

"Know him?" the student asked, incredulously. "I worked with him. He's the whole reason I decided to get my doctorate in biochemistry. Wish he'd told me he wasn't going to be here before I switched."

"What were you working on?" Alex nonchalantly asked.

"A new protocol for treating women prone to having babies prematurely. Dr. Hoffel was brilliant," the student said, the sparkle returning to his eyes. "Come on, I want to show you something." Without waiting for their answer, fully expecting them to follow, he bounded up the stairs.

"Ladies first." Alex smiled, gesturing upward, knowing Sharon was as exhausted as him.

She rolled her eyes, took two steps at a time up the stairs after the student, and on first floor followed him out of the building and along a walkway into the School of Medicine. Making sharp turns along long hallways and finally heading out the opposite side from which they entered, they went through a courtyard and into the University Hospital. Yet, their journey did not end there. Along clean and crowded hallways and out the northeast doors, the young man turned west, past a parking garage and went into the bowels of the Primary Children's Medical Center. On the second floor, he stopped. "In here," he said, outside a closed, neonatal care unit.

"See them?" The student pointed to four tiny babies with hands not much bigger than Alex's thumbnail. "They're premies. Babies that didn't get the benefit of Dr. Hoffel's protocol. Now, come down here." He led Alex and Sharon further down the hall and to a nursery, where more than a dozen normal-sized babies slept. "See those five in the corner? They're quintuplets. All full term and normal. Born healthy two weeks ago."

"Two weeks?" Sharon asked. "Isn't that a little long for them to still be in the hospital after a healthy birth?"

"That's part of Dr. Hoffel's protocol. Though fully developed and totally healthy, they were only five pounds each when they were born. Dr. Hoffel won't let them go home until they each weigh seven."

"What is this protocol you keep talking about?" Alex asked.

"I didn't get in on the initial research, so I don't know yet what's in the formula he gives his patients. But, treatment starts as soon as a risky pregnancy is discovered, – especially if there's going to be multiple births. I've only worked with him six months, but I've seen him handle over twenty successful births."

"All multiples?"

"Most of them."

"Any failures?"

"Just one. A little boy born with a defective heart. He was sent to cardiology immediately, but they couldn't save him. You friends of Dr. Hoffel's?"

"Yes," Alex told him, "we're traveling through the area and were hoping to catch up with him."

"Sorry." The student's enthusiasm was waning. "They said he was already in Guatemala."

The sky was a hazy, polluted blue as Alex and Sharon walked back the way they had come and toward the parking garage behind the Eccles Institute. "That was sure a waste of time," Sharon observed. "Maybe we should just go with what we have to that professor of yours."

Chapter Forty-three

Salt Lake City, Utah
February 1857

By 1857, the Temple grounds were enclosed by a high rock wall. The Temple's foundation was slowly taking shape, and the adobe Tabernacle, large enough for two-thousand people, was finished. A block away, Brigham Young's mansions, the Lion and Beehive, stood as evidence of his wealth and power. Modern and sophisticated, the city's Council House and Social Hall looked like they had been built in contemporary England. An array of other public buildings were under construction, and despite hard times, the entire city was blossoming with new businesses.

Though on the surface all seemed to be getting better, currents of trouble churned between the Mormons and Gentiles. Tensions mounted. As was encouraged by their leaders, Mormons distrusted nonbelievers and believed Federal officials were governing Utah without their consent. Tempers flared. Between Mormons and Gentiles accusatory letters were exchanged, and each dispute bred another. Gentiles declared Mormon missionaries to the Indians rude and lawless, a curse to any civilized community. Jim Bridger accused them of forcibly taking Fort Bridger from him and threatening his life. Gentiles who had Washington's ear were talking against them, and Washington was listening.

Republican politicians compared Mormon polygamy to slavery, calling them the "the twin relics of barbarism." Fearing the consequences of those accusations, the Mormons reorganized the Nauvoo Legion, the army they organized in Illinois to defend their city-state of Nauvoo, and began training a militia.

John had spent the winter working on the Temple's foundation. In exchange for his labor, he did not have to pay Church tithing. With the money John saved from that which would otherwise go to tithing, they added to the house two more rooms and a kitchen. He had been given forty acres when they arrived and, with Anna and Hattie's help, had made the most of the gift. The family was living comfortably, and their future was promising.

One night in February, John came home with news, and everything changed. They were sitting in front of the fire after supper when he told them, "I never said anything about it before," he began, "but Brothers Jacob and Jeremy weren't too happy when I told them I wouldn't take a second wife." He looked at Anna. "I didn't want them blaming you, but, seems they did anyway. Jacob got so nasty about it, I hit him."

Without telling them what Jacob had called Anna or mentioning he had knocked Jacob clear across Jeremy's study for it, John did admit, "It's all I can do to be civil to them anymore." He got up, went to the fireplace, and slowly filled and packed his pipe. Touching a stick to the fire, he lit the pipe, then told them, "I thought that was end of the matter, – but it wasn't. They've found a way to get back at us."

"How?" Anna asked, her hand clutching his arm. "What are they going to do?"

"They're making us move to Cedar City."

"Cedar City!" Hattie exclaimed. "That's more than two-hundred and fifty miles south of here."

"What about our house?" Anna asked, already fearing the answer. Seeing hurt and resignation in John's eyes, she knew, even before he told her. They would have to give up their house. "We don't have a choice, do we?"

He shook his head. "No." Lightly touching the narrow, stone mantle, he looked about the room and into his family's distraught and searching eyes. "There's nothing we can do."

"Did you try Elder Ira?" Anna hopefully asked.

John wryly nodded, his lips twisting in disgust. "Before I got a word out of my mouth, Ira congratulated me on our selection. Told me how important to the Church getting the Cedar City area populated was. Told me how we were chosen to go because Jacob and Jeremy personally recommended us, then reminded me the Church was counting on us."

"When do we have to leave?" Anna asked.

"As soon as the weather turns."

"What about all the work we put into this place?" Hattie asked.

"Are they going to let us sell it?" Anna knew from having seen other families moved that selling was not often allowed.

John rubbed his hand over his face. Shoulders drooping, face drawn, he looked into the fire. "We're expected to consecrate everything we can't take with us, including the house."

"What do you mean, 'consegrate'?" Lizzy asked.

"That means we have to give our homestead to the Church and that we get nothing for it."

"Nothing?" Hattie asked. "What are we supposed to live on?"

"We'll get along. We can keep our personal possessions, our livestock, and whatever we need to get us down there. We'll have enough to make a new start, but that's about all. It's been decided. They're drawing up the papers tonight, and in the morning I'm to sign them."

Reluctantly and out of sorts, John knocked on Jeremy's front door at midmorning. Jeremy was to handle the consecration and was to have the papers waiting. One of Jeremy's oldest sons came to the door and showed John to the study. It was a small room with pine and leather furnishings. A stuffed elk head hung over the mantle. It was the same room in which they last met and in which John slugged Jacob. To John's surprise, Jacob was there.

"Morning, Brother John," Jacob cheerfully greeted, as if nothing had happened between them. His smile was shallow, and he did not shake John's hand.

Jeremy was standing beside a small, pine desk near a window. He gave no greeting at all and wasted no time in getting to business. "The papers are drawn up and ready for you." Jeremy pointed to documents of transfer on the desk. "You probably won't understand them, but you can read them if you like."

There was much in the fine print John did not understand, but he did know this: he was giving up everything he owned except that which he could take with him in his wagon. He paused. Everything they had worked for the last two and a half years was lost. They would leave the valley with barely more than what they brought in. He did not trust Jeremy and certainly did not trust Jacob. "Has anyone else looked at this?" he asked, preferring to involve someone else.

"This is the same form we all use," Jeremy told him, "drafted and approved by the Church. There's no need for anyone else to look at it."

"But, what about this?" John pointed to a section that was incomplete, the one identifying the person to whom the property was being given.

"What about what?" Jeremy asked, impatiently.

Not to be intimidated, John held the paper up to him and pointed to the section again. "This," he said, equally impatiently. "It doesn't say who gets the property."

"The Church does," Jeremy said. "Isn't that what you agreed to do?"

"So why doesn't the paper say so?"

"Look, John," Jeremy patronizingly continued, using his hands seemingly to draw John a picture, "Brigham Young is the Church's trustee. His name will go there."

"Why isn't it there now?" John pressed.

"Because Brother Brigham prefers to complete these things himself. Doesn't he, Brother Jacob?"

"Why, yes," Jacob confirmed. "I've never known Brother Brigham to put his name to a document that hasn't been signed first."

"You see?" Jeremy pushed. "I'll take the papers to him this afternoon if you like."

"What do we need Brother Jacob for?" John pressed.

"He'll be one of the witnesses. I'll have my son be the other. We want everything to be legal, don't we?" Jeremy walked to the door, spoke to a woman outside, and returned. "He'll be here in a minute."

Though uncomfortable about signing a document that was incomplete and having Jacob be a witness, John did not see that he had a choice. Jacob and Jeremy were Church elders. He did not dare question their honesty aloud. He had already lost almost everything, there was no reason to risk losing more. He signed, and as he left, the front door closed behind him.

"The fool." Jacob grinned. He lit a cigar while Jeremy poured each of them a brandy. Stepping to the desk, joking at John's expense, they filled in the blank sections of the agreement with their own names, making John's property their own.

On the day John and Anna were to leave, a midday meeting in the Tabernacle was called. Though the meeting would delay their departure by hours, maybe even a day, their attendance was required. Brigham Young was speaking, and most urgently of all, he was speaking to them.

"I know some of you are discouraged," Brigham acknowledged. "But, keep heart. The Church is your future, the future of all people. I beseech you to have faith, to prove yourself in God's eyes. Men have come to me asking if they could serve God better by finding gold or discovering silver. I say, don't even try. We, as good members of the Church, will soon own all the wealth on earth.

"After we have conquered the world and the truths of Mormonism are universally acknowledged, we will have all the wealth we desire. In just a few years, no people but we will be alive. Gold will be as plentiful as silver, silver as plentiful as brass. There will be as much brass as stone, and stone as plenty as wood. This gold and silver and other precious metals and stones will beautify our temples and will be made our holy vessels, while each man of you will have all the wealth he can enjoy. All you need be is faithful in these days before the world is ours.

"Work for each other. Do for each other. Hold your brothers and sisters responsible for their sins and help them atone for them. If we are to rule the world, we must become independent of the Gentiles. Reject their goods. Pay them nothing. Do not rely on them or help them. Consume only what we produce. For, when the Gentiles are gone, there will be only us.

"The Gentiles suspect what we have planned, so there will be war with them. I have sent missionaries to Las Vegas to mine and smelt lead for ammunition and to Southern Utah to process iron from the mountains. To strengthen our hold on these lands and squeeze out the Gentiles, there must be additional settlement. Some of you will leave immediately. Others will follow. Be proud, for you are being sent to conquer the Kingdom of God."

Chapter Forty-four
Berkeley, California
8:00 p.m.
April 23

An hour before Alex and Sharon reached the campus of the University of California, Berkeley, Alex called his friend, Kevin. Kevin was working late and would meet them in his office.

They arrived at Dwinelle Hall, made their way through its infamously, unintelligible layout, and were at the top of the stairs on seventh floor, outside Room 7233, Classics Department. A clutch of zealous graduate students were mingled there arguing about something in Greek. Alex did not hesitate to interrupt them. "Is Professor James around?"

Obviously irritated by his interruption, one of them brusquely gestured southwest, "Corner office."

"Alex!" Kevin James greeted him warmly, when Alex and Sharon entered his office, "Haven't seen you in ages."

Kevin was an expert in mythology, and Alex tapped into his expertise whenever a story called for it. He was in his mid-forties. His long, ash blond hair was thinning, uncombed, and carelessly tied in back. His short beard was dark and unkempt, looking as if he hadn't bothered to shave for several days. He was wearing loose and ill fitting, khaki pants and an untucked, short-sleeved, tan shirt with brown and black snake designs.

"This is Sharon Marshall," Alex introduced. "We need your help."

"Come on in. Sit down," Kevin invited, seating himself behind his cluttered desk.

Alex told Kevin of Kim and Wayne's disappearances, what happened at the storage facility, and of the two men in the Impala chasing them. He handed Kevin the mysterious gold medallion but did not give him a chance to examine it, shoving at him the list of cryptic numbers.

"Samson Project – Inventory," Kevin read aloud from the list. "I'll have to take some time with this," he told them, setting it aside. He picked up the gold medallion and briefly examined both sides. Instantly recognizing the figures impressed on them, he asked, "You say the man who owned and hid this was Mormon? Wayne did you say his name was? It's Wayne and his wife who are missing? Right?"

"Yes, do you know what the figures mean?"

"I do happen to know," Kevin told them. "Symbols of the eagle and bee are nothing new to Mormons or to the State of Utah. Harry Edwards used both of them in designing the state's seal way back in 1896. The only difference is that the Mormon's use a beehive as the bee symbol rather than the red crown that appears on this medallion. The beehive is one of the Mormon's oldest symbols.

"I'll show you." Kevin walked to the large bookshelf beside the door and took from it the Book of Mormon. Quickly thumbing through it, looking for a particular phrase, he paused at Ether 2:3, reading, "'and they did also carry with them deseret, which by interpretation, is a honey bee: and thus they did carry with them swarms of bees.'"

Kevin explained. "The original Deseret people were the people who migrated to Egypt from the Middle East and created Egypt's civilization. The Egyptians they became claimed that their king, and he alone, possessed the secret of resurrection, – the Bee its symbol. They called their king, their land and their empire, 'Deseret,' meaning the thing that first nourishes when an old world is destroyed and new one begun. Deseret was also the name the Mormons gave to the nation state they tried to cut out of the western United States in the mid-eighteen hundreds.

"Min, the figure on the medallion holding the red crown, the Deseret, could mean a number of things. But, that eagle, the symbol of the Tribe of Dan, when linked to the Mormons, means only one thing. It's referring to the Sons of Dan.

"Who are the Sons of Dan?" Sharon asked.

"The Sons of Dan was a group of thugs organized by Joseph Smith around 1838 to do his dirty work. Smith was in all kinds of trouble. The Gentiles knew him as a scoundrel and an adulterer who claimed he was having conversations with God. They threatened him and his followers and completely forced them out of Independence, Missouri in the mid 1830's. His settlement in Kirtland, Ohio didn't do so well, either, so he started a bank and began issuing his own paper currency. When he stopped making payment on the paper he issued, that bank failed. People lost substantial sums of money and weren't very happy with him. Some of them sued him. Members of the Church began dropping away, and when the Kirtland settlement collapsed, he fled to Far West, Missouri.

"By 1838, the Church was in serious financial trouble. Smith decided to remedy the problem by requiring all of his followers to transfer their property to the Church. When some of them refused, he called them 'dissenters' and turned on them. Choosing only zealous followers who thrived on violence, he formed the Sons of Dan to drive the dissenters out. Blood was spilled, and when the job inside the Church was done, the Sons of Dan turned against enemies outside the Church.

"That turning point seemed to be Sidney Rigdon's Salt Sermon in 1838." Squint eyed, Kevin peered across the room at the cluttered bookshelf next to the door. "I think I have that speech here somewhere." His gaze focused on a dusty, voluminous, paperback on the bottom shelf. "There," he pointed. "Would you mind, Alex? Bottom shelf, eighth from the left."

He thumbed quickly through the well worn pages. "Sidney Rigdon was one of two counselors to Joseph Smith, which made him part of the First Presidency. It also made him very powerful. Whatever Rigdon said was as good as if it had come from the Prophet himself. First turning against, then threatening the remaining Mormon dissenters, Rigdon borrowed a portion of the Sermon on the Mount and told them, 'Ye are the salt of the earth; but if the salt have lost his savor, wherewith shall it be salted? It is thenceforth good for nothing, but to be cast out, and to be trodden under the foot of men.' Rigdon put his foot in something brown and foul and turned on the Gentiles, vowing they would trample on the Mormons no more, basically declaring a war of extermination against them. The Mormons were to attack the Gentiles and their families in their homes and follow them until the last drop of Gentile blood was spilled. They were to keep killing until one party or the other was utterly destroyed."

Kevin silently scanned the rest of Rigdon's speech, then read from its conclusion: "'This day, then, proclaim ourselves free with a purpose and determination that never can be broke. No, never! No, never! No, never!' As Rigdon intended," Kevin told them, looking up from the speech, "dissenters within the Church become a mortal threat, and Gentiles took his words as a declaration of war. Dissenters were killed, and the war between Mormons and Gentiles intensified. If the Mormon's did not do everything they were told to do, or they did not keep their deeds secret, they would forfeit their lives. The Sons of Dan became the Army of Elohim and the scourge of anyone who got in the way."

"Why did they chose the name 'Dan'?" Alex asked.

Kevin turned in his chair and took a bible from one of the few shelves behind him. Turning to Jeremiah 8: 15-17, he read:

"'We looked for peace, but no good came; and for a time of health, and behold trouble! 'The snorting of his horses was heard from Dan: the whole land trembled at the sound of the neighing of his strong ones; for they are come, and have devoured the land, and all that is in it; the city, and those that dwell therein.'" Kevin looked up from the pages. "The Sons of Dan were going to wipe the dissenters and Gentiles from the earth." He paused for effect, then told them, they were called the 'Sons of Dan' or 'Danites' mostly through the late 1830s and 40s. Once out West, when they were working for Brigham Young, they became 'Destroying' or 'Avenging Angels.'"

"Avenging Angels?" Sharon blurted. "I remember my grandmother talking about the Avenging Angels, something about Great Grandfather John and bad things."

"She say anything else? Like, what 'bad things'?" Alex asked.

"That's all I remember. I'll call Mother. See if she knows anything about them."

"Be careful," Kevin told them, "This medallion of Wayne's isn't an old one from out of your grandmother's past. From the looks of it, it's brand new."

"You mean to tell us Wayne belongs to a group that descended from the Sons of Dan and the Avenging Angels? That he's a murderer like they were?"

Kevin hesitated. "I hate to believe it, but at the very least, it looks like the Sons of Dan may well have been revived and that Wayne joined them. If that's true," Kevin added, "when Wayne met with Hank Blanchard ready to divulge the secrets he was sworn to keep, he committed a grievous sin. His disappearance may well mean he's dead."

Sharon blanched. She had denied the possibility until that moment. Gathering within her strength to ask the question so dear to her, she sighed, "What about Kim? Would they have killed her, too?"

Kevin's kind eyes studied her, and he hesitated. "If the group we're dealing with is truly a continuation of the Sons of Dan or the Avenging Angels, Kim would not be the first woman they've killed. But, we can't be certain she's dead. At least not yet."

Alex took her hand in his to comfort her, "Don't worry, Sharon, we'll find Kim, – maybe even Wayne," he told her. "But, we've got to hurry. He looked at Kevin. "Let's see what we can learn from the inventory," he pressed, "starting from the title. Why would they name the project 'Samson'?"

"For any number of reasons," Kevin considered. "However, 'Samson' usually refers to a character in the Bible. You're familiar with the story, the strong man who was destroyed by Delilah."

"But, what has he to do with bees?" Sharon asked. "Wayne told Hank the whole thing was about 'bees'."

"Ever heard of Samson's Riddle?" Kevin asked.

"No, I haven't."

"As the story goes, Samson posed this riddle to his enemies, the Philistines:'Out of the eater came something to eat, – out of the strong came something sweet.' When the Philistines couldn't come up with the answer, they went to Samson's wife. She told them Samson had discovered the carcass of a lion infested with bees and that he ate the honeycomb."

"What does that mean?" Alex asked, the lesson of Samson's riddle lost on him.

"There's a Greek myth I've always thought explained the lesson of Samson's riddle: When Proteus, the Sea God, teaches Aristaeus, son of Apollo and Cyrene, protector and healer, how to remedy the loss of his bees, Proteus says, 'Kill a heifer and bury its carcass in the earth. The buried heifer will give the things thou seekest....' After

Aristaeus had killed and buried the heifer, 'swarms of bees hive out of the putrid beef: one life snuffed out brought to birth a thousand.'"

Alex and Sharon stared at him. "And,...?" Sharon finally asked, expecting him to tell them what all it had to do with Wayne and Kim.

"There's no 'and'. I don't know what Samson and the bees have to do with this new breed of Dan. I don't know what they're up to. But it means something, or they wouldn't have titled the inventory 'Samson'." Wayne responded.

"All this material to work with and no place to go. All we have is a new riddle," Alex observed. Restless and frustrated, he stood and started pacing. "Bees, heifers, Samsons, eagles," he murmured, trying to find among the various clues even a semblance of reason.

"I think I'll call Mother, see if she knows anything about Grandma's Avenging Angels." Sharon told them. She went into the hall, stood next to an open, exterior window, and dialed. "Mom?" she began, when a familiar voice answered.

Inside the office, Kevin implored Alex, "I find this whole thing fascinating. Why don't you let me help you and Sharon? What a topic for a new book, 'The Resurrection of Dan.'"

Alex grinned. "You want to go with us?"

Kevin beamed. "If I may."

"What about your obligations here? What about finals? Isn't it about that time of the year?"

"I'll take emergency leave. My doctoral student can handle my classes. What do you say?"

"Are you kidding? You're like a walking web. We'd be grateful for your help."

Over the phone, Sharon's mother, Susan, told her, "I don't think your grandmother knew much about the Sons of Dan or the Avenging Angels. Only stories her own mother and grandmother told her. She did leave me something that might help, though, Great Grandma Anna's diary. She found it wrapped in leather and glued to the bottom of Grandma Anna's rocking chair, beneath the leather seat. Must have been there for years."

"Did Grandma Anna say anything about Avenging Angels?"

"You know, I always meant to read what Grandma Anna wrote, but never seemed to find time. Why? What's so important?"

"Oh, just a case I'm working on." The last thing in the world Sharon wanted to do was tell her mother Kim was missing, but if she must, she would tell her in person. "Want a couple of overnight visitors?"

"Sure, I'll move the kids into one room and get the spare bedrooms ready. What time do you think you'll be here?"

"We're still in San Francisco, so probably not before nine or ten in the morning."

"When are you going to sleep?"

"We'll sleep in the car, then rest when we get there."

"Okay dear. I'll see you then. Drive carefully."

Sharon hesitated by the open window. Refreshed by the evening breeze buffeting the campus, she blankly gazed along the lighted Cross Campus Road and into the circular parking lot below. Vaguely following the movements of a white car that ignored the equally spaced white stripes, she watched it drive up to the sidewalk outside the lighted entrance and stop. Barely glancing as two men in sport coats, a balding one, muscle bound and short, and a stocky redhead with a jaw that could bite through bone, emerged. They wore starched, white shirts and narrow, dark ties. As the redhead got out of the car his jacket opened to a holster and revolver.

She looked closer. As they hurried around the corner of the less than distinguished concrete hall and up the north steps, it hit Sharon who they were. "My God!" she blurted, suddenly aware. "It's the Impala! Alex," she shouted, bursting into Kevin's office, "they found us!"

Chapter Forty-five

New York City
3:00 a.m. Saturday
April 24

Chunky pools of vomit commingled with urine coating the walls and floor around the open fixture the guards called a toilet. At various other locations along the holding cell walls, a man in his late twenties, victimized by a lifetime of drugs, was evacuating himself, and the sound of his constant retching was driving Hank Blanchard mad. "Good God, Man!" Hank shouted at him. The three others in the cell had taken refuge on a bench in the far corner. "You really oughta do something about that."

The cell was unbearable, the day Hank spent there hell. "Where's my lawyer?" he yelled. His attorney had come to the precinct to arrange bail immediately after receiving Hank's call, but obstacle after obstacle had been put before him, and the bond hearing was postponed until late that morning. Claustrophobic, filthy, and frightened, Hank was losing patience.

"Sit down," a tall, white man in tailored evening attire and much too clean for a place like this told Hank. Sitting next to him, was a black man, whose revulsion for all of them was so intense he reeked of it. Hank's fourth cell mate was a derelict of the sort found sleeping next to a dumpster. Had they not been cornered by vomit and forced to sit on the same bench, none of them would have had anything to do with the others. "You can't stop that man by yelling at him. He's sick," the tall man continued.

Realizing he was right, Hank gave up and joined them. Finding a small space at the end of the bench to sit down, about the only place left in the cell Mr. Regurgitation had left unspoiled, he told them, "Sorry, I just want to get out of here."

"You're the guy accused of that murder at Madison Square Garden, aren't you?" the tall man confirmed.

"Self-defense," Hank said.

"I'm sure it was," the man said, skeptically.

"What are you in here for? Embezzlement?"

The tall man had been brought in about midnight, handcuffed and ruffled. "Felony trespass," he said, his voice replete with disgust. "I was invited to this fundraiser for that self-righteous Presidential candidate of ours. Paid my $10,000 for dinner just to see for myself what went on, then made the mistake of letting the people at my table know I wasn't going to vote for him. Said I didn't want another right wing fanatic in the White House. When I argued he'd lied about nuclear weapons in the Mideast and told them all he was after was control of their oil, I became a leper to my dinner companions." He leaned into Hank's ear, whispering, "An undesirable. They gave me about a minute to eat my salad before security jumped on me and sent me here.

"Ahh-hh-hh," he sighed, "for the old days, when there was such a thing as free speech."

"Shut up! I'm tired a' guys like you."

Hank looked up, startled. The challenge came from the derelict, who suddenly sobered and came alive.

"You're nothin' but a traitor!" he shouted. He lunged with driving fist at the man in the tuxedo, his vile, tattered jacket brushing Hank's nose.

"Hey," Hank said, trying to pull him off. "It's just politics."

"Guard!" the black man shouted, getting out of the way.

A three-inch knife fell from the derelict's ankle, slid across the floor and into a puddle of vomit. Trying to keep it away from him, Hank kicked the knife toward the cell door. He followed it to kick it again and was tackled.

The derelict pinned him, pressing his face against the cold, filthy concrete, and reaching for the knife. Prostrate, helpless beneath the much larger man, Hank could do nothing to defend himself as the derelict grabbed his hair and wrenched back his head. Caged light from the ceiling was reflecting off the blade. The blade moved closer, the light flashed, and then disappeared.

To be continued…..

About the author...

Shawna Ryan was born and raised in the Northwest. After obtaining her law degree, she was a corporate attorney and a trial attorney. Though she has traveled extensively, her home is still in the Northwest. She recently retired from practice to devote more time to writing. Always having been interested in the philosophies of religion, she enjoys researching and writing about the histories behind them.

She is a descendant of Catholics, Mormons, Methodists, Baptists, and other Protestants and tries to be both critical and objective about them all. The inspirations for the research that led to her new serial, KINGDOM, were Shawna's great grandmothers, who converted to Mormonism in 1854 and who were among the first European converts to immigrate to Utah. Some of the anecdotes in KINGDOM were based are their own stories.

KINGDOM - Book 1 is Shawna's fourth thriller. She is also the author of Destiny's Damned, Satan's Scat, and Triumvirate of the Damned, a thriller trilogy. The initial inspiration for the trilogy was the writings of Joseph Campbell, a well known and respected mythologist who was brilliant in his fields of comparative mythology and comparative religions.

Shawna's goal is to write thrillers which are fun to read and which inspire their readers to talk about them with friends. Shawna's favorite thriller writers are Douglas Preston and Lincoln Child.

Other Solstice titles you may enjoy...

I Am His Mother
By: Carlos Solorzano

For centuries religious denominations have argued the theological message of Jesus' teachings while historians have argued over what could be considered as historical fact from the biblical accounts of Jesus' life. Non-canonical texts are discovered every so many years, which only leads to more speculation as to who Jesus Christ really was. Such debates never seem to end. What if, however, we were able to speak to the woman who carried Him in her womb, gave birth to Him and raised Him prior to His public ministry? What if she were able to write down her maternal reflections of what it was like to see this most famous figure go from the child that lived in her own home to the teacher that continues to influence the lives of billions of people everywhere? What if her personal memoir this was in fact the latest undiscovered document from the ancient world? Author Carlos Solorzano takes on such a journey with I Am His Mother, the memoir of Mary the Mother of Jesus based right out of the portions of the Gospel where Mary played a key role in the life of Jesus Christ.

An Early Apocalypse
By: Carlos Solorzano

Seven years after his encounter in the past Joaquin Alameda is now settled into middle aged life with a loving family and a flourishing career. He is now more secure than ever in his faith as well as in his sense of self-worth. However, he is no fool and upon returning from the past had long wondered when Lucifer would fulfill his promise to strike at him again. Joaquin's fear was certainly well warranted as the Prince of Darkness is now obsessed with exacting his revenge on the man who thwarted his perfect plan. To do so, he will unleash the anitchrist prior to his appointed time in order to test Joaquin's faith in ways that he never thought possible in order to deliver him personally to Lucifer in hell. How will Joaquin withstand the challenge of a man with no equal during a time when the only true threat to the antichrist, the returning Christ, is not expected to return due to the fact that prophecy must be fulfilled as it is written?

Due Date
By: Nancy Wood

Surrogate mother Shelby McDougall just fell for the biggest con of all—a scam that risks her life and the lives of her unborn twins.
Twenty-three year-old Shelby McDougall is facing a mountain of student debt and a memory she'd just as soon forget. A *Rolling Stone* ad for a surrogate mother offers her a way to erase the loans and right her karmic place in the cosmos. Within a

month, she's signed a contract, relocated to Santa Cruz, California, and started fertility treatments.

But intended parents Jackson and Diane Entwistle have their own secret agenda—one that has nothing to do with diapers and lullabies. With her due date looming, and the clues piling up, Shelby must save herself and her twins. As she uses her wits to survive, Shelby learns the real meaning of the word "family."

For more Solstice title go to:

http://store.solsticepublishing.com/bookstore/